The JUNIOR CLASSICS

VOLUME TEN • POETRY • READING GUIDE • INDEXES

Boris Artzybasheff

She left lonely forever
The Kings of the sea.

[See page 298]

The JUNIOR CLASSICS

Edited by MABEL WILLIAMS *and* MARCIA DALPHIN.

With Introduction by WILLIAM ALLAN NEILSON, *Former President of Smith College; Introduction to First Edition by* CHARLES W. ELIOT, *Former President of Harvard University*

Popular Edition

ILLUSTRATED

VOLUME
TEN

POETRY
READING GUIDE
INDEXES

P. F. COLLIER & SON CORPORATION

P. F. COLLIER & SON CORPORATION

sixty-second printing, 1959

CEIFB

MANUFACTURED IN THE UNITED STATES OF AMERICA

CONTENTS

NURSERY RHYMES

PAGE

Sing a Song of Sixpence 3

Illustration by Randolph Caldecott

A Diller, A Dollar 3

Simple Simon 4

Daffy-Down-Dilly 4

Little Boy Blue 4

When I Was a Bachelor 4

Great A, Little a 5

Illustration by L. Leslie Brooke

Little Miss Muffet 5

Little Jack Horner 5

Ding, Dong, Bell 5

Pussy-Cat, Pussy-Cat 6

Humpty Dumpty 6

Old King Cole 6

The North Wind Doth Blow 6

Higgley Piggley 7

Come, Let's to Bed 7

Curly Locks! Curly Locks! 7

The Queen of Hearts 7

CONTENTS

PAGE

Blow, Wind, Blow! 7
Diddle, Diddle Dumpling 8
There Was an Old Woman Who Lived in a Shoe 8
Jack Sprat Could Eat No Fat 8
Pease Pudding Hot 8
Jack and Jill 8
Solomon Grundy 8
Little Polly Flinders 9
I Had a Little Nut-Tree 9
Taffy Was a Welshman 9
Little Bo-Peep 9
Illustration by L. Leslie Brooke
Mistress Mary, Quite Contrary 10
Where Are You Going, My Pretty Maid? 10
There Was an Old Woman Toss'd Up in a Basket 10
I Had a Little Pony 10
Bye, Baby Bunting 11
There Was an Old Woman Lived under a Hill 11
Illustration by L. Leslie Brooke
To Market, To Market 11
There Was a Crooked Man 11
This Is the Way the Ladies Ride 12
Illustrations by L. Leslie Brooke
Hushaby, Baby 12
Rockabye, Baby 12
Hey! Diddle, Diddle 13
The Lion and the Unicorn 13
Ride a Cock-Horse 13
There Was a Little Man 13

CONTENTS

PAGE

There Was a Man, and He Had Nought 13

The Three Little Kittens 13

Goosey, Goosey, Gander 14

Illustration by L. Leslie Brooke

The Fox and His Wife 14

Old Mother Hubbard 16

A Frog He Would A-Wooing Go 18

Illustration by Randolph Caldecott

The House That Jack Built 20

Illustrations by Randolph Caldecott

RIDDLES

Two Legs Sat Upon Three Legs 23

Illustration by Charles Folkard

As I Went through the Garden Gap 23

Thirty White Horses 23

Arthur O' Bower 23

Hick-a-more, Hack-a-more 24

Long Legs, Crooked Thighs 24

Flour of England, Fruit of Spain 24

Little Nancy Etticote 24

I Have a Little Sister 24

As I Was Going to St. Ives 24

POEMS OF CHILDHOOD AND YOUTH

NATURE'S YEAR

Piping down the Valleys Wild . . . . . . *William Blake* 27

Illustration by Pamela Bianco

Nearly Ready . . . . *Mary Mapes Dodge* 28

March . . . . *William Wordsworth* 28

Spring . . . . *Thomas Nashe* 29

CONTENTS

PAGE

The Spicebush in March . . . . *Sara Teasdale* 29

Spring Quiet . . . . *Christina G. Rossetti* 30

The Dandelions . . . . *Helen Gray Cone* 30

The Wind in a Frolic . . . . *William Howitt* 31

Who Has Seen the Wind? . . . . . . *Christina G. Rossetti* 32

The Procession of the Flowers . . . . . . *Sydney Dobell* 33

The Grass . . . . *Emily Dickinson* 34

June . . . . *James Russell Lowell* 34

Summer Days . . . . *Christina G. Rossetti* 36

How the Leaves Came Down . . . . . . *Susan Coolidge* 36

The Morns Are Meeker Than They Were . *Emily Dickinson* 37

Autumn Fires . . . . *Robert Louis Stevenson* 38

Fog . . . . *Carl Sandburg* 38

Illustration by James Daugherty

The Frost . . . . *Hannah Flagg Gould* 39

Rhyme of November Stars . . . . *Sara Teasdale* 40

Windy Nights . . . . *Robert Louis Stevenson* 40

Winter . . . . *William Shakespeare* 41

A Song of Winter . . . . *Anonymous* 41

Velvet Shoes . . . . *Elinor Wylie* 42

Stopping by Woods on a Snowy Evening . . . *Robert Frost* 43

O Lady Moon . . . . *Christina G. Rossetti* 43

The Wind and the Moon . . . . *George Macdonald* 44

Lady Moon . . . . *Lord Houghton* 45

The Night Will Never Stay . . . . *Eleanor Farjeon* 46

The Old Horse in the City . . . . *Vachel Lindsay* 46

Yet Gentle Will the Griffin Be . . . . . . *Vachel Lindsay* 47

Illustration by George Richards

The Moon's the North Wind's Cooky . . . *Vachel Lindsay* 48

CONTENTS

PAGE

Stars . . . . *Sara Teasdale* 48

Illustration by Dorothy Lathrop

Canis Major . . . . *Robert Frost* 49

Donnybrook . . . . *James Stephens* 49

Light the Lamps Up, Lamplighter! . . . . *Eleanor Farjeon* 50

THE WORLD OF CREATURES

All Things Bright and Beautiful . . *Cecil Frances Alexander* 51

Illustration by Corydon Bell

The Butterfly's Ball . . . . *William Roscoe* 52

The Spider and the Fly . . . . *Mary Howitt* 54

To the Grasshopper and the Cricket . . . . . *Leigh Hunt* 56

The Bee . . . . *Emily Dickinson* 56

A Dream . . . . *William Blake* 57

All Things Wait Upon Thee . . . . *Christina G. Rossetti* 58

Nature's Friend . . . . *William H. Davies* 58

The Housekeeper . . . . *Charles Lamb* 59

A Narrow Fellow in the Grass . . . . . *Emily Dickinson* 59

A Friend in the Garden . . . . . . *Juliana Horatia Ewing* 60

Seal Lullaby . . . . *Rudyard Kipling* 61

Answer to a Child's Question . . . *Samuel Taylor Coleridge* 61

A Bird Came down the Walk . . . . . . *Emily Dickinson* 62

The Last Word of a Bluebird . . . . *Robert Frost* 62

An Epitaph on a Robin Redbreast . . . . *Samuel Rogers* 63

Who Stole the Bird's Nest? . . . . . . *Lydia Maria Child* 63

Robin Redbreast . . . . *William Allingham* 66

The Owl . . . . *Alfred, Lord Tennyson* 67

The Eagle . . . . *Alfred, Lord Tennyson* 67

The City Mouse and the Garden Mouse . *Christina G. Rossetti* 67

CONTENTS

PAGE

The Cow . . . . *Robert Louis Stevenson* 68
A Dirge for a Righteous Kitten . . . . . *Vachel Lindsay* 68
The Kitten and the Falling Leaves . . *William Wordsworth* 68
A Child's Pet . . . . *William H. Davies* 69
The Lamb . . . . *William Blake* 70
A Fable . . . . *Ralph Waldo Emerson* 71
Poor Dog Tray . . . . *Thomas Campbell* 71
The Blood Horse . . . . *Barry Cornwall* 72
The Runaway . . . . *Robert Frost* 73
The Tiger . . . . *William Blake* 74

FAIRYLAND

Over Hill, Over Dale . . . . *William Shakespeare* 75
Where the Bee Sucks . . . . *William Shakespeare* 75
Come unto These Yellow Sands . . . . *William Shakespeare* 76
Full Fathom Five . . . . *William Shakespeare* 76
The Wee, Wee Man . . . . *Anonymous* 76
The Arming of Pigwiggen . . . . *Michael Drayton* 77
Robin Goodfellow . . . . *Anonymous* 78
The Visitor . . . . *Rachel Field* 80
Illustrations by the Author
The Visitor . . . . *Patrick R. Chalmers* 81
Berries . . . . *Walter de la Mare* 83
The Fairies . . . . *William Allingham* 85
Illustration by Boris Artzybasheff
The Fairies of the Caldon Low . . . . *Mary Howitt* 86
A Fairy Went A-Marketing . . . . *Rose Fyleman* 89

FUN AND NONSENSE

John Gilpin . . . . *William Cowper* 90
Illustrations by Randolph Caldecott

CONTENTS

PAGE

Topsy-Turvy World . . . . *William B. Rands* 97

An Elegy on the Death of a Mad Dog . . *Oliver Goldsmith* 98

Captain Reece . . . . *William S. Gilbert* 99

The Yarn of the Nancy Bell . . . . . . *William S. Gilbert* 102
Illustration by the Author

Robinson Crusoe's Story . . . . *Charles E. Carryl* 105

Little Billee . . . . *William Makepeace Thackeray* 107

The Story of Augustus Who Would Not
Have Any Soup . . . . *Heinrich Hoffman* 108
Illustrations by the Author

Clean Clara . . . . *William B. Rands* 109

The Owl and the Pussy Cat . . . . *Edward Lear* 111
Illustrations by the Author

The Pobble Who Has No Toes . . . . . . *Edward Lear* 112

The Jumblies . . . . *Edward Lear* 113

The Courtship of the Yonghy-Bonghy-Bô . . . *Edward Lear* 115

Jabberwocky . . . . *Lewis Carroll* 118
Illustration by Sir John Tenniel

The Walrus and the Carpenter . . . . *Lewis Carroll* 119
Illustration by Sir John Tenniel

The Mad Gardener's Song . . . . *Lewis Carroll* 122
Illustration by Harry Furniss

The Three Badgers . . . . *Lewis Carroll* 124

The Duel . . . . *Eugene Field* 126

The Man in the Moon . . . . *James Whitcomb Riley* 127

The Ship of Rio . . . . *Walter de la Mare* 129
Illustration by W. Heath Robinson

The Plaint of the Camel . . . . *Charles E. Carryl* 130

Sage Counsel . . . . *Sir Arthur Quiller-Couch* 131

The Chimpanzee . . . . *Oliver Herford* 131

The Ant . . . . *Oliver Herford* 132

CONTENTS

PAGE

A Bunny Romance . . . . *Oliver Herford* 132

Illustration by the Author

The Elf and the Dormouse . . . . *Oliver Herford* 134

Illustration by Warren Chappell

The Python . . . . *Hilaire Belloc* 135

The Frog . . . . *Hilaire Belloc* 136

The Yak . . . . *Hilaire Belloc* 136

The Vowels: An Enigma . . . . *Jonathan Swift* 137

A Riddle . . . . *Hannah More* 137

A Riddle . . . . *Catherine Fanshawe* 138

At Home and at Play

The Land of Story-Books . . . . . . *Robert Louis Stevenson* 139

Woodcut by Gwen Raverat

Travel . . . . *Robert Louis Stevenson* 140

The Land of Counterpane . . . . . *Robert Louis Stevenson* 141

The Hens . . . . *Elizabeth Madox Roberts* 141

The Pasture . . . . *Robert Frost* 142

Winter-Time . . . . *Robert Louis Stevenson* 142

The Lost Doll . . . . *Charles Kingsley* 143

The Children's Hour . . . . *Henry Wadsworth Longfellow* 143

Good Night and Good Morning . . . . . *Lord Houghton* 145

Nurse's Song . . . . *William Blake* 145

Old Gaelic Lullaby . . . . *Anonymous* 146

Willie Winkie . . . . *William Miller* 146

Wynken, Blynken, and Nod . . . . *Eugene Field* 147

Lullaby of an Infant Chief . . . . *Sir Walter Scott* 148

The Ogre . . . . *Walter de la Mare* 149

Before Sleeping . . . . *Anonymous* 151

Cradle Hymn . . . . *Martin Luther* 151

CONTENTS

FRIENDS

PAGE

Little Gustava . . . . *Celia Thaxter* 152
Illustration by Warren Chappell

A Midsummer Song . . . . *Richard Watson Gilder* 154

Farm-Yard Song . . . . *John Townsend Trowbridge* 154

Thanksgiving Day . . . . *Lydia Maria Child* 156

A Visit from St. Nicholas . . . . *Clement C. Moore* 157

Hiawatha's Childhood . . . . *Henry Wadsworth Longfellow* 158
Illustration by Nancy Barnhart

The Little Black Boy . . . . *William Blake* 161

The Lost Shoe . . . . *Walter de la Mare* 162
Illustration by Florence Wyman Ivins

The Chimney Sweeper . . . . *William Blake* 163

The Pin . . . . *Ann Taylor* 164

Meddlesome Matty . . . . *Ann Taylor* 165

Meg Merrilies . . . . *John Keats* 166

An Old Woman of the Roads . . . . *Padraic Colum* 167

Seumas Beg . . . . *James Stephens* 168
Illustration by Florence Wyman Ivins

Sam . . . . *Walter de la Mare* 169

Portrait by a Neighbor . . . . *Edna St. Vincent Millay* 170

OLD BALLADS AND STORIES

Bonnie George Campbell . . . . *Anonymous* 171
Illustration by Warren Chappell

Sir Patrick Spens . . . . *Anonymous* 172

Bonny Barbara Allan . . . . *Anonymous* 175

Hynde Horn . . . . *Anonymous* 176

The Pied Piper of Hamelin . . . . *Robert Browning* 178
Illustration by Warren Chappell

God's Judgment on a Wicked Bishop . . . . *Robert Southey* 186

The Inchcape Rock . . . . *Robert Southey* 188

CONTENTS

		PAGE
A Story for a Child	*Bayard Taylor*	190
The Wreck of the Hesperus	*Henry Wadsworth Longfellow*	192
Lucy Gray	*William Wordsworth*	194
The Farewell	*Robert Burns*	196
Gathering Song of Donald Dhu	*Sir Walter Scott*	197
Lord Ullin's Daughter	*Thomas Campbell*	198
Allen-A-Dale	*Sir Walter Scott*	200
The King of Denmark's Ride	*Caroline Elizabeth Norton*	201
Lochinvar	*Sir Walter Scott*	202
Lepanto	*Gilbert K. Chesterton*	203
The Destruction of Sennacherib	*George Gordon, Lord Byron*	207
How They Brought the Good News from Ghent to Aix	*Robert Browning*	208
The Harp that Once Through Tara's Halls	*Thomas Moore*	209
The Minstrel-Boy	*Thomas Moore*	210
Ye Mariners of England	*Thomas Campbell*	210
After Blenheim	*Robert Southey*	211
The Skeleton in Armor	*Henry Wadsworth Longfellow*	213
Columbus	*Joaquin Miller*	217
The Landing of the Pilgrim Fathers	*Felicia Dorothea Hemans*	219
Paul Revere's Ride	*Henry Wadsworth Longfellow*	220
Concord Hymn	*Ralph Waldo Emerson*	223
Old Ironsides	*Oliver Wendell Holmes*	224
Barbara Frietchie	*John Greenleaf Whittier*	224
Nancy Hanks	*Rosemary Benét*	226
O Captain! My Captain!	*Walt Whitman*	227
The Ghosts of the Buffaloes	*Vachel Lindsav*	228

CONTENTS

Romance and Adventure

PAGE

The Song of Wandering Aengus . . . . *William Butler Yeats* 231

Illustration by Wilfred Bromhall

The Vagabond . . . . *Robert Louis Stevenson* 232

Romance . . . . *Robert Louis Stevenson* 233

The Passionate Shepherd to His Love . . *Christopher Marlowe* 233

O, Wert Thou in the Cauld Blast . . . . . *Robert Burns* 234

Time, You Old Gypsy Man . . . . *Ralph Hodgson* 235

Tarantella . . . . *Hilaire Belloc* 236

Romance . . . . *Walter J. Turner* 237

Arabia . . . . *Walter de la Mare* 237

The Outlaw . . . . *Sir Walter Scott* 238

Smugglers' Song . . . . *Rudyard Kipling* 240

The Wraggle Taggle Gypsies . . . . *Anonymous* 241

Tom o' Bedlam . . . . *Anonymous* 242

Tewkesbury Road . . . . *John Masefield* 243

If Once You Have Slept on an Island . . . . *Rachel Field* 243

The Sea Gypsy . . . . *Richard Hovey* 244

Sea Fever . . . . *John Masefield* 244

Eel-Grass . . . . *Edna St. Vincent Millay* 245

A Visit from the Sea . . . . *Robert Louis Stevenson* 245

The Northern Seas . . . . *William Howitt* 246

The Sailor's Consolation . . . . *Charles Dibdin* 247

The Bell Buoy . . . . *Rudyard Kipling* 248

A Sea Song . . . . *Allan Cunningham* 250

Messmates . . . . *Henry Newbolt* 251

Drake's Drum . . . . *Henry Newbolt* 252

The Old Ships . . . . *James Elroy Flecker* 252

Requiem . . . . *Robert Louis Stevenson* 253

CONTENTS

LOOKING FORWARD

PAGE

Orpheus with His Lute . . . . . . *William Shakespeare* 257
Illustration by H. J. Ford

Hark! Hark! the Lark . . . . *William Shakespeare* 258

Fidele . . . . *William Shakespeare* 258

Jog On, Jog On . . . . *William Shakespeare* 259

Cardinal Wolsey's Speech to Cromwell . . *William Shakespeare* 259

Shall I Compare Thee to a Summer's Day? *William Shakespeare* 260

Integer Vitae . . . . *Thomas Campion* 260

Sweet Content . . . . *Thomas Dekker* 261

Folding the Flocks . . . . *John Fletcher* 262

To Meadows . . . . *Robert Herrick* 263

To Daffodils . . . . *Robert Herrick* 263

Going A-Maying . . . . *Robert Herrick* 264

Death, the Leveler . . . . *James Shirley* 266

Song: On May Morning . . . . *John Milton* 266

Evening in Paradise . . . . *John Milton* 267

On His Blindness . . . . *John Milton* 267

Song of the Emigrants in Bermuda . . . . *Andrew Marvell* 267

Divine Ode . . . . *Joseph Addison* 269

Peace . . . . *Henry Vaughan* 269

The Shepherd Boy Sings in the Valley of Humiliation . . . . *John Bunyan* 270

Solitude . . . . *Alexander Pope* 270

The Seasons . . . . *William Blake* 271

Night . . . . *William Blake* 273

Lucy . . . . *William Wordsworth* 275

Daffodils . . . . *William Wordsworth* 276

The Solitary Reaper . . . . *William Wordsworth* 277

CONTENTS

PAGE

Breathes There the Man . . . . *Sir Walter Scott* 278

Kubla Khan . . . . *Samuel Taylor Coleridge* 278

Abou Ben Adhem. . . . . *Leigh Hunt* 280

The Cloud . . . . *Percy Bysshe Shelley* 280

To a Skylark . . . . *Percy Bysshe Shelley* 282

To Night . . . . *Percy Bysshe Shelley* 286

To Autumn . . . . *John Keats* 287

Winter . . . . *John Keats* 288

La Belle Dame Sans Merci . . . . *John Keats* 288

Ode on a Grecian Urn . . . . *John Keats* 290

Autumn . . . . *Thomas Hood* 291

Early Spring . . . . *Alfred, Lord Tennyson* 292

Bugle Song . . . . *Alfred, Lord Tennyson* 294

Prospice . . . . *Robert Browning* 294

The Forsaken Merman . . . . *Matthew Arnold* 295

Illustration by Boris Artzybasheff

The Shepherdess . . . . *Alice Meynell* 299

Up-Hill . . . . *Christina G. Rossetti* 299

Bredon Hill . . . . *A. E. Housman* 300

To a Waterfowl . . . . *William Cullen Bryant* 301

Thanatopsis . . . . *William Cullen Bryant* 302

Forbearance . . . . *Ralph Waldo Emerson* 304

The Snow Storm . . . . *Ralph Waldo Emerson* 304

Daybreak . . . . *Henry Wadsworth Longfellow* 305

The Day is Done . . . . . . *Henry Wadsworth Longfellow* 306

Hymn to the Night . . . . . *Henry Wadsworth Longfellow* 307

Snow-Bound . . . . *John Greenleaf Whittier* 308

The Chambered Nautilus . . . . . . *Oliver Wendell Holmes* 311

CONTENTS

PAGE

The Last Leaf . . . . *Oliver Wendell Holmes* 312
To One in Paradise . . . . *Edgar Allan Poe* 313
To Helen . . . . *Edgar Allan Poe* 314
The Shepherd of King Admetus . . . . *James Russell Lowell* 314
Sources 316

Acknowledgments 319
Reading Guide 329
Biographical List of Artists 361
Index of Titles 371
Index of Authors 380

Nursery Rhymes

NURSERY RHYMES

Sing a song of sixpence,
  A bag full of rye;
Four and twenty blackbirds
  Baked in a pie;

When the pie was open'd,
  The birds began to sing;
Was not that a dainty dish
  To set before the king?

The king was in the counting-house,
  Counting out his money;
The queen was in the parlor,
  Eating bread and honey;

The maid was in the garden,
  Hanging out the clothes,
There came a little blackbird,
  And snapped off her nose.

A diller, a dollar,
A ten o'clock scholar,
What makes you come so soon?
You used to come at ten o'clock,
But now you come at noon.

Simple Simon met a pieman,
Going to the fair;
Says Simple Simon to the pieman,
"Let me taste your ware."

Says the pieman to Simple Simon,
"Show me first your penny."
Says Simple Simon to the pieman,
"Indeed I have not any."

Simple Simon went a-fishing
For to catch a whale;
All the water he had got
Was in his mother's pail!

Daffy-Down-Dilly has come up to town
In a yellow petticoat and a green gown.

Little Boy Blue, come blow your horn;
The sheep's in the meadow, the cow's in the corn.
"Where's the little boy that looks after the sheep?"
"He's under the hay-cock, fast asleep."
"Will you wake him?" "No, not I;
For if I do, he'll be sure to cry."

When I was a bachelor I lived by myself,
And all the meat I got I put upon a shelf;
The rats and the mice did lead me such a life
That I went to London to get myself a wife.

The streets were so broad and the lanes were so narrow,
I could not get my wife home without a wheelbarrow;
The wheelbarrow broke, my wife got a fall,
Down tumbled wheelbarrow, little wife. and all.

Great A, little a,
  Bouncing B!
The cat's in the cupboard,
  And can't see me.

Little Miss Muffet
Sat on a tuffet,
Eating of curds and whey;
There came a spider,
And sat down beside her,
And frightened Miss Muffet away.

Little Jack Horner
Sat in a corner,
Eating a Christmas pie.
He put in his thumb,
And took out a plum,
And said, "What a good boy am I."

Ding, dong, bell,
Pussy's in the well!
Who put her in?—
Little Tommy Lin.
Who pulled her out?—
Dog with long snout.
What a naughty boy was that
To drown poor pussy-cat,
Who never did any harm,
But killed the mice in his father's barn.

Pussy-cat, pussy-cat, where have you been?
I've been up to London to look at the queen.
Pussy-cat, pussy-cat, what did you there?
I frighten'd a little mouse under the chair.

Humpty Dumpty sat on a wall;
Humpty Dumpty had a great fall;
All the king's horses and all the king's men
Couldn't put Humpty Dumpty back again.

Old King Cole
Was a merry old soul,
And a merry old soul was he;
He called for his pipe,
And he called for his bowl,
And he called for his fiddlers three.

Every fiddler, he had a fiddle,
And a very fine fiddle had he;
Twee tweedle dee, tweedle dee, went the fiddlers.
Oh, there's none so rare
As can compare
With King Cole and his fiddlers three!

The north wind doth blow,
  And we shall have snow,
And what will poor Robin do then?
  Poor thing!

He'll sit in a barn,
  And to keep himself warm,
Will hide his head under his wing.
  Poor thing!

Higgley Piggley,
  My black hen,
She lays eggs
  For gentlemen;
Sometimes nine,
  And sometimes ten.
Higgley Piggley,
  My black hen!

Come, let's to bed, says Sleepy-head;
  Tarry awhile, says Slow;
Put on the pan, says Greedy Nan,
  Let's sup before we go.

Curly locks! Curly locks! wilt thou be mine?
Thou shalt not wash dishes, nor yet feed the swine,
But sit on a cushion and sew a fine seam,
And feed upon strawberries, sugar, and cream!

The Queen of Hearts,
She made some tarts,
    All on a summer's day;
The Knave of Hearts,
He stole those tarts,
    And took them clean away.

The King of Hearts
Called for the tarts,
    And beat the Knave full sore;
The Knave of Hearts
Brought back the tarts,
    And vowed he'd steal no more.

Blow, wind, blow! and go, mill, go!
That the miller may grind his corn;
That the baker may take it,
And into rolls make it,
And send us some hot in the morn.

Diddle, diddle dumpling, my son John,
He went to bed with his stockings on;
One shoe off, and one shoe on,
Diddle, diddle dumpling, my son John.

There was an old woman who lived in a shoe;
She had so many children she didn't know what to do;
She gave them some broth without any bread;
She whipped them all soundly and put them to bed.

Jack Sprat could eat no fat,
His wife could eat no lean;
And so between them both, you see,
They licked the platter clean.

Pease pudding hot,
Pease pudding cold,
Pease pudding in the pot,
Nine days old.

Some like it hot,
Some like it cold,
Some like it in the pot,
Nine days old.

Jack and Jill went up the hill
To fetch a pail of water;
Jack fell down and broke his crown,
And Jill came tumbling after.

Solomon Grundy,
Born on Monday,
Christened on Tuesday,
Married on Wednesday,
Took ill on Thursday,
Worse on Friday,
Died on Saturday,
Buried on Sunday.
This is the end of
Solomon Grundy.

Leslie Brooke

Then up she took her little crook.

[See page 9]

Little Polly Flinders
Sat among the cinders
   Warming her pretty little toes.
Her mother came and caught her,
And whipped her little daughter
   For spoiling her nice new clothes.

I had a little nut-tree, nothing would it bear
But a silver nutmeg and a golden pear;
The King of Spain's daughter came to visit me,
And all was because of my little nut-tree.
I skipp'd over water, I danced over sea,
And all the birds in the air couldn't catch me.

Taffy was a Welshman, Taffy was a thief;
Taffy came to my house and stole a piece of beef;
I went to Taffy's house, Taffy was not at home;
Taffy came to my house and stole a marrow-bone.
I went to Taffy's house, Taffy was not in;
Taffy came to my house and stole a silver pin;
I went to Taffy's house, Taffy was in bed,
I took up a poker and flung it at his head.

Little Bo-Peep has lost her sheep,
   And can't tell where to find them;
Leave them alone, and they'll come home,
   And bring their tails behind them.

Little Bo-Peep fell fast asleep,
   And dreamt she heard them bleating;
But when she awoke, she found it a joke,
   For they were still a-fleeting.

Then up she took her little crook,
   Determin'd for to find them;
She found them indeed, but it made her heart bleed,
   For they'd left all their tails behind 'em.

Mistress Mary, quite contrary,
  How does your garden grow?
With cockle-shells, and silver bells,
  And pretty maids all a-row.

"Where are you going, my pretty maid?"
"I'm going a-milking, sir," she said.
"May I go with you, my pretty maid?"
"You're kindly welcome, sir," she said.
"What is your father, my pretty maid?"
"My father's a farmer, sir," she said.

"Say, will you marry me, my pretty maid?"
"Yes, if you please, kind sir," she said.
"What is your fortune, my pretty maid?"
"My face is my fortune, sir," she said.
"Then I can't marry you, my pretty maid!"
"Nobody asked you, sir," she said.

There was an old woman toss'd up in a basket
  Nineteen times as high as the moon;
Where she was going I couldn't but ask it,
  For in her hand she carried a broom.

"Old woman, old woman, old woman," quoth I,
  "O whither, O whither, O whither so high?"
"To brush the cobwebs off the sky!"
  "Shall I go with thee?" "Ay, bye-and-bye."

I had a little pony
  They called him Dapple-gray.
I lent him to a lady,
  To ride a mile away.
She whipped him, she slashed him,
  She rode him through the mire.
I would not lend my pony now,
  For all the lady's hire.

Bye, Baby Bunting!
Father's gone a-hunting,
Gone to fetch a rabbit-skin,
To wrap the Baby Bunting in.

There was an old woman
  Lived under a hill,
And if she's not gone
  She lives there still.

To market, to market, to buy a fat pig;
Home again, home again, dancing a jig.
Ride to the market to buy a fat hog;
Home again, home again, jiggety-jog.

There was a crooked man, and he went a crooked mile,
He found a crooked sixpence against a crooked stile:
He bought a crooked cat, which caught a crooked mouse,
And they all lived together in a little crooked house.

This is the way the ladies ride:
Tri, tre, tre, tree,
Tri, tre, tre, tree!
This is the way the ladies ride:
Tri, tre, tre, tri-tre-tre-tree!

This is the way the gentlemen ride:
Gallop-a-trot,
Gallop-a-trot!
This is the way the gentlemen ride:
Gallop-a-gallop-a-trot!

This is the way the farmers ride:
Hobbledy-hoy,
Hobbledy-hoy!
This is the way the farmers ride:
Hobbledy hobbledy-hoy!

Hushaby, baby, thy cradle is green;
Father's a nobleman, mother's a queen;
Sister's a lady, and wears a gold ring;
Brother's a drummer, and drums for the king.

Rockabye, baby, on the tree top;
When the wind blows the cradle will rock;
When the bough breaks the cradle will fall;
Down will come baby, bough, cradle, and all.

Hey! diddle, diddle,
The cat and the fiddle,
The cow jumped over the moon;
The little dog laugh'd
To see the sport,
While the dish ran after the spoon.

The lion and the unicorn
Were fighting for the crown;
The lion beat the unicorn
All round the town.

Some gave them white bread,
And some gave them brown;
Some gave them plum-cake,
And sent them out of town.

Ride a cock-horse
To Banbury Cross,
To see a fine lady
Upon a white horse.
Rings on her fingers,
Bells on her toes,
She shall have music
Wherever she goes.

There was a little man,
And he had a little gun,
And his bullets were made of lead, lead, lead;
He went to the brook
And saw a little duck,
And he shot it right through the head, head, head.

He carried it home
To his old wife Joan,
And bid her a fire for to make, make, make;
To roast the little duck
He had shot in the brook,
And he'd go and fetch her the drake, drake, drake.

Goosey, goosey, gander,
Where shall I wander?
Upstairs, downstairs,
And in my lady's chamber.
There I met an old man
That would not say his prayers;
I took him by the left leg,
And threw him downstairs.

There was a man, and he had nought,
And robbers came to rob him;
He crept up to the chimney-pot,
And then they thought they had him.

But he got down on t'other side,
And then they could not find him.
He ran fourteen miles in fifteen days,
And never looked behind him.

THE THREE LITTLE KITTENS

Three little kittens lost their mittens;
And they began to cry,
O mother dear,
We very much fear
That we have lost our mittens.
What, lost your mittens!
You naughty kittens!
Then you shall have no pie.
Mee-ow, mee-ow, mee-ow.
No, you shall have no pie.

The three little kittens found their mittens,
And they began to cry,
O mother dear,
See here, see here;

See, we have found our mittens.
What, found your mittens,
You darling kittens,
Then you shall have some pie.
Purr-r, purr-r,
Then you shall have some pie.

THE FOX AND HIS WIFE

The fox and his wife they had a great strife,
They never ate mustard in all their whole life;
They ate their meat without fork or knife,
And loved to be picking a bone, e-oh!

The fox jumped up on a moonlight night;
The stars they were shining, and all things bright;
Oh, ho! said the fox, it's a very fine night
For me to go through the town, e-ho!

The fox when he came to yonder stile,
He lifted his lugs and he listened a while!
Oh, ho! said the fox, it's but a short mile
From this unto yonder wee town, e-ho!

The fox when he came to the farmer's gate,
Who should he see but the farmer's drake;
I love you well for your master's sake,
And long to be picking your bone, e-ho!

The gray goose she ran round the hay-stack,
Oh, ho! said the fox, you are very fat;
You'll grease my beard and ride on my back
From this into yonder wee town, e-ho!

Old Gammer Hipple-hopple hopped out of bed,
She opened the casement, and popped out her head;
Oh! husband, oh! husband, the gray goose is dead,
And the fox is gone through the town, oh!

Then the old man got up in his red cap,
And swore he would catch the fox in a trap;
But the fox was too cunning, and gave him the slip,
And ran through the town, the town, oh!

When he got up to the top of the hill,
He blew his trumpet both loud and shrill,
For joy that he was safe
  Through the town, oh!

When the fox came back to his den,
He had young ones both nine and ten
"You're welcome home, daddy, you may go again,
If you bring us such nice meat
  From the town, oh!"

OLD MOTHER HUBBARD

Old Mother Hubbard
Went to the cupboard
  To get her poor dog a bone;
But when she came there
The cupboard was bare,
  And so the poor dog had none.

She went to the baker's
  To buy him some bread,
But when she came back
  The poor dog was dead.

She went to the joiner's
  To buy him a coffin,
But when she came back
  The poor dog was laughing.

She took a clean dish
  To get him some tripe,
But when she came back
  He was smoking his pipe.

She went to the fishmonger's
  To buy him some fish,
And when she came back
  He was licking the dish.

She went to the ale-house
  To get him some beer,
But when she got back
  The dog sat in a chair.

She went to the tavern
  For white wine and red,
But when she came back
  The dog stood on his head.

She went to the hatter's
  To buy him a hat,
But when she came back
  He was feeding the cat.

She went to the barber's
  To buy him a wig,
But when she came back
  He was dancing a jig.

She went to the fruiterer's
  To buy him some fruit,
But when she came back
  He was playing the flute.

She went to the tailor's
  To buy him a coat,
But when she came back
  He was riding a goat.

She went to the cobbler's
  To buy him some shoes,
But when she came back
  He was reading the news.

She went to the seamstress
  To buy him some linen,
But when she came back
  The dog was spinning.

She want to the hosier's
  To buy him some hose,
But when she came back
  He was dress'd in his clothes.

The dame made a curtsey,
  The dog made a bow;
The dame said, "Your servant,"
  The dog said, "Bow, wow."

A FROG HE WOULD A-WOOING GO

A frog he would a-wooing go,
  Sing, heigho, says Rowley,
Whether his mother would let him or no;
With a rowley, powley, gammon, and spinach,
  Heigho, says Anthony Rowley.

So off he marched with his opera hat,
  Heigho, says Rowley,
And on the way he met with a rat,
  With a rowley, powley, etc.

"Pray, Mr. Rat, will you go with me,"
  Heigho, says Rowley,
"Pretty Miss Mouse for to see?"
  With a rowley, powley, etc.

And when they came to mouse's hall,
  Heigho, says Rowley,
They gave a loud knock, and they gave a loud call
  With a rowley, powley, etc.

"Pray, Miss Mouse, are you within?"
  Heigho, says Rowley;
"Yes, kind sir, I am sitting to spin,"
  With a rowley, powley, etc.

"Pray, Miss Mouse, will you give us some beer?"
  Heigho, says Rowley;
"For Froggy and I are fond of good cheer,"
  With a rowley, powley, etc.

"Pray, Mr. Frog, will you give us a song?"
  Heigho, says Rowley,
"But let it be something that's not very long."
  With a rowley, powley, etc.

"Indeed, Miss Mouse," replied Mr. Frog.
  Heigho, says Rowley,
"A cold has made me as hoarse as a Hog."
  With a rowley, powley, etc.

"Since you have caught cold," Miss Mouse said
  Heigho, say Rowley,
"I'll sing you a song that I have just made,"
  With a rowley, powley, etc.

Now while they all were a merry-making,
  Heigho, says Rowley,
The cat and her kittens came tumbling in,
  With a rowley, powley, etc.

The cat she seized the rat by the crown,
  Heigho, says Rowley,
The kittens they pulled the little mouse down,
  With a rowley, powley, etc.

This put poor frog in a terrible fright,
  Heigho, says Rowley,
So he took up his hat and wished them good-night,
  With a rowley, powley, etc.

But as Froggy was crossing over a brook,
  Heigho, says Rowley,
A lily-white duck came and gobbled him up,
  With a rowley, powley, etc.

So there was an end of one, two, and three,
  Heigho, says Rowley,
The rat, the mouse, and the little Frog-ee!
With a rowley, powley, gammon, and spinach,
  Heigho, says Anthony Rowley.

THE HOUSE THAT JACK BUILT

1. This is the house that Jack built.

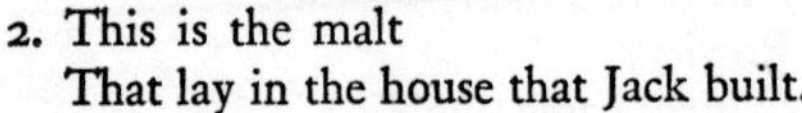

2. This is the malt
   That lay in the house that Jack built.

3. This is the rat,
   That ate the malt,
   That lay in the house that Jack built.

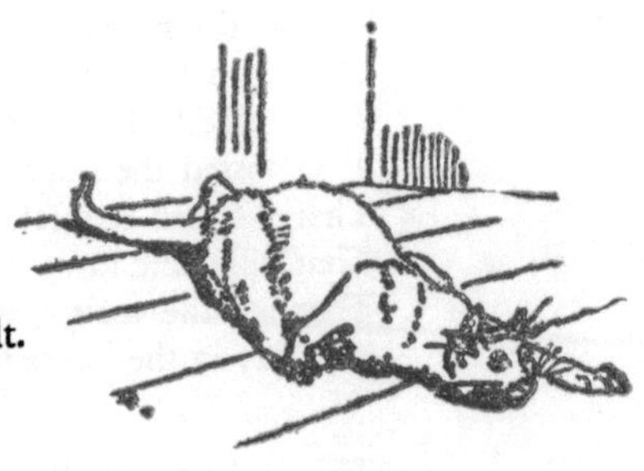

4. This is the cat,
That kill'd the rat,
That ate the malt,
That lay in the house that Jack built.

5. This is the dog,
That worried the cat,
That kill'd the rat,
That ate the malt,
That lay in the house that Jack built.

6. This is the cow with the crumpled horn,
That toss'd the dog,
That worried the cat,
That kill'd the rat,
That ate the malt,
That lay in the house that Jack built.

7. This is the maiden all forlorn,
That milk'd the cow with the crumpled horn,
That toss'd the dog,
That worried the cat,
That kill'd the rat,
That ate the malt,
That lay in the house that Jack built.

8. This is the man all tatter'd and torn,
That kissed the maiden all forlorn,
That milk'd the cow with the crumpled horn,
That tossed the dog,
That worried the cat,
That kill'd the rat,
That ate the malt,
That lay in the house that Jack built,

9. This is the priest all shaven and shorn,
That married the man all tatter'd and torn,
That kiss'd the maiden all forlorn,
That milk'd the cow with the crumpled horn,
That tossed the dog,
That worried the cat,
That kill'd the rat,
That ate the malt,
That lay in the house that Jack built.

10. This is the cock that crow'd in the morn,
That waked the priest all shaven and shorn,
That married the man all tatter'd and torn,
That kiss'd the maiden all forlorn,
That milk'd the cow with the crumpled horn,
That toss'd the dog,
That worried the cat,
That kill'd the rat,
That ate the malt,
That lay in the house that Jack built.

11. This is the farmer sowing his corn,
That kept the cock that crow'd in the morn,
That waked the priest all shaven and shorn,
That married the man all tatter'd and torn,
That kissed the maiden all forlorn,
That milk'd the cow with the crumpled horn,
That tossed the dog,
That worried the cat,
That kill'd the rat,
That ate the malt,
That lay in the house that Jack built.

RIDDLES

Two legs sat upon three legs,
With one leg in his lap;
In comes four legs,
And runs away with one leg.
Up jumps two legs,
Catches up three legs,
Throws it after four legs,
And makes him bring back one leg.

[*One leg is a leg of mutton; two legs, a man; three legs, a stool; four legs, a dog*

As I went through the garden gap,
Who should I meet but Dick Red-cap!
A stick in his hand, a stone in his throat,
If you'll tell me this riddle, I'll give you a groat.

[*A cherry*

Thirty white horses upon a red hill,
Now they tramp, now they champ, now they stand still.

[*Teeth and gums*

Arthur O'Bower has broken his band,
He comes roaring up the land—
The King of Scots, with all his power,
Cannot turn Arthur of the Bower!

[*A storm of wind*

Hick-a-more, Hack-a-more,
On the king's kitchen door;
All the king's horses,
And all the king's men,
Couldn't drive Hick-a-more, Hack-a-more,
Off the king's kitchen door!

[*Sunshine*

Long legs, crooked thighs,
Little head, and no eyes.

[*Pair of tongs*

Flour of England, fruit of Spain,
Met together in a shower of rain;
Put in a bag tied round with a string,
If you'll tell me this riddle, I'll give you a ring.

[*A plum-pudding*

Little Nancy Etticote,
In a white petticoat,
With a red nose;
The longer she stands
The shorter she grows.

[*A candle*

I have a little sister, they call her Peep, Peep;
She wades the waters deep, deep, deep;
She climbs the mountains high, high, high;
Poor little creature she has but one eye.

[*A star*

As I was going to St. Ives,
I met a man with seven wives;
Every wife had seven sacks,
Every sack had seven cats,
Every cat had seven kits:
Kits, cats, sacks, and wives,
How many were there going to St. Ives?

[*One*

Poems of Childhood and Youth

NATURE'S YEAR

PIPING DOWN THE VALLEYS WILD

By William Blake

Piping down the valleys wild,
  Piping songs of pleasant glee,
On a cloud I saw a child,
  And he laughing said to me:

"Pipe a song about a lamb!"
  So I piped with merry cheer.
"Piper, pipe that song again";
  So I piped: he wept to hear.

"Drop thy pipe, thy happy pipe;
  Sing thy songs of happy cheer!"
So I sang the same again.
  While he wept with joy to hear.

"Piper, sit thee down and write
  In a book that all may read."
So he vanished from my sight;
  And I plucked a hollow reed.

And I made a rural pen,
  And I stained the water clear,
And I wrote my happy songs
  Every child may joy to hear.

NEARLY READY

By Mary Mapes Dodge

In the snowing and the blowing,
  In the cruel sleet,
Little flowers begin their growing
  Far beneath our feet.
Softly taps the Spring, and cheerly,
  "Darlings, are you here?"
Till they answer, "We are nearly,
  Nearly ready, dear."

"Where is Winter, with his snowing?
  "Tell us, Spring," they say.
Then she answers, "He is going,
  Going on his way.
Poor old Winter does not love you;
  But his time is past;
Soon my birds shall sing above you—
  Set you free at last."

MARCH

By William Wordsworth

The cock is crowing,
The stream is flowing,
The small birds twitter,
The lake doth glitter,
The green field sleeps in the sun;
The oldest and youngest
Are at work with the strongest;
The cattle are grazing,
Their heads never raising;
There are forty feeding like one!

Like an army defeated
The snow hath retreated,
And now doth fare ill
On the top of the bare hill;
The plowboy is whooping—anon—anon;

There's joy in the mountains;
There's life in the fountains;
Small clouds are sailing,
Blue sky prevailing;
The rain is over and gone!

SPRING

By Thomas Nashe

Spring, the sweet Spring, is the year's pleasant king;
Then blooms each thing, then maids dance in a ring,
Cold doth not sting, the pretty birds do sing,
  Cuckoo, jug-jug, pu-we, to-witta-woo!

The palm and may make country houses gay,
Lambs frisk and play, the shepherds pipe all day,
And we hear aye birds tune this merry lay,
  Cuckoo, jug-jug, pu-we, to-witta-woo!

The fields breathe sweet, the daisies kiss our feet,
Young lovers meet, old wives a-sunning sit,
In every street, these tunes our ears do greet,
  Cuckoo, jug-jug, pu-we, to-witta-woo!
    Spring, the sweet Spring!

THE SPICEBUSH IN MARCH

By Sara Teasdale

Spicebush, yellow spicebush, tell me
  Where you found so much clear gold?
Every branch and every twig
  Has as much as it can hold,
Flaunting before tattered winter
  Your new dress the wind whips round—
Color, color! You were first,
  You dredged and drew it from the ground!

SPRING QUIET

By Christina G. Rossetti

Gone were but the Winter,
 Come were but the Spring,
I would go to a covert
 Where the birds sing.

Where in the whitethorn
 Singeth a thrush,
And a robin sings
 In the holly-bush.

Full of fresh scents,
 Are the budding boughs
Arching high over
 A cool green house:

Full of sweet scents,
 And whispering air
Which sayeth softly:
 "We spread no snare;

"Here dwell in safety,
 Here dwell alone,
With a clear stream
 And a mossy stone.

"Here the sun shineth
 Most shadily;
Here is heard an echo
 Of the far sea,
 Though far off it be."

THE DANDELIONS

By Helen Gray Cone

Upon a showery night and still,
 Without a sound of warning,
A trooper band surprised the hill,
 And held it in the morning.
We were not waked by bugle-notes,
 No cheer our dreams invaded,
And yet, at dawn, their yellow coats
 On the green slopes paraded.

We careless folk the deed forgot;
  Till one day, idly walking,
We marked upon the self-same spot
  A crowd of vet'rans talking.
They shook their trembling heads and gray
  With pride and noiseless laughter;
When, well-a-day! they blew away,
  And ne'er were heard of after!

THE WIND IN A FROLIC

By William Howitt

The wind one morning sprang up from sleep,
Saying, "Now for a frolic! now for a leap!
Now for a madcap galloping chase!
I'll make a commotion in every place!"
So it swept with a bustle right through a great town,
Cracking the signs and scattering down
Shutters; and whisking, with merciless squalls,
Old women's bonnets and gingerbread stalls.
There never was heard a lustier shout,
As the apples and oranges trundled about;
And the urchins that stand with their thievish eyes
For ever on watch, ran off each with a prize.

Then away to the field it went, blustering and humming,
And the cattle all wondered whatever was coming;
It plucked by the tails the grave matronly cows,
And tossed the colts' manes all over their brows;
Till, offended at such an unusual salute,
They all turned their backs, and stood sulky and mute.

So on it went capering and playing its pranks,
Whistling with reeds on the broad river's banks,
Puffing the birds as they sat on the spray,
Or the traveler grave on the king's highway.
It was not too nice to hustle the bags
Of the beggar, and flutter his dirty rags;

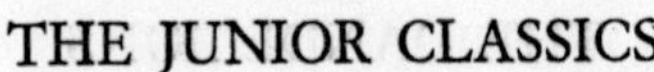

'Twas so bold that it feared not to play its joke
With the doctor's wig or the gentleman's cloak.
Through the forest it roared, and cried gaily, "Now,
You sturdy old oaks, I'll make you bow!"
And it made them bow without more ado,
Or it cracked their great branches through and through.

Then it rushed like a monster on cottage and farm,
Striking their dwellers with sudden alarm;
And they ran out like bees in a midsummer swarm;—
There were dames with their kerchiefs tied over their caps,
To see if their poultry were free from mishaps;
The turkeys they gobbled, the geese screamed aloud,
And the hens crept to roost in a terrified crowd;
There was rearing of ladders, and logs laying on,
Where the thatch from the roof threatened soon to be gone.

But the wind had swept on, and had met in a lane
With a schoolboy, who panted and struggled in vain;
For it tossed him and twirled him, then passed, and he stood
With his hat in a pool and his shoes in the mud.
Then away went the wind in its holiday glee,
And now it was far on the billowy sea,
And the lordly ships felt its staggering blow,
And the little boats darted to and fro.
But lo! it was night, and it sank to rest
On the sea-bird's rock in the gleaming West,
Laughing to think, in its fearful fun,
How little of mischief it really had done.

WHO HAS SEEN THE WIND?

By Christina G. Rossetti

Who has seen the wind?
Neither I nor you:
But when the leaves hang trembling,
The wind is passing through.

Who has seen the wind?
Neither you nor I:
But when the trees bow down their heads
The wind is passing by.

THE PROCESSION OF THE FLOWERS

By Sydney Dobell

First came the primrose,
On the bank high,
Like a maiden looking forth
From the window of a tower
When the battle rolls below,
So looked she,
And saw the storms go by.

Then came the wind-flower
In the valley left behind,
As a wounded maiden pale
With purple streaks of woe
When the battle has roll'd by
Wanders to and fro,
So tottered she,
Dishevell'd in the wind.

Then came the daisies,
On the first of May,
Like a bannered show's advance
While the crowd runs by the way,
With ten thousand flowers about them
They came trooping through the fields.

As a happy people come,
So came they;
As a happy people come
When the war has rolled away,
With dance and tabor, pipe and drum,
And all make holiday.

Then came the cowslip
Like a dancer in the fair,
She spread her little mat of green,
And on it danced she.
With a fillet bound about her brow,
A fillet round her happy brow,
A golden fillet round her brow,
And rubies in her hair

THE GRASS

By Emily Dickinson

The grass so little has to do—
A sphere of simple green,
With only butterflies to brood,
And bees to entertain,

And stir all day to pretty tunes
The breezes fetch along,
And hold the sunshine in its lap
And bow to everything;

And thread the dews all night, like pearls,
And make itself so fine—
A duchess were too common
For such a noticing.

And even when it dies, to pass
In odors so divine,
As lowly spices gone to sleep,
Or amulets of pine.

And then to dwell in sovereign barns,
And dream the days away—
The grass so little has to do,
I wish I were a hay!

JUNE

By James Russell Lowell

And what is so rare as a day in June?
  Then, if ever come perfect days;
Then Heaven tries the earth if it be in tune,
  And over it softly her warm ear lays:
Whether we look, or whether we listen,
We hear life murmur, or see it glisten;
Every clod feels a stir of might,
  An instinct within it that reaches and towers,
And, groping blindly above it for light,
  Climbs to a soul in grass and flowers;

The flush of life may well be seen
  Thrilling back over hills and valleys;
The cowslip startles in meadows green,
  The buttercup catches the sun in its chalice,
And there's never a leaf nor a blade too mean
  To be some happy creature's palace;
The little bird sits at his door in the sun,
  Atilt like a blossom among the leaves,
And lets his illumined being o'errun
  With the deluge of summer it receives;
His mate feels the eggs beneath her wings,
And the heart in her dumb breast flutters and sings;
He sings to the wide world and she to her nest—
In the nice ear of Nature which song is the best?

Now is the high tide of the year,
  And whatever of life hath ebbed away
Comes flooding back with a ripply cheer,
  Into every bare inlet and creek and bay;
Now the heart is so full that a drop overfills it,
We are happy now because God wills it;
No matter how barren the past may have been,
'Tis enough for us now that the leaves are green;
We sit in the warm shade and feel right well
How the sap creeps up and the blossoms swell;
We may shut our eyes, but we cannot help knowing
That skies are clear and grass is growing;
The breeze comes whispering in our ear,
That dandelions are blossoming near,
That maize has sprouted, that streams are flowing,
That the river is bluer than the sky,
That the robin is plastering his house hard by;
And if the breeze kept the good news back,
For other couriers we should not lack;
  We could guess it all by yon heifer's lowing,
And hark! how clear bold chanticleer,
Warmed with the new wine of the year,
  Tells all in his lusty crowing!

SUMMER DAYS

By Christina G. Rossetti

Winter is cold-hearted;
Spring is yea and nay;
Autumn is a weathercock;
Blown every way:
Summer days for me
When every leaf is on its tree,

When Robin's not a beggar,
And Jenny Wren's a bride,
And larks hang, singing, singing, singing,
Over the wheat-fields wide,
And anchored lilies ride,
And the pendulum spider,
Swings from side to side,

And blue-black beetles transact business,
And gnats fly in a host,
And furry caterpillars hasten
That no time be lost,
And moths grow fat and thrive,
And lady birds arrive.

Before green apples blush,
Before green nuts embrown,
Why, one day in the country
Is worth a month in town—
Is worth a day and a year
Of the dusty, musty, lag-last fashion
That days drone elsewhere.

HOW THE LEAVES CAME DOWN

By Susan Coolidge

I'll tell you how the leaves came down.
The great Tree to his children said:
"You're getting sleepy, Yellow and Brown,
Yes, very sleepy, little Red.
It is quite time to go to bed."

"Ah!" begged each silly, pouting leaf,
"Let us a little longer stay;
Dear Father Tree, behold our grief!
'Tis such a very pleasant day,
We do not want to go away."

So, for just one more merry day
To the great Tree the leaflets clung,
Frolicked and danced, and had their way,
Upon the autumn breezes swung,
Whispering all their sports among—

"Perhaps the great Tree will forget,
And let us stay until the spring,
If we all beg, and coax, and fret."
But the great Tree did no such thing;
He smiled to hear their whispering.

"Come, children, all to bed," he cried;
And ere the leaves could urge their prayer,
He shook his head, and far and wide,
Fluttering and rustling everywhere,
Down sped the leaflets through the air.

I saw them; on the ground they lay,
Golden and red, a huddled swarm,
Waiting till one from far away,
White bedclothes heaped upon her arm,
Should come to wrap them safe and warm.

The great bare Tree looked down and smiled.
"Good night, dear little leaves," he said.
And from below each sleepy child
Replied, "Good night," and murmurèd,
"It is so nice to go to bed!"

THE MORNS ARE MEEKER THAN THEY WERE

By Emily Dickinson

The morns are meeker than they were,
The nuts are getting brown;
The berry's cheek is plumper,
The rose is out of town.

The maple wears a gayer scarf,
The field a scarlet gown.
Lest I should be old-fashioned,
I'll put a trinket on.

AUTUMN FIRES

By Robert Louis Stevenson

In the other gardens
And all up the vale,
From the autumn bonfires
See the smoke trail!

Pleasant summer over
And all the summer flowers,
The red fire blazes,
The gray smoke towers.

Sing a song of seasons!
Something bright in all!
Flowers in the summer,
Fires in the fall!

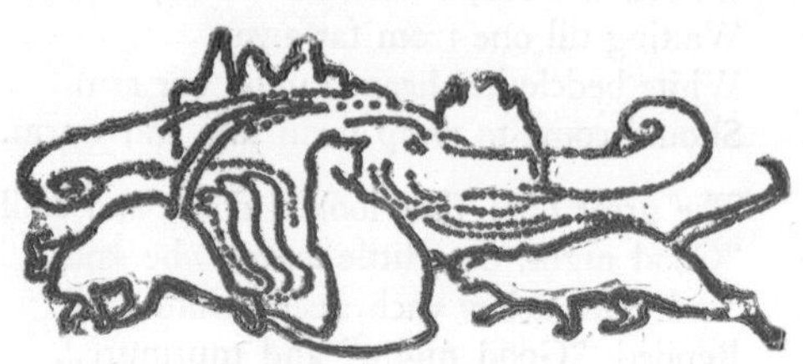

FOG

By Carl Sandburg

The fog comes
on little cat feet.

It sits looking
over harbor and city
on silent haunches
and then, moves on.

THE FROST

By Hannah Flagg Gould

The Frost looked forth, one still, clear night,
And whispered, "Now I shall be out of sight;
So through the valley and over the height,
In silence I'll take my way:
I will not go on with that blustering train,
The wind and the snow, the hail and the rain,
Who makes so much bustle and noise in vain,
But I'll be as busy as they."

Then he flew to the mountain and powdered its crest;
He lit on the trees, and their boughs he dressed
In diamond beads—and over the breast
Of the quivering lake he spread
A coat of mail, that it need not fear
The downward point of many a spear
That hung on its margin far and near,
Where a rock could rear its head.

He went to the windows of those who slept,
And over each pane, like a fairy, crept;
Wherever he breathed, wherever he slept,
By the light of the moon were seen
Most beautiful things—there were flowers and trees;
There were bevies of birds and swarms of bees;
There were cities with temples and towers, and these
All pictured in silver sheen!

But he did one thing that was hardly fair;
He peeped in the cupboard, and finding there
That all had forgotten for him to prepare—
"Now just to set them a-thinking,
I'll bite this basket of fruit," said he,
"This costly pitcher I'll burst in three,
And the glass of water they've left for me
Shall *'tchich!'* to tell them I'm drinking."

RHYME OF NOVEMBER STARS

By Sara Teasdale

The noiseless marching of the stars
Sweeps above me all night long;
Up the skies, over the skies,
Passes the uncounted throng,
Without haste, without rest,
From the east to the west:
Vega, Deneb, white Altair
Shine like crystals in the air,
And the lonely Fomalhaut
In the dark south, paces low.
Now the timid Pleiades
Leave the shelter of the trees,
While toward the north, mounting high,
Gold Capella, like a queen,
Watches over her demesne
Stretching toward the kingly one,
Dusky, dark Aldebaran.
Betelguese and Rigel burn
In their wide wheel, slow to turn,
And in the sharp November frost
Bright Sirius, with his blue light
Completes the loveliness of night.

WINDY NIGHTS

By Robert Louis Stevenson

Whenever the moon and stars are set,
Whenever the wind is high,
All night long in the dark and wet,
A man goes riding by.
Late in the night when the fires are out,
Why does he gallop and gallop about?

Whenever the trees are crying aloud,
And ships are tossed at sea,
By, on the highway, low and loud,
By at the gallop goes he.
By at the gallop he goes, and then
By he comes back at the gallop again.

WINTER

By William Shakespeare

When icicles hang by the wall,
And Dick the shepherd blows his nail,
And Tom bears logs into the hall,
And milk comes frozen home in pail,
When blood is nipt, and ways be foul,
Then nightly sings the staring owl,
Tuwhoo!
Tuwhit! Tuwhoo! A merry note!
While greasy Joan doth keel the pot.

When all around the wind doth blow,
And coughing drowns the parson's saw,
And birds sit brooding in the snow,
And Marian's nose looks red and raw;
When roasted crabs hiss in the bowl,
Then nightly sings the staring owl,
Tuwhoo!
Tuwhit! Tuwhoo! A merry note!
While greasy Joan doth keel the pot.

A SONG OF WINTER

Anonymous

Cold cold!
Cold tonight is broad Moylurg,
Higher the snow than the mountain-range,
The deer cannot get at their food.

Cold till Doom!
The storm has spread over all:
A river is each furrow upon the slope,
Each ford a full pool.

A great tidal sea is each loch,
A full loch is each pool:
Horses cannot get over the ford of Ross,
No more can two feet get there.

The fish of Ireland are a-roaming,
There is no strand which the wave does not pound,
Not a town there is in the land,
Not a bell is heard, no crane talks.

The wolves of Cuan-wood get
Neither rest nor sleep in their lair,
The little wren cannot find
Shelter in her nest on the slope of Lon.

Keen wind and cold ice
Has burst upon the little company of birds,
The blackbird cannot get a lee to her liking,
Shelter for its side in Cuan-wood.

Cozy our pot on its hook,
Crazy the hut on the slope of Lon:
The snow has crushed the wood here,
Toilsome to climb up Ben-bo.

Glenn Rye's ancient bird
From the bitter wind gets grief;
Great her misery and her pain,
The ice will get into her mouth.

From flock and from down to rise—
Take it to heart—were folly for thee;
Ice in heaps on every ford—
That is why I say "cold"!

VELVET SHOES

By Elinor Wylie

Let us walk in the white snow
  In a soundless space;
With footsteps quiet and slow,
  At a tranquil pace,
  Under veils of white lace.

I shall go shod in silk,
  And you in wool,
White as a white cow's milk,
  More beautiful
  Than the breast of a gull.

We shall walk through the still town
  In a windless peace;
We shall step upon white down,
  Upon silver fleece,
  Upon softer than these.

We shall walk in velvet shoes:
  Wherever we go
Silence will fall like dews
  On white silence below.
  We shall walk in the snow.

STOPPING BY WOODS ON A SNOWY EVENING

By Robert Frost

Whose woods these are I think I know.
His house is in the village though;
He will not see me stopping here
To watch his woods fill up with snow.

The little horse must think it queer
To stop without a farmhouse near
Between the woods and frozen lake
The darkest evening of the year.

He gives his harness bells a shake
To ask if there is some mistake.
The only other sound's the sweep
Of easy wind and downy flake.

The woods are lovely, dark and deep.
But I have promises to keep,
And miles to go before I sleep,
And miles to go before I sleep.

O LADY MOON

By Christina G. Rossetti

O Lady Moon, your horns point toward the east:
  Shine, be increased;
O Lady Moon, your horns point toward the west:
  Wane, be at rest.

THE WIND AND THE MOON

By George Macdonald

Said the Wind to the Moon, "I will blow you out!
You stare
In the air
As if crying 'Beware,'
Always looking what I am about:
I hate to be watched; I will blow you out!"

The Wind blew hard, and out went the Moon.
So, deep
On a heap
Of clouds, to sleep,
Down lay the Wind, and slumbered soon,
Muttering low, "I've done for that Moon!"

He turned in his bed: she was there again!
On high
In the sky,
With her one ghost-eye
The Moon shone white and alive and plain:
Said the Wind, "I will blow you out again!"

The wind blew hard, and the Moon grew slim.
"With my sledge
And my wedge
I have knocked off her edge!
I will blow," said the Wind, "right fierce and grim,
And the creature will soon be slimmer than slim!"

He blew and he blew, and she thinned to a thread.
"One puff
More's enough
To blow her to snuff!
One good puff more where the last was bred,
And glimmer, glimmer, glum will go that thread!"

He blew a great blast, and the thread was gone.
In the air
Nowhere
Was a moonbeam bare;
Larger and nearer the shy stars shone:
Sure and certain the Moon was gone!

The Wind he took to his revels once more;
On down
And in town,
A merry-mad clown,
He leaped and holloed with whistle and roar—
When there was that glimmering thread once more!

He flew in a rage—he danced and blew;
But in vain
Was the pain
Of his bursting brain,
For still the Moon-scrap the broader grew
The more that he swelled his big cheeks and blew.

Slowly she grew—till she filled the night,
And shone
On her throne
In the sky alone,
A matchless, wonderful, silvery light,
Radiant and lovely, the queen of the night.

Said the Wind: "What a marvel of power am I!
With my breath,
In good faith,
I blew her to death!—
First blew her away right out of the sky,
Then blew her in: what a strength am I!"

But the Moon she knew naught of the silly affair:
For, high
In the sky,
With her one white eye,
Motionless miles above the air,
She never had heard the great Wind blare.

LADY MOON

By Lord Houghton

Lady Moon, Lady Moon, where are you roving?
"Over the sea."
Lady Moon, Lady Moon, whom are you loving?
"All that love me."

Are you not tired with rolling, and never
Resting to sleep?
Why look so pale and so sad, as forever
Wishing to weep?

"Ask me not this, little child, if you love me:
You are too bold:
I must obey my dear Father above me,
And do as I'm told."

Lady Moon, Lady Moon, where are you roving?
"Over the sea."
Lady Moon, Lady Moon, whom are you loving?
"All that love me."

THE NIGHT WILL NEVER STAY

By Eleanor Farjeon

The night will never stay,
The night will still go by,
Though with a million stars
You pin it to the sky;
Though you bind it with the blowing wind
And buckle it with the moon,
The night will slip away
Like sorrow or a tune.

THE OLD HORSE IN THE CITY

By Vachel Lindsay

The moon's a peck of corn. It lies
Heaped up for me to eat.
I wish that I might climb the path
And taste that supper sweet.

Men feed me straw and scanty grain
And beat me till I'm sore.
Some day I'll break the halter-rope
And smash the stable-door,

Run down the street and mount the hill
Just as the corn appears.
I've seen it rise at certain times
For years and years and years.

YET GENTLE WILL THE GRIFFIN BE

By Vachel Lindsay

The moon? It is a griffin's egg,
Hatching tomorrow night.
And how the little boys will watch
With shouting and delight
To see him break the shell and stretch
And creep across the sky.
The boys will laugh. The little girls,
I fear, may hide and cry.
Yet gentle will the griffin be,
Most decorous and fat,
And walk up to the Milky Way
And lap it like a cat.

THE MOON'S THE NORTH WIND'S COOKY

By Vachel Lindsay

The Moon's the North Wind's cooky.
He bites it, day by day,
Until there's but a rim of scraps
That crumble all away.

The South Wind is a baker.
He kneads clouds in his den,
And bakes a crisp new moon that . . . greedy
North . . . Wind . . . eats . . . again!

STARS

By Sara Teasdale

Alone in the night
  On a dark hill
With pines around me
  Spicy and still,

And a heaven full of stars
  Over my head,
White and topaz
  And misty red;

Myriads with beating
  Hearts of fire
That aeons
  Cannot vex or tire;

Up the dome of heaven
  Like a great hill,
I watch them marching
  Stately and still,

And I know that I
  Am honored to be
Witness
  Of so much majesty.

Dorothy Lathrop

A heaven full of stars.

[See page 48]

CANIS MAJOR

By Robert Frost

The Great Overdog,
  That heavenly beast
With a star in one eye,
  Gives a leap in the East.

He dances upright
  All the way to the West,
And never once drops
  On his forefeet to rest.

I'm a poor Underdog;
  But tonight I will bark,
With the Great Overdog
  That romps through the dark.

DONNYBROOK

By James Stephens

I saw the moon, so broad and bright,
Sailing high on a frosty night!

And the air shone silvery between
The pearly queen and the silver queen!

And here a white, and there a white
Cloud mist swam in a mist of light!

And, all encrusted in the sky,
High, and higher, and yet more high,

Was gold and gold that glimmered through
The hollow vault, the vault of blue:

And then I knew—that God was good,
And the world was fair! And, where I stood,

I bent the knee, and bent the head;
And said my prayers and went to bed.

LIGHT THE LAMPS UP, LAMPLIGHTER

By Eleanor Farjeon

Light the lamps up, Lamplighter,
The people are in the street—
    Without a light
    They have no sight,
And where will they plant their feet?
Some will tread in the gutter,
And some in the mud—oh dear!
Light the lamps up, Lamplighter,
Because the night is here.

Light the candles, Grandmother,
The children are going to bed—
    Without a wick
    They'll stumble and stick,
And where will they lay their head?
Some will lie on the staircase,
And some in the hearth—oh dear!
Light the candles, Grandmother,
Because the night is here.

Light the stars up, Gabriel,
The cherubs are out to fly—
    If heaven is blind
    How will they find
Their way across the sky?
Some will splash in the Milky Way,
Or bump on the moon—oh dear!
Light the stars up, Gabriel,
Because the night is here.

THE WORLD OF CREATURES

ALL THINGS BRIGHT AND BEAUTIFUL

By Cecil Frances Alexander

All things bright and beautiful,
  All creatures great and small,
All things wise and wonderful,
  The Lord God made them all.

Each little flower that opens,
  Each little bird that sings,
He made their glowing colors,
  He made their tiny wings.

The rich man in his castle,
  The poor man at his gate,
God made them, high or lowly,
  And order'd their estate.

The sunset and the morning,
  The river running by,
The purple-headed mountain,
  That brightens up the sky—

The cold wind in the winter,
The pleasant summer sun,
The ripe fruits in the garden—
He made them every one.

The tall trees in the greenwood,
The meadows where we play,
The rushes by the water
We gather every day.

He gave us eyes to see them,
And lips that we might tell,
How great is God Almighty,
Who has made all things well.

THE BUTTERFLY'S BALL

By William Roscoe

"Come, take up your hats, and away let us haste
To the Butterfly's Ball and the Grasshopper's Feast:
The trumpeter, Gadfly, has summoned the crew,
And the revels are now only waiting for you."

So said little Robert, and pacing along,
His merry companions came forth in a throng,
And on the smooth grass by the side of a wood,
Beneath a broad oak that for ages has stood,
Saw the children of earth and the tenants of air
For an evening's amusement together repair.

And there came the Beetle, so blind and so black,
Who carried the Emmet, his friend on his back;
And there was the Gnat and the Dragon-fly too,
With all their relations, green, orange, and blue.

And there came the Moth, with his plumage of down,
And the Hornet, in jacket of yellow and brown,
Who with him the Wasp, his companion, did bring:
They promised that evening to lay by their sting.

And the sly little Dormouse crept out of his hole,
And brought to the Feast his blind brother, the Mole.
And the Snail, with his horns peeping out of his shell,
Came from a great distance—the length of an ell.

A mushroom their table, and on it was laid
A water-dock leaf, which a tablecloth made.
The viands were various, to each of their taste,
And the Bee brought her honey to crown the repast.

Then close on his haunches, so solemn and wise,
The Frog from a corner looked up to the skies;
And the Squirrel, well-pleased such diversions to see,
Mounted high overhead and looked down from a tree.

Then out came a Spider, with fingers so fine,
To show his dexterity on the tight-line.
From one branch to another his cobwebs he slung,
Then quick as an arrow he darted along.

But just in the middle—oh! shocking to tell,
From his rope, in an instant, poor Harlequin fell.
Yet he touched not the ground, but with talons outspread,
Hung suspended in air, at the end of a thread.

Then the Grasshopper came, with a jerk and a spring,
Very long was his leg, though but short was his wing;
He took but three leaps, and was soon out of sight,
Then chirped his own praises the rest of the night.

With step so majestic, the Snail did advance,
And promised the gazers a minuet to dance;
But they all laughed so loud that he pulled in his head,
And went to his own little chamber to bed.
Then as evening gave way to the shadows of night,
Their watchman, the Glow-worm, came out with a light.

"Then home let us hasten while yet we can see,
For no watchman is waiting for you and for me."
So said little Robert, and pacing along,
His merry companions returned in a throng.

THE SPIDER AND THE FLY

By Mary Howitt

"Will you walk into my parlor?"
  Said a spider to a fly;
" 'Tis the prettiest little parlor
  That ever you did spy.
The way into my parlor
  Is up a winding stair,
And I have many pretty things
  To show when you are there."
"Oh, no, no!" said the little fly,
  "To ask me is in vain;
For who goes up your winding stair
  Can ne'er come down again."

"I'm sure you must be weary
  With soaring up so high;
Will you rest upon my little bed?"
  Said the spider to the fly.
"There are pretty curtains drawn around,
  The sheets are fine and thin;
And if you like to rest awhile,
  I'll snugly tuck you in."
"Oh, no, no!" said the little fly,
  "For I've often heard it said,
They never, never wake again
  Who sleep upon your bed."

Said the cunning spider to the fly,
  "Dear friend, what shall I do
To prove the warm affection
  I've always felt for you?
I have within my pantry
  Good store of all that's nice;
I'm sure you're very welcome—
  Will you please to take a slice?"
"Oh, no, no!" said the little fly,
  "Kind sir, that cannot be;
I've heard what's in your pantry,
  And I do not wish to see."

"Sweet creature," said the spider,
  "You're witty and you're wise;
How handsome are your gauzy wings,
  How brilliant are your eyes.
I have a little looking-glass
  Upon my parlor shelf;
If you'll step in one moment, dear,
  You shall behold yourself."
"I thank you, gentle sir," she said,
  "For what you're pleased to say,
And bidding you good morning, now,
  I'll call another day."

The spider turned him round about,
  And went into his den,
For well he knew the silly fly
  Would soon be back again;
So he wove a subtle thread
  In a little corner sly,
And set his table ready
  To dine upon the fly.
He went out to his door again,
  And merrily did sing,
"Come hither, hither, pretty fly,
  With the pearl and silver wing;
Your robes are green and purple,
  There's a crest upon your head;
Your eyes are like the diamond bright,
  But mine are dull as lead."

Alas, alas! how very soon
  This silly little fly,
Hearing his wily, flattering words,
  Came slowly flitting by:
With buzzing wings she hung aloft,
  Then near and nearer drew—
Thought only of her brilliant eyes,
  And green and purple hue;
Thought only of her crested head—
  Poor foolish thing! At last
Up jumped the cunning spider,
  And fiercely held her fast.

He dragged her up his winding stair,
  Into his dismal den
Within his little parlor—but
  She ne'er came out again!
And now, dear little children
  Who may this story read,
To idle, silly, flattering words,
  I pray you, ne'er give heed:
Unto an evil counselor
  Close heart and ear and eye,
And learn a lesson from this tale
  Of the spider and the fly.

TO THE GRASSHOPPER AND THE CRICKET

By Leigh Hunt

Green little vaulter in the sunny grass,
Catching your heart up at the feel of June—
Sole voice that's heard amidst the lazy noon
When even the bees lag at the summoning brass;
And you, warm little housekeeper, who class
With those who think the candles come too soon,
Loving the fire, and with your tricksome tune
Nick the glad silent moments as they pass!

O sweet and tiny cousins, that belong,
One to the fields, the other to the hearth,
Both have your sunshine; both, though small, are strong
At your clear hearts; and both seem given to earth
To sing in thoughtful ears this natural song—
In doors and out, summer and winter, mirth.

THE BEE

By Emily Dickinson

Like trains of cars on tracks of plush
  I hear the level bee:
A jar across the flower goes,
  Their velvet masonry

Withstands until the sweet assault
  Their chivalry consumes,
While he, victorious, tilts away
  To vanquish other blooms.

His feet are shod with gauze,
  His helmet is of gold;
His breast, a single onyx
  With chrysoprase, inlaid.

His labor is a chant,
  His idleness a tune;
Oh, for a bee's experience
  Of clovers and of noon!

A DREAM

By William Blake

Once a dream did weave a shade
O'er my Angel-guarded bed,
That an emmet lost its way
Where on grass methought I lay.

Troubled, 'wildered, and forlorn,
Dark, benighted, travel-worn,
Over many a tangled spray,
All heart-broke I heard her say:

"O my children! do they cry?
Do they hear their father sigh?
Now they look abroad to see:
Now return and weep for me."

Pitying, I dropped a tear;
But I saw a glow-worm near,
Who replied: "What wailing wight
Calls the watchman of the night?

"I am set to light the ground,
While the beetle goes his round:
Follow now the beetle's hum;
Little wanderer, hie thee home."

ALL THINGS WAIT UPON THEE

By Christina G. Rossetti

Innocent eyes not ours
And made to look on flowers,
Eyes of small birds, and insects small;
Morn after summer morn
The sweet rose on her thorn
Opens her bosom to them all.

The last and least of things,
That soar on quivering wings,
Or crawl among the grass blades out of sight
Have just as clear a right
To their appointed portion of delight
As queens or kings.

NATURE'S FRIEND

By William H. Davies

Say what you like,
All things love me!
I pick no flowers—
That wins the Bee.

The Summer's Moths
Think my hand one
To touch their wings
With Wind and Sun.

The garden Mouse
Comes near to play;
Indeed, he turns
His eyes away.

The Wren knows well
I rob no nest;
When I look in,
She still will rest.

The hedge stops Cows,
Or they would come
After my voice
Right to my home.

The Horse can tell,
  Straight from my lip,
My hand could not
  Hold any whip.

Say what you like
  All things love me!
Horse, Cow, and Mouse,
  Bird, Moth and Bee.

THE HOUSEKEEPER

By Charles Lamb

The frugal snail, with forecast of repose,
Carries his house with him where'er he goes;
Peeps out—and if there comes a shower of rain,
Retreats to his small domicile again.
Touch but a tip of him, a horn—'tis well—
He curls up in his sanctuary Shell,
He's his own landlord, his own tenant; stay
Long as he will, he dreads no Quarter Day.

Himself he boards and lodges; both invites
And feasts himself; sleeps with himself o'nights.
He spares the upholsterer trouble to procure
Chattels; himself is his own furniture,
And his sole riches. Wheresoe'er he roam—
Knock when you will—he's sure to be at home.

A NARROW FELLOW IN THE GRASS

By Emily Dickinson

A narrow fellow in the grass
Occasionally rides;
You may have met him—did you not?
His notice sudden is.

The grass divides as with a comb,
A spotted shaft is seen;
And then it closes at your feet
And opens further on.

He likes a boggy acre,
A floor too cool for corn.
Yet when a child, and barefoot,
I more than once, at morn,

Have passed, I thought, a whip-lash
Unbraiding in the sun—
When, stooping to secure it,
It wrinkled, and was gone.

Several of nature's people
I know, and they know me;
I feel for them a transport
Of cordiality;

But never met this fellow,
Attended or alone,
Without a tighter breathing,
And zero at the bone.

A FRIEND IN THE GARDEN

By Juliana Horatia Ewing

He is not John the gardener,
  And yet the whole day long
Employs himself most usefully,
  The flower-beds among.

He is not Tom the pussycat,
  And yet the other day,
With stealthy stride and glistening eye,
  He crept upon his prey.

He is not Dash the dear old dog,
  And yet perhaps, if you
Took pains with him and petted him,
  You'd come to love him too.

He's not a Blackbird, though he chirps,
  And though he once was black;
And now he wears a loose grey coat,
  All wrinkled on the back.

He's got a very dirty face,
And very shining eyes;
He sometimes comes and sits indoors;
He looks—and p'r'aps is—wise.

But in a sunny flower-bed
He has his fixed abode;
He eats the things that eat my plants—
He is a friendly TOAD.

SEAL LULLABY

By Rudyard Kipling

Oh, hush thee, my baby, the night is behind us,
And black are the waters that sparkled so green,
The moon o'er the combers, looks downward to find us
At rest in the hollows that rustle between.
Where billow meets billow, there soft be thy pillow;
Ah, weary wee flipperling, curl at thy ease!
The storm shall not wake thee, nor shark overtake thee,
Asleep in the arms of the slow-swinging seas.

ANSWER TO A CHILD'S QUESTION

By Samuel Taylor Coleridge

Do you ask what the birds say? The sparrow, the dove,
The linnet, and thrush say, "I love and I love!"
In the winter they're silent, the wind is so strong:
What it says I don't know, but it sings a loud song.
But green leaves and blossoms, and sunny warm weather,
And singing and loving, all come back together;
Then the lark is so brimful of gladness and love,
The green fields below him, the blue sky above,
That he sings, and he sings, and forever sings he,
"I love my Love, and my Love loves me."

A BIRD CAME DOWN THE WALK

By Emily Dickinson

A bird came down the walk:
He did not know I saw;
He bit an angle-worm in halves
And ate the fellow, raw.

And then he drank a dew
From a convenient grass,
And then hopped sidewise to the wall
To let a beetle pass.

He glanced with rapid eyes
That hurried all abroad—
They looked like frightened beads, I thought;
He stirred his velvet head

Like one in danger; cautious,
I offered him a crumb,
And he unrolled his feathers
And rowed him softer home

Than oars divide the ocean,
Too silver for a seam,
Or butterflies, off banks of noon,
Leap, plashless, as they swim.

THE LAST WORD OF A BLUEBIRD

By Robert Frost

As I went out a Crow
In a low voice said "Oh,
I was looking for you.
How do you do?
I just came to tell you
To tell Lesley (will you?)
That her little Bluebird
Wanted me to bring word
That the north wind last night,
That made the stars bright
And made the ice on the trough,
Almost made him cough
His tail feathers off.

He just had to fly
But he sent her Good-bye,
And said to be good,
And wear her red hood,
And look for skunk tracks
In the snow with an ax—
And do everything
And perhaps in the spring
He would come back and sing!"

AN EPITAPH ON A ROBIN REDBREAST

By Samuel Rogers

Tread lightly here; for here, 'tis said,
When piping winds are hush'd around,
A small note wakes from underground,
Where now his tiny bones are laid.

No more in lone or leafless groves,
With ruffled wing and faded breast,
His friendless, homeless spirit roves;
Gone to the world where birds are blest

Where never cat glides o'er the green,
Or school-boy's giant form is seen;
But love, and joy, and smiling Spring
Inspire their little souls to sing!

WHO STOLE THE BIRD'S NEST?

By Lydia Maria Child

"To-whit! to-whit! to-whee!
Will you listen to me?
Who stole four eggs I laid,
And the nice nest I made?"

"Not I," said the cow; "Moo-oo!
Such a thing I'd never do.
I gave you a wisp of hay,
But didn't take your nest away.
Not I," said the cow, "Moo-oo!
Such a thing I'd never do."

"To-whit! to-whit! to-whee!
Will you listen to me?
Who stole four eggs I laid,
And the nice nest I made?"

"Bob-o'-link! Bob-o'-link!
Now, what do you think?
Who stole a nest away
From the plum-tree, today?"

"Not I," said the dog; "Bow-wow!
I wouldn't be so mean, anyhow!
I gave hairs the nest to make,
But the nest I did not take.
Not I," said the dog, "Bow-wow!
I'm not so mean, anyhow."

"To-whit! to-whit! to-whee!
Will you listen to me?
Who stole four eggs I laid,
And the nice nest I made?"

"Bob-o'-link! Bob-o'-link!
Now what do you think?
Who stole a nest away
From the plum-tree, today?"

"Coo-coo! Coo-coo! Coo-coo!
Let me speak a word, too!
Who stole that pretty nest
From little yellow-breast?"

"Not I," said the sheep; "Oh, no!
I wouldn't treat a poor bird so.
I gave wool the nest to line,
But the nest was none of mine.
Baa! Baa!" said the sheep; "Oh, no,
I wouldn't treat a poor bird so."

"To-whit! to-whit! to-whee!
Will you listen to me?
Who stole four eggs I laid,
And the nice nest I made?"

"Bob-o'-link! Bob-o'-link!
Now, what do you think?

Who stole a nest away
From the plum-tree, today?"

"Coo-coo! Coo-coo! Coo-coo!
Let me speak a word, too!
Who stole that pretty nest
From little yellow-breast?"

"Caw! Caw!" cried the crow;
"I should like to know
What thief took away
A bird's nest today?"

"Cluck! Cluck!" said the hen,
"Don't ask me again.
Why, I haven't a chick
Would do such a trick.
We all gave her a feather,
And she wove them together.
I'd scorn to intrude
On her and her brood.
Cluck! Cluck!" said the hen,
"Don't ask me again."

"Chirr-a-whirr; Chirr-a-whirr!
All the birds make a stir!
Let us find out his name
And all cry 'For shame!' "

"I would not rob a bird,"
Said little Mary Green;
"I think I never heard
Of anything so mean."

"It is very cruel, too,"
Said little Alice Neal;
"I wonder if he knew
How sad the bird would feel?"

A little boy hung down his head,
And went and hid behind the bed;
For he stole that pretty nest
From poor little yellow-breast;
And he felt so full of shame,
He didn't like to tell his name.

ROBIN REDBREAST

By William Allingham

Good-bye, good-bye to Summer!
  For Summer's nearly done;
The garden smiling faintly,
  Cool breezes in the sun;
Our thrushes now are silent,
  Our swallows flown away—
But Robin's here in coat of brown,
  And scarlet breast-knot gay.
    Robin, Robin Redbreast,
      O Robin dear!
    Robin sings so sweetly
      In the falling of the year.

Bright yellow, red, and orange,
  The leaves come down in hosts;
The trees are Indian princes,
  But soon they'll turn to ghosts;
The scanty pears and apples
  Hang russet on the bough;
It's Autumn, Autumn, Autumn late,
  'Twill soon be Winter now.
    Robin, Robin Redbreast,
      O Robin dear!
    And what will this poor Robin do?
      For pinching days are near.

The fireside for the cricket,
  The wheat-stock for the mouse,
When trembling night-winds whistle
  And moan all round the house.
The frosty ways like iron,
  The branches plumed with snow—
Alas! in Winter dead and dark,
  Where can poor Robin go?
    Robin, Robin Redbreast,
      O Robin dear!
    And a crumb of bread for Robin,
      His little heart to cheer!

THE OWL

By Alfred, Lord Tennyson

When cats run home and light is come,
And dew is cold upon the ground,
And the far-off stream is dumb,
And the whirring sail goes round,
And the whirring sail goes round;
Alone and warming his five wits,
The white owl in the belfry sits.

When merry milkmaids click the latch,
And rarely smells the new-mown hay,
And the cock hath sung beneath the thatch
Twice or thrice his roundelay,
Twice or thrice his roundelay;
Alone and warming his five wits,
The white owl in the belfry sits.

THE EAGLE

By Alfred, Lord Tennyson

He clasps the crag with crooked hands;
Close to the sun in lonely lands,
Ring'd with the azure world, he stands.

The wrinkled sea beneath him crawls;
He watches from his mountain walls,
And like a thunderbolt he falls.

THE CITY MOUSE AND THE GARDEN MOUSE

By Christina Rossetti

The city mouse lives in a house—
  The garden mouse lives in a bower,
He's friendly with the frogs and toads,
  And sees the pretty plants in flower.

The city mouse eats bread and cheese—
  The garden mouse eats what he can;
We will not grudge him seeds and stocks,
  Poor little timid furry man.

THE COW

By Robert Louis Stevenson

The friendly cow all red and white,
  I love with all my heart:
She gives me cream with all her might,
  To eat with apple-tart.

She wanders lowing here and there,
  And yet she cannot stray;
All in the pleasant open air,
  The pleasant light of day;

And blown by all the winds that pass
  And wet with all the showers,
She walks among the meadow grass
  And eats the meadow flowers.

A DIRGE FOR A RIGHTEOUS KITTEN

By Vachel Lindsay

Ding-dong, ding-dong, ding-dong.
Here lies a kitten good, who kept
A kitten's proper place.
He stole no pantry eatables,
Nor scratched the baby's face.
He let the alley-cats alone.
He had no yowling vice.
His shirt was always laundried well,
He freed the house of mice.
Until his death he had not caused
His little mistress tears,
He wore his ribbon prettily,
He washed behind his ears.
Ding-dong, ding-dong, ding-dong.

THE KITTEN AND THE FALLING LEAVES

By William Wordsworth

See the kitten on the wall,
Sporting with the leaves that fall,
Withered leaves—one—two—and three—
From the lofty elder tree!
Through the calm and frosty air
Of this morning bright and fair,
Eddying round and round they sink
Softly, slowly: one might think,
From the motions that are made,
Every little leaf conveyed
Sylph or fairy hither tending—
To this lower world descending,
Each invisible and mute,
In his wavering parachute.
But the kitten, how she starts!
Crouches, stretches, paws and darts!
First at one, and then its fellow,
Just as light and just as yellow;
There are many now—now one—
Now they stop and there are none.
What intenseness of desire
In her upward eye of fire!
With a tiger-leap, half-way
Now she meets the coming prey;
Lets it go as fast, and then
Has it in her power again:
Now she works with three or four,
Like an Indian conjuror;
Quick as he in feats of art,
Far beyond in joy of heart.

A CHILD'S PET

By William H. Davies

When I sailed out of Baltimore
  With twice a thousand head of sheep,
They would not eat, they would not drink,
  But bleated o'er the deep.

Inside the pens we crawled each day,
  To sort the living from the dead;
And when we reached the Mersey's mouth,
  Had lost five hundred head.

Yet every night and day one sheep,
  That had no fear of man or sea,
Stuck through the bars its pleading face,
  And it was stroked by me.

And to the sheep-men standing near,
  "You see," I said, "this one tame sheep:
It seems a child has lost her pet,
  And cried herself to sleep."

So every time we passed it by,
  Sailing to England's slaughter-house,
Eight ragged sheep-men—tramps and thieves—
  Would stroke that sheep's black nose.

THE LAMB

By William Blake

Little Lamb, who made thee?
Dost thou know who made thee,
Gave thee life, and bid thee feed
By the stream and o'er the mead;
Gave thee clothing of delight,
Softest clothing, woolly, bright;
Gave thee such a tender voice
Making all the vales rejoice;
  Little Lamb, who made thee?
  Dost thou know who made thee?

Little Lamb, I'll tell thee.
Little Lamb, I'll tell thee.
He is callèd by thy name,
For He calls Himself a Lamb—
He is meek and He is mild;
He became a little child.
I a child, and thou a lamb,
We are callèd by His name.
  Little Lamb, God bless thee;
  Little Lamb. God bless thee.

A FABLE

By Ralph Waldo Emerson

The mountain and the squirrel
Had a quarrel,
And the former called the latter "Little Prig";
Bun replied,
"You are doubtless very big;
But all sorts of things and weather
Must be taken in together,
To make up a year
And a sphere.
And I think it no disgrace
To occupy my place.
If I'm not so large as you,
You are not so small as I,
And not half so spry.

"I'll not deny you make
A very pretty squirrel track;
Talents differ; all is well and wisely put;
If I cannot carry forests on my back,
Neither can you crack a nut."

POOR DOG TRAY

By Thomas Campbell

On the green banks of Shannon, when Shulah was nigh,
No blithe Irish lad was so happy as I;
No harp like my own could so cheerily play,
And wherever I went was my poor dog Tray.

When at last I was forced from my Shulah to part,
She said, while the sorrow was big at her heart,
"O, remember your Shulah when far, far away,
And be kind, my dear Pat, to our poor dog Tray."

When the road was so dark, and the wind was so cold,
And Pat and his dog were growing weary and old,
How snugly we slept in my old coat of grey!
And he licked me for kindness—my poor dog Tray.

Though my wallet was scant, I remembered his case,
Nor refused my last crust to his pitiful face;
But he died at my feet on a cold winter's day,
And I played a sad lament for my poor dog Tray.

Where now shall I go? Poor, forsaken, and blind,
Can I find one to guide me, so faithful and kind?
To my dear native village, so far, far away,
I can never return with my poor dog Tray!

THE BLOOD HORSE

By Barry Cornwall

Gamarra is a dainty steed,
Strong, black, and of a noble breed,
Full of fire, and full of bone,
With all his line of fathers known;
Fine his nose, his nostrils thin,
But blown abroad by the pride within!
His mane is like a river flowing,
And his eyes like embers glowing
In the darkness of the night,
And his pace as swift as light.

Look—how 'round his straining throat
Grace and shifting beauty float;
Sinewy strength is in his reins,
And the red blood gallops through his veins:
Richer, redder, never ran
Through the boasting heart of man.
He can trace his lineage higher
Than the Bourbon dare aspire—
Douglas, Guzman, or the Guelph,
Or O'Brien's blood itself!

He, who hath no peer, was born,
Here, upon a red March morn;
But his famous fathers dead
Were Arabs all, and Arab bred,
And the last of that great line
Trod like one of a race divine!

And yet—he was but friend to one,
Who fed him at the set of sun,
By some lone fountain fringed with green:
With him, a roving Bedouin,
He lived (none else would he obey
Through all the hot Arabian day)—
And died untamed upon the sands
Where Balkh amidst the desert stands!

THE RUNAWAY

By Robert Frost

Once when the snow of the year was beginning to fall,
We stopped by a mountain pasture to say, "Whose colt?"
A little Morgan had one forefoot on the wall,
The other curled at his breast. He dipped his head
And snorted to us. And then he had to bolt.
We heard the miniature thunder where he fled,
And we saw him, or thought we saw him, dim and gray,
Like a shadow against the curtain of falling flakes.
"I think the little fellow's afraid of the snow.
He isn't winter-broken. It isn't play
With the little fellow at all. He's running away.
I doubt if even his mother could tell him, 'Sakes,
It's only weather.' He'd think she didn't know!
Where is his mother? He can't be out alone."
And now he comes again with a clatter of stone
And mounts the wall again with whited eyes
And all his tail that isn't hair up straight.
He shudders his coat as if to throw off flies.
"Whoever it is that leaves him out so late,
When other creatures have gone to stall and bin,
Ought to be told to come and take him in."

THE TIGER

By William Blake

Tiger, tiger, burning bright,
In the forests of the night,
What immortal hand or eye
Could frame thy fearful symmetry?

In what distant deeps or skies
Burnt the fire of thine eyes?
On what wings dare he aspire?
What the hand dare seize the fire?

And what shoulder, and what art,
Could twist the sinews of thy heart?
And when thy heart began to beat,
What dread hand and what dread feet?

What the hammer? What the chain?
In what furnace was thy brain?
What the anvil? What dread grasp
Dare its deadly terrors clasp?

When the stars threw down their spears,
And water'd heaven with their tears,
Did He smile his work to see?
Did He who made the lamb make thee?

Tiger, tiger, burning bright
In the forests of the night,
What immortal hand or eye
Dare frame thy fearful symmetry?

FAIRYLAND

OVER HILL, OVER DALE

By William Shakespeare

Over hill, over dale,
  Through bush, through brier,
Over park, over pale,
  Through flood, through fire,
I do wander everywhere,
Swifter than the moon's sphere;
And I serve the fairy queen,
To dew her orbs upon the green:
The cowslips tall her pensioners be;
    In their gold coats spots you see;
    Those be rubies, fairy favors,
    In those freckles live their savors;
I must go seek some dew-drops here,
And hang a pearl in every cowslip's ear.

WHERE THE BEE SUCKS

By William Shakespeare

Where the bee sucks, there suck I;
In a cowslip's bell I lie;
There I couch when owls do cry.
On the bat's back I do fly
After summer, merrily:
Merrily, merrily shall I live now,
Under the blossom that hangs on the bough.

COME UNTO THESE YELLOW SANDS

By William Shakespeare

Come unto these yellow sands,
And then take hands;
Curt'sied when you have, and kissed—
The wild waves whist—
Foot it featly here and there;
And, sweet sprites, the burthen bear.
Hark, Hark!
Bow-wow.
The watch-dogs bark:
Bow-wow.
Hark, hark! I hear
The strain of strutting Chanticleer
Cry, Cock-a-diddle-dow.

FULL FATHOM FIVE

By William Shakespeare

Full fathom five thy father lies;
  Of his bones are coral made;
Those are pearls that were his eyes:
  Nothing of him that doth fade
But doth suffer a sea-change
Into something rich and strange.
Sea-nymphs hourly ring his knell:
  Hark! now I hear them,—
    Ding-dong, bell.

THE WEE, WEE MAN

Anonymous

As I was walking by my lane,
  Atween a water and a wa,
There sune I spied a wee, wee man—
  He was the least that ere I saw.

His legs were scant a shathmont's length,
  And sma and limber was his thie;
Between his een there was a span,
  Betwixt his shoulders there was ells three.

He has tane up a meikle stane,
  And flang't as far as I cold see;
Ein thouch I had been Wallace wicht,
  I dought na lift it to my knie.

"O wee, wee man, but ye be strang!
  Tell me whar may thy dwelling be?"
"I dwell beneth that bonnie bouir—
  Oh, will ye gae wi me and see?"

On we lap, and awa we rade,
  Till we cam to a bonny green;
We lichted syne to bait our steid,
  And out there came a lady sheen.

Wi four and twentie at her back,
  A comely cled in glistering green;
Thouch there the king of Scots had stude,
  The warst micht weil hae been his queen.

On syne we past wi wondering cheir,
  Till we cam to a bonny ha;
The roof was o' the beaten gowd,
  The flure was o' the crystal a'.

When we cam there, wi wee, wee knichts
  War ladies dancing, jimp and sma;
But in the twinkling of an eie
  Baith green and ha war clein awa.

THE ARMING OF PIGWIGGEN

By Michael Drayton

He quickly arms him for the field,
A little cockle-shell his shield,
Which he could very bravely yield,
  Yet could it not be pierced:
His spear a bent both stiff and strong,
And well near of two inches long;
The pile was of a horsefly's tongue,
  Whose sharpness naught reversed.

And put him on a coat of mail,
Which was of a fish's scale,
That when his foe should him assail,
  No point should be prevailing.
His rapier was a hornet's sting,
It was a very dangerous thing;
For if he chanc'd to hurt the king,
  It would be long in healing.

His helmet was a beetle's head,
Most horrible and full of dread,
That able was to strike one dead,
  Yet it did well become him:
And for a plume a horse's hair,
Which being tossèd by the air,
Had forced to strike his foe with fear,
  And turn his weapon from him.

Himself he on an earwig set,
Yet scarce he on his back could get,
So oft and high he did curvet
  Ere he himself could settle:
He made him turn, and stop, and bound,
To gallop, and to trot the round,
He scarce could stand on any ground,
  He was so full of mettle.

ROBIN GOODFELLOW

Anonymous

From Oberon, in fairy land,
  The king of ghosts and shadows there,
Mad Robin I, at his command,
  Am sent to view the night-sports here.
    What revel rout
    Is kept about,
  In every corner where I go,
    I will o'ersee,
    And merry be,
  And make good sport, with ho, ho, ho!

More swift than lightning can I fly
About this airy welkin soon,
And, in a minute's space, descry
Each thing that's done below the moon.
There's not a hag
Or ghost shall wag,
Or cry 'ware goblins! where I go;
But, Robin, I
Their feats will spy,
And send them home with ho, ho, ho!

Whene'er such wanderers I meet,
As from their night-sports they trudge home,
With counterfeiting voice I greet,
And call them on with me to roam;
Through woods, through lakes,
Through bogs, through brakes,
Or else, unseen, with them I go,
All in the nick
To play some trick,
And frolic it, with ho, ho, ho!

Sometimes I meet them like a man,
Sometimes an ox, sometimes a hound;
And to a horse I turn me can,
To trip and trot about them round.
But if to ride,
My back they stride,
More swift than wind away I go,
O'er hedge and lands,
Through pools and ponds,
I hurry, laughing, ho, ho, ho!

By wells and rills, in meadows green,
We nightly dance our heyday guise;
And to our fairy King and Queen,
We chant our moonlight minstrelsies,
When larks 'gin sing,
Away we fling;
And babes new born steal as we go;
And elf in bed,
We leave instead,
And wend us laughing, ho, ho, ho!

From hag-bred Merlin's time have I
  Thus nightly revell'd to and fro;
And for my pranks men call me by
  The name of Robin Goodfellow.
    Fiends, ghosts, and sprites,
    Who haunt the nights,
  The hags and goblins do me know;
    And beldames old
    My feats have told,
  So *valé, valé!* ho, ho, ho!

THE VISITOR

By Rachel Field

Feather-footed and swift as a mouse
An elfin gentleman came to our house;
Knocked his wee brown knuckles upon our door;
Bowed till his peaked cap swept the floor.
His shiny eyes blinked bright at me
As he asked for bread and a sup of tea,

"And plenty of honey, please," he said,
"For I'm fond of honey on my bread!"
Cross-legged he sat, with never a word,
But the old black kettle sang like a bird;
The red geranium burst in bloom
With the blaze of firelight in the room,
The china rattled on every shelf,
And the broom danced merrily all by itself.
Quick to the pantry then I ran
For to serve that elfin gentleman.
I brewed him tea, I brought him bread
With clover honey thickly spread.
One sip he took, one elfin bite,
But his ears they twitched with sheer delight.
He smacked his lips and he smiled at me.
"May good luck follow you, child!" said he.
He circled me round like a gay green flame
Before he was off the way he came,
Leaving me there in the kitchen dim,
Sighing and staring after him,
With the fire low and the tea grown cold,
And the moon through the window sharp and old,
Only before me—instead of honey,
That bread was golden with thick-spread money!

THE VISITOR

By Patrick R. Chalmers

The white goat Amaryllis,
  She wandered at her will
At time of daffodillies
  Afar and up the hill:
We hunted and we holloa'd
  And back she came at dawn,
But what d'you think had followed?—
  A little, pagan Faun!

His face was like a berry,
  His ears were high and pricked:
Tip-tap—his hoofs came merry
  As up the hill he clicked;

A junket for his winning
  We set in dairy delf;
He ate it—pert and grinning
  As Christian as yourself!

He stayed about the steading
  A fortnight, say, or more;
A blanket for his bedding
  We spread beside the door;
And when the cocks crowed clearly
  Before the dawn was ripe,
He'd call the milkmaids cheerly
  Upon a reedy pipe!

That fortnight of his staying
  The work went smooth as silk:
The hens were all in laying,
  The cows were all in milk;
And then—and then one morning
  The maids woke up at day
Without his oaten warning—
  And found he'd gone away.

He left no trace behind him;
  But still the milkmaids deem
That they, perhaps, may find him
  With butter and with cream:
Beside the door they set them
  In bowl and golden pat,
But no one comes to get them—
  Unless, maybe, the cat.

The white goat Amaryllis,
  She wanders at her will
At time of daffodillies,
  Away up Woolcombe hill;
She stays until the morrow,
  Then back she comes at dawn;
But never—to our sorrow—
  The little, pagan Faun.

BERRIES

By Walter de la Mare

There was an old woman
  Went blackberry picking
Along the hedges
  From Weep to Wicking.
Half a pottle—
  No more she had got,
When out steps a Fairy
  From her green grot;
And says, "Well, Jill,
  Would 'ee pick 'ee mo?"
And Jill, she curtseys,
  And looks just so.
"Be off," says the Fairy,
  "As quick as you can,
Over the meadows
  To the little green lane,
That dips to the hayfields
  Of Farmer Grimes:
I've berried those hedges
  A score of times;
Bushel on bushel
  I'll promise 'ee, Jill,
This side of supper
  If 'ee pick with a will."
She glints very bright,
  And speaks her fair;
Then lo, and behold!
  She had faded in air.

Be sure Old Goodie
  She trots betimes
Over the meadows
  To Farmer Grimes.
And never was queen
  With jewellery rich
As those same hedges
  From twig to ditch;
Like Dutchmen's coffers,
  Fruit, thorn, and flower—

They shone like William
  And Mary's bower.
And be sure Old Goodie
  Went back to Weep,
So tired with her basket
  She scarce could creep.

When she comes in the dusk
  To her cottage door,
There's Towser wagging
  As never before,
To see his Missus
  So be glad to be
Come from her fruit-picking
  Back to he.
As soon as next morning
  Dawn was gray,
The pot on the hob
  Was simmering away;
And all in a stew
  And a hugger-mugger
Towser and Jill
  A-boiling of sugar,
And the dark clear fruit
  That from Faerie came,
For syrup and jelly
  And blackberry jam.

Twelve jolly gallipots
  Jill put by;
And one little teeny one
  One inch high;
And that she's hidden
  A good thumb deep,
Half way over
  From Wicking to Weep.

THE FAIRIES

By William Allingham

Up the airy mountain
  Down the rushy glen,
We daren't go a-hunting,
  For fear of little men;
Wee folk, good folk,
  Trooping all together;
Green jacket, red cap,
  And white owl's feather.
Down along the rocky shore
  Some make their home,
They live on crispy pancakes
  Of yellow tide-foam;
Some in the reeds
  Of the black mountain-lake,
With frogs for their watch-dogs,
  All night awake.

High on the hill-top
  The old King sits;
He is now so old and gray
  He's nigh lost his wits.
With a bridge of white mist
  Columbkill he crosses,
On his stately journeys
  From Slieveleague to Rosses;
Or going up with music,
  On cold starry nights,
To sup with the Queen,
  Of the gay Northern Lights.

They stole little Bridget
  For seven years long;
When she came down again
  Her friends were all gone.
They took her lightly back
  Between the night and morrow;
They thought that she was fast asleep,
  But she was dead with sorrow.

They have kept her ever since
  Deep within the lake,
On a bed of flag leaves,
  Watching till she wake.
By the craggy hill-side,
  Through the mosses bare,
They have planted thorn trees
  For pleasure here and there.
Is any man so daring
  As dig them up in spite?
He shall find the thornies set
  In his bed at night.

Up the airy mountain,
  Down the rushy glen,
We daren't go a-hunting
  For fear of little men;
Wee folk, good folk,
  Trooping all together;
Green jacket, red cap,
  And white owl's feather.

THE FAIRIES OF THE CALDON LOW

By Mary Howitt

"And where have you been, my Mary,
  And where have you been from me?"
"I've been to the top of the Caldon Low,
  The midsummer-night to see!"

"And what did you see, my Mary,
  All up on the Caldon Low?"
"I saw the glad sunshine come down,
  And I saw the merry winds blow."

"And what did you hear, my Mary,
  All up on the Caldon Hill?"
"I heard the drops of the waters made,
  And the ears of the green corn fill."

"Oh! tell me all, my Mary,
  All, all that ever you know;
For you must have seen the fairies
  Last night on the Caldon Low."

Boris Artzybasheff

He shall find the thornies set
In his bed at night.

[See page 86]

He shall find the thornies set
In his bed at night.

[See page 86]

"Then take me on your knee, mother;
And listen, mother of mine.
A hundred fairies danced last night,
And the harpers they were nine.

"And their harp-strings rung so merrily
To their dancing feet so small;
But oh! the words of their talking
Were merrier far than all."

"And what were the words, my Mary,
That then you heard them say?"
"I'll tell you all, my mother;
But let me have my way.

"Some of them played with the water,
And rolled it down the hill;
'And this,' they said, 'shall speedily turn
The poor old miller's mill:

"'For there has been no water
Ever since the first of May;
And a busy man will the miller be
At the dawning of the day.

"'Oh! the miller, how he will laugh
When he sees the mill-dam rise!
The jolly old miller, how he will laugh,
Till the tears fill both his eyes!'

"And some they seized the little winds
That sounded over the hill;
And each put a horn into his mouth,
And blew both loud and shrill:

"'And there,' they said, 'the merry winds go,
Away from every horn;
And they shall clear the mildew dank
From the blind old widow's corn.

"'Oh! the poor blind widow,
Though she has been blind so long,
She'll be blithe enough when the mildew's gone,
And the corn stands tall and strong.'

"And some they brought the brown lint-seed,
And flung it down from the Low;
"'And this,' they said, 'by the sunrise,
In the weaver's croft shall grow.

"'Oh! the poor lame weaver,
How he will laugh outright,
When he sees his dwindling flax-field
And full of flowers by night!'

"And then outspoke a brownie,
With a long beard on his chin;
'I have spun up all the tow,' said he,
'And I want some more to spin.

"'I've spun a piece of hempen cloth,
And I want to spin another;
A little sheet for Mary's bed,
And an apron for her mother.'

"With that I could not help but laugh,
And I laughed out loud and free;
And then on the top of the Caldon Low
There was no one left but me.

"And all on the top of the Caldon Low
The mists were cold and gray,
And nothing I saw but the mossy stones
That round about me lay.

"But coming down from the hill-top,
I heard afar below.
How busy the jolly miller was
And how the wheel did go.

"And I peeped into the widow's field,
And, sure enough, were seen
The yellow ears of the mildewed corn,
All standing stout and green.

"And down to the weaver's croft I stole,
To see if the flax were sprung;
But I met the weaver at his gate,
With the good news on his tongue.

"Now this is all I heard, mother,
  And all that I did see;
So, pr'ythee, make my bed, mother,
  For I'm tired as I can be."

A FAIRY WENT A-MARKETING

By Rose Fyleman

A Fairy went a-marketing—
  She bought a little fish;
She put it in a crystal bowl
  Upon a golden dish.
An hour she sat in wonderment
  And watched its silver gleam,
And then she gently took it up
  And slipped it in a stream.

A fairy went a-marketing—
  She bought a colored bird;
It sang the sweetest, shrillest song
  That ever she had heard.
She sat beside its painted cage
  And listened half the day,
And then she opened wide the door
  And let it fly away.

A fairy went a-marketing—
  She bought a winter gown
All stitched about with gossamer
  And lined with thistledown.
She wore it all afternoon
  With prancing and delight,
Then gave it to a little frog
  To keep him warm at night.

A fairy went a-marketing—
  She bought a gentle mouse
To take her tiny messages,
  To keep her tiny house.
All day she kept its busy feet
  Pit-patting to and fro
And then she kissed its silken ears,
  Thanked it, and let it go.

FUN AND NONSENSE

JOHN GILPIN

By William Cowper

John Gilpin was a citizen
  Of credit and renown,
A train-band captain eke was he
  Of famous London Town.

John Gilpin's spouse said to her dear,
  "Though wedded we have been
These twice ten tedious years, yet we
  No holiday have seen.

"Tomorrow is our wedding day,
  And we will then repair
Unto the Bell at Edmonton,
  All in a chaise and pair.

"My sister and my sister's child,
  Myself, and children three,
Will fill the chaise; so you must ride
  On horseback after we."

He soon replied, "I do admire
  Of womankind but one,
And you are she, my dearest dear,
  Therefore it shall be done.

"I am a linendraper bold,
  As all the world doth know,
And my good friend, the Calender,
  Will lend his horse to go."

Quoth Mistress Gilpin, "That's well said;
  And, for that wine is dear,
We will be furnish'd with our own,
  Which is both bright and clear."

John Gilpin kiss'd his loving wife;
  O'erjoy'd was he to find
That, though on pleasure she was bent,
  She had a frugal mind.

The morning came, the chaise was brought,
  But yet was not allow'd
To drive up to the door, lest all
  Should say that she was proud.

So three doors off the chaise was stay'd,
  Where they did all get in,
Six precious souls, and all agog
  To dash through thick and thin.

Smack went the whip, round went the wheels;
  Were never folks so glad:
The stones did rattle underneath,
  As if Cheapside were mad.

John Gilpin, at his horse's side,
  Seized fast the flowing mane,
And up he got, in haste to ride,
  But soon came down again;

For saddle-tree scarce reach'd had he,
  His journey to begin,
When, turning round his head, he saw
  Three customers come in.

So down he came; for loss of time
  Although it grieved him sore,
Yet loss of pence, full well he knew,
  Would trouble him much more.

'Twas long before the customers
Were suited to their mind,
When Betty, screaming, came downstairs,
"The wine is left behind!"

"Good lack!" quoth he, "Yet bring it me,
My leathern belt likewise,
In which I bear my trusty sword
When I do exercise."

Now Mistress Gilpin (careful soul!)
Had two stone bottles found,
To hold the liquor that she loved,
And keep it safe and sound.

Each bottle had a curling ear,
Through which the belt he drew,
And hung a bottle on each side,
To make his balance true.

Then over all, that he might be
Equipp'd from top to toe,
His long red cloak, well-brush'd and neat,
He manfully did throw.

Now see him mounted once again
Upon his nimble steed,
Full slowly pacing o'er the stones,
With caution and good heed.

But finding soon a smoother road
Beneath his well-shod feet,
The snorting beast began to trot,
Which gall'd him in his seat.

So, "Fair and softly!" John he cried,
But John he cried in vain;
That trot became a gallop soon,
In spite of curb and rein.

So stooping down, as needs he must
Who cannot sit upright,
He grasp'd the mane with both his hands,
And eke with all his might.

His horse, who never in that sort
  Had handled been before,
What thing upon his back had got
  Did wonder more and more.

Away went Gilpin, neck or nought;
  Away went hat and wig;
He little dreamt, when he set out,
  Of running such a rig.

The wind did blow, the cloak did fly
  Like streamer long and gay,
Till loop and button failing both,
  At last it flew away.

Then might all people well discern
  The bottles he had slung;
A bottle swinging at each side,
  As hath been said or sung.

The dogs did bark, the children scream'd,
  Up flew the windows all;
And every soul cried out: "Well done!"
  As loud as he could bawl.

Away went Gilpin—who but he?
  His fame soon spread around,
"He carries weight; he rides a race!
  'Tis for a thousand pound!"

And still, as fast as he drew near,
  'Twas wonderful to view
How in a trice the turnpike men
  Their gates wide open threw.

And now, as he went bowing down
  His reeking head full low,
The bottles twain behind his back
  Were shatter'd at a blow.

Down ran the wine into the road,
  Most piteous to be seen,
Which made his horse's flanks to smoke
  As they had basted been.

But still he seem'd to carry weight,
  With leathern girdle braced;
For all might see the bottle-necks
  Still dangling at his waist.

Thus all through merry Islington
  These gambols he did play,
Until he came unto the Wash
  Of Edmonton so gay;

And there he threw the Wash about
  On both sides of the way,
Just like unto a trundling mop,
  Or a wild goose at play.

At Edmonton his loving wife
  From the balcony spied
Her tender husband, wondering much
  To see how he did ride.

"Stop, stop, John Gilpin! Here's the house!"
  They all at once did cry;
"The dinner waits, and we are tired":
  Said Gilpin, "So am I!"

But yet his horse was not a whit
  Inclined to tarry there;
For why? his owner had a house
  Full ten miles, off, at Ware.

So like an arrow swift he flew,
  Shot by an archer strong;
So did he fly—which brings me to
  The middle of my song.

Away went Gilpin, out of breath,
  And sore against his will
Till at his friend the Calender's
  His horse at last stood still.

The Calender, amazed to see
  His neighbor in such trim,
Laid down his pipe, flew to the gate,
  And thus accosted him.

"What news? what news? your tidings tell!
  Tell me you must and shall—
Say, why bare-headed you are come,
  Or why you come at all?"

Now Gilpin had a pleasant wit,
  And loved a timely joke;
And thus unto the Calender
  In merry guise he spoke:

"I came, because your horse would come;
  And, if I well forbode,
My hat and wig will soon be here,
  They are upon the road."

The Calender, right glad to find
  His friend in merry pin,
Return'd him not a single word,
  But to the house went in;

Whence straight he came, with hat and wig,
  A wig that flow'd behind;
A hat not much the worse for wear;
  Each comely in its kind.

He held them up, and in his turn
  Thus show'd his ready wit:
"My head is twice as big as yours,
  They therefore needs must fit.

"But let me scrape the dirt away,
  That hangs upon your face;
And stop and eat, for well you may
  Be in a hungry case."

Said John, "It is my wedding day,
  And all the world would stare,
If wife should dine at Edmonton,
  And I should dine at Ware!"

So, turning to his horse, he said,
  "I am in haste to dine;
'Twas for your pleasure you came here,
  You shall go back for mine."

Ah, luckless speech, and bootless boast!
  For which he paid full dear;
For, while he spake, a braying ass
  Did sing most loud and clear;

Whereat his horse did snort, as he
  Had heard a lion roar,
And gallop'd off with all his might,
  As he had done before.

Away went Gilpin, and away
  Went Gilpin's hat and wig;
He lost them sooner than at first,
  For why?—they were too big.

Now Mistress Gilpin, when she saw
  Her husband posting down
Into the country far away
  She pull'd out half-a-crown;

And thus unto the youth she said,
  That drove them to the Bell,
"This shall be yours, when you bring back
  My husband safe and well."

The youth did ride, and soon did meet
  John coming back amain;
Whom in a trice he tried to stop,
  By catching at his rein;

But not performing what he meant,
  And gladly would have done,
The frighten'd steed he frighten'd more,
  And made him faster run.

Away went Gilpin, and away
  Went postboy at his heels,
The postboy's horse right glad to miss
  The lumbering of the wheels.

Six gentlemen upon the road
  Thus seeing Gilpin fly,
With postboy scampering in the rear
  They raised the hue and cry:

"Stop thief! stop thief!—a highwayman!"
  Not one of them was mute;
And all and each that pass'd that way
  Did join in the pursuit.

And now the turnpike gates again
  Flew open in short space:
The toll-men thinking as before
  That Gilpin rode a race.

And so he did, and won it too!
  For he got first to town;
Nor stopp'd till where he had got up
  He did again get down.

—Now let us sing, Long live the King,
  And Gilpin, long live he;
And, when he next doth ride abroad,
  May I be there to see!

TOPSY-TURVY WORLD

By William B. Rands

If the butterfly courted the bee,
  And the owl the porcupine;
If churches were built in the sea,
  And three times one were nine;

If the pony rode his master,
  If the buttercups ate the cows,
If the cats had the dire disaster
  To be worried, sir, by the mouse;
If Mamma, sir, sold the baby
  To a gypsy for half a crown;
If a gentleman, sir, was a lady—
  The world would be Upside-down!
If any or all of these wonders
  Should ever come about,
I should not consider them blunders,
  For I should be Inside-out:

Chorus

Ba-ba, black wool
  Have you any sheep?
Yes, sir, a packful,
  Creep, mouse, creep!
Four-and-twenty little maids
  Hanging out the pie,
Out jumped the honey-pot,
  Guy Fawkes, Guy!
Cross latch, cross latch,
  Sit and spin the fire;
When the pie was opened,
  The bird was on the brier!

AN ELEGY ON THE DEATH OF A MAD DOG

By Oliver Goldsmith

Good people all, of every sort,
  Give ear unto my song;
And if you find it wondrous short—
  It cannot hold you long.

In Islington there was a Man,
  Of whom the world might say,
That still a godly race he ran—
  Whene'er he went to pray.

A kind and gentle heart he had,
To comfort friends and foes:
The naked every day he clad—
When he put on his clothes.

And in that town a Dog was found,
As many dogs there be,
Both mongrel, puppy, whelp, and hound,
And curs of low degree.

This Dog and Man at first were friends;
But when a pique began,
The Dog, to gain some private ends
Went mad, and bit the Man.

Around from all the neighboring streets
The wondering neighbors ran,
And swore the Dog had lost his wits,
To bite so good a Man!

The wound it seem'd both sore and sad
To every Christian eye:
And while they swore the Dog was mad,
They swore the Man would die.

But soon a wonder came to light,
That show'd the rogues they lied—
The Man recover'd of the bite,
The Dog it was that died!

CAPTAIN REECE

By William S. Gilbert

Of all the ships upon the blue,
No ship contained a better crew
Than that of worthy Captain Reece,
Commanding of *The Mantelpiece*.

He was adored by all his men,
For worthy Captain Reece, R.N.,
Did all that lay within him to
Promote the comfort of his crew.

If ever they were dull or sad,
Their captain danced to them like mad,
Or told, to make the time pass by,
Droll legends of his infancy.

A feather-bed had every man,
Warm slippers and hot-water can,
Brown Windsor from the captain's store,
A valet, too, to every four.

Did they with thirst in summer burn,
Lo, seltzogenes at every turn,
And on all very sultry days
Cream ices handed round on trays.

Then currant wine and ginger-pops
Stood handily on all the "tops";
And also, with amusement rife,
A "Zoetrope, or Wheel of Life."

New volumes came across the sea
From Mister Mudie's libraree;
The *Times* and *Saturday Review*
Beguiled the leisure of the crew.

Kind-hearted Captain Reece, R.N.,
Was quite devoted to his men;
In point of fact, good Captain Reece
Beatified *The Mantelpiece.*

One summer eve, at half-past ten,
He said (addressing all his men):
"Come, tell me, please, what I can do
To please and gratify my crew.

"By any reasonable plan
I'll make you happy if I can;
My own convenience count as nil:
It is my duty, and I will."

Then up and answered William Lee
(The kindly captain's coxswain he,
A nervous, shy, low-spoken man),
He cleared his throat and thus began:

"You have a daughter, Captain Reece,
Ten female cousins and a niece,
A ma, if what I'm told is true,
Six sisters, and an aunt or two.

"Now, somehow, sir, it seems to me
More friendly like we all should be,
If you united of 'em to
Unmarried members of the crew.

"If you'd ameliorate our life,
Let each select from them a wife;
And as for nervous me, old pal,
Give me your own enchanting gal!"

Good Captain Reece, that worthy man,
Debated on his coxswain's plan:
"I quite agree," he said, "O Bill;
It is my duty, and I will.

"My daughter, that enchanting gurl,
Has just been promised to an Earl,
And all my other famillee
To peers of various degree.

"But what are dukes and viscounts to
The happiness of all my crew?
The word I gave you I'll fulfill;
It is my duty, and I will.

"As you desire it shall befall;
I'll settle thousands on you all,
And I shall be, despite my hoard,
The only bachelor on board."

The boatswain of *The Mantelpiece,*
He blushed and spoke to Captain Reece:
"I beg your honor's leave," he said:
"If you would wish to go and wed,

"I have a widowed mother who
Would be the very thing for you—
She long has loved you from afar;
She washes for you, Captain R."

The Captain saw the dame that day—
Addressed her in this playful way—
"And did it want a wedding ring?
It was a tempting ickle sing!

"Well, well, the chaplain I will seek,
We'll all be married this day week
At yonder church upon the hill;
It is my duty, and I will!"

The sisters, cousins, aunts, and niece,
And widowed ma of Captain Reece,
Attended there as they were bid;
It was their duty, and they did.

THE YARN OF THE "NANCY BELL"

By William S. Gilbert

'Twas on the shores that round our coast
  From Deal to Ramsgate span,
That I found alone, on a piece of stone,
  An elderly naval man.

His hair was weedy, his beard was long,
  And weedy and long was he;
And I heard this wight, on the shore recite,
  In a singular minor key:

"Oh, I am a cook and a captain bold,
And the mate of the *Nancy* brig,
And a bo'sun tight, and a midshipmite,
And the crew of the captain's gig."

And he shook his fists and he tore his hair,
Till I really felt afraid,
For I couldn't help thinking the man had been drinking,
And so I simply said:

"Oh, elderly man, it's little I know
Of the duties of men of the sea,
And I'll eat my hand if I understand
However you can be

"At once a cook, and a captain bold,
And the mate of the *Nancy* brig,
And a bo'sun tight, and a midshipmite,
And the crew of the captain's gig."

Then he gave a hitch to his trousers, which
Is a trick all seamen larn,
And having got rid of a thumping quid,
He spun this painful yarn:

" 'Twas in the good ship *Nancy Bell*
That we sailed to the Indian Sea,
And there on a reef we come to grief,
Which has often occurred to me.

"And pretty nigh all o' the crew was drowned
(There was seventy-seven o' soul),
And only ten of the *Nancy's* men
Said 'Here' to the muster-roll.

"There was me, and the cook, and the captain bold
And the mate of the *Nancy* brig,
And the bo'sun tight, and a midshipmite,
And the crew of the captain's gig.

"For a month we'd neither wittles nor drink,
Till a-hungry we did feel,
So we drawed a lot, and, accordin', shot
The captain for our meal.

"The next lot fell to the *Nancy's* mate,
And a delicate dish he made;
Then our appetite with the midshipmite
We seven survivors stayed.

"And then we murdered the bo'sun tight,
And he much resembled pig;
Then we wittled free, did the cook and me,
On the crew of the captain's gig.

"Then only the cook and me was left,
And the delicate question, 'Which
Of us two goes to the kettle?' arose,
And we argued it out as sich.

"For I loved that cook as a brother, I did,
And the cook he worshipped me;
But we'd both be blowed if we'd either be stowed
In the other chap's hold, you see.

" 'I'll be eat if you dines off me,' says Tom.
'Yes, that,' says I, 'you'll be—
I'm boiled if I die, my friend,' quoth I;
And 'Exactly so,' quoth he.

"Says he: 'Dear James, to murder me
Were a foolish thing to do,
For don't you see that you can't cook *me,*
While I can—and will—cook *you!*'

"So he boils the water, and takes the salt
And the pepper in portions true
(Which he never forgot), and some chopped shalot,
And some sage and parsley too.

" 'Come here,' says he, with a proper pride,
Which his smiling features tell,
' 'Twill soothing be if I let you see
How extremely nice you'll smell.'

"And he stirred it round and round and round,
And he sniffed at the foaming froth;
While I ups witn his heels, and smothers his squeals
In the scum of the boiling broth.

"And I ate that cook in a week or less,
And—as I eating be
The last of his chops, why I almost drops,
For a wessel in sight I see.

• • •

"And I never larf, and I never smile,
And I never lark nor play;
But sit and croak, and a single joke
I have—which is to say:

"Oh, I am a cook and a captain bold
And the mate of the *Nancy* brig,
And a bo'sun tight, and a midshipmite,
And the crew of the captain's gig!"

ROBINSON CRUSOE'S STORY

By Charles E. Carryl

The night was thick and hazy
When the "Piccadilly Daisy"
Carried down the crew and captain in the sea;
And I think the water drowned 'em;
For they never, never found 'em,
And I know they didn't come ashore with me.

Oh! 'twas very sad and lonely
When I found myself the only
Population of this cultivated shore;
But I've made a little tavern
In a rocky little cavern,
And I sit and watch for people at the door.

I spent no time in looking
For a girl to do my cooking,
As I'm quite a clever hand at making stews;
But I had that fellow Friday
Just to keep the tavern tidy,
And to put a Sunday polish on my shoes.

I have a little garden
That I'm cultivating lard in,
And the things I eat are rather tough and dry;
For I live on toasted lizards,
Prickly pears, and parrot gizzards,
And I'm really very fond of beetle-pie.

The clothes I had were furry,
And it made me fret and worry
When I found the moths were eating off the hair;
And I had to scrape and sand 'em,
And I boiled 'em and I tanned 'em,
Till I got the fine morocco suit I wear.

I sometimes seek diversion
In a family excursion
With the few domestic animals you see;
And we take along a carrot
As refreshment for the parrot,
And a little can of jungleberry tea.

Then we gather as we travel,
Bits of moss and dirty gravel,
And we chip off little specimens of stone;
And we carry home as prizes
Funny bugs, of handy sizes,
Just to give the day a scientific tone.

If the roads are wet and muddy
We remain at home and study—
For the Goat is very clever at a sum—
And the Dog, instead of fighting,
Studies ornamental writing,
While the Cat is taking lessons on the drum.

We retire at eleven,
And we rise again at seven;
And I wish to call attention, as I close,
To the fact that all the scholars
Are correct about their collars,
And particular in turning out their toes.

LITTLE BILLEE

By William Makepeace Thackeray

There were three sailors of Bristol city
Who took a boat and went to sea.
But first with beef and captain's biscuits
And pickled pork they loaded she.

There was gorging Jack and guzzling Jimmy,
And the youngest he was little Billee.
Now when they got as far as the Equator
They'd nothing left but one split pea.

Says gorging Jack to guzzling Jimmy,
"I am extremely hungaree."
To gorging Jack says guzzling Jimmy,
"We've nothing left, us must eat we."

Says gorging Jack to guzzling Jimmy,
"With one another we shouldn't agree!
There's little Bill, he's young and tender,
We're old and tough, so let's eat he."

"Oh, Billy, we're going to kill and eat you,
So undo the button of your chemie."
When Bill received this information
He used his pocket-handkerchie.

"First let me say my catechism,
Which my poor mammy taught to me."
"Make haste, make haste," says guzzling Jimmy
While Jack pulled out his snickersnee.

So Billy went up to the main-top gallant mast,
And down he fell on his bended knee.
He scarce had come to the twelfth commandment
When up he jumps. "There's land I see:

"Jerusalem and Madagascar,
And North and South Amerikee:
There's the British flag a-riding at anchor,
With Admiral Napier, K. C. B."

So when they got aboard the Admiral's,
He hanged fat Jack and flogged Jimmee;
And as for little Bill he made him
The captain of a Seventy-three!

THE STORY OF AUGUSTUS, WHO WOULD NOT HAVE ANY SOUP

By Heinrich Hoffman

Augustus was a chubby lad;
Fat, ruddy checks Augustus had;
And everybody saw with joy
The plump and hearty, healthy boy.
He ate and drank as he was told,
And never let his soup get cold.

But one day, one cold winter's day,
He screamed out—"Take the soup away!
O take the nasty soup away!
I won't have any soup today."

Next day begins his tale of woes;
Quite lank and lean Augustus grows.
Yet, though he feels so weak and ill,
The naughty fellow cries out still—
"Not any soup for me, I say:
O take the nasty soup away!
I won't have any soup today."

The third day comes; O what a sin!
To make himself so pale and thin.
Yet, when the soup is put on table,
He screams as loud as he is able—
"Not any soup for me, I say:
O take the nasty soup away!
I won't have any soup today."

Look at him, now the fourth day's come!
He scarcely weighs a sugar-plum;
He's like a little bit of thread,
And on the fifth day, he was—dead!

CLEAN CLARA

By William B. Rands

What! not know our Clean Clara?
Why, the hot folks in Sahara,
And the cold Esquimaux,
Our little Clara know;
Clean Clara, the Poet sings,
Cleaned a hundred thousand things!

She cleaned the keys of the harpsichord,
She cleaned the hilt of the family sword,
She cleaned my lady, she cleaned my lord.
All the pictures in their frames,
Knights with daggers and stomachered dames—
Cecils, Godfreys, Montforts, Graemes,
Winifreds—all those nice old names!

She cleaned the works of the eight-day clock,
She cleaned the spring of a secret lock,
She cleaned the mirror, she cleaned the cupboard;
All the books she India-rubbered!

She cleaned the Dutch tiles in the place,
She cleaned some very old-fashioned lace;
The Countess of Miniver came to her,
"Pray, my dear, will you clean my fur?"
All her cleanings are admirable;
To count your teeth you will be able,
If you look in the walnut table!

She cleaned the tent-stitch and the sampler,
She cleaned the tapestry, which was ampler:
Joseph going down into the pit,
And the Shunammite woman with the boy in a fit;

You saw the reapers, *not* in the distance,
And Elisha coming to the child's assistance,
With the house on the wall that was built for the prophet,
The chair, the bed, and the bolster of it;
The eyebrows all had a twirl reflective,
Just like an eel: to spare invective
There was plenty of color, but no perspective.

However, Clara cleaned it all,
With a curious lamp, that hangs in the hall;
She cleaned the drops of the chandeliers,
Madam in mittens was moved to tears.

She cleaned the cage of the cockatoo,
The oldest bird that ever grew;
I should say a thousand years old would do—
I'm sure he look'd it, but nobody knew;
She cleaned the china, she cleaned the delf,
She cleaned the baby, she cleaned herself!

Tomorrow morning she means to try
To clean the cobwebs from the sky;
Some people say the girl will rue it,
But my belief is she will do it.

So I've made up my mind to be there to see,
There's a beautiful place in the walnut-tree;
The bough is as firm as a solid rock;
She brings out her broom at six o'clock.

THE OWL AND THE PUSSY-CAT

By Edward Lear

The Owl and the Pussy-Cat went to sea
  In a beautiful pea-green boat;
They took some honey, and plenty of money
  Wrapped up in a five-pound note.
The Owl looked up to the moon above,
  And sang to a small guitar:
"Oh lovely Pussy! O Pussy, my love,
  What a beautiful Pussy you are
    You are,
    You are!
  What a beautiful Pussy you are!"

Pussy said to the Owl: "You elegant fowl,
  How charmingly sweet you sing!
Oh, let us be married—too long we have tarried—
  But what shall we do for a ring?"
They sailed away for a year and a day
  To the land where the bong tree grows;
And there in a wood, a piggy-wig stood
  With a ring at the end of his nose,
    His nose,
    His nose.
  With a ring at the end of his nose.

"Dear Pig, are you willing to sell for one shilling
Your ring?" Said the piggy, "I will."
So they took it away, and were married next day
By the turkey who lives on the hill.
They dined upon mince and slices of quince,
Which they ate with a runcible spoon,
And hand in hand on the edge of the sand
They danced by the light of the moon,
The moon,
The moon.
They danced by the light of the moon.

THE POBBLE WHO HAS NO TOES

By Edward Lear

The Pobble who has no toes
Had once as many as we;
When they said, "Some day you may lose them all";
He replied, "Fish fiddle-de-dee!"
And his Aunt Jobiska made him drink
Lavender water tinged with pink;
For she said, "The World in general knows
There's nothing so good for a Pobble's toes!"

The Pobble who has no toes,
Swam across the Bristol Channel;
But before he set out he wrapped his nose
In a piece of scarlet flannel.
For his Aunt Jobiska said, "No harm
Can come to his toes if his nose is warm;
And it's perfectly known that a Pobble's toes
Are safe—provided he minds his nose."

The Pobble swam fast and well,
And when boats or ships came near him,
He tinkledy-binkledy-winkled a bell
So that all the world could hear him.
And all the Sailors and Admirals cried,
When they saw him nearing the further side—
"He has gone to fish, for his Aunt Jobiska's
Runcible Cat with crimson whiskers!"

But before he touched the shore—
  The shore of the Bristol Channel,
A sea-green Porpoise carried away
  His wrapper of scarlet flannel.
And when he came to observe his feet,
Formerly garnished with toes so neat,
His face at once became forlorn
On perceiving that all his toes were gone!

And nobody ever knew,
  From that dark day to the present,
Whoso had taken the Pobble's toes,
  In a manner so far from pleasant.
Whether the shrimps or crawfish gray,
Or crafty Mermaids stole them away,
Nobody knew; and nobody knows
How the Pobble was robbed of his twice five toes!

The Pobble who has no toes
  Was placed in a friendly Bark,
And they rowed him back, and carried him up
  To his Aunt Jobiska's Park.
And she made him a feast, at his earnest wish,
Of eggs and buttercups fried with fish;
And she said, "It's a fact the whole world knows,
That Pobbles are happier without their toes."

THE JUMBLIES

By Edward Lear

They went to sea in a sieve, they did,
  In a sieve they went to sea:
In spite of all their friends could say,
On a winter's morn, on a stormy day,
  In a sieve they went to sea.
And when the sieve turned round and round,
And every one cried, "You'll all be drowned!"
They called aloud, "Our sieve ain't big;
But we don't care a button, we don't care a fig:
  In a sieve we'll go to sea!"
      Far and few, far and few,
        Are the lands where the Jumblies live;
      Their heads are green, and their hands are blue,
        And they went to sea in a sieve.

They sailed away in a sieve, they did,
  In a sieve they sailed so fast,
With only a beautiful pea-green veil
Tied with a ribbon, by way of a sail,
  To a small tobacco-pipe mast.
And every one said who saw them go,
"Oh! won't they be soon upset, you know?
For the sky is dark, and the voyage is long;
And, happen what may, it's extremely wrong
  In a sieve to sail so fast."
    Far and few, far and few,
      Are the lands where the Jumblies live;
    Their heads are green, and their hands are blue,
      And they went to sea in a sieve.

The water it soon came in, it did,
  The water it soon came in;
So, to keep them dry, they wrapped their feet
In a pinky paper all folded neat;
  And they fastened it down with a pin.
And they passed the night in a crockery jar;
And each of them said: "How wise we are!
Though the sky be dark and the voyage long
Yet we never can think we were rash or wrong,
  While round in our sieve we spin."
    Far and few, far and few,
      Are the lands where the Jumblies live;
    Their heads are green, and their hands are blue,
      And they went to sea in a sieve.

And all night long they sailed away;
  And when the sun went down,
They whistled and warbled a moony song
To the echoing sound of a coppery gong,
  In the shade of the mountains brown.
"O Timballoo! How happy we are
When we live in a sieve and a crockery jar!
And all night long, in the moonlight pale,
We sail away with a pea-green sail
  In the shade of the mountains brown."
    Far and few, far and few,
      Are the lands where the Jumblies live;
    Their heads are green, and their hands are blue,
      And they went to sea in a sieve.

They sailed to the Western Sea, they did—
  To a land all covered with trees;
And they bought an owl, and a useful cart,
And a pound of rice, and a cranberry-tart,
  And a hive of silvery bees;
And they bought a pig, and some green jackdaws,
And a lovely monkey with lollipop paws.
And forty bottles of ring-bo-ree,
  And no end of Stilton cheese.
    Far and few, far and few,
      Are the lands where the Jumblies live;
    Their heads are green, and their hands are blue,
      And they went to sea in a sieve.

And in twenty years they all came back—
  In twenty years or more;
And every one said, "How tall they've grown!
For they've been to the Lakes, and the Torrible Zone,
  And the hills of the Chankly Bore."
And they drank their health, and gave them a feast
Of dumplings made of beautiful yeast;
And every one said, "If we only live,
We, too, will go to sea in a sieve,
  To the hills of the Chankly Bore."
    Far and few, far and few,
      Are the lands where the Jumblies live;
    Their heads are green, and their hands are blue,
      And they went to sea in a sieve.

THE COURTSHIP OF THE YONGHY-BONGHY-BÒ

By Edward Lear

On the Coast of Coromandel
  Where the early pumpkins blow,
    In the middle of the woods
  Lived the Yonghy-Bonghy-Bò,
Two old chairs, and half a candle,
One old jug without a handle—
    These were all his worldly goods:
    In the middle of the woods,
    These were all the worldly goods
  Of the Yonghy-Bonghy-Bò,
  Of the Yonghy-Bonghy-Bò.

Once, among the Bong-trees walking
  Where the early pumpkins blow,
    To a little heap of stones
  Came the Yonghy-Bonghy-Bò,
There he heard a Lady talking,
To some milk-white Hens of Dorking—
    " 'Tis the Lady Jingly Jones!
    On that little heap of stones
    Sits the Lady Jingly Jones!"
  Said the Yonghy-Bonghy-Bò,
  Said the Yonghy-Bonghy-Bò.

"Lady Jingly! Lady Jingly!
  Sitting where the pumpkins blow,
    Will you come and be my wife?"
  Said the Yonghy-Bonghy-Bò,
"I am tired of living singly—
On this coast so wild and shingly—
    I'm a-weary of my life;
    If you'll come and be my wife,
    Quite serene would be my life!"
  Said the Yonghy-Bonghy-Bò,
  Said the Yonghy-Bonghy-Bò.

"On this Coast of Coromandel
  Shrimps and watercresses grow
    Prawns are plentiful and cheap,"
  Said the Yonghy-Bonghy-Bò,
"You shall have my chairs and candle,
And my jug without a handle!
    Gaze upon the rolling deep
    (Fish is plentiful and cheap);
    As the sea, my love is deep!"
  Said the Yonghy-Bonghy-Bò,
  Said the Yonghy-Bonghy-Bò.

Lady Jingly answered sadly,
  And her tears began to flow—
    "Your proposal comes too late,
  Mr. Yonghy-Bonghy-Bò.
I would be your wife most gladly!"
(Here she twirled her fingers madly),

"But in England I've a mate!
Yes! you've asked me far too late,
For in England I've a mate,
Mr. Yonghy-Bonghy-Bò!
Mr. Yonghy-Bonghy-Bò!

"Mr. Jones (his name is Handel—
Handel Jones, Esquire, & Co.)
Dorking fowls delights to send,
Mr. Yonghy-Bonghy-Bò!
Keep, oh keep your chairs and candle,
And your jug without a handle—
I can merely be your friend!
Should my Jones more Dorkings send,
I will give you three, my friend!
Mr. Yonghy-Bonghy-Bò!
Mr. Yonghy-Bonghy-Bò!

"Though you've such a tiny body,
And your head so large doth grow—
Though your hat may blow away,
Mr. Yonghy-Bonghy-Bò!
Though you're such a Hoddy Doddy,
Yet I wish that I could modi-
fy the words I needs must say!
Will you please to go away?
That is all I have to say,
Mr. Yonghy-Bonghy-Bò!
Mr. Yonghy-Bonghy-Bò!"

Down the slippery slopes of Myrtle,
Where the early pumpkins blow,
To the calm and silent sea
Fled the Yonghy-Bonghy-Bò.
There, beyond the Bay of Gurtle,
Lay a large and lively Turtle.
"You're the Cove," he said, "for me;
On your back beyond the sea,
Turtle, you shall carry me!"
Said the Yonghy-Bonghy-Bò,
Said the Yonghy-Bonghy-Bò.

Through the silent-roaring ocean
 Did the Turtle swiftly go;
  Holding fast upon his shell,
 Rode the Yonghy-Bonghy-Bò,
With a sad primeval motion
Towards the sunset isles of Boshen
  Still the Turtle bore him well.
  Holding fast upon his shell,
  "Lady Jingly Jones, farewell!"
 Sang the Yonghy-Bonghy-Bò,
 Sang the Yonghy-Bonghy-Bò.

From the Coast of Coromandel
 Did that Lady never go;
  On that heap of stones she mourns
 For the Yonghy-Bonghy-Bò.
On the Coast of Coromandel,
In his jug without a handle
  Still she weeps, and daily moans;
  On that little heap of stones
  To her Dorking Hens she moans,
 For the Yonghy-Bonghy-Bò,
 For the Yonghy-Bonghy-Bò.

JABBERWOCKY

By Lewis Carroll

'Twas brillig, and the slithy toves
 Did gyre and gimble in the wabe;
All mimsy were the borogoves,
 And the mome raths outgrabe.

"Beware the Jabberwock, my son!
 The jaws that bite, the claws that catch!
Beware the Jubjub bird, and shun
 The frumious Bandersnatch!"

He took his vorpal sword in hand:
 Long time the manxome foe he sought—
So rested he by the Tumtum tree,
 And stood awhile in thought.

Sir John Tenniel

The vorpal blade went snicker-snack!

[See page 119]

And as in uffish thought he stood,
  The Jabberwock, with eyes of flame,
Came whiffling through the tulgey wood,
  And burbled as it came!

One, two! One, two! And through and through
  The vorpal blade went snicker-snack!
He left it dead, and with its head
  He went galumphing back.

"And hast thou slain the Jabberwock?
  Come to my arms, my beamish boy!
O frabjous day! Callooh! Callay!"
  He chortled in his joy.

'Twas brillig, and the slithy toves
  Did gyre and gimble in the wabe;
All mimsy were the borogoves,
  And the mome raths outgrabe.

THE WALRUS AND THE CARPENTER

By Lewis Carroll

The sun was shining on the sea,
  Shining with all its might:
He did his very best to make
  The billows smooth and bright—
And this was odd, because it was
  The middle of the night.

The moon was shining sulkily,
  Because she thought the sun
Had got no business to be there
  After the day was done—
"It's very rude of him," she said,
  "To come and spoil the fun!"

The sea was wet as wet could be,
  The sands were dry as dry.
You could not see a cloud, because
  No cloud was in the sky:
No birds were flying overhead—
  There were no birds to fly.

The Walrus and the Carpenter
  Were walking close at hand;
They wept like anything to see
  Such quantities of sand:
"If this were only cleared away,"
  They said, "it *would* be grand!"

"If seven maids with seven mops
  Swept it for half a year,
Do you suppose," the Walrus said,
  "That they could get it clear?"
"I doubt it," said the Carpenter,
  And shed a bitter tear.

"O Oysters, come and walk with us!"
  The Walrus did beseech.
"A pleasant talk, a pleasant walk,
  Along the briny beach:
We cannot do with more than four,
  To give a hand to each."

The eldest Oyster looked at him,
  But never a word he said:
The eldest Oyster winked his eye,
  And shook his heavy head—
Meaning to say he did not choose
  To leave the oyster-bed.

But four young Oysters hurried up,
  All eager for the treat:
Their coats were brushed, their faces washed,
  Their shoes were clean and neat—
And this was odd, because, you know,
  They hadn't any feet.

Four other Oysters followed them,
  And yet another four;
And thick and fast they came at last,
  And more, and more, and more—
All hopping through the frothy waves,
  And scrambling to the shore.

The Walrus and the Carpenter
  Walked on a mile or so,
And then they rested on a rock
  Conveniently low:
And all the little Oysters stood
  And waited in a row.

"The time has come," the Walrus said,
  "To talk of many things:
Of shoes—and ships—and sealing-wax—
  Of cabbages—and kings—
And why the sea is boiling hot—
  And whether pigs have wings."

"But wait a bit," the Oysters cried,
  "Before we have our chat;
For some of us are out of breath,
  And all of us are fat!"
"No hurry!" said the Carpenter.
  They thanked him much for that.

"A loaf of bread," the Walrus said,
  "Is what we chiefly need:
Pepper and vinegar besides
  Are very good indeed—
Now, if you're ready, Oysters dear,
  We can begin to feed."

"But not on us!" the Oysters cried,
  Turning a little blue.
"After such kindness, that would be
  A dismal thing to do!"
"The night is fine," the Walrus said.
  "Do you admire the view?

"It was so kind of you to come!
  And you were very nice!"
The Carpenter said nothing but
  "Cut us another slice.
I wish you were not quite so deaf—
  I've had to ask you twice!"

"It seems a shame," the Walrus said,
  "To play them such a trick.
After we've brought them out so far,
  And made them trot so quick!"
The Carpenter said nothing but
  "The butter's spread too thick!"

"I weep for you," the Walrus said:
  "I deeply sympathize."
With sobs and tears he sorted out
  Those of the largest size,
Holding his pocket-handkerchief
  Before his streaming eyes.

"O Oysters," said the Carpenter,
  "You've had a pleasant run!
Shall we be trotting home again?"
  But answer came there none—
And this was scarcely odd, because
  They'd eaten every one.

THE MAD GARDENER'S SONG

By Lewis Carroll

He thought he saw an Elephant,
  That practised on a fife:
He looked again, and found it was
  A letter from his wife.
"At length I realize," he said,
  "The bitterness of Life!"

He thought he saw a Buffalo
  Upon the chimney-piece:
He looked again, and found it was
  His Sister's Husband's Niece.
"Unless you leave this house," he said,
  "I'll send for the Police!"

He thought he saw a Rattlesnake
  That questioned him in Greek:
He looked again, and found it was
  The Middle of Next Week.
"The one thing I regret," he said,
  "Is that it cannot speak!"

He thought he saw a Banker's Clerk,
  Descending from the bus:
He looked again, and found it was
  A Hippopotamus:
"If this should stay to dine," he said,
  "There won't be much for us!"

He thought he saw a Kangaroo
  That worked a coffee-mill:
He looked again, and found it was
  A Vegetable-Pill.
"Were I to swallow this," he said,
  "I should be very ill!"

He thought he saw a Coach-and-Four
  That stood beside his bed:
He looked again, and found it was
  A Bear without a Head.

"Poor thing," he said, "poor silly thing!
  It's waiting to be fed!"

He thought he saw an Albatross
  That fluttered round the lamp:
He looked again, and found it was
  A Penny-Postage-Stamp.
"You'd best be getting home," he said:
  "The nights are very damp!"

He thought he saw a Garden-Door
  That opened with a key:
He looked again, and found it was
  A Double Rule of Three:
"And all its mystery," he said,
  "Is clear as day to me!"

He thought he saw an Argument
  That proved he was the Pope:
He looked again, and found it was
  A Bar of Mottled Soap.
"A fact so dread," he faintly said,
  "Extinguishes all hope!"

THE THREE BADGERS

By Lewis Carroll

There be three Badgers on a mossy stone
  Beside a dark and covered way:
Each dreams himself a monarch on his throne,
  And so they stay and stay—
Though their old Father languishes alone,
  They stay, and stay, and stay.

There be three Herrings loitering around,
  Longing to share that mossy seat:
Each Herring tries to sing what she has found
  That makes Life seem so sweet.
Thus, with a grating and uncertain sound,
  They bleat, and bleat, and bleat.

The Mother-Herring, on the salt sea-wave,
  Sought vainly for her absent ones:
The Father-Badger, writhing in a cave,
  Shrieked out "Return, my sons!
You shall have buns," he shrieked, "if you'll behave!
  Yea, buns, and buns, and buns!"

"I fear," said she, "your sons have gone astray.
  My daughters left me while I slept."
"Yes'm," the Badger said: "it's as you say.
  They should be better kept."
Thus the poor parents talked the time away,
  And wept, and wept, and wept.

"Oh dear, beyond our dearest dreams,
Fairer than all that fairest seems!
To feast the rosy hours away,
To revel in a roundelay!
    How blest would be
    A life so free—
Ipwergis-Pudding to consume,
And drink the subtle Azzigoom!

"And if, in other days and hours,
Mid other fluffs and other flowers,
The choice were given me how to dine—
'Name what thou wilt: it shall be thine!'
    Oh, then I see
    The life for me—
Ipwergis-Pudding to consume,
And drink the subtle Azzigoom!"

The Badgers did not care to talk to Fish:
  They did not dote on Herrings' songs:
They never had experienced the dish
  To which that name belongs:
"And oh, to pinch their tails," (this was their wish,)
  "With tongs, yea, tongs, and tongs!"

"And are not these the Fish," the Eldest sighed,
  "Whose Mother dwells beneath the foam?"
"They *are* the Fish!" the Second one replied.
  "And they have left their home!"
"Oh, wicked Fish," the Youngest Badger cried,
  "To roam, yea, roam, and roam!"

Gently the Badgers trotted to the shore—
  The sandy shore that fringed the bay:
Each in his mouth a living Herring bore—
  Those aged ones waxed gay:
Clear rang their voices through the ocean's roar,
  "Hooray, hooray, hooray!"

THE DUEL

By Eugene Field

The gingham dog and the calico cat
Side by side on the table sat;
'Twas half-past twelve, and (what do you think!)
Nor one nor t'other had slept a wink!
  The old Dutch clock and the Chinese plate
  Appeared to know as sure as fate
There was going to be a terrible spat.
  (*I wasn't there; I simply state*
  What was told me by the Chinese plate!)

The gingham dog went "Bow-wow-wow!"
And the calico cat replied "Mee-ow!"
The air was littered, an hour or so,
With bits of gingham and calico,
  While the old Dutch clock in the chimney-place
  Up with its hands before its face,
For it always dreaded a family row!
  (*Now mind: I'm only telling you*
  What the old Dutch clock declares is true!)

The Chinese plate looked very blue,
And wailed, "Oh, dear! what shall we do?"
But the gingham dog and the calico cat
Wallowed this way and tumbled that,
  Employing every tooth and claw
  In the awfullest way you ever saw—
And, Oh! How the gingham and calico flew!
  (*Don't fancy I exaggerate!*
  I got my news from the Chinese plate!)

Next morning, where the two had sat,
They found no trace of dog or cat;
And some folks think unto this day
That burglars stole that pair away!
  But the truth about the cat and pup
  Is this: they ate each other up!
Now what do you really think of that!
  (The old Dutch clock it told me so,
  And that is how I came to know.)

THE MAN IN THE MOON

By James Whitcomb Riley

Said the Raggedy Man, on a hot afternoon:
  "My!
    Sakes!
      What a lot o' mistakes
Some little folks makes on The Man in the Moon!
But people that's be'n to *see* him, like *me,*
And calls on him frequent and intimuttly,
Might drop a few facts that would interest you
  Clean!
    Through!—
      If you wanted 'em to—
  Some *actual* facts that might interest you!

"O The Man in the Moon has a crick in his back;
  Whee!
    Whimm!
      Ain't you sorry for him?
And a mole on his nose that is purple and black;
And his eyes are so weak that they water and run
If he dares to *dream* even he looks at the sun—
So he jes' dreams of stars, as the doctors advise—
  My!
    Eyes!
      But isn't he wise—
To jes' dream of stars, as the doctors advise?

"And the Man in the Moon has a boil on his ear—
  Whee!
    Whing!
      What a singular thing!
I know! but these facts are authentic, my dear—
There's a boil on his ear; and a corn on his chin—
He calls it a dimple—but dimples stick in—
Yet it might be a dimple turned over, you know!
  Whang!
    Ho!
      Why, certainly so!—
  It might be a dimple turned over, you know!

"And the Man in the Moon has a rheumatic knee—
  Gee!
    Whizz!
      What a pity that is!
And his toes have worked round where his heels ought to be—
So whenever he wants to go north he goes *south,*
And comes back with porridge-crumbs all round his mouth,
And he brushes them off with a Japanese fan,
  Whing!
    Whann!
      What a marvelous man!
  What a very remarkably marvelous man!

"And The Man in the Moon," sighed The Raggedy Man,
  "Gits!
    So!
      Sullonesome, you know—
Up there by hisse'f sence creation began!—
That when I call on him and then come away,
He grabs me and holds me and begs me to stay—
Till—*Well!* if it wasn't fer *Jimmy-cum-jim,*
  Dadd!
    Limb!
      I'd go pardners with him—
Jes' jump my job here and be pardners with *him!*"

THE SHIP OF RIO

By Walter de la Mare

There was a ship of Rio
  Sailed out into the blue,
And nine and ninety monkeys
  Were all her jovial crew.
From bo'sun to the cabin boy,
  From quarter to caboose,
There weren't a stitch of calico
  To breech 'em—tight or loose;
From spar to deck, from deck to keel,
  From barnacle to shroud.
There weren't one pair of reach-me-downs
  To all that jabbering crowd.
But wasn't it a gladsome sight,
  When roared the deep-sea gales,
To see them reef her fore and aft,
  A-swinging by their tails!
Oh, wasn't it a gladsome sight,
  When glassy calm did come,
To see them squatting tailor-wise
  Around a keg of rum!
Oh, wasn't it a gladsome sight,
  When in she sailed to land,
To see them all a-scampering skip
  For nuts across the sand!

THE PLAINT OF THE CAMEL

By Charles E. Carryl

"Canary-birds feed on sugar and seed,
Parrots have crackers to crunch;
And as for the poodles, they tell me the noodles
Have chickens and cream for their lunch.
But there's never a question
About MY digestion—
ANYTHING does for me!

"Cats, you're aware, can repose in a chair,
Chickens can roost upon rails;
Puppies are able to sleep in a stable,
And oysters can slumber in pails.
But no one supposes
A poor Camel dozes—
ANY PLACE does for me!

"Lambs are enclosed where it's never exposed,
Coops are constructed for hens;
Kittens are treated to houses well heated,
And pigs are protected by pens.
But a Camel comes handy
Wherever it's sandy—
ANYWHERE does for me!

"People would laugh if you rode a giraffe,
Or mounted the back of an ox;
It's nobody's habit to ride on a rabbit,
Or try to bestraddle a fox.
But as for a Camel, he's
Ridden by families—
ANY LOAD does for me!

"A snake is as round as a hole in the ground,
And weasels are wavy and sleek;
And no alligator could ever be straighter
Than lizards that live in a creek,
But a Camel's all lumpy
And bumpy and humpy—
ANY SHAPE does for me!"

SAGE COUNSEL

By Sir Arthur Quiller-Couch

The Lion is the beast to fight:
He leaps along the plain,
And if you run with all your might,
He runs with all his mane.
I'm glad I'm not a Hottentot,
But if I were, with outward cal-lum
I'd either faint upon the spot
Or hie me up a leafy pal-lum.

The Chamois is the beast to hunt:
He's fleeter than the wind,
And when the Chamois is in front
The hunter is behind.
The Tyrolese make famous cheese
And hunt the Chamois o'er the chaz-zums;
I'd choose the former, if you please,
For precipices give me spaz-zums.

The Polar Bear will make a rug
Almost as white as snow:
But if he gets you in his hug,
He rarely lets you go.
And polar ice looks very nice,
With all the colors of a prissum:
But, if you'll follow my advice,
Stay home and learn your catechissum.

THE CHIMPANZEE

By Oliver Herford

Children, behold the Chimpanzee:
He sits on the ancestral tree
From which we sprang in ages gone.
I'm glad we sprang: had we held on,
We might, for aught that I can say,
Be horrid Chimpanzees today.

THE ANT

By Oliver Herford

My child, ob-serve the use-ful Ant,
How hard she works each day;
She works as hard as ad-a-mant
(That's very hard, they say).
She has no time to gal-li-vant;
She has no time to play.
Let Fi-do chase his tail all day;
Let Kit-ty play at tag;
She has no time to throw away,
She has no tail to wag;
She hur-ries round from morn till night;
She nev-er, nev-er sleeps;
She seiz-es ev-er-y thing in sight,
She drags it home with all her might,
And all she takes she keeps.

A BUNNY ROMANCE

By Oliver Herford

The Bunnies are a feeble folk
Whose weakness is their strength,
To shun a gun a Bun will run
To almost any length.

Now once, when war alarms were rife
In the ancestral wood
Where the kingdom of the Bunnies
For centuries had stood,
The king, for fear long peace had made
His subjects over-bold,
To wake the glorious spirit
Of timidity of old,
Announced one day he would bestow
Princess Bunita's hand
On the Bunny who should prove himself
Most timid in the land.

Next day a proclamation
Was posted in the wood
"To the Flower of Timidity,
The Pick of Bunnyhood:
His Majesty the Bunny king,
Commands you to appear
At a tournament—at such a date
In such and such a year—
Where his Majesty will then bestow
Princess Bunita's hand
On the Bunny who will prove himself
Most timid in the land."

Then every timid Bunny's heart
Swelled with exultant fright
At the thought of doughty deeds of fear
And prodigies of flight.
For the motto of the Bunnies
As perhaps you are aware,
Is "Only the faint-hearted
Are deserving of the fair."

They fell at once to practicing,
These Bunnies, one and all,
Till some would almost die of fright
To hear a petal fall.
And one enterprising Bunny
Got up a special class
To teach the art of fainting
At your shadow on the grass.

At length—at length—at length
The moment is at hand!
And trembling all from head to foot
A hundred Bunnies stand.
And a hundred Bunny mothers
With anxiety turn gray
Lest their offspring dear should lose their fear
And linger in the fray.

Never before in Bunny lore
Was such a stirring sight
As when the bugle sounded
To begin the glorious flight!
A hundred Bunnies, like a flash,
All disappeared from sight
Like arrows from a hundred bows—
None swerved to left or right.
Some north, some south, some east, some west—
And none of them, 'tis plain,
Till he has gone around the earth
Will e'er be seen again.

It may be in a hundred weeks,
Perchance a hundred years.
Whenever it may be, 'tis plain
The one who first appears
Is the one who ran the fastest;
He wins the Princess' hand,
And gains the glorious title of
"Most timid in the Land."

THE ELF AND THE DORMOUSE

By Oliver Herford

Under a toadstool crept a wee Elf,
Out of the rain, to shelter himself.

Under the toadstool sound asleep,
Sat a big Dormouse all in a heap.

Trembled the wee Elf, frightened, and yet
Fearing to fly away lest he get wet.

To the next shelter—maybe a mile!
Sudden the wee Elf smiled a wee smile,

Tugged till the toadstool toppled in two.
Holding it over him, gayly he flew.

Soon he was safe home, dry as could be.
Soon woke the Dormouse—"Good gracious me!

"Where is my toadstool?" loud he lamented.
—And that's how umbrellas first were invented.

THE PYTHON

By Hilaire Belloc

A Python I should not advise—
It needs a doctor for its eyes,
  And has the measles yearly.
However, if you feel inclined
To get one (to improve your mind,
  And not from fashion merely),
Allow no music near its cage;
And when it flies into a rage,
  Chastise it most severely.

I had an Aunt in Yucatan
Who bought a Python from a man
  And kept it for a pet.
She died because she never knew
These simple little rules and few—
  The snake is living yet.

THE FROG

By Hilaire Belloc

Be kind and tender to the Frog,
And do not call him names,
As "Slimy-skin," or "Polly-wog,"
Or likewise, "Uncle James,"

Or "Gape-a-grin," or "Toad-gone-wrong,"
Or "Billy Bandy-knees":
The Frog is justly sensitive
To epithets like these.

No animal will more repay
A treatment kind and fair,
At least so lonely people say
Who keep a Frog (and, by the way,
They are extremely rare).

THE YAK

By Hilaire Belloc

As a friend to the children, commend me the Yak;
You will find it exactly the thing;
It will carry and fetch, you can ride on its back,
Or lead it about with a string.

The Tartar who dwells on the plains of Thibet
(A desolate region of snow),
Has for centuries made it a nursery pet,
And surely the Tartar should know!

Then tell your papa where the Yak can be got,
And if he is awfully rich,
He will buy you the creature—or else he will not,
(I cannot be positive which).

THE VOWELS: AN ENIGMA

By Jonathan Swift

We are little airy creatures,
All of different voice and features;
One of us in glass is set,
One of us you'll find in jet,
T'other you may see in tin,
And the fourth a box within;
If the fifth you should pursue,
It can never fly from you.

A RIDDLE

By Hannah More

I'm a strange contradiction; I'm new, and I'm old,
I'm often in tatters, and oft decked with gold.
Though I never could read, yet lettered I'm found;
Though blind, I enlighten; though loose, I am bound,
I'm always in black, and I'm always in white;
I'm grave and I'm gay, I am heavy and light—
In form too I differ—I'm thick and I'm thin,
I've no flesh and bones, yet I'm covered with skin;
I've more points than the compass, more stops than the flute;
I sing without voice, without speaking confute.
I'm English, I'm German, I'm French, and I'm Dutch;
Some love me too fondly, some slight me too much;
I often die soon, though I sometimes live ages,
And no monarch alive has so many pages.

[*A book*.

A RIDDLE

By Catherine M. Fanshawe

'Twas whispered in Heaven, 'twas muttered in hell,
And echo caught faintly the sound as it fell;
On the confines of earth 'twas permitted to rest,
And the depths of the ocean its presence confess'd;
'Twill be found in the sphere when 'tis riven asunder,
Be seen in the lightning and heard in the thunder;
'Twas allotted to man with his earliest breath,
Attends him at birth and awaits him at death,
Presides o'er his happiness, honor and health,
Is the prop of his house, and the end of his wealth.
In the heaps of the miser 'tis hoarded with care,
But is sure to be lost on his prodigal heir;
It begins every hope, every wish it must bound,
With the husbandman toils, and with monarchs is crowned;
Without it the soldier and seaman may roam,
But woe to the wretch who expels it from home!
In the whispers of conscience its voice will be found,
Nor e'er in the whirlwind of passion be drowned;
'Twill soften the heart; but though deaf be the ear,
It will make him acutely and instantly hear.
Set in shade, let it rest like a delicate flower;
Ah! breathe on it softly, it dies in an hour.

[*The letter H.*

AT HOME AND AT PLAY

THE LAND OF STORY-BOOKS

By Robert Louis Stevenson

At evening when the lamp is lit,
Around the fire my parents sit;
They sit at home and talk and sing,
And do not play at anything.

Now, with my little gun, I crawl
All in the dark along the wall,
And follow round the forest track
Away behind the sofa back.

There, in the night, where none can spy,
All in my hunter's camp I lie,
And play at books that I have read
Till it is time to go to bed.

These are the hills, these are the woods,
These are my starry solitudes;
And there the river by whose brink
The roaring lions come to drink.

I see the others far away,
As if in firelit camp they lay,
And I, like to an Indian scout,
Around their party prowled about.

So, when my nurse comes in for me,
Home I return across the sea,
And go to bed with backward looks
At my dear land of Story-books.

TRAVEL

By Robert Louis Stevenson

I should like to rise and go
Where the golden apples grow—
Where below another sky
Parrot islands anchored lie,
And, watched by cockatoos and goats,
Lonely Crusoes building boats—
Where in sunshine reaching out
Eastern cities, miles about,
Are with mosque and minaret
Among sandy gardens set,
And the rich goods from near and far
Hang for sale in the bazaar—
Where the Great Wall round China goes,
And on one side the desert blows,
And with bell and voice and drum,
Cities on the other hum—
Where are forests, hot as fire,
Wide as England, tall as a spire,
Full of apes and cocoanuts
And the negro hunters' huts—
Where the knotty crocodile
Lies and blinks in the Nile,
And the red flamingo flies
Hunting fish before his eyes:—
Where in jungles, near and far,
Man-devouring tigers are,
Lying close and giving ear
Lest the hunt be drawing near,
Or a comer-by be seen
Swinging in a palanquin—
Where among the desert sands
Some deserted city stands,
All its children, sweep and prince,
Grown to manhood ages since,
Not a foot in street or house,
Not a stir of child or mouse,
And when kindly falls the night,
In all the town no spark of light.

There I'll come when I'm a man
With a camel caravan;
Light a fire in the gloom
Of some dusty dining room;
See the pictures on the walls,
Heroes, fights and festivals;
And in a corner find the toys
Of the old Egyptian boys.

THE LAND OF COUNTERPANE

By Robert Louis Stevenson

When I was sick and lay a-bed,
I had two pillows at my head,
And all my toys beside me lay
To keep me happy all the day.

And sometimes for an hour or so
I watched my leaden soldiers go,
With different uniforms and drills,
Among the bed-clothes, through the hills;

And sometimes sent my ships in fleets
All up and down among the sheets;
Or brought my trees and houses out,
And planted cities all about.

I was the giant great and still
That sits upon the pillow-hill,
And sees before him, dale and plain,
The pleasant land of counterpane.

THE HENS

By Elizabeth Madox Roberts

The night was coming very fast;
It reached the gate as I ran past.

The pigeons had gone to the tower of the church
And all the hens were on their perch,

Up in the barn, and I thought I heard
A piece of a little purring word.

I stopped inside, waiting and staying,
To try to hear what the hens were saying.

They were asking something, that was plain,
Asking it over and over again.

One of them moved and turned around,
Her feathers made a ruffled sound,

A ruffled sound, like a bushful of birds,
And she said her little asking words.

She pushed her head close into her wing,
But nothing answered anything.

THE PASTURE

By Robert Frost

I'm going out to clean the pasture spring;
I'll only stop to rake the leaves away
(And wait to watch the water clear, I may):
I shan't be gone long.—You come too.

I'm going out to fetch the little calf
That's standing by the mother. It's so young,
It totters when she licks it with her tongue.
I shan't be gone long.—You come too.

WINTER-TIME

By Robert Louis Stevenson

Late lies the wintry sun a-bed,
A frosty, fiery sleepy-head;
Blinks but an hour or two; and then,
A blood-red orange, sets again.

Before the stars have left the skies,
At morning in the dark I rise;
And, shivering in my nakedness,
By the cold candle, bathe and dress.

Close by the jolly fire I sit
To warm my frozen bones a bit;
Or, with a reindeer-sled, explore
The colder countries round the door.

When, to go out, my nurse doth wrap
Me in my comforter and cap,
The cold wind burns my face, and blows
Its frosty pepper up my nose.

Black are my steps on silver sod;
Thick blows my frosty breath abroad;
And tree and house, and hill and lake,
Are frosted like a wedding-cake.

THE LOST DOLL

By Charles Kingsley

I once had a sweet little doll, dears,
The prettiest doll in the world;
Her cheeks were so red and white, dears,
And her hair was so charmingly curled.
But I lost my poor little doll, dears,
As I played on the heath one day;
And I cried for her more than a week, dears,
But I never could find where she lay.

I found my poor little doll, dears,
As I played on the heath one day;
Folks say she is terribly changed, dears,
For her paint is all washed away,
And her arms trodden off by the cows, dears,
And her hair not the least bit curled;
Yet for old sakes' sake, she is still, dears,
The prettiest doll in the world.

THE CHILDREN'S HOUR

By Henry Wadsworth Longfellow

Between the dark and the daylight,
When night is beginning to lower,
Comes a pause in the day's occupations,
That is known as the children's hour.

I hear in the chamber above me
  The patter of little feet,
The sound of a door that is opened,
  And voices soft and sweet.

From my study I see in the lamplight,
  Descending the broad hall stair,
Grave Alice and laughing Allegra,
  And Edith with golden hair.

A whisper and then a silence,
  Yet I know by their merry eyes
They are plotting and planning together
  To take me by surprise.

A sudden rush from the stairway,
  A sudden raid from the hall,
By three doors left unguarded,
  They enter my castle wall.

They climb up into my turret,
  O'er the arms and back of my chair;
If I try to escape, they surround me;
  They seem to be everywhere.

They almost devour me with kisses,
  Their arms about me entwine,
Till I think of the Bishop of Bingen
  In his Mouse-Tower on the Rhine.

Do you think, O blue-eyed banditti,
  Because you have scaled the wall,
Such an old mustache as I am
  Is not a match for you all?

I have you fast in my fortress,
  And will not let you depart,
But put you into the dungeon
  In the round-tower of my heart.

And there will I keep you forever,
  Yes, forever and a day,
Till the walls shall crumble to ruin,
  And moulder in dust away.

GOOD NIGHT AND GOOD MORNING

By Lord Houghton

A fair little girl sat under a tree
Sewing as long as her eyes could see;
Then smoothed her work and folded it right,
And said, "Dear work, good night, good night!"

Such a number of rooks came over her head
Crying, "Caw, caw!" on their way to bed;
She said, as she watched their curious flight,
"Little black things, good night, good night!"

The horses neighed, and the oxen lowed;
The sheep's "Bleat, bleat!" came over the road,
All seeming to say, with quiet delight,
"Good little girl, good night, good night!"

She did not say to the sun, "Good night!"
Though she saw him there like a ball of light;
For she knew he had God's own time to keep
All over the world, and never could sleep.

The tall, pink Fox-glove bowed his head—
The Violets curtsied, and went to bed;
And good little Lucy tied up her hair,
And said, on her knees, her favorite prayer.

And while on her pillow she softly lay,
She knew nothing more till again it was day,
And all things said to the beautiful sun,
"Good morning, good morning! our work is begun."

NURSE'S SONG

By William Blake

When the voices of children are heard on the green,
  And laughing is heard on the hill,
My heart is at rest within my breast,
  And everything else is still.

"Then come home, my children, the sun is gone down,
  And the dews of night arise;
Come, come, leave off play, and let us away
  Till the morning appears in the skies."

"No, no, let us play, for it is yet day,
And we cannot go to sleep;
Besides, in the sky the little birds fly,
And the hills are all cover'd with sheep."

"Well, well, go and play till the light fades away,
And then go home to bed."
The little ones leaped and shouted and laugh'd
And all the hills echoèd.

OLD GAELIC LULLABY

Anonymous

Hush! the waves are rolling in,
White with foam, white with foam;
Father toils amid the din;
But baby sleeps at home.

Hush! the winds roar hoarse and deep—
On they come, on they come!
Brother seeks the wandering sheep;
But baby sleeps at home.

Hush! the rain sweeps o'er the knowes,
Where they roam, where they roam;
Sister goes to seek the cows;
But baby sleeps at home.

WILLIE WINKIE

By William Miller

Wee Willie Winkie rins through the town,
Up-stairs and doon-stairs in his nicht-gown,
Tirlin' at the window, cryin' at the lock,
"Are the weans in their bed?—for it's noo ten o'clock."

Hey, Willie Winkie! are ye comin' ben?
The cat's singin' gay thrums to the sleepin' hen,
The doug's speldered on the floor, and disna gie a cheep;
But here's a waukrife laddie that winna fa' asleep.

Onything but sleep, ye rogue! glow'rin' like the moon,
Rattlin' in an airn jug wi' an airn spoon,
Rumblin', tumblin', roun' about, crowin' like a cock,
Skirlin' like a kenna-what—wauknin' sleepin' folk.

Hey, Willie Winkie! the wean's in a creel!
Waumblin' aff a body's knee like a vera eel,
Ruggin' at the cat's lug, and ravellin' a' her thrums—
Hey, Willie Winkie!—See, there he comes!

Wearie is the mither that has a storie wean,
A wee stumpie stoussie that canna rin his lane,
That has a battle aye wi' sleep before he'll close an ee;
But a kiss frae aff his rosy lips gies strength anew to me.

WYNKEN, BLYNKEN, AND NOD

By Eugene Field

Wynken, Blynken, and Nod one night
  Sailed off in a wooden shoe—
Sailed on a river of crystal light,
  Into a sea of dew.
"Where are you going, and what do you wish?"
  The old moon asked the three.
"We have come to fish for the herring fish
  That live in this beautiful sea;
  Nets of silver and gold have we!"
          Said Wynken,
          Blynken,
          And Nod.

The old moon laughed and sang a song,
  As they rocked in the wooden shoe,
And the wind that sped them all night long
  Ruffled the waves of dew.
The little stars were the herring fish
  That lived in the beautiful sea—
"Now cast your nets wherever you wish—
  Never afeard are we!"
  So cried the stars to the fishermen three;
          Wynken,
          Blynken,
          And Nod.

All night long their nets they threw
  To the stars in the twinkling foam—
Then down from the skies came the wooden shoe,
  Bringing the fishermen home;
'Twas all so pretty a sail it seemed
  As if it could not be,
And some folks thought 'twas a dream they'd dreamed
  Of sailing that beautiful sea—
  But I shall name you the fishermen three:
        Wynken,
        Blynken,
        And Nod.

Wynken and Blynken are two little eyes,
  And Nod is a little head,
And the wooden shoe that sailed the skies
  Is a wee one's trundle-bed.
So shut your eyes while mother sings
  Of wonderful sights that be,
And you shall see the beautiful things
  As you rock in the misty sea,
  Where the old shoe rocked the fishermen three;
        Wynken,
        Blynken,
        And Nod.

LULLABY OF AN INFANT CHIEF

By Sir Walter Scott

O, hush thee, my baby, thy sire was a knight,
Thy mother a lady both lovely and bright;
The woods and the glens from the tower which we see,
They all are belonging, dear baby, to thee.

O, fear not the bugle, though loudly it blows,
It calls but the warders that guard thy repose;
Their bows would be bended, their blades would be red,
Ere the step of a foeman draws near to thy bed.

O, hush thee, my baby, the time will soon come
When thy sleep shall be broken by trumpet and drum;
Then hush thee, my darling, take rest while you may,
For strife comes with manhood, and waking with day.

THE OGRE

By Walter de la Mare

'Tis moonlight on Trebarwith Sands
And moonlight on their seas,
Lone in a cove a cottage stands
Enclustered in with trees.

Snuffing its thin faint smoke afar—
An Ogre prowls, and he
Smells supper, for where humans are
Rich dainties too may be.

Small, with thin smoke ascending up,
Three casements and a door:
The Ogre eager is to sup,
And here seems dainty store.

Sweet as a larder to a mouse,
So to him staring down,
Seemed the small-windowed moonlit house,
With jasmine overgrown.

He snorted, as the billows snort
In darkness of the night,
Betwixt his lean locks tawny-swart,
He glowered on the sight.

Into the garden sweet with peas,
He put his wooden shoe,
And bending back the apple trees
Crept covetously through;

Then, stooping, with a gloating eye
Stared through the lattice small,
And spied two children which did lie
Asleep, against the wall.

Into their dreams no shadow fell
Of his disastrous thumb
Groping discreet, and gradual,
Across the quiet room.

But scarce his nail had scraped the cot
  Wherein these children lay,
As though his malice were forgot,
  It suddenly did stay—

As faintly on the quiet air
  There fell a music sweet,
That stirred with fear his matted hair
  And stayed his prowling feet.

For she who in the kitchen sat
  Darning by the fire,
Guileless of what he would be at,
  Sang sweet as wind or wire:

"Lullay, thou little tiny child,
  By-by, lullay, lullie;
Jesu in glory, meek and mild,
  This night remember thee!

"Fiend, witch, and goblin, foul and wild,
  He deems them smoke to be;
Lullay, thou little tiny child,
  By-by, lullay, lullie!"

The Ogre lifted up his eyes
  Into the moon's pale ray,
And gazed upon her leopard-wise,
  Cruel and clear as day;

He snarled in gluttony and fear.
  The wind blows dismally—
"Jesu in storm my lambs be near,
  By-by, lullay, lullie!"

And like a ravenous beast which sees
  The hunter's icy eye,
So did this wretch in wrath confess
  Sweet Jesu's mastery.

With gaunt locks dangling crouched he, then
  Drew backward from his prey,
Through tangled apple-boughs again
  He wrenched and rent his way.

Shrill on the sea-sands, white with foam,
He heard the sea-birds' wail,
And strode, enormous, swiftly home,
Whinnying down the dale.

BEFORE SLEEPING

Anonymous

Matthew, Mark, Luke, and John,
Bless the bed that I lie on.
Before I lay me down to sleep
I give my soul to Christ to keep.
Four corners to my bed,
Four angels there aspread,
Two to foot, and two to head,
And four to carry me when I'm dead.
I go by sea, I go by land,
The Lord made me with His right hand.
If any danger come to me,
Sweet Jesus Christ deliver me.
He's the branch and I'm the flower,
Pray God send me a happy hour,
And if I die before I wake,
I pray that Christ my soul will take.

CRADLE HYMN

By Martin Luther

Away in a manger, no crib for a bed,
The little Lord Jesus laid down his sweet head.
The stars in the bright sky looked down where he lay—
The little Lord Jesus asleep on the hay.

The cattle are lowing, the baby awakes,
But little Lord Jesus, no crying he makes.
I love thee, Lord Jesus! look down from the sky,
And stay by my cradle till morning is nigh.

FRIENDS

LITTLE GUSTAVA

By Celia Thaxter

I

Little Gustava sits in the sun,
Safe in the porch, and the little drops run
From the icicles under the eaves so fast,
For the bright spring sun shines warm at last
    And glad is little Gustava.

II

She wears a quaint little scarlet cap,
And a little green bowl she holds in her lap,
Filled with bread and milk to the brim,
And a wreath of marigolds round the rim.
    "Ha ha!" laughs little Gustava.

III

Up comes her little gray coaxing cat
With her little pink nose, and she mews, "What's that?"
Gustava feeds her—she begs for more;
And a little brown hen walks in at the door.
    "Good day!" cries little Gustava.

IV

She scatters crumbs for the little brown hen.
There comes a rush and a flutter, and then
Down fly her little white doves so sweet,
With their snowy wings and crimson feet:
"Welcome!" cries little Gustava.

V

So dainty and eager they pick up the crumbs.
But who is this through the doorway comes?
Little Scotch terrier, little dog Rags.
Looks in her face, and his funny tail wags:
"Ha, ha!" laughs little Gustava.

VI

"You want some breakfast too?" and down
She sets her bowl on the brick floor brown;
And little dog Rags drinks up her milk,
While she strokes his shaggy locks like silk:
"Dear Rags!" says little Gustava.

VII

Waiting without stood sparrow and crow,
Cooling their feet in the melting snow:
"Won't you come in, good folk?" she cried.
But they were too bashful, and stood outside
Though "Pray come in!" cried Gustava.

VIII

So the last she threw them, and knelt on the mat
With doves and biddy and dog and cat.
And her mother came to the open house-door
"Dear little daughter, I bring you some more.
My merry little Gustava!"

IX

Kitty and terrier, biddy and doves,
All things harmless Gustava loves.
The shy, kind creatures 'tis joy to feed,
And oh, her breakfast is sweet indeed
To happy little Gustava!

A MIDSUMMER SONG

By Richard Watson Gilder

Oh, father's gone to market-town: he was up before the day,
And Jamie's after robins, and the man is making hay,
And whistling down the hollow goes the boy that minds the mill,
While mother from the kitchen-door is calling with a will,
  "Polly!—Polly!—The cows are in the corn!
    Oh, where's Polly?"

From all the misty morning air there comes a summer sound,
A murmur as of waters, from skies and trees and ground.
The birds they sing upon the wing, the pigeons bill and coo;
And over hill and hollow rings again the loud halloo:
  "Polly!—Polly!—The cows are in the corn!
    Oh, where's Polly?"

Above the trees, the honey-bees swarm by with buzz and boom,
And in the field and garden a thousand blossoms bloom.
Within the farmer's meadow a brown-eyed daisy blows,
And down at the edge of the hollow a red and thorny rose.
  But "Polly!—Polly!—The cows are in the corn!
    Oh, where's Polly?"

How strange at such a time of day the mill should stop its clatter!
The farmer's wife is listening now, and wonders what's the matter.
Oh, wild the birds are singing in the wood and on the hill,
While whistling up the hollow goes the boy that minds the mill.
  But "Polly!—Polly!—The cows are in the corn!
    Oh, where's Polly?"

FARM-YARD SONG

By John Townsend Trowbridge

Over the hill the farm-boy goes,
His shadow lengthens along the land,
A giant staff in a giant hand;
In the poplar-tree, above the spring,
The katydid begins to sing;
    The early dews are falling;
Into the stone-heap darts the mink;
The swallows skim the river's brink;

And home to the woodland fly the crows,
When over the hill the farm-boy goes,
Cheerily calling—
"Co', boss! co', boss! co'! co'! co'!"
Farther, farther over the hill,
Faintly calling, calling still—
"Co', boss! co', boss! co'! co'!"

Into the yard the farmer goes,
With grateful heart, at the close of day;
Harness and chain are hung away;
In the wagon-shed stand yoke and plow;
The straw's in the stack, the hay in the mow;
The cooling dews are falling;
The friendly sheep his welcome bleat,
The pigs come grunting to his feet,
The whinnying mare her master knows,
When into the yard the farmer goes,
His cattle calling—
"Co', boss! co', boss! co'! co'! co'!"
While still the cow-boy, far away,
Goes seeking those that have gone astray—
"Co', boss! co', boss! co'! co'!"

Now to her task the milkmaid goes.
The cattle come crowding through the gate,
Lowing, pushing, little and great;
About the trough, by the farm-yard pump,
The frolicsome yearlings frisk and jump,
While the pleasant dews are falling;
The new milch heifer is quick and shy,
But the old cow waits with tranquil eye;
And the white stream into the bright pail flows,
When to her task the milkmaid goes,
Soothingly calling—
"So, boss! so, boss! so! so! so!"
The cheerful milkmaid takes her stool,
And sits and milks in the twilight cool,
Saying, "So! so, boss! so! so!"

To supper at last the farmer goes.
The apples are pared, the paper read,
The stories are told, then all to bed.

Without, the crickets' ceaseless song
Makes shrill the silence all night long;
The heavy dews are falling.
The housewife's hand has turned the lock;
Drowsily ticks the kitchen clock;
The household sinks to deep repose;
But still in sleep the farm-boy goes
Singing, calling—
"Co', boss! co', boss! co'! co'! co'!"
And oft the milkmaid in her dreams,
Drums in the pail with the flashing streams,
Murmuring, "So, boss! so!"

THANKSGIVING DAY

By Lydia Maria Child

Over the river and through the wood,
To grandfather's house we go;
The horse knows the way
To carry the sleigh
Through the white and drifted snow.
Over the river and through the wood—
O, how the wind does blow!
It stings the toes,
And bites the nose,
As over the ground we go.

Over the river and through the wood,
To have a first-rate play.
Hear the bells ring,
"Ting-a-ling-ding!"
Hurrah for Thanksgiving Day!
Over the river and through the wood
Trot fast, my dapple-gray!
Spring over the ground,
Like a hunting-hound!
For this is Thanksgiving Day.

Over the river and through the wood,
And straight through the barnyard gate.
We seem to go
Extremely slow—
It is so hard to wait!
Over the river and through the wood—
Now grandmother's cap I spy!
Hurrah for the fun!
Is the pudding done?
Hurrah for the pumpkin-pie!

A VISIT FROM ST. NICHOLAS

By Clement C. Moore

'Twas the night before Christmas, when all through the house
Not a creature was stirring, not even a mouse.
The stockings were hung by the chimney with care,
In hopes that St. Nicholas soon would be there.
The children were nestled all snug in their beds,
While visions of sugar-plums danced in their heads;
And mamma in her kerchief, and I in my cap,
Had just settled our brains for a long winter's nap—
When out on the lawn there arose such a clatter,
I sprang from my bed to see what was the matter.
Away to the window I flew like a flash,
Tore open the shutters and threw up the sash.
The moon on the breast of the new-fallen snow
Gave a luster of midday to objects below;
When what to my wondering eyes should appear
But a miniature sleigh and eight tiny reindeer!
With a little old driver, so lively and quick,
I knew in a moment it must be St. Nick.
More rapid than eagles his coursers they came,
And he whistled, and shouted, and called them by name:
"Now, Dasher! now, Dancer! now, Prancer and Vixen!
On, Comet! On, Cupid! On, Donder and Blitzen—
To the top of the porch, to the top of the wall,
Now, dash away, dash away, dash away all!"
As dry leaves that before the wild hurricane fly
When they meet with an obstacle mount to the sky,

So up to the house-top the coursers they flew,
With a sleigh full of toys—and St. Nicholas, too.
And then, in a twinkling, I heard on the roof
The prancing and pawing of each little hoof.
As I drew in my head, and was turning around,
Down the chimney St. Nicholas came with a bound:
He was dressed all in fur from his head to his foot,
And his clothes were all tarnished with ashes and soot;
A bundle of toys he had flung on his back,
And he looked like a peddler just opening his pack.
His eyes, how they twinkled! his dimples, how merry!
His cheeks were like roses, his nose like a cherry;
His droll little mouth was drawn up like a bow,
And the beard on his chin was as white as the snow.
The stump of a pipe he held tight in his teeth,
And the smoke it encircled his head like a wreath.
He had a broad face and a little round belly
That shook when he laughed, like a bowl full of jelly.
He was chubby and plump—a right jolly old elf—
And I laughed when I saw him, in spite of myself;
A wink of his eye, and a twist of his head,
Soon gave me to know I had nothing to dread.
He spoke not a word, but went straight to his work,
And filled all the stockings; then turned with a jerk,
And laying his finger aside of his nose,
And giving a nod, up the chimney he rose.
He sprang to his sleigh, to his team gave a whistle,
And away they all flew like the down of a thistle;
But I heard him exclaim, ere they drove out of sight,
"Happy Christmas to all, and to all a good night!"

HIAWATHA'S CHILDHOOD

By Henry Wadsworth Longfellow

By the shores of Gitche Gumee,
By the shining Big-Sea-Water,
Stood the wigwam of Nokomis,
Daughter of the moon, Nokomis.
Dark behind it rose the forest,
Rose the black and gloomy pine-trees,
Rose the firs with cones upon them;

Bright before it beat the water,
Beat the clear and sunny water,
Beat the shining Big-Sea-Water.

There the wrinkled old Nokomis
Nursed the little Hiawatha,
Rocked him in his linden cradle,
Bedded soft in moss and rushes,
Safely bound with reindeer sinews;
Stilled his fretful wail by saying,
"Hush! the Naked Bear will hear thee!"
Lulled him into slumber, singing,
"Ewa-yea! my little owlet!
Who is this that lights the wigwam?
With his great eyes lights the wigwam?
Ewa-yea my little owlet!"

Many things Nokomis taught him
Of the stars that shine in heaven;
Showed him Ishkoodah, the comet,
Ishkoodah, with fiery tresses;
Showed the Death-Dance of the spirits,
Warriors with their plumes and war-clubs,
Flaring far away to northward
In the frosty nights of winter;
Showed the broad, white road in heaven,
Pathway of the ghosts, the shadows,
Running straight across the heavens,
Crowded with the ghosts, the shadows.

At the door, on summer evenings,
Sat the little Hiawatha;
Heard the whispering of the pine-trees,
Heard the lapping of the water,
Sounds of music, words of wonder;
"Minnie-wawa!" said the pine-trees,
"Mudway-aushka!" said the water;
Saw the fire-fly, Wah-wah-taysee,
Flitting through the dusk of evening,
With the twinkle of its candle
Lighting up the brakes and bushes,
And he sang the song of children,
Sang the song Nokomis taught him:

"Wah-wah-taysee, little fire-fly,
Little, flitting, white-fire insect,
Little, dancing, white-fire creature,
Light me with your little candle,
Ere upon my bed I lay me,
Ere in sleep I close my eyelids!"

Saw the moon rise from the water
Rippling, rounding from the water,
Saw the flecks and shadows on it,
Whispered, "What is that, Nokomis?"
And the good Nokomis answered:
"Once a warrior, very angry,
Seized his grandmother, and threw her
Up into the sky at midnight;
Right against the moon he threw her;
'Tis her body that you see there."

Saw the rainbow in the heaven,
In the eastern sky, the rainbow,
Whispered, "What is that, Nokomis?"
And the good Nokomis answered:
" 'Tis the heaven of flowers you see there;
All the wild-flowers of the forest,
All the lilies of the prairie,
When on earth they fade and perish,
Blossom in that heaven above us."

When he heard the owls at midnight,
Hooting, laughing in the forest,
"What is that?" he cried in terror;
"What is that," he said, "Nokomis?"
And the good Nokomis answered:
"That is but the owl and owlet,
Talking in their native language,
Talking, scolding at each other."
Then the little Hiawatha
Learned of every bird its language,
Learned their names and all their secrets,
How they built their nests in summer,
Where they hid themselves in winter,
Talked with them whene'er he met them,
Called them "Hiawatha's Chickens."
Of all beasts he learned the language,

Nancy Barnhart

Where the squirrels hid their acorns.

[See page 161]

Learned their names and all their secrets,
How the beavers built their lodges,
Where the squirrels hid their acorns,
How the reindeer ran so swiftly,
Why the rabbit was so timid,
Talked with them whene'er he met them,
Called them "Hiawatha's Brothers."

THE LITTLE BLACK BOY

By William Blake

My mother bore me in the southern wild,
And I am black, but O, my soul is white!
White as an angel is the English child,
But I am black, as if bereaved of light.

My mother taught me underneath a tree,
And, sitting down before the heat of day,
She took me on her lap and kissed me,
And, pointing to the East, began to say:

"Look at the rising sun: there God does live,
And gives his light, and gives his heat away,
And flowers and trees and beasts and men receive
Comfort in morning, joy in the noonday.

"And we are put on earth a little space,
That we may learn to bear the beams of love;
And these black bodies and this sunburnt face
Are but a cloud, and like a shady grove.

"For when our souls have learn'd the heat to bear,
The clouds will vanish, we shall hear His voice,
Saying, 'Come out from the grove, my love and care,
And round my golden tent like lambs rejoice.' "

Thus did my mother say, and kissèd me,
And thus I say to little English boy.
When I from black and he from white cloud free,
And round the tent of God like lambs we joy,

I'll shade him from the heat till he can bear
To lean in joy upon our Father's knee;
And then I'll stand and stroke and stroke his silver hair,
And be like him, and he will then love me.

THE LOST SHOE

By Walter de la Mare

Poor little Lucy
By some mischance,
Lost her shoe
As she did dance:
'Twas not on the stairs,
Not in the hall;
Not where they sat
At supper at all.
She looked in the garden,
But there it was not;
Henhouse, or kennel,
Or high dovecote.
Dairy and meadow,
And wild woods through
Showed not a trace
Of Lucy's shoe.
Bird nor bunny
Nor glimmering moon
Breathed a whisper
Of where 'twas gone.
It was cried and cried,
Oyez and Oyez!
In French, Dutch, Latin,
And Portuguese.

Ships the dark seas
  Went plunging through,
But none brought news,
  Of Lucy's shoe;
And still she patters
  In silk and leather,
O'er snow, sand, shingle,
  In every weather;
Spain, and Africa;
  Hindustan,
Java, China,
  And lamped Japan;
Plain and desert,
  She hops-hops through,
Pernambuco
  To gold Peru;
Mountain and forest,
  And river too,
All the world over
  For her lost shoe.

THE CHIMNEY SWEEPER

By William Blake

When my mother died I was very young,
And my father sold me while yet my tongue
Could scarcely cry " 'weep! 'weep! 'weep! 'weep!"
So your chimneys I sweep, and in soot I sleep.

There's little Tom Dacre, who cried when his head,
That curled like a lamb's back, was shaved: so I said
"Hush, Tom! never mind it, for when your head's bare
You know that the soot cannot spoil your white hair."

And so he was quiet, and that very night,
As Tom was a-sleeping, he had such a sight!
That thousands of sweepers, Dick, Joe, Ned, and Jack,
Were all of them locked up in coffins of black.

And by came an Angel who had a bright key,
And he opened the coffins and set them all free;
Then down a green plain leaping, laughing, they run,
And wash in a river, and shine in the Sun.

Then naked and white, all their bags left behind,
They rise upon clouds and sport in the wind;
And the Angel told Tom, if he'd be a good boy,
He'd have God for his father, and never want joy.

And so Tom awoke; and we rose in the dark,
And got with our bags and our brushes to work.
Tho' the morning was cold, Tom was happy and warm;
So if all do their duty they need not fear harm.

THE PIN

By Ann Taylor

"Dear me! what signifies a pin,
  Wedged in a rotten board?
I'm certain that I won't begin,
  At ten years old, to hoard;
I never will be called a miser,
That I'm determined," said Eliza.

So onward tripped the little maid,
  And left the pin behind,
Which very snug and quiet lay,
  To its hard fate resigned;
Nor did she think (a careless chit)
'Twas worth her while to stoop for it.

Next day a party was to ride,
  To see an air balloon;
And all the company beside
  Were dressed and ready soon;
But she a woeful case was in,
For want of just a single pin.

In vain her eager eyes she brings,
  To every darksome crack;
There was not one, and yet her things
  Were dropping off her back.
She cut her pincushion in two,
But no, not one had fallen through.

At last, as hunting on the floor,
  Over a crack she lay,
The carriage rattled to the door,
  Then rattled fast away;
But poor Eliza was not in,
For want of just—a single pin!

There's hardly anything so small,
  So trifling or so mean,
That we may never want at all,
  For service unforeseen;
And wilful waste, depend upon't,
Brings, almost always, woeful want!

MEDDLESOME MATTY

By Ann Taylor

One ugly trick has often spoiled,
  The sweetest and the best;
Matilda, though a pleasant child,
  One ugly trick possessed,
Which, like a cloud before the skies,
Hid all her better qualities.

Sometimes she'd lift the tea-pot lid,
  To peep at what was in it;
Or tilt the kettle, if you did
  But turn your back a minute.
In vain you told her not to touch,
Her trick of meddling grew so much.

Her grandmamma went out one day,
  And by mistake she laid
Her spectacles and snuff-box gay
  Too near the little maid;
"Ah! well," thought she, "I'll try them on,
As soon as grandmamma is gone."

Forthwith she placed upon her nose
  The glasses large and wide;
And looking round, as I suppose,
  The snuff-box too she spied:
"Oh! what a pretty box is that;
I'll open it," said little Matt.

"I know what grandmamma would say,
'Don't meddle with it, dear';
But then, she's far enough away,
And no one else is near:
Besides, what can there be amiss
In opening such a box as this?"

So thumb and finger went to work
To move the stubborn lid,
And presently a mighty jerk
The mighty mischief did;
For all at once, ah! woeful case,
The snuff came puffing in her face.

Poor eyes, and nose, and mouth, beside,
A dismal sight presented;
In vain, as bitterly she cried,
Her folly she repented.
In vain she ran about for ease;
She could no nothing now but sneeze.

She dashed the spectacles away,
To wipe her tingling eyes,
And as in twenty bits they lay,
Her grandmamma she spies.
"Heydey! and what's the matter now?"
Says grandmamma, with lifted brow.

Matilda, smarting with the pain,
And tingling still, and sore,
Made many a promise to refrain
From meddling evermore.
And 'tis a fact, as I have heard,
She ever since has kept her word.

MEG MERRILIES

By John Keats

Old Meg she was a Gypsy,
And lived upon the moors:
Her bed it was the brown heath turf,
And her house was out of doors.

Her apples were swart blackberries,
  Her currants pods o' broom;
Her wine was dew of the wild white rose,
  Her book a churchyard tomb.

Her brothers were the craggy hills,
  Her sisters larchen trees—
Alone with her great family
  She lived as she did please.

No breakfast had she many a morn,
  No dinner many a noon,
And 'stead of supper she would stare
  Full hard against the moon.

But every morn of woodbine fresh
  She made her garlanding,
And every night the dark glen yew
  She wove, and she would sing.

And with her fingers old and brown
  She plaited mats o' rushes,
And gave them to the cottagers
  She met among the bushes.

Old Meg was brave as Margaret Queen
  And tall as Amazon:
An old red blanket cloak she wore;
  A chip hat had she on.
God rest her aged bones somewhere—
  She died full long agone!

AN OLD WOMAN OF THE ROADS

By Padraic Colum

O, to have a little house!
  To own the hearth and stool and all!
The heaped-up sods upon the fire,
  The pile of turf against the wall!

To have a clock with weights and chains
  And pendulum swinging up and down!
A dresser filled with shining delph,
  Speckled and white and blue and brown!

I could be busy all the day
  Clearing and sweeping hearth and floor,
And fixing on their shelf again
  My white and blue and speckled store!

I could be quiet there at night
  Beside the fire and by myself,
Sure of a bed, and loth to leave
  The ticking clock and the shining delph!

Och! but I'm weary of mist and dark,
  And roads where there's never a house or bush,
And tired I am of bog and road
  And the crying wind and the lonesome hush!

And I am praying to God on high,
  And I am praying Him night and day,
For a little house—a house of my own—
  Out of the wind's and the rain's way.

SEUMAS BEG

By James Stephens

A man was sitting underneath a tree
Outside the village, and he asked me what
Name was upon this place, and said that he
Was never here before. He told a lot
Of stories to me, too. His nose was flat.
I asked him how it happened, and he said
The first mate of the Mary Ann done that
With a marlin-spike one day, but he was dead,
And jolly good job, too; and he'd have gone
A long way to have killed him, and he had
A gold ring in one ear; the other one
"Was bit off by a crocodile, bedad."
That's what he said. He taught me how to chew.
He was a real nice man. He liked me, too.

Florence Wyman Ivins

And he had a gold ring in one ear.

[See page 168]

SAM

By Walter de la Mare

When Sam goes back in memory,
  It is to where the sea
Breaks on the shingle, emerald-green,
  In white foam, endlessly;

He says—with small brown eye on mine—
  "I used to keep awake,
And lean from my window in the moon,
  Watching those billows break.

And half a million tiny hands,
  And eyes, like sparks of frost,
Would dance and come tumbling into the moon,
  On every breaker tossed.

And all across from star to star,
  I've seen the watery sea,
With not a single ship in sight,
  Just ocean there, and me;

And heard my father snore. And once,
  As sure as I'm alive,
Out of those wallowing, moon-flecked waves
  I saw a mermaid dive;

Head and shoulders above the wave,
  Plain as I now see you,
Combing her hair, now back, now front,
  Her two eyes peeping through;

Calling me, 'Sam!' quietlike—'Sam!' . . .
  But me . . . I never went,
Making believe I kind of thought
  'Twas some one else she meant . . .

Wonderful lovely there she sat,
  Singing the night away,
All in the solitudinous sea
  Of that there lonely bay.

"P'r'aps," and he'd smooth his hairless mouth,
  "P'r'aps, if 'twere now, my son,
P'r'aps, if I heard a voice say, 'Sam!' . . .
  Morning would find me gone."

PORTRAIT BY A NEIGHBOR

By Edna St. Vincent Millay

Before she has her floor swept
  Or her dishes done,
Any day you'll find her
  A-sunning in the sun!

It's long after midnight
  Her key's in the lock,
And you never see her chimney smoke
  Till past ten o'clock!

She digs in her garden
  With a shovel and a spoon,
She weeds her lazy lettuce
  By the light of the moon.

She walks up the walk
  Like a woman in a dream,
She forgets she borrowed butter
  And pays you back cream!

Her lawn looks like a meadow,
  And if she mows the place
She leaves the clover standing
  And the Queen Anne's lace!

OLD BALLADS AND STORIES

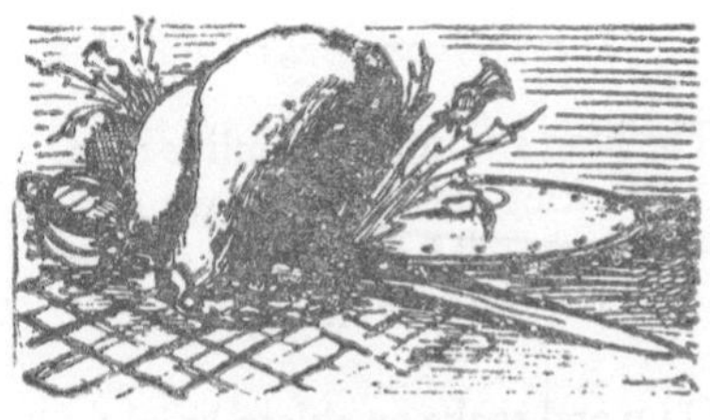

BONNIE GEORGE CAMPBELL

Anonymous

Hie upon Hielands,
  and laigh upon Tay,
Bonnie George Campbell
  rode out on a day.

Saddled and bridled
  and booted rade he;
Toom[1] hame cam' the saddle,
  but never cam' he.

Down cam' his auld mither,
  greetin' fu' sair,
And down cam' his bonny wife,
  wringin' her hair:—

"My meadow lies green,
  and my corn is unshorn,
My barn is to build
  and my babe is unborn."

Saddled and bridled
  and booted rade he;
Toom hame cam' the saddle
  but never cam' he.

[1]Empty.

SIR PATRICK SPENS

Anonymous

The king sits in Dunfermline toun,
Drinking the blude-red wine:
"O whare will I get a skeely skipper
To sail this new ship of mine?"

O up and spake an eldern knight,
Sat at the king's right knee—
"Sir Patrick Spens is the best sailor
That ever sailed the sea."

Our king has written a braid letter,
And sealed it with his hand,
And sent it to Sir Patrick Spens
Was walking on the strand.

"To Noroway, to Noroway,
To Noroway o'er the faem;
The king's daughter of Noroway,
'Tis thou maun bring her hame."

The first word that Sir Patrick read,
Sae loud loud laughèd he;
The neist word that Sir Patrick read,
The tear blinded his e'e.

"O wha is this has done this deed,
And tauld the king o' me,
To send us out, at this time o' year,
To sail upon the sea?

"Be it wind, be it weet, be it hail, be it sleet,
Our ship must sail the faem;
The king's daughter of Noroway,
'Tis we must fetch her hame."

They hoysed their sails on Monenday morn,
Wi' a' the speed they may;
And they hae landed in Noroway,
Upon a Wodensday.

They hadna been a week, a week
  In Noroway but twae,
When that the lords o' Noroway
  Began aloud to say:

"Ye Scottishmen spend a' our king's gowd,
  And a' our queenis fee."
"Ye lie, ye lie, ye liars loud!
  Fu' loud I hear ye lie!

"For I hae brought as much white monie
  As gane my men and me—
And I hae brought a half-fou' o' gude red gowd
  Out o'er the sea wi' me.

"Make ready, make ready, my merry men, a'!
  Our gude ship sails the morn."
"Now, ever, alack, my master dear,
  I fear a deadly storm!

"I saw the new moon, late yestreen,
  Wi' the auld moon in her arm;
And if we gang to sea, master,
  I fear we'll come to harm."

They hadna sail'd a league, a league,
  A league but barely three,
When the lift grew dark, and the wind blew loud,
  And gurly grew the sea.

The ankers brak, and the top-masts lap,
  It was sic a deadly storm;
And the waves cam' o'er the broken ship
  Till a' her sides were torn.

"O where will I get a gude sailor,
  To take my helm in hand,
Till I get up to the tall top-mast;
  To see if I can spy land?"

"O here am I, a sailor gude,
  To take the helm in hand,
Till ye get up to the tall top-mast:
  But I fear you'll ne'er spy land."

He hadna gane a step, a step,
 A step but barely ane,
When a bout flew out of our goodly ship,
 And the salt sea it came in.

"Gae, fetch a web o' the silken claith,
 Another o' the twine,
And wap them into our ship's side,
 And letna the sea come in."

They fetch'd a web o' the silken claith.
 Another o' the twine,
And they wapped them round that gude ship's side,
 But still the sea came in.

O laith, laith were our gude Scots lords
 To wet their cork-heeled shoon!
But lang ere a' the play was play'd
 They wat their hats aboon.

And mony was the feather-bed
 That floated on the faem,
And mony was the gude lord's son
 That never mair came hame.

The ladyes wrang their fingers white—
 The maidens tore their hair;
A' for the sake of their true loves—
 For them they'll see na mair.

O lang lang may the ladyes sit,
 Wi' their fans into their hand,
Before they see Sir Patrick Spens
 Come sailing to the strand!

And lang lang may the maidens sit,
 Wi' the goud kaims in their hair,
A' waiting for their ain dear loves—
 For them they'll see na mair.

O forty miles off Aberdour,
 'Tis fifty fathoms deep,
And there lies gude Sir Patrick Spens,
 Wi' the Scots lords at his feet.

BONNY BARBARA ALLAN

Old Ballad

It was in and about the Martinmas time,
  When the green leaves were a falling,
That Sir John Graeme, in the West Country,
  Fell in love with Barbara Allan.

He sent his man down through the town,
  To the place where she was dwelling:
"O haste and come to my master dear,
  Gin ye be Barbara Allan."

O hooly,[1] hooly rose she up,
  To the place where he was lying,
And when she drew the curtain by,
  "Young man, I think you're dying."

"O it's I'm sick, and very, very sick,
  And 'tis a' for Barbara Allan":
"O the better for me ye's never be,
  Tho' your heart's blood were a-spilling."

"O dinna ye mind, young man," said she,
  "When ye was in the tavern a-drinking,
That ye made the healths gae round and round,
  And slighted Barbara Allan?"

He turned his face unto the wall,
  And death was with him dealing:
"Adieu, adieu, my dear friends all,
  And be kind to Barbara Allan."

And slowly, slowly raise she up,
  And slowly, slowly left him,
And sighing said, she could not stay,
  Since death of life had reft him.

She had not gane a mile but twa,
  When she heard the dead-bell ringing,
And every jow that the dead-bell gied,
  It cry'd, Woe to Barbara Allan!

[1] Softly.

"O mother, mother, make my bed!
O make it saft and narrow!
Since my love died for me today,
I'll die for him tomorrow."

HYNDE HORN

Old Ballad

"Oh, it's Hynde Horn fair, and it's Hynde Horn free;
Oh, where were you born, and in what countrie?"
"In a far distant countrie I was born;
But of home and friends I am quite forlorn."

Oh, it's seven long years he served the king,
But wages from him he ne'er got a thing:
Oh, it's seven long years he served, I ween,
And all for love of the king's daughter Jean.

Oh, he gave to his love a silver wand,
Her sceptre of rule over fair Scotland;
With three singing laverocks set thereon,
For to mind her of him when he was gone.

And his love gave to him a gay gold ring,
With three shining diamonds set therein;
Oh, his love gave to him this gay gold ring,
Of virtue and value above all thing;

Saying—"While the diamonds do keep their hue,
You will know that my love holds fast and true;
But when the diamonds grow pale and wan,
I'll be dead, or wed to another man."

Then the sails were spread, and away sail'd he;
Oh, he sail'd away to a far countrie;
And when he had been seven years to sea,
Hynde Horn look'd to see how his ring might be.

But when Hynde Horn look'd the diamonds upon,
Oh, he saw that they were both pale and wan;
And at once he knew, from their alter'd hue,
That his love was dead or had proved untrue.

Oh, the sails were spread, and away sail'd he
Back over the sea to his own countrie;
Then he left the ship when it came to land,
And he met an auld beggar upon the strand.

"What news, thou auld beggar man?" said he;
"For full seven years I've been over the sea."
Then the auld man said—"The strangest of all
Is the curious wedding in our king's hall.

"For there a king's daughter, came frae the wast,
Has been married to him these nine days past;
But unto him a wife the bride winna be,
For love of Hynde Horn, far over the sea."

"Now, auld man, give to me your begging weed,
And I will give to thee my riding steed;
And, auld man, give to me your staff of tree,
And my scarlet cloak I will give to thee.

"And you must teach me the auld beggar's rôle,
As he goes his rounds and receives his dole."
The auld man he did as young Hynde Horn said,
And taught him the way to beg for his bread.

Then Hynde Horn bent him to his staff of tree,
And to the king's palace away hobbled he;
And when he arrived at the king's palace gate,
To the porter he thus his petition did state:

"Good porter, I pray, for Saints Peter and Paul,
And for sake of the Saviour who died for us all,
For one cup of wine, and one bit of bread,
To an auld man with travel and hunger bestead.

"And ask the fair bride, for the sake of Hynde Horn,
To hand them to one so sadly forlorn."
Then the porter for pity the message convey'd,
And told the fair bride all the beggar man said.

And when she did hear it, she tripp'd down the stair,
And in her fair hands did lovingly bear
A cup of red wine, and a farle of cake,
To give the old man, for loved Hynde Horn's sake.

And when she came to where Hynde Horn did stand,
With joy he did take the cup from her hand;
Then pledged the fair bride, the cup out did drain,
Dropp'd in it the ring, and return'd it again.

"Oh, found you that ring by sea or on land,
Or got you that ring off a dead man's hand?"
"Oh, I found not that ring by sea or on land,
But I got that ring from a fair lady's hand.

"As a pledge of true love she gave it to me,
Full seven years ago, as I sail'd o'er the sea;
But now that the diamonds are chang'd in their hue,
I know that my love has to me proved untrue."

"Oh, I will cast off my gay costly gown,
And follow thee on from town unto town,
And I will take the gold combs from my hair,
And follow my true love for ever mair."

"You need not cast off your gay costly gown,
To follow me on from town unto town;
You need not take the gold combs from your hair,
For Hynde Horn has gold enough, and to spare."

He stood up erect, let his beggar weed fall,
And shone there the foremost and noblest of all;
Then the bridegrooms were chang'd, and the lady re-wed,
To Hynde Horn thus come back, like one from the dead.

THE PIED PIPER OF HAMELIN

By Robert Browning

Hamelin Town's in Brunswick,
By famous Hanover city;
  The River Weser, deep and wide,
  Washes its walls on the southern side;
  A pleasanter spot you never spied;
But, when begins my ditty,
  Almost five hundred years ago,
  To see the townsfolk suffer so,
From vermin, was a pity.

Rats!
They fought the dogs and killed the cats,
And bit the babies in the cradles,
And ate the cheeses out of the vats,
And licked the soup from the cook's own ladles,
Split open the kegs of salted sprats,
Made nests inside men's Sunday hats,
And even spoiled the women's chats,
By drowning their speaking
With shrieking and squeaking
In fifty different sharps and flats.

At last the people in a body
To the Town Hall came flocking;
" 'Tis clear," cried they, "our Mayor's a noddy;
And as for our Corporation—shocking
To think we buy gowns lined with ermine
For dolts that can't or won't determine
What's best to rid us of our vermin!
You hope, because you're old and obese,
To find in the furry civic robe ease?
Rouse up, sirs! Give your brains a racking
To find the remedy we're lacking,
Or, sure as fate, we'll send you packing!"
At this the Mayor and Corporation
Quaked with a mighty consternation.

An hour they sat in council;
At length the Mayor broke silence;
"For a guilder I'd my ermine gown sell;
I wish I were a mile hence!
It's easy to bid one rack one's brain—
I'm sure my poor head aches again,
I've scratched it so, and all in vain.
Oh for a trap, a trap, a trap!"
Just as he said this, what should hap
At the chamber door, but a gentle tap.
"Bless us!" cried the Mayor, "what's that?"
(With the Corporation as he sat,
Looking little though wondrous fat;
Nor brighter was his eye, nor moister
Than a too-long-opened oyster,
Save when at noon his paunch grew mutinous
For a plate of turtle green and glutinous.)

"Only a scraping of shoes on the mat?
Anything like the sound of a rat
Makes my heart go pit-a-pat!"

"Come in!" the Mayor cried, looking bigger,
And in did come the strangest figure!
His queer long coat, from heel to head
Was half of yellow and half of red,
And he himself was tall and thin,
With sharp blue eyes, each like a pin,
And light loose hair, yet swarthy skin,
No tuft on cheek nor beard on chin,
But lips where smiles went out and in;
There was no guessing his kith and kin;
And nobody could enough admire
The tall man and his quaint attire.
Quoth one: "It's as if my great-grandsire,
Starting up at the Trump of Doom's tone,
Had walked this way from his painted tomb-stone!"

He advanced to the council table:
And, "Please your honors," said he, "I'm able,
By means of a secret charm, to draw
  All creatures living beneath the sun,
  That creep, or swim, or fly, or run,
After me so as you never saw!
And I chiefly use my charm
On creatures that do people harm,
The mole, the toad, the newt, the viper;
And people call me the Pied Piper."
  (And here they noticed round his neck
  A scarf of red and yellow stripe
To match his coat of the selfsame cheque;
  And at the scarf's end hung a pipe;
And his fingers, they noticed, were ever straying
As if impatient to be playing
Upon his pipe, as low it dangled
Over his vesture so old-fangled.)
"Yet" said he, "poor piper as I am,
In Tartary I freed the Cham,
  Last June, from his huge swarm of gnats;
I eased in Asia the Nizam
  Of a monstrous brood of vampire bats:

And as for what your brain bewilders,
  If I can rid your town of rats
Will you give me a thousand guilders?"
"One? fifty thousand!"—was the exclamation
Of the astonished Mayor and Corporation.

Into the street the Piper stept,
  Smiling first a little smile,
As if he knew what magic slept
  In his quiet pipe the while;
Then, like a musical adept,
To blow the pipe his lips he wrinkled,
And green and blue his sharp eyes twinkled,
Like a candle flame where salt is sprinkled;
And ere three shrill notes the pipe had uttered,
You heard as if an army muttered;
And the muttering grew to a grumbling;
And the grumbling grew to a mighty rumbling;
And out of the houses the rats came tumbling.
Great rats, small rats, lean rats, brawny rats,
Brown rats, black rats, gray rats, tawny rats,

Grave old plodders, gay young friskers,
  Fathers, mothers, uncles, cousins,
Cocking tails, and pricking whiskers,
  Families by tens and dozens,
Brothers, sisters, husbands, wives—
Followed the Piper for their lives.
From street to street he piped, advancing,
And step for step, they followed dancing,
Until they came to the River Weser,
  Wherein all plunged and perished!
—Save one, who stout as Julius Caesar,
Swam across and lived to carry
  (As he, the manuscript he cherished)
To Rat-land home his commentary:
Which was, "At the first shrill notes of the pipe,
I heard a sound as of scraping tripe,
And putting apples, wondrous ripe,
Into a cider-press's gripe:
And a moving away of pickle-tub boards,
And a leaving ajar of conserve-cupboards,
And a drawing the corks of train-oil-flasks,

And a breaking the hoops of butter-casks:
And it seemed as if a voice
(Sweeter far than by harp or by psaltery
Is breathed) called out, 'Oh, rats, rejoice!
  The world is grown to one vast drysaltery!
So munch on, crunch on, take your nuncheon,
Breakfast, supper, dinner, luncheon!'
And just as a bulky sugar-puncheon,
All ready staved, like a great sun shone
Glorious, scarce an inch before me,
Just as methought it said, 'Come, bore me!'
—I found the Weser rolling o'er me."

You should have heard the Hamelin people
Ringing the bells till they rocked the steeple.
"Go," cried the Mayor, "and get long poles,
Poke out the nests, and block up the holes!
Consult with carpenters and builders,
And leave in our town not even a trace
Of the rats!" When suddenly, up the face
Of the Piper perked in the market-place,
With a "First, if you please, my thousand guilders!"

A thousand guilders! The Mayor looked blue;
So did the Corporation, too.
For council dinners made rare havoc
With Claret, Moselle, Vin-de-Grave, Hock;
And half the money would replenish
Their cellar's biggest butt with Rhenish.
To pay this sum to a wandering fellow,
With a gypsy coat of red and yellow!
"Beside," quoth the Mayor, with a knowing wink
"Our business was done at the river's brink;
We saw with our eyes the vermin sink,
And what's dead can't come to life, I think.
So friend, we're not the folks to shrink
From the duty of giving you something to drink,
And a matter of money to put in your poke;
But, as for the guilders, what we spoke
Of them, as you very well know, was in joke.
Beside, our losses have made us thrifty.
A thousand guilders! Come, take fifty!"

The Piper's face fell, and he cried,
"No trifling! I can't wait, beside!
I've promised to visit by dinner-time
Bagdad, and accept the prime
Of the Head-Cook's pottage, all he's rich in,
For having left, in the Caliph's kitchen,
Of a nest of scorpions no survivor:
With him I proved no bargain-driver,
With you, don't think I'll bate a stiver!
And folks who put me in a passion
May find me pipe after another fashion."

"How!" cried the Mayor, "d'ye think I'll brook
Being worse treated than a cook?
Insulted by a lazy ribald
With idle pipe and vesture piebald?
You threaten us, fellow? Do your worst,
Blow your pipe there till you burst!"

Once more he stept into the street,
  And to his lips again
Laid his long pipe of smooth straight cane;
  And ere he blew three notes (such sweet
Soft notes as yet musician's cunning
  Never gave the enraptured air)
There was a rustling that seemed like a bustling
Of merry crowds justling at pitching and hustling,
Small feet were pattering, wooden shoes clattering,
Little hands clapping and little tongues chattering.
And, like fowls in a farmyard when barley is scattering,
Out came the children running.
And all the little boys and girls,
With rosy cheeks and flaxen curls,
And sparkling eyes and teeth like pearls,
Tripping and skipping, ran merrily after
The wonderful music with shouting and laughter.

The Mayor was dumb, and the Council stood
As if they were changed into blocks of wood,
Unable to move a step, or cry
To the children merrily skipping by,
And could only follow with the eye
That joyous crowd at the Piper's back.
And now the Mayor was on the rack,

And the wretched Council's bosoms beat,
As the Piper turned from the High Street
To where the Weser rolled its waters
Right in the way of their sons and daughters!
However, he turned from south to west,
And to Koppelberg Hill his steps addressed,
And after him the children pressed;
Great was the joy in every breast.
"He never can cross that mighty top!
He's forced to let the piping drop,
And we shall see our children stop!"
When, lo, as they reached the mountain-side,
A wondrous portal opened wide,
As if a cavern was suddenly hollowed;
And the Piper advanced, and the children followed,
And when all were in to the very last,
The door in the mountain-side shut fast.
Did I say all? No! One was lame,
 And could not dance the whole of the way;
And in after years, if you would blame
 His sadness, he was used to say—
"It's dull in our town since my playmates left!
I can't forget that I'm bereft
Of all the pleasant sights they see,
Which the Piper also promised me.

For he led us, he said, to a joyous land,
Joining the town and just at hand,
Where waters gushed and fruit trees grew,
And flowers put forth a fairer hue,
And everything was strange and new;
The sparrows were brighter than peacocks here,
And their dogs outran our fallow deer,
And honey-bees had lost their stings,
And horses were born with eagles' wings;
And just as I became assured
My lame foot would be speedily cured,
The music stopped, and I stood still,
And found myself outside the hill,
Left alone against my will,
To go now limping as before,
And never hear of that country more!"

Alas, alas for Hamelin!
  There came into many a burgher's pate
  A text which says that heaven's gate
  Opes to the rich at as easy rate
As the needle's eye takes a camel in!
The Mayor sent East, West, North and South,
To offer the Piper, by word of mouth,
  Wherever it was man's lot to find him.
Silver and gold to his heart's content,
If he'd only return the way he went,
  And bring the children behind him.

But when they saw 'twas a lost endeavor,
And Piper and dancers were gone forever,
They made a decree that lawyers never
  Should think their records dated duly
If, after the day of the month and the year,
These words did not as well appear:
"And so long after what happened here
  On the Twenty-second of July,
Thirteen hundred and seventy-six."
And the better in memory to fix
The place of the children's last retreat,
They called it the Pied Piper's Street—
Where any one playing on pipe or tabor
Was sure for the future to lose his labor.

Nor suffered they hostelry or tavern
To shock with mirth a street so solemn;
But opposite the place of the cavern
They wrote the story on a column,
And on the great church-window painted
The same, to make the world acquainted
How their children were stolen away,
And there it stands to this very day.

And I must not omit to say
That in Transylvania there's a tribe
Of alien people who ascribe
The outlandish ways and dress
On which their neighbors lay such stress,
To their fathers and mothers having risen
Out of some subterraneous prison
Into which they were trepanned
Long ago in a mighty band
Out of Hamelin town in Brunswick land,
But how or why, they don't understand.

So, Willy, let you and me be wipers
Of scores out with all men—especially pipers!
And, whether they pipe us free from rats or from mice,
If we've promised them aught, let us keep our promise!

GOD'S JUDGMENT ON A WICKED BISHOP

By Robert Southey

The summer and autumn had been so wet,
That in winter the corn was growing yet:
'Twas a piteous sight to see, all around,
The grain lie rotting on the ground.

Every day the starving poor
Crowded around Bishop Hatto's door;
For he had a plentiful last-year's store,
And all the neighborhood could tell
His granaries were furnished well.

At last Bishop Hatto appointed a day
To quiet the poor without delay;
He bade them to his great barn repair,
And thev should have food for the winter there.

Rejoiced such tidings good to hear,
The poor folk flocked from far and near;
The great barn was full as it could hold
Of women and children, and young and old.

Then, when he saw it could hold no more,
Bishop Hatto he made fast the door;
And, while for mercy on Christ they call,
He set fire to the barn, and burnt them all.

"I' faith, 'tis an excellent bonfire!" quoth he;
"And the country is greatly obliged to me
For ridding it, in these times forlorn,
Of rats that only consume the corn."

So then to his palace returnèd he,
And he sat down to supper merrily,
And he slept that night like an innocent man;
But Bishop Hatto never slept again.

In the morning, as he entered the hall,
Where his picture hung against the wall,
A sweat like death all over him came,
For the rats had eaten it out of the frame.

As he looked, there came a man from his farm—
He had a countenance white with alarm:
"My Lord, I opened your granaries this morn,
And the rats had eaten all your corn."

Another came running presently,
And he was pale as pale could be.
"Fly! my Lord Bishop, fly!" quoth he,
"Ten thousand rats are coming this way—
The Lord forgive you for yesterday!"

"I'll go to my tower in the Rhine," replied he;
" 'Tis the safest place in Germany—
The walls are high, and the shores are steep,
And the tide is strong, and the water deep."

Bishop Hatto fearfully hastened away,
And he crossed the Rhine without delay,
And reached his tower, and barred with care
All the windows, and doors, and loop-holes there.

He laid him down and closed his eyes,
But soon a scream made him arise;
He started, and saw two eyes of flame
On his pillow, from whence the screaming came.

He listened and looked—it was only the cat;
But the Bishop he grew more fearful for that,
For she sat screaming, mad with fear,
At the army of rats that were drawing near.

For they have swum over the river so deep,
And they have climbed the shores so steep,
And now by thousands up they crawl
To the holes and the windows in the wall.

Down on his knees the Bishop fell,
And faster and faster his beads did he tell,
As louder and louder, drawing near,
The saw of their teeth without he could hear.

And in at the windows, and in at the door,
And through the walls by thousands they pour;
And down from the ceiling and up through the floor,
From the right and the left, from behind and before,
From within and without, from above and below—
And all at once to the Bishop they go.

They have whetted their teeth against the stones,
And now they pick the Bishop's bones;
They gnawed the flesh from every limb,
For they were sent to do judgment on him!

THE INCHCAPE ROCK

By Robert Southey

No stir in the air, no stir in the sea,
The ship was still as she could be;
Her sails from heaven received no motion;
Her keel was steady in the ocean.

Without either sign or sound of their shock,
The waves flow'd over the Inchcape Rock;
So little they rose, so little they fell,
They did not move the Inchcape Bell.

The Abbot of Aberbrothok
Had placed that Bell on the Inchcape Rock;
On a buoy in the storm it floated and swung,
And over the waves its warning rung.

When the Rock was hid by the surge's swell,
The mariners heard the warning Bell;
And then they knew the perilous Rock,
And blest the Abbot of Aberbrothok.

The Sun in heaven was shining gay;
All things were joyful on that day;
The sea-birds scream'd as they wheel'd round.
And there was joyance in their sound.

The buoy of the Inchcape Bell was seen
A darker speck on the ocean green;
Sir Ralph the Rover walk'd his deck,
And he fix'd his eye on the darker speck.

He felt the cheering power of spring;
It made him whistle, it made him sing;
His heart was mirthful to excess,
But the Rover's mirth was wickedness.

His eye was on the Inchcape float;
Quoth he, "My men, put out the boat,
And row me to the Inchcape Rock,
And I'll plague the Abbot of Aberbrothok."

The boat is lower'd, the boatmen row,
And to the Inchcape Rock they go;
Sir Ralph bent over from the boat,
And he cut the Bell from the Inchcape float.

Down sunk the Bell with a gurgling sound;
The bubbles rose and burst around;
Quoth Sir Ralph, "The next who comes to the Rock
Won't bless the Abbot of Aberbrothok."

Sir Ralph the Rover sail'd away;
He scour'd the seas for many a day;
And now, grown rich with plunder'd store,
He steers his course for Scotland's shore.

So thick a haze o'erspreads the sky,
They cannot see the Sun on high;
The wind hath blown a gale all day;
At evening it hath died away.

On the deck the Rover takes his stand;
So dark it is they see no land.
Quoth Sir Ralph, "It will be lighter soon,
For there is the dawn of the rising Moon."

"Canst hear," said one, "the breakers roar?
For methinks we should be near the shore."
"Now where we are I cannot tell,
But I wish I could hear the Inchcape Bell."

They hear no sound; the swell is strong;
Though the wind hath fallen, they drift along,
Till the vessel strikes with a shivering shock—
"O God! it is the Inchcape Rock!"

Sir Ralph the Rover tore his hair;
He curs'd himself in his despair;
The waves rush in on every side;
The ship is sinking beneath the tide.

But, even in his dying fear,
One dreadful sound could the Rover hear—
A sound as if, with the Inchcape Bell,
The fiends below were ringing his knell.

A STORY FOR A CHILD

By Bayard Taylor

Little one, come to my knee!
  Hark, how the rain is pouring
Over the roof, in the pitch-black night,
  And the wind in the woods a-roaring!

Hush, my darling, and listen,
  Then pay for the story with kisses;
Father was lost in the pitch-black night,
  In just such a storm as this is!

High up on the lonely mountains,
  Where the wild men watched and waited;
Wolves in the forest, and bears in the bush,
  And I on my path belated.

The rain and the night together
  Came down, and the wind came after,
Bending the props of the pine-tree roof,
  And snapping many a rafter.

I crept along in the darkness,
  Stunned, and bruised, and blinded—
Crept to a fir with thick-set boughs,
  And a sheltering rock behind it.

There from the blowing and raining,
  Crouching, I sought to hide me:
Something rustled, two green eyes shone,
  And a wolf lay down beside me.

Little one, be not frightened;
  I and the wolf together,
Side by side, through the long, long night,
  Hid from the awful weather.

His wet fur pressed against me;
  Each of us warmed the other;
Each of us felt, in the stormy dark,
  That beast and man was brother.

And when the falling forest
  No longer crashed in warning,
Each of us went from our hiding-place
  Forth in the wild, wet morning.

Darling, kiss me in payment!
  Hark, how the wind is roaring;
Father's house is a better place
  When the stormy rain is pouring!

THE WRECK OF THE HESPERUS

By Henry Wadsworth Longfellow

It was the schooner Hesperus
That sailed the wintry sea;
And the skipper had taken his little daughter
To bear him company.

Blue were her eyes as the fairy-flax,
Her cheeks like the dawn of day,
And her bosom white as the hawthorn buds,
That ope in the month of May.

The skipper he stood beside the helm,
His pipe was in his mouth,
And he watched how the veering flaw did blow
The smoke now west, now south.

Then up and spake an old sailor
Had sailed to the Spanish main,
"I pray thee put into yonder port,
For I fear a hurricane.

"Last night the moon had a golden ring,
And tonight no moon we see!"
The skipper he blew a whiff from his pipe,
And a scornful laugh laughed he.

Colder and colder blew the wind,
A gale from the northeast;
The snow fell hissing in the brine,
And the billows frothed like yeast.

Down came the storm, and smote amain
The vessel in its strength;
She shuddered and paused like a frightened steed,
Then leaped her cable's length.

"Come hither! Come hither! my little daughter,
And do not tremble so;
For I can weather the roughest gale,
That ever wind did blow."

He wrapped her warm in his seaman's coat
Against the stinging blast;
He cut a rope from a broken spar,
And bound her to the mast.

"O father! I hear the church-bells ring;
Oh, say, what may it be?"
" 'Tis a fog-bell on a rock-bound coast!"
And he steered for the open sea.

"O father! I hear the sound of guns;
Oh, say, what may it be?"
"Some ship in distress, that cannot live
In such an angry sea!"

"O father! I see a gleaming light;
Oh, say, what may it be?"
But the father answered never a word,
A frozen corpse was he.

Lashed to the helm, all stiff and stark,
With his face turned to the skies,
The lantern gleamed through the gleaming snow
On his fixed and glassy eyes.

Then the maiden clasped her hands and prayed
That savèd she might be;
And she thought of Christ, who stilled the waves
On the Lake of Galilee.

And fast through the midnight dark and drear,
Through the whistling sleet and snow,
Like a sheeted ghost the vessel swept
Towards the reef of Norman's Woe.

And ever the fitful gusts between
A sound came from the land;
It was the sound of the trampling surf
On the rocks and the hard sea-sand.

The breakers were right beneath her bows,
She drifted a dreary wreck,
And a whooping billow swept the crew
Like icicles from her deck.

She struck where the white and fleecy waves
Looked soft as carded wool,
But the cruel rocks they gored her side
Like the horns of an angry bull.

Her rattling shrouds, all sheathed in ice,
With the masts went by the board;
Like a vessel of glass she stove and sank—
Ho! ho! the breakers roared!

At daybreak, on the bleak sea-beach
A fisherman stood aghast
To see the form of a maiden fair
Lashed close to a drifting mast.

The salt sea was frozen on her breast,
The salt tears in her eyes;
And he saw her hair, like the brown sea-weed,
On the billows fall and rise.

Such was the wreck of the Hesperus
In the midnight and the snow!
Christ save us all from a death like this
On the reef of Norman's Woe!

LUCY GRAY

By William Wordsworth

Oft I had heard of Lucy Gray:
  And, when I crossed the wild,
I chanced to see, at break of day,
  The solitary child.

No mate, no comrade Lucy knew;
  She dwelt on a wide moor,
The sweetest thing that ever grew
  Beside a human door!

Youth yet may spy the fawn at play,
  The hare upon the green;
But the sweet face of Lucy Gray
  Will never more be seen.

"Tonight will be a stormy night—
You to the town must go;
And take a lantern, Child, to light
Your mother through the snow."

"That, Father, will I gladly do:
'Tis scarcely afternoon—
The minster-clock has just struck two,
And yonder is the moon!"

At this the Father raised his hook,
And snapped a fagot-brand.
He plied his work—and Lucy took
The lantern in her hand.

Not blither is the mountain roe:
With many a wanton stroke
Her feet disperse the powdery snow,
That rises up like smoke.

The storm came on before its time:
She wandered up and down:
And many a hill did Lucy climb:
But never reached the town.

The wretched parents all that night
Went shouting far and wide;
But there was neither sound nor sight
To serve them for a guide.

At daybreak on the hill they stood
That overlooked the moor;
And thence they saw the bridge of wood,
A furlong from their door.

They wept—and, turning homeward, cried,
"In heaven we all shall meet";
When in the snow the mother spied
The print of Lucy's feet.

Then downwards from the steep hill's edge
They tracked the footmarks small:
And through the broken hawthorn hedge,
And by the low stone wall;

And then an open field they crossed—
  The marks were still the same—
They tracked them on, nor ever lost;
  And to the bridge they came.

They followed from the snowy bank
  Those footmarks, one by one,
Into the middle of the plank;
  And further there were none!

—Yet some maintain that to this day
  She is a living child;
That you may see sweet Lucy Gray
  Upon the lonesome wild.

O'er rough and smooth she trips along,
  And never looks behind;
And sings a solitary song
  That whistles in the wind.

THE FAREWELL

By Robert Burns

It was a' for our rightfu' King,
  We left fair Scotland's strand;
It was a' for our rightfu' King
  We e'er saw Irish land,
      My dear;
  We e'er saw Irish land.

Now a' is done that men can do,
  And a' is done in vain;
My love and native land farewell,
  For I maun cross the main,
      My dear;
  For I maun cross the main.

He turn'd him right and round about
  Upon the Irish shore;
And gae his bridle-reins a shake,
  With adieu for evermore,
      My dear;
  With adieu for evermore.

The sodger from the wars returns,
  The sailor frae the main;
But I hae parted frae my love,
  Never to meet again,
      My dear;
  Never to meet again.

When day is gane, and night is come,
  And a' folk bound to sleep;
I think on him that's far awa',
  The lee-lang night, and weep,
      My dear;
  The lee-lang night, and weep.

GATHERING SONG OF DONALD DHU

By Sir Walter Scott

Pibroch of Donuil Dhu,
  Pibroch of Donuil,
Wake thy wild voice anew,
  Summon Clan Conuil.
Come away, come away,
  Hark to the summons!
Come in your war-array,
  Gentles and commons.

Come from deep glen, and
  From mountain so rocky;
The war-pipe and pennon
  Are at Inverlochy.
Come every hill-plaid, and
  True heart that wears one,
Come every steel blade, and
  Strong hand that bears one.

Leave untended the herd,
  The flock without shelter;
Leave the corpse uninterr'd,
  The bride at the altar;
Leave the deer, leave the steer,
  Leave nets and barges:
Come with your fighting gear,
  Broadswords and targes.

Come as the winds come, when
  Forests are rended;
Come as the waves come, when
  Navies are stranded:
Faster come, faster come,
  Faster and faster,
Chief, vassal, page and groom,
  Tenant and master.

Fast they come, fast they come;
  See how they gather!
Wide waves the eagle plume
  Blended with heather.
Cast your plaids, draw your blades,
  Forward each man set!
Pibroch of Donuil Dhu
  Knell for the onset!

LORD ULLIN'S DAUGHTER

By Thomas Campbell

A Chieftain to the Highlands bound
  Cries "Boatman, do not tarry!
And I'll give thee a silver pound
  To row us o'er the ferry!"

"Now who be ye, would cross Lochgyle
  This dark and stormy water?"
"O I'm the chief of Ulva's isle,
  And this, Lord Ullin's daughter.

"And fast before her father's men
  Three days we've fled together,
For should he find us in the glen,
  My blood would stain the heather.

"His horsemen hard behind us ride—
  Should they our steps discover,
Then who will cheer my bonny bride
  When they have slain her lover!"

Out spoke the hardy Highland wight
  "I'll go, my chief, I'm ready:
It is not for your silver bright,
  But for your winsome lady:

"And by my word! the bonny bird
  In danger shall not tarry;
So though the waves are raging white
  I'll row you o'er the ferry."

By this the storm grew loud apace,
  The water-wraith was shrieking;
And in the scowl of heaven each face
  Grew dark as they were speaking.

But still as wilder blew the wind
  And as the night grew drearer,
Adown the glen rode armèd men,
  Their trampling sounded nearer.

"O haste thee, haste!" the lady cries,
  "Though tempests round us gather;
I'll meet the raging of the skies,
  But not an angry father."

The boat has left a stormy land,
  A stormy sea before her—
When, O! too strong for human hand
  The tempest gather'd o'er her.

And still they row'd amidst the roar
  Of waters fast prevailing:
Lord Ullin reach'd that fatal shore—
  His wrath was changed to wailing.

For, sore dismay'd through storm and shade
  His child he did discover:
One lovely hand she stretch'd for aid,
  And one was round her lover.

"Come back! come back!" he cried in grief
  "Across this stormy water:
And I'll forgive your Highland chief,
  My daughter!—O my daughter!"

'Twas vain: the loud waves lash'd the shore,
  Return or aid preventing:
The waters wild went o'er his child,
  And he was left lamenting.

ALLEN-A-DALE

By Sir Walter Scott

Allen-a-Dale has no fagot for burning,
Allen-a-Dale has no furrow for turning,
Allen-a-Dale has no fleece for the spinning,
Yet Allen-a-Dale has red gold for the winning.
Come, read me my riddle! come, hearken my tale;
And tell me the craft of bold Allen-a-Dale.

The Baron of Ravensworth prances in pride,
And he views his domains upon Arkindale side,
The mere for his net, and the land for his game,
The chase for the wild, and the park for the tame;
Yet the fish of the lake, and the deer of the vale,
Are less free to Lord Dacre than Allen-a-Dale!

Allen-a-Dale was ne'er belted a knight,
Though his spur be as sharp, and his blade be as bright;
Allen-a-Dale is no baron or lord,
Yet twenty tall yeomen will draw at his word;
And the best of our nobles his bonnet will vail,
Who at Rere-cross on Stanmore meets Allen-a-Dale.

Allen-a-Dale to his wooing is come;
The mother, she ask'd of his household and home:
"Though the castle of Richmond stand fair on the hill,
My hall," quoth bold Allen, "shows gallanter still;
'Tis the blue vault of heaven, with its crescent so pale,
And with all its bright spangles!" said Allen-a-Dale.

The father was steel, and the mother was stone;
They lifted the latch, and they bade him be gone;
But loud, on the morrow, their wail and their cry:
He had laugh'd on the lass with his bonny black eye.
And she fled to the forest to hear a love-tale,
And the youth it was told by was Allen-a-Dale!

THE KING OF DENMARK'S RIDE

By Caroline Elizabeth Norton

Word was brought to the Danish king,
(Hurry!)
That the love of his heart lay suffering,
And pined for the comfort his voice would bring
(Oh! ride as if you were flying!)
Better he loves each golden curl
On the brow of that Scandinavian girl
Than his rich crown-jewels of ruby and pearl;
And his Rose of the Isles is dying!

Thirty nobles saddled with speed;
(Hurry!)
Each one mounted a gallant steed
Which he kept for battle and days of need;
(Oh! ride as though you were flying!)
Spurs were stuck in the foaming flank,
Worn-out chargers staggered and sank:
Bridles were slackened and girths were burst;
But, ride as they would, the king rode first,
For his Rose of the Isles lay dying.

His nobles are beaten, one by one;
(Hurry!)
They have fainted, and faltered, and homeward gone;
His little fair page now follows alone,
For strength and for courage trying.
The king looked back at that faithful child,
Wan was the face that answering smiled.
They passed the drawbridge with clattering din,
Then he dropped, and only the king rode in
Where his Rose of the Isles lay dying.

The king blew a blast on his bugle-horn,
(Silence!)
No answer came, but faint and forlorn
An echo returned on the cold gray morn,
Like the breath of a spirit sighing;
The castle portal stood grimly wide;
None welcomed the king from that weary ride!

For, dead in the light of the dawning day,
The pale sweet form of the welcomer lay,
  Who had yearned for his voice while dying.

The panting steed with a drooping crest
    Stood weary;
The king returned from the chamber of rest,
The thick sobs choking in his breast,
  And that dumb companion eyeing,
The tears gushed forth, which he strove to check;
He bowed his head on his charger's neck—
"O steed that every nerve didst strain,
Dear steed! our ride hath been in vain
  To the halls where my love lay dying."

LOCHINVAR

By Sir Walter Scott

Oh, young Lochinvar is come out of the West;
Through all the wide Border his steed was the best;
And save his good broadsword he weapons had none;
He rode all unarmed, and he rode all alone.
So faithful in love, and so dauntless in war,
There never was knight like the young Lochinvar.

He stayed not for brake, and he stopped not for stone;
He swam the Eske river where ford there was none;
But, ere he alighted at Netherby gate,
The bride had consented, the gallant came late:
For a laggard in love, and a dastard in war,
Was to wed the fair Ellen of brave Lochinvar.

So boldly he entered the Netherby hall,
'Mong bridesmen and kinsmen, and brothers and all.
Then spoke the bride's father, his hand on his sword
(For the poor craven bridegroom said never a word),
"Oh, come ye in peace here, or come ye in war,
Or to dance at our bridal, young Lord Lochinvar?"

"I long wooed your daughter, my suit you denied.
Love swells like the Solway, but ebbs like its tide;
And now I am come, with this lost love of mine
To lead but one measure, drink one cup of wine.
There are maidens in Scotland more lovely by far
That would gladly be bride to the young Lochinvar."

The bride kissed the goblet; the knight took it up:
He quaffed off the wine, and he threw down the cup.
She looked down to blush, and she looked up to sigh,
With a smile on her lips and a tear in her eye.
He took her soft hand ere her mother could bar—
"Now tread we a measure!" said young Lochinvar.

So stately his form, and so lovely her face,
That never a hall such a galliard did grace;
While her mother did fret, and her father did fume,
And the bridegroom stood dangling his bonnet and plume;
And the bride-maidens whispered, " 'Twere better by far
To have matched our fair cousin with young Lochinvar."

One touch to her hand, and one in her ear,
When they reached the hall door and the charger stood near;
So light to the croup the fair lady he swung,
So light to the saddle before her he sprung!
"She is won! we are gone, over bank, bush, and scaur!
They'll have fleet steeds that follow!" quoth young Lochinvar.

There was mounting 'mong Graemes of the Netherby clan;
Forsters, Fenwicks, and Musgraves, they rode and they ran;
There was racing and chasing on Cannobie Lee;
But the lost bride of Netherby ne'er did they see.
So daring in love, and so dauntless in war,
Have ye e'er heard of gallant like young Lochinvar?

LEPANTO

By Gilbert K. Chesterton

White founts falling in the Courts of the sun,
And the Soldan of Byzantium is smiling as they run;
There is laughter like the fountains in that face of all men feared,
It stirs the forest darkness, the darkness of his beard;
It curls the blood-red crescent, the crescent of his lips;
For the inmost sea of all the earth is shaken with his ships.
They have dared the white republics up the capes of Italy,
They have dashed the Adriatic round the Lion of the Sea,
And the Pope has cast his arms abroad for agony and loss,
And called the kings of Christendom for swords about the Cross.
The cold queen of England is looking in the glass;
The shadow of the Valois is yawning at the Mass;

From evening isles fantastical rings faint the Spanish gun,
And the Lord upon the Golden Horn is laughing in the sun.

Dim drums throbbing in the hills half heard,
Where only on a nameless throne a crownless prince has stirred,
Where, risen from a doubtful seat and half-attainted stall,
The last knight of Europe takes weapons from the wall.
The last and lingering troubadour to whom the bird has sung,
That once went singing southward when all the world was young.
In that enormous silence, tiny and unafraid,
Comes up along a winding road the noise of the Crusade.
Strong gongs groaning as the guns boom far,
Don John of Austria is going to the war,
Stiff flags straining in the night-blasts cold
In the gloom black-purple, in the glint old-gold,
Torchlight crimson on the copper kettle-drums,
Then the tuckets, then the trumpets, then the cannon, and he comes.
Don John laughing in the brave beard curled,
Spurning of his stirrups like the thrones of all the world,
Holding his head up for a flag of all the free.
Love-light of Spain—hurrah!
Death-light of Africa!
Don John of Austria
Is riding to the sea.

Mahound is in his paradise above the evening star,
(Don John of Austria is going to the war.)
He moves a mighty turban on the timeless houri's knees,
His turban that is woven of the sunsets and the seas.
He shakes the peacock gardens as he rises from his ease,
And he strides among the tree-tops and is taller than the trees;
And his voice through all the garden is a thunder sent to bring
Black Azrael and Ariel and Ammon on the wing.
Giants and the Genii,
Multiplex of wing and eye,
Whose strong obedience broke the sky
When Solomon was king.

They rush in red and purple from the red clouds of the morn,
From temples where the yellow gods shut up their eyes in scorn;
They rise in green robes roaring from the green hells of the sea
Where fallen skies and evil hues and eyeless creatures be;
On them the sea-wolves cluster and the gray sea-forests curl,
Splashed with a splendid sickness, the sickness of the pearl;

They swell in sapphire smoke out of the blue cracks of the ground—
They gather and they wonder and give worship to Mahound.
And he saith, "Break up the mountains where the hermit-folk
can hide,
And sift the red and silver sands lest bone of saint abide,
And chase the Giaours flying night and day, not giving rest,
For that which was our trouble comes again out of the west.
We have set the seal of Solomon on all things under sun,
Of knowledge and of sorrow and endurance of things done,
But a noise is in the mountains, in the mountains, and I know
The voice that shook our palaces—four hundred years ago:
It is he that saith not 'Kismet'; it is he that knows not Fate;
It is Richard, it is Raymond, it is Godfrey at the gate!
It is he whose loss is laughter when he counts the wager worth,
Put down your feet upon him, that our peace be on the earth."
For he heard drums groaning and he heard guns jar,
(Don John of Austria is going to the war.)
Sudden and still-hurrah!
Bolt from Iberia!
Don John of Austria
Is gone by Alcalar.

St. Michael's on his Mountain in the sea-roads of the north
(Don John of Austria is girt and going forth.)
Where the gray seas glitter and the sharp tides shift
And the sea-folk labor and the red sails lift.
He shakes his lance of iron and he claps his wings of stone;
The noise is gone through Normandy; the noise is gone alone;
The North is full of tangled things and texts and aching eyes,
And dead is all the innocence of anger and surprise,
And Christian killeth Christian in a narrow dusty room,
And Christian dreadeth Christ that hath a newer face of doom,
And Christian hateth Mary that God kissed in Galilee—
But Don John of Austria is riding to the sea.
Don John calling through the blast and the eclipse
Crying with the trumpet, with the trumpet to his lips,
Trumpet that sayeth ha!
Domino gloria!
Don John of Austria
Is shouting to the ships.

King Philip's in his closet with the Fleece about his neck
(Don John of Austria is armed upon the deck.)
The walls are hung with velvet that is black and soft as sin,
And little dwarfs creep out of it and little dwarfs creep in.
He holds a crystal phial that has colors like the moon,
He touches, and it tingles, and he trembles very soon,
And his face is as a fungus of a leprous white and gray
Like plants in the high houses that are shuttered from the day,
And death is in the phial and the end of noble work,
But Don John of Austria has fired upon the Turk.
Don John's hunting, and his hounds have bayed—
Booms away past Italy the rumor of his raid.
Gun upon gun, ha! ha!
Gun upon gun, hurrah!
Don John of Austria
Has loosed the cannonade.

The Pope was in his chapel before day or battle broke,
(Don John of Austria is hidden in the smoke.)
The hidden room in man's house where God sits all the year,
The secret window whence the world looks small and very dear.
He sees as in a mirror on the monstrous twilight sea
The crescent of his cruel ships whose name is mystery;
They fling great shadows foe-wards, making Cross and Castle dark,
They veil the plumèd lions in the galleys of St. Mark;
And above the ships are palaces of brown, black-bearded chiefs,
And below the ships are prisons where, with multitudinous griefs,
Christian captives, sick and sunless, all a laboring race repines
Like a race in sunken cities, like a nation in the mines.
They are lost like slaves that sweat, and in the skies of morning hung
The stair-ways of the tallest gods when tyranny was young.
They are countless, voiceless, hopeless as those fallen or fleeing on
Before the high Kings' horses in the granite of Babylon.
And many a one grows witless in his quiet room in hell
Where a yellow face looks inward through the lattice of his cell,
And he finds his God forgotten, and he seeks no more a sign—
(But Don John of Austria has burst the battle-line!)
Don John pounding from the slaughter-painted poop,
Purpling all the ocean like a bloody pirate's sloop,
Scarlet running over on the silvers and the golds,
Breaking of the hatches up and bursting of the holds,
Thronging of the thousands up that labor under sea
White for bliss and blind for sun and stunned for liberty.

Vivat Hispania!
Domino Gloria!
Don John of Austria
Has set his people free!

Cervantes on his galley sets the sword back in the sheath
(Don John of Austria rides homeward with a wreath.)
And he sees across a weary land a straggling road in Spain,
Up which a lean and foolish knight for ever rides in vain,
And he smiles, but not as Sultans smile, and settles back the blade . .
(But Don John of Austria rides home from the Crusade.)

THE DESTRUCTION OF SENNACHERIB

By George Gordon, Lord Byron

The Assyrian came down like a wolf on the fold,
And his cohorts were gleaming in purple and gold;
And the sheen of their spears was like stars on the sea,
When the blue wave rolls nightly on deep Galilee.

Like the leaves of the forest when the Summer is green,
That host with their banners at sunset were seen:
Like the leaves of the forest when Autumn hath blown,
That host on the morrow lay withered and strown.

For the Angel of Death spread his wings on the blast,
And breathed in the face of the foe as he passed;
And the eyes of the sleepers waxed deadly and chill,
And their hearts but once heaved, and forever grew still!

And there lay the steed with his nostril all wide,
But through it there rolled not the breath of his pride;
And the foam of his gasping lay white on the turf.
And cold as the spray of the rock-beating surf.

And there lay the rider distorted and pale,
With the dew on his brow, and the rust on his mail.
And the tents were all silent, the banners alone,
The lances unlifted, the trumpet unblown.

And the widows of Ashur are loud in their wail,
And the idols are broke in the temple of Baal;
And the might of the Gentile, unsmote by the sword,
Hath melted like snow in the glance of the Lord!

HOW THEY BROUGHT THE GOOD NEWS FROM GHENT TO AIX

By Robert Browning

I sprang to the stirrup, and Joris, and he;
I galloped, Dirck galloped, we galloped all three;
"Good speed!" cried the watch as the gate-bolts undrew;
"Speed!" echoed the wall to us galloping through;
Behind shut the postern, the lights sank to rest,
And into the midnight we galloped abreast.

Not a word to each other; we kept the great pace
Neck by neck, stride by stride, never changing our place;
I turned in my saddle and made its girth tight,
Then shortened each stirrup, and set the pique right,
Rebuckled the cheek-strap, chained slacker the bit,
Nor galloped less steadily Roland a whit.

'Twas moonset at starting; but while we drew near
Lokeren, the cocks crew and twilight dawned clear;
At Boom, a great yellow star came out to see;
At Düffeld, 'twas morning as plain as could be;
And from Mecheln church-steeple we heard the half-chime,
So Joris broke silence with, "Yet there is time!"

At Aershot, up leaped of a sudden the sun,
And against him the cattle stood black every one
To stare through the mist at us galloping past,
And I saw my stout galloper Roland at last,
With resolute shoulders, each butting away
The haze, as some bluff river headland its spray;

And his low head and crest, just one sharp ear bent back
For my voice, and the other pricked out on his track;
And one eye's black intelligence—ever that glance
O'er its white edge at me, his own master, askance!
And the thick, heavy spume-flakes which aye and anon
His fierce lips shook upward in galloping on.

By Hasselt, Dirck groaned; and cried Joris, "Stay spur!
Your Roos galloped bravely, the fault's not in her,
We'll remember at Aix"—for one heard the quick wheeze
Of her chest, saw the stretched neck and staggering knees,

And sunk tail, and horrible heave of the flank,
As down on her haunches she shuddered and sank.

So, we were left galloping, Joris and I,
Past Looz and past Tongres, no cloud in the sky;
The broad sun above laughed a pitiless laugh,
'Neath our feet broke the brittle bright stubble like chaff;
Till over by Dalhem a dome-spire sprang white,
And "Gallop," gasped Joris, "for Aix is in sight!"

"How they'll greet us!"—and all in a moment his roan
Rolled neck and croup over, lay dead as a stone;
And there was my Roland to bear the whole weight
Of the news which alone could save Aix from her fate,
With nostrils like pits full of blood to the brim,
And with circles of red for his eye-sockets' rim.

Then I cast loose my buffcoat, each holster let fall,
Shook off both my jack-boots, let go belt and all,
Stood up in the stirrup, leaned, patted his ear,
Called my Roland his pet-name, my horse without peer;
Clapped my hands, laughed and sang, any noise, bad or good,
Till at length into Aix Roland galloped and stood.

And all I remember is—friends flocking round
As I sat with his head 'twist my knees on the ground;
And no voice but was praising this Roland of mine,
As I poured down his throat our last measure of wine,
Which (the burgesses voted by common consent)
Was no more than his due who brought good news from Ghent.

THE HARP THAT ONCE THROUGH TARA'S HALLS

By Thomas Moore

The harp that once through Tara's halls
  The soul of music shed,
Now hangs as mute on Tara's walls
  As if that soul were fled.
So sleeps the pride of former days,
  So glory's thrill is o'er,
And hearts, that once beat high for praise,
  Now feel that pulse no more.

No more to chiefs and ladies bright
 The harp of Tara swells:
The chord alone, that breaks at night,
 Its tale of ruin tells.
Thus Freedom now so seldom wakes,
 The only throb she gives
Is when some heart indignant breaks,
 To show that still she lives.

THE MINSTREL-BOY

By Thomas Moore

The Minstrel-Boy to the war is gone,
 In the ranks of death you'll find him;
His father's sword he has girded on,
 And his wild harp slung behind him.
"Land of song!" said the warrior-bard,
 "Though all the world betrays thee,
One sword, at least, thy rights shall guard,
 One faithful harp shall praise thee!"

The Minstrel fell!—but the foeman's chain
 Could not bring his proud soul under;
The harp he loved ne'er spoke again,
 For he tore its chords asunder;
And said, "No chains shall sully thee,
 Thou soul of love and bravery!
Thy songs were made for the pure and free,
 They shall never sound in slavery!"

YE MARINERS OF ENGLAND

By Thomas Campbell

Ye mariners of England,
That guard our native seas;
Whose flag has braved, a thousand years,
The battle and the breeze!
Your glorious standard launch again
To match another foe!
And sweep through the deep,
While the stormy winds do blow;
While the battle rages loud and long,
And the stormy winds do blow.

The spirits of your fathers
Shall start from every wave;
For the deck it was their field of fame,
And Ocean was their grave.
Where Blake and mighty Nelson fell,
Your manly hearts shall glow,
As ye sweep through the deep,
While the stormy winds do blow;
While the battle rages loud and long,
And the stormy winds do blow.

Britannia needs no bulwarks,
No towers along the steep;
Her march is o'er the mountain-waves,
Her home is on the deep.
With thunders from her native oak,
She quells the floods below—
As they roar on the shore,
When the stormy winds do blow;
When the battle rages loud and long
And the stormy winds do blow.

The meteor flag of England
Shall yet terrific burn;
Till danger's troubled night depart,
And the star of peace return.
Then, then, ye ocean warriors!
Our song and feast shall flow
To the fame of your name,
When the storm has ceased to blow;
And the fiery fight is heard no more
And the storm has ceased to blow.

AFTER BLENHEIM

By Robert Southey

It was a summer evening;
  Old Kaspar's work was done,
And he before his cottage door
  Was sitting in the sun;
And by him sported on the green
His little grandchild Wilhelmine.

She saw her brother Peterkin
  Roll something large and round
Which he beside the rivulet
  In playing there had found;
He came to ask what he had found
That was so large and smooth and round.

Old Kaspar took it from the boy,
  Who stood expectant by;
And then the old man shook his head,
  And with a natural sigh
" 'Tis some poor fellow's skull," said he,
"Who fell in the great victory.

"I find them in the garden,
  For there's many here about;
And often when I go to plow
  The plowshare turns them out.
For many thousand men," said he,
"Were slain in that great victory."

"Now tell us what 'twas all about,"
  Young Peterkin he cries;
And little Wilhelmine looks up
  With wonder-waiting eyes;
"Now tell us all about the war,
And what they fought each other for?"

"It was the English," Kaspar cried,
  "Who put the French to rout;
But what they fought each other for
  I could not well make out.
But everybody said," quoth he,
"That 'twas a famous victory.

"My father lived at Blenheim then,
  Yon little stream hard by;
They burned his dwelling to the ground,
  And he was forced to fly:
So with his wife and child he fled,
Nor had he where to rest his head.

"With fire and sword the country round
  Was wasted far and wide,
And many a childing mother then
  And new-born baby died:
But things like that, you know, must be
At every famous victory.

"They say it was a shocking sight
  After the field was won;
For many thousand bodies here
  Lay rotting in the sun;
But things like that, you know, must be
After a famous victory.

"Great praise the Duke of Marlboro' won
  And our good Prince Eugene";
—"Why, 'twas a very wicked thing!"
  Said little Wilhelmine;
"Nay . . . nay . . . my little girl," quoth he,
"It was a famous victory!

"And everybody praised the Duke
  Who this great fight did win."
—"But what good came of it at last?"
  Quoth little Peterkin:—
"Why, that I cannot tell," said he,
"But 'twas a famous victory."

THE SKELETON IN ARMOR

By Henry Wadsworth Longfellow

"Speak! speak! thou fearful guest!
Who, with thy hollow breast
Still in rude armor drest,
  Comest to daunt me!
Wrapt not in Eastern balms,
But with thy fleshless palms
Stretched, as if asking alms,
  Why dost thou haunt me?"

Then from those cavernous eyes
Pale flashes seemed to rise,
As when the Northern skies
  Gleam in December;
And, like the water's flow
Under December's snow,
Came a dull voice of woe
  From the heart's chamber.

"I was a Viking old!
My deeds, though manifold,
No Skald in song has told,
  No Saga taught thee!
Take heed that in thy verse
Thou dost the tale rehearse,
Else dread a dead man's curse;
  For this I sought thee.

"Far in the Northern Land,
By the wild Baltic's strand,
I, with my childish hand,
  Tamed the gerfalcon;
And, with my skates fast-bound,
Skimmed the half-frozen Sound,
That the poor whimpering hound
  Trembled to walk on.

"Oft to his frozen lair
Tracked I the grizzly bear,
While from my path the hare
  Fled like a shadow;
Oft through the forest dark
Followed the were-wolf's bark,
Until the soaring lark
  Sang from the meadow.

"But when I older grew,
Joining a corsair's crew,
O'er the dark sea I flew
  With the marauders.
Wild was the life we led;
Many the souls that sped,
Many the hearts that bled,
  By our stern orders.

"Many a wassail-bout
Wore the long Winter out;
Often our midnight shout
  Set the cocks crowing,
As we the Berserk's tale
Measured in cups of ale,
Draining the oaken pail
  Filled to o'erflowing.

"Once as I told in glee
Tales of the stormy sea,
Soft eyes did gaze on me,
  Burning yet tender;
And as the white stars shine
On the dark Norway pine,
On that dark heart of mine
  Fell their soft splendor.

"I wooed the blue-eyed maid,
Yielding, yet half afraid,
And in the forest's shade
  Our vows were plighted.
Under its loosened vest
Fluttered her little breast,
Like birds within their nest
  By the hawk frighted.

"Bright in her father's hall
Shields gleamed upon the wall,
Loud sang the minstrels all,
  Chanting his glory;
When of old Hildebrand
I asked his daughter's hand,
Mute did the minstrels stand
  To hear my story.

"While the brown ale he quaffed,
Loud then the champion laughed,
And as the wind-gusts waft
  The sea-foam brightly,
So the loud laugh of scorn,
Out of those lips unshorn,
From the deep drinking-horn
  Blew the foam lightly.

"She was a Prince's child,
I but a Viking wild,
And though she blushed and smiled,
  I was discarded!
Should not the dove so white
Follow the sea-mew's flight?
Why did they leave that night
  Her nest unguarded?

"Scarce had I put to sea,
Bearing the maid with me—
Fairest of all was she
  Among the Norsemen!—
When on the white sea-strand,
Waving his armed hand,
Saw we old Hildebrand,
  With twenty horsemen.

"Then launched they to the blast,
Bent like a reed each mast,
Yet we were gaining fast,
  When the wind failed us;
And with a sudden flaw
Came round the gusty Skaw,
So that our foe we saw
  Laugh as he hailed us.

"And as to catch the gale
Round veered the flapping sail,
'Death!' was the helmsman's hail,
  'Death without quarter!'
Midships with iron keel
Struck we her ribs of steel;
Down her black hulk did reel
  Through the black water!

"As with his wings aslant,
Sails the fierce cormorant,
Seeking some rocky haunt,
  With his prey laden,
So toward the open main,
Beating to sea again,
Through the wild hurricane,
  Bore I the maiden.

"Three weeks we westward bore,
And when the storm was o'er,
Cloud-like we saw the shore
  Stretching to leeward;
There for my lady's bower
Built I the lofty tower
Which to this very hour
  Stands looking seaward.

"There lived we many years;
Time dried the maiden's tears;
She had forgot her fears,
  She was a mother;
Death closed her mild blue eyes;
Under that tower she lies;
Ne'er shall the sun arise
  On such another.

"Still grew my bosom then,
Still as a stagnant fen!
Hateful to me were men,
  The sunlight hateful!
In the vast forest here,
Clad in my warlike gear,
Fell I upon my spear,
  Oh, death was grateful!

"Thus, seamed with many scars,
Bursting these prison bars,
Up to its native stars
  My soul ascended!
There from the flowing bowl
Deep drinks the warrior's soul,
Skoal! to the Northland! *skoal!*"
  Thus the tale ended.

COLUMBUS

By Joaquin Miller

Behind him lay the gray Azores,
  Behind the Gates of Hercules;
Before him not the ghost of shores,
  Before him only shoreless seas.

The good mate said: "Now must we pray,
  For lo! the very stars are gone.
Brave Admiral, speak, what shall I say?"
  "Why, say 'Sail on! sail on! and on!' "

"My men grow mutinous day by day;
  My men grow ghastly wan and weak."
The stout mate thought of home; a spray
  Of salt wave washed his swarthy cheek.
"What shall I say, brave Admiral, say,
  If we sight naught but seas at dawn?"
"Why, you shall say at break of day,
  'Sail on! sail on! sail on! and on!' "

They sailed and sailed, as winds might blow,
  Until at last the blanched mate said:
"Why, now not even God would know
  Should I and all my men fall dead.
These very winds forget their way,
  For God from these dread seas is gone.
Now speak, brave Admiral, speak and say"—
  He said: "Sail on! sail on! and on!"

They sailed. They sailed. Then spake the mate:
  "This mad sea shows his teeth tonight.
He curls his lip, he lies in wait,
  With lifted teeth, as if to bite!
Brave Admiral, say but one good word:
  What shall we do when hope is gone?"
The words leapt like a leaping sword:
    "Sail on! sail on! sail on! and on!"

Then, pale and worn, he kept his deck,
  And peered through darkness. Ah, that night
Of all dark nights! And then a speck—
  A light! a light! a light! a light!
It grew, a starlit flag unfurled!
  It grew to be Time's burst of dawn.
He gained a world; he gave that world
  Its grandest lesson: "On! sail on!"

THE LANDING OF THE PILGRIM FATHERS IN NEW ENGLAND

By Felicia Dorothea Hemans

The breaking waves dash'd high
  On a stern and rock-bound coast,
And the woods against a stormy sky
  Their giant branches toss'd;

And the heavy night hung dark
  The hills and waters o'er,
When a band of exiles moor'd their bark
  On the wild New England shore.

Not as the conqueror comes,
  They, the true-hearted, came;
Not with the roll of the stirring drums,
  And the trumpet that sings of fame;

Not as the flying come,
  In silence and in fear—
They shook the depths of the desert gloom
  With their hymns of lofty cheer.

Amidst the storm they sang,
  And the stars heard and the sea;
And the sounding aisles of the dim woods rang
  To the anthem of the free!

The ocean eagle soar'd
  From his nest by the white wave's foam;
And the rocking pines of the forest roar'd—
  This was their welcome home!

There were men with hoary hair
  Amidst that pilgrim band;—
Why had they come to wither there,
  Away from their childhood's land?

There was woman's fearless eye,
  Lit by her deep love's truth;
There was manhood's brow serenely high,
  And the fiery heart of youth.

What sought they thus afar?—
  Bright jewels of the mine?
The wealth of seas, the spoils of war?—
  They sought a faith's pure shrine!

Ay, call it holy ground,
  The soil where first they trod.
They have left unstain'd what there they found—
  Freedom to worship God.

PAUL REVERE'S RIDE

By Henry Wadsworth Longfellow

Listen, my children, and you shall hear
Of the midnight ride of Paul Revere,
On the eighteenth of April, in Seventy-Five:
Hardly a man is now alive
Who remembers that famous day and year.

He said to his friend—"If the British march
By land or sea from the town tonight,
Hang a lantern aloft in the belfry-arch
Of the North Church tower, as a signal-light—
One if by land, and two if by sea;
And I on the opposite shore will be,
Ready to ride and spread the alarm
Through every Middlesex village and farm,
For the country folk to be up and to arm."

Then he said good night, and with muffled oar
Silently row'd to the Charlestown shore,
Just as the moon rose over the bay,
Where swinging wide at her moorings lay
The *Somerset,* British man-of-war:
A phantom ship, with each mast and spar
Across the moon, like a prison-bar,
And a huge, black hulk, that was magnified
By its own reflection in the tide.

Meanwhile his friend, through alley and street
Wanders and watches with eager ears,
Till in the silence around him he hears
The muster of men at the barrack-door,

The sound of arms, and the tramp of feet,
And the measured tread of the grenadiers
Marching down to their boats on the shore.

Then he climb'd the tower of the Old North Church,
Up the wooden stairs, with stealthy tread,
To the belfry-chamber overhead,
And startled the pigeons from their perch
On the somber rafters, that round him made
Masses and moving shapes of shade;
Up the light ladder, slender and tall,
To the highest window in the wall,
Where he paused to listen and look down
A moment on the roofs of the town,
And the moonlight flowing over all.

Beneath, in the churchyard, lay the dead
In their night-encampment on the hill,
Wrapp'd in silence so deep and still,
That he could hear, like a sentinel's tread,
The watchful night-wind as it went
Creeping along from tent to tent,
And seeming to whisper, "All is well!"

A moment only he feels the spell
Of the place and the hour, the secret dread
Of the lonely belfry and the dead;
For suddenly all his thoughts are bent
On a shadowy something far away,
Where the river widens to meet the bay—
A line of black, that bends and floats
On the rising tide, like a bridge of boats.

Meanwhile, impatient to mount and ride,
Booted and spurr'd, with a heavy stride,
On the opposite shore walk'd Paul Revere.
Now he patted his horse's side,
Now gazed on the landscape far and near,
Then impetuous stamp'd the earth,
And turn'd and tighten'd his saddle-girth;
But mostly he watch'd with eager search
The belfry-tower of the Old North Church,
As it rose above the graves on the hill,
Lonely, and spectral, and somber, and still.

And, lo! as he looks, on the belfry's height,
A glimmer, and then a gleam of light!
He springs to the saddle, the bridle he turns,
But lingers and gazes, till full on his sight
A second lamp in the belfry burns!
A hurry of hoofs in a village street,
A shape in the moonlight, a bulk in the dark,
And beneath from the pebbles, in passing, a spark
Struck out by a steed that flies fearless and fleet:
That was all! And yet, through the gloom and the light,
The fate of a nation was riding that night;
And the spark struck out by that steed, in his flight,
Kindled the land into flame with its heat.

It was twelve by the village clock,
When he cross'd the bridge into Medford town,
He heard the crowing of the cock,
And the barking of the farmer's dog,
And felt the damp of the river-fog,
That rises when the sun goes down.

It was one by the village clock,
When he rode into Lexington.
He saw the gilded weathercock
Swim in the moonlight as he pass'd,
And the meeting-house windows, blank and bare,
Gaze at him with a spectral glare,
As if they already stood aghast
At the bloody work they would look upon.

It was two by the village clock,
When he came to the bridge in Concord town.
He heard the bleating of the flock,
And the twitter of birds among the trees,
And felt the breath of the morning-breeze
Blowing over the meadows brown.
And one was safe and asleep in his bed
Who at the bridge would be first to fall,
Who that day would be lying dead,
Pierced by a British musket-ball.

You know the rest. In the books you have read
How the British regulars fired and fled;
How the farmers gave them ball for ball,

From behind each fence and farmyard-wall,
Chasing the red-coats down the lane,
Then crossing the fields to emerge again
Under the trees at the turn of the road,
And only pausing to fire and load.

So through the night rode Paul Revere;
And so through the night went his cry of alarm
To every Middlesex village and farm—
A cry of defiance, and not of fear—
A voice in the darkness, a knock at the door,
And a word that shall echo for evermore!
For, borne on the night-wind of the Past,
Through all our history, to the last,
In the hour of darkness, and peril, and need,
The people will waken and listen to hear
The hurrying hoof-beat of that steed,
And the midnight message of Paul Revere.

CONCORD HYMN

By Ralph Waldo Emerson

By the rude bridge that arched the flood,
Their flag to April's breeze unfurled,
Here once the embattled farmers stood
And fired the shot heard round the world.

The foe long since in silence slept;
Alike the conqueror silent sleeps;
And Time the ruined bridge has swept
Down the dark stream which seaward creeps.

On this green bank, by this soft stream,
We set today a votive stone;
That memory may their deed redeem,
When, like our sires, our sons are gone.

Spirit, that made those heroes dare
To die, and leave their children free,
Bid Time and Nature gently spare
The shaft we raise to them and thee.

OLD IRONSIDES

By Oliver Wendell Holmes

Ay, tear her tattered ensign down!
Long has it waved on high,
And many an eye has danced to see
That banner in the sky;
Beneath it rung the battle shout,
And burst the cannon's roar—
The meteor of the ocean air
Shall sweep the clouds no more.

Her deck, once red with heroes' blood,
Where knelt the vanquished foe,
When winds were hurrying o'er the flood,
And waves were white below,
No more shall feel the victor's tread,
Or know the conquered knee—
The harpies of the shore shall pluck
The eagle of the sea!

Oh, better that her shattered hulk
Should sink beneath the wave;
Her thunders shook the mighty deep,
And there should be her grave;
Nail to the mast her holy flag,
Set every threadbare sail,
And give her to the god of storms,
The lightning and the gale!

BARBARA FRIETCHIE

By John Greenleaf Whittier

Up from the meadows rich with corn,
Clear in the cool September morn,

The clustered spires of Frederick stand
Green-walled by the hills of Maryland.

Round about them orchards sweep,
Apple and peach tree fruited deep,

Fair as a garden of the Lord
To the eyes of the famished rebel horde,

On that pleasant morn of the early fall
When Lee marched over the mountain wall—

Over the mountains, winding down,
Horse and foot into Frederick town.

Forty flags with their silver stars,
Forty flags with their crimson bars,

Flapped in the morning wind; the sun
Of noon looked down, and saw not one.

Up rose old Barbara Frietchie then,
Bowed with her fourscore years and ten;

Bravest of all in Frederick town,
She took up the flag the men hauled down;

In her attic window the staff she set,
To show that one heart was loyal yet.

Up the street came the rebel tread,
Stonewall Jackson riding ahead.

Under his slouch hat left and right
He glanced: the old flag met his sight.

"Halt!"—the dust-brown ranks stood fast;
"Fire!"—out blazed the rifle-blast.

It shivered the window, pane and sash;
It rent the banner with seam and gash.

Quick, as it fell, from the broken staff,
Dame Barbara snatched the silken scarf;

She leaned far out on the window-sill,
And shook it forth with a royal will.

"Shoot, if you must, this old gray head,
But spare your country's flag," she said.

A shade of sadness, a blush of shame,
Over the face of the leader came;

The nobler nature within him stirred
To life at that woman's deed and word:

"Who touches a hair of yon gray head
Dies like a dog! March on!" he said.

All day long through Frederick street
Sounded the tread of marching feet;

All day long that free flag tossed
Over the heads of the rebel host.

Ever its torn folds rose and fell
On the loyal winds that loved it well;

And through the hill-gaps sunset light
Shone over it with a warm good night.

Barbara Frietchie's work is o'er,
And the rebel rides on his raids no more.

Honor to her! and let a tear
Fall, for her sake, on Stonewall's bier.

Over Barbara Frietchie's grave,
Flag of freedom and union wave!

Peace and order and beauty draw
Round thy symbol of light and law;

And ever the stars above look down
On thy stars below in Frederick town.

NANCY HANKS

By Rosemary Benét

If Nancy Hanks
Came back as a ghost,
Seeking news
Of what she loved most,
She'd ask first
"Where's my son?
What's happened to Abe?
What's he done?

"Poor little Abe,
Left all alone
Except for Tom,
Who's a rolling stone;
He was only nine
The year I died.
I remember still
How hard he cried.

"Scraping along
In a little shack,
With hardly a shirt
To cover his back,
And a prairie wind
To blow him down,
Or pinching times
If he went to town.

"You wouldn't know
About my son?
Did he grow tall?
Did he have fun?
Did he learn to read?
Did he get to town?
Do you know his name?
Did he get on?"

O CAPTAIN! MY CAPTAIN!

By Walt Whitman

O Captain! my Captain! our fearful trip is done,
The ship has weathered every rack, the prize we sought is won,
The port is near, the bells I hear, the people all exulting,
While follow eyes the steady keel, the vessel grim and daring;
But O heart! heart! heart!
O the bleeding drops of red,
Where on the deck my Captain lies,
Fallen cold and dead.

O Captain! my Captain! rise up and hear the bells;
Rise up—for you the flag is flung—for you the bugle trills,
For you bouquets and ribboned wreaths—for you the shores a-crowding,
For you they call, the swaying mass, their eager faces turning;
Here Captain! dear father!
This arm beneath your head!
It is some dream that on the deck
You've fallen cold and dead.

My Captain does not answer, his lips are pale and still,
My father does not feel my arm, he has no pulse nor will;
The ship is anchored safe and sound, its voyage closed and done,
From fearful trip the victor ship comes in with object won;
Exult, O shores! and ring, O bells!
But I, with mournful tread,
Walk the deck my Captain lies,
Fallen cold and dead.

THE GHOSTS OF THE BUFFALOES

By Vachel Lindsay

Last night at black midnight I woke with a cry,
The windows were shaking, there was thunder on high,
The floor was a-tremble, the door was ajar,
White fires, crimson fires, shone from afar.
I rushed to the dooryard. The city was gone.
My home was a hut without orchard or lawn.
It was mud-smear and logs near a whispering stream,
Nothing else built by man could I see in my dream . . .
Then . . .
Ghost-kings came headlong, row upon row,
Gods of the Indians, torches aglow.

They mounted the bear and the elk and the deer,
And eagles gigantic, aged and sere,
They rode long-horn cattle, they cried "A-la-la."
They lifted the knife, the bow, and the spear,
They lifted ghost torches from dead fires below,
The midnight made grand with the cry "A-la-la."
The midnight made grand with a red-god charge,
A red-god show,
A red-god show,
"A-la-la, a-la-la, a-la-la, a-la-la."

With bodies like bronze, and terrible eyes
Came the rank and the file, with catamount cries,
Gibbering, yipping, with hollow-skull clacks,
Riding white bronchos with skeleton backs,
Scalp-hunters, beaded and spangled and bad,
Naked and lustful and foaming and mad,

Flashing primeval demoniac scorn,
Blood-thirst and pomp amid darkness reborn,
Power and glory that sleep in the grass
While the winds and the snows and the great rains pass.

They crossed the gray river, thousands abreast,
They rode in infinite lines to the west,
Tide upon tide of strange fury and foam,
Spirits and wraiths, the blue was their home,
The sky was their goal where the star-flags were furled,
And on past those far golden splendors they whirled.
They burned to dim meteors, lost in the deep,
And I turned in dazed wonder, thinking of sleep.

And the wind crept by,
Alone, unkempt, unsatisfied,
The wind cried and cried—
Muttered of massacres long past,
Buffaloes in shambles vast...
An owl said: "Hark, what is a-wing?"
I heard a cricket carolling,
I heard a cricket carolling,
I heard a cricket carolling.
Then...
Snuffing the lighting that crashed from on high
Rose royal old buffaloes, row upon row.
The lords of the prairie came galloping by.
And I cried in my heart "A-la-la, a-la-la,
A red-god show,
A red-god show,
A-la-la, a-la-la, a-la-la, a-la-la."

Buffaloes, buffaloes; thousands abreast,
A scourge and amazement, they swept to the west.
With black bobbing noses, with red rolling tongues,
Coughing forth steam from their leather-wrapped lungs,
Cows with their calves, bulls, big and vain,
Goring the laggards, shaking the mane,
Stamping flint feet, flashing moon eyes.
Pompous and owlish, shaggy and wise.

Like sea-cliffs and caves resounded their ranks
With shoulders like waves, and undulant flanks.
Tide upon tide of strange fury and foam,
Spirits and wraiths, the blue was their home,
The sky was their goal where the star-flags are furled,
And on past those far golden splendors they whirled.
They burned to dim meteors, lost in the deep,
And I turned in dazed wonder, thinking of sleep.

I heard a cricket's cymbals play,
A scarecrow lightly flapped his rags,
And a pan that hung by his shoulder rang,
Rattled and thumped in a listless way,
And now the wind in the chimney sang,
The wind in the chimney,
The wind in the chimney,
The wind in the chimney,
  Seemed to say:—
"Dream, boy, dream,
If you anywise can.
To dream is the work
Of beast or man.
Life is the west-going dream-storms' breath,
Life is a dream, the sigh of the skies,
The breath of the stars, that nod on their pillows
With their golden hair mussed over their eyes."

The locust played on his musical wing,
Sang to his mate of love's delight.
I heard the whippoorwill's soft fret.
I heard a cricket carolling,
I heard a cricket carolling,
I heard a cricket say: "Good-night, good-night,
Good-night, good-night . . . good-night."

ROMANCE AND ADVENTURE

THE SONG OF WANDERING AENGUS

By William Butler Yeats

I went out to the hazel wood,
Because a fire was in my head,
And cut and peeled a hazel wand,
And hooked a berry to a thread;
And when white moths were on the wing,
And moth-like stars were flickering out,
I dropped the berry in a stream
And caught a little silver trout.

When I had laid it on the floor
I went to blow the fire a-flame,
But something rustled on the floor,
And someone called me by my name:
It had become a glimmering girl
With apple blossom in her hair,
Who called me by my name and ran
And faded through the brightening air.

Though I am old with wandering
Through hollow lands and hilly lands,
I will find out where she has gone,
And kiss her lips and take her hands;
And walk among long dappled grass,
And pluck till time and times are done
The silver apples of the moon,
The golden apples of the sun.

THE VAGABOND

By Robert Louis Stevenson

Give to me the life I love,
  Let the lave go by me,
Give the jolly heaven above
  And the byway nigh me.
Bed in the bush with stars to see,
  Bread I dip in the river—
There's the life for a man like me,
  There's the life for ever.

Let the blow fall soon or late,
  Let what will be o'er me;
Give the face of earth around
  And the road before me.
Wealth I seek not, hope nor love,
  Nor a friend to know me;
All I seek, the heaven above
  And the road below me.

Or let autumn fall on me
  Where afield I linger,
Silencing the bird on tree,
  Biting the blue finger.
White as meal the frosty field—
  Warm the fireside haven—
Not to autumn will I yield,
  Not to winter even!

Let the blow fall soon or late,
  Let what will be o'er me;
Give the face of earth around,
  And the road before me.

Wealth I ask not, hope nor love,
  Nor a friend to know me;
All I ask, the heaven above
  And the road below me.

ROMANCE

By Robert Louis Stevenson

I will make you brooches and toys for your delight,
Of bird-song at morning and star-shine at night.
I will make a palace fit for you and me,
Of green days in forests and blue days at sea.

I will make my kitchen, and you shall keep your room,
Where white flows the river and bright blows the broom,
And you shall wash your linen and keep your body white
In rainfall at morning and dewfall at night.

And this shall be for music when no one else is near
The fine song for singing, the rare song to hear!
That only I remember, that only you admire,
Of the broad road that stretches and the roadside fire.

THE PASSIONATE SHEPHERD TO HIS LOVE

By Christopher Marlowe

Come live with me and be my love,
And we will all the pleasures prove
That hills and valleys, dales and fields,
And woods or steepy mountain yields.

And we will sit upon the rocks,
Seeing the shepherds feed their flocks
By shallow rivers to whose falls
Melodious birds sing madrigals.

And I will make thee beds of roses
And a thousand fragrant posies,
A cap of flowers, and a kirtle
Embroider'd all with leaves of myrtle.

A gown made of the finest wool,
Which from our pretty lambs we pull,
Fair-linèd slippers for the cold,
With buckles of the purest gold.

A belt of straw and ivy-buds
With coral clasps and amber studs,
An' if these pleasures may thee move,
Come live with me, and be my love.

Thy silver dishes for thy meat
As precious as the gods do eat,
Shall on an ivory table be
Prepar'd each day for thee and me.

The shepherd-swains shall dance and sing
For thy delight each May-morning:
If these delights thy mind may move,
Then live with me, and be my love.

O WERT THOU IN THE CAULD BLAST

By Robert Burns

O wert thou in the cauld blast,
  On yonder lea, on yonder lea,
My plaidie to the angry airt,
  I'd shelter thee, I'd shelter thee;
Or did Misfortune's bitter storms
  Around thee blaw, around thee blaw,
Thy bield[1] should be my bosom,
  To share it a', to share it a'.

Or were I in the wildest waste
  Of earth and air, of earth and air,
The desert were a Paradise,
  If thou wert there, if thou wert there.
Or were I Monarch o' the globe,
  Wi' thee to reign, wi' thee to reign,
The only jewel in my crown
  Wad be my Queen, wad be my Queen.

[1] Shelter.

TIME, YOU OLD GYPSY MAN

By Ralph Hodgson

Time, you old gypsy man,
Will you not stay,
Put up your caravan
Just for one day?

All things I'll give you
Will you be my guest,
Bells for your jennet
Of silver the best,
Goldsmiths shall beat you
A great golden ring,
Peacocks shall bow to you,
Little boys sing,
Oh, and sweet girls will
Festoon you with may.
Time, you old gypsy,
Why hasten away?

Last week in Babylon,
Last night in Rome,
Morning, and in the crush
Under Paul's dome;
Under Paul's dial
You tighten your rein—
Only a moment,
And off once again;
Off to some city
Now blind in the womb,
Off to another
Ere that's in the tomb.

Time, you old gypsy man,
Will you not stay,
Put up your caravan
Just for one day?

TARANTELLA

By Hilaire Belloc

Do you remember an Inn, Miranda?
Do you remember an Inn?
And the tedding and the spreading
Of the straw for a bedding,
And the fleas that tease in the High Pyrenees,
And the wine that tasted of the tar?
And the cheers and the jeers of the young muleteers
(Under the dark of the vine verandah)?
Do you remember an Inn, Miranda,
Do you remember an Inn?
And the cheers and the jeers of the young muleteers
Who hadn't got a penny,
And who weren't paying any,
And the hammer at the doors and the Din?
And the Hip! Hop! Hap!
Of the clap
Of the hands to the twirl and the swirl
Of the girl gone chancing,
Glancing,
Dancing,
Backing and advancing,
Snapping of the clapper to the spin
Out and in—
And the Ting, Tong, Tang of the guitar!
Do you remember an Inn,
Miranda?
Do you remember an Inn?
    Never more;
    Miranda,
    Never more.
    Only the high peaks hoar:
    And Aragon a torrent at the door.
    No sound
    In the walls of the Halls where falls
    The tread
    Of the feet of the dead to the ground.
    No sound:
    Only the boom
    Of the far Waterfall like Doom.

ROMANCE

By Walter J. Turner

When I was but thirteen or so
  I went into a golden land,
Chimborazo, Cotopaxi
  Took me by the hand.

My father died, my brother too,
  They passed like fleeting dreams,
I stood where Popocatepetl
  In the sunlight gleams.

I dimly heard the master's voice
  And boys far-off at play,
Chimborazo, Cotopaxi
  Had stolen me away.

I walked in a great golden dream
  The town streets, to and fro—
Shining Popocatepetl
  Gleamed with his cap of snow.

I walked home with a gold dark boy
  And never a word I'd say,
Chimborazo, Cotopaxi
  Had taken my breath away:

I gazed entranced upon his face
  Fairer than any flower—
O shining Popocatepetl,
  It was thy magic hour:

The houses, people, traffic seemed
  Thin fading dreams by day,
Chimborazo, Cotopaxi,
  They had stolen my soul away!

ARABIA

By Walter de la Mare

Far are the shades of Arabia,
  Where the Princes ride at noon,
'Mid the verdurous vales and thickets,
  Under the ghost of the moon;

And so dark is that vaulted purple
Flowers in the forest rise
And toss into blossom 'gainst the phantom stars
Pale in the noonday skies.

Sweet is the music of Arabia
In my heart, when out of dreams
I still in the thick clear mirk of dawn
Descry her gliding streams;
Hear her strange lutes on the green banks
Ring loud with the grief and delight
Of the dim-silked, dark-haired Musicians
In the brooding silence of night.

They haunt me—her lutes and her forests;
No beauty on earth I see
But shadowed with that dream recalls
Her loveliness to me:
Still eyes look coldly upon me,
Cold voices whisper and say—
"He is crazed with the spell of far Arabia,
They have stolen his wits away."

THE OUTLAW

By Sir Walter Scott

O, Brignall banks are wild and fair,
And Greta woods are green,
And you may gather garlands there,
Would grace a summer queen.
And as I rode by Dalton Hall
Beneath the turrets high,
A Maiden on the castle wall
Was singing merrily—
"O, Brignall banks are fresh and fair,
And Greta woods are green;
I'd rather rove with Edmund there
Than reign our English queen."

—"If, Maiden, thou wouldst wend with me,
To leave both tower and town,
Thou first must guess what life lead we,
That dwell by dale and down?

And if thou canst that riddle read,
  As read full well you may,
Then to the greenwood shalt thou speed
  As blithe as Queen of May."
Yet sung she, "Brignall banks are fair,
  And Greta woods are green;
I'd rather rove with Edmund there,
  Than reign our English queen.

"I read you by your bugle horn
  And by your palfrey good,
I read you for a Ranger sworn,
  To keep the king's greenwood."
—"A Ranger, lady, winds his horn,
  And 'tis at peep of light;
His blast is heard at merry morn,
  And mine at dead of night."
Yet sung she, "Brignall banks are fair,
  And Greta woods are gay;
I would I were with Edmund there,
  To reign his Queen of May!

"With burnish'd brand and musketoon,
  So gallantly you come,
I read you for a bold dragoon
  That lists the tuck of drum."
—"I list no more the tuck of drum,
  No more the trumpet hear;
But when the beetle sounds his hum,
  My comrades take the spear.
And O! though Brignall banks be fair
  And Greta woods be gay,
Yet mickle must the maiden dare,
  Would reign my Queen of May!

"Maiden! a nameless life I lead,
  A nameless death I'll die!
The fiend, whose lantern lights the mead
  Were better mate than I!
And when I'm with my comrades met
  Beneath the greenwood bough,
What once we were we all forget,
  Nor think what we are now."

Chorus

"Yet Brignall banks are fresh and fair,
And Greta woods are green,
And you may gather garlands there
Would grace a summer queen."

SMUGGLERS' SONG

By Rudyard Kipling

If you wake at midnight, and hear a horse's feet,
Don't go drawing back the blind, or looking in the street,
Them that ask no questions isn't told a lie.
Watch the wall, my darling, while the Gentlemen go by!
Five and twenty ponies,
Trotting through the dark—
Brandy for the Parson,
'Baccy for the Clerk;
Laces for a lady, letters for a spy.
And watch the wall, my darling, while the Gentlemen go by!

Running round the woodlump if you chance to find
Little barrels, roped and tarred, all full of brandy-wine,
Don't you shout to come and look, nor use 'em for your play.
Put the brushwood back again—and they'll be gone next day!

If you see the stable-door setting open wide;
If you see a tired horse lying down inside;
If your mother mends a coat cut about and tore;
If the lining's wet and warm—don't you ask no more!

If you meet King George's men, dressed in blue and red,
You be careful what you say, and mindful what is said.
If they call you "pretty maid," and chuck you 'neath the chin,
Don't you tell where no one is, nor yet where no one's been!

Knocks and footsteps round the house—whistles after dark—
You've no call for running out till the house-dogs bark.
Trusty's here, and Pincher's here, and see how dumb they lie—
They don't fret to follow when the Gentlemen go by!

If you do as you've been told, likely there's a chance,
You'll be give a dainty doll, all the way from France,

With a cap of Valenciennes, and a velvet hood—
A present from the Gentlemen, along o' being good!
Five and twenty ponies,
Trotting through the dark—
Brandy for the Parson,
'Baccy for the Clerk.
Them that ask no questions isn't told a lie—
Watch the wall, my darling, while the Gentlemen go by!

THE WRAGGLE TAGGLE GYPSIES

Anonymous

There were three gypsies a-come to my door,
And down stairs ran this a-lady, O!
One sang high, and another sang low,
And the other sang, Bonny, bonny Biscay, O!

Then she pulled off her silk-finished gown
And put on hose of leather, O!
The ragged, ragged rags about our door—
She's gone with the wraggle taggle gypsies, O!

It was late last night, when my lord came home,
Enquiring for his a-lady, O!
The servants said, on every hand:
"She's gone with the wraggle taggle gypsies, O!"

"O saddle to me my milk-white steed,
Go and fetch me my pony, O!
That I may ride and seek my bride,
Who is gone with the wraggle taggle gypsies, O!"

O he rode high and he rode low,
He rode through woods and copses too,
Until he came to an open field,
And there he espied his a-lady, O!

"What makes you leave your house and land?
What makes you leave your money, O?
What makes you leave your new-wedded lord;
To go with the wraggle taggle gypsies, O!"

"What care I for my house and my land?
What care I for my money, O?
What care I for my new-wedded lord?
I'm off with the wraggle taggle gypsies, O!"

"Last night you slept on a goose-feather bed,
With the sheet turned down so bravely, O!
And tonight you'll sleep in a cold open field,
Along with the wraggle taggle gypsies, O!"

"What care I for a goose-feather bed,
With the sheet turned down so bravely, O?
For tonight I shall sleep in a cold open field,
Along with the wraggle taggle gypsies, O!"

TOM O'BEDLAM

Anonymous

The moon's my constant mistress,
And the lovely owl my marrow;
The flaming drake,
And the night-crow, make
Me music to my sorrow.

I know more than Apollo;
For oft, when he lies sleeping,
I behold the stars
At mortal wars,
And the rounded welkin weeping.

The moon embraces her shepherd,
And the Queen of Love her warrior;
While the first does horn
The stars of the morn,
And the next the heavenly farrier.

With a heart of furious fancies,
Whereof I am commander:
With a burning spear,
And a horse of air,
To the wilderness I wander;

With a knight of ghosts and shadows,
I summoned am to Tourney:
Ten leagues beyond
The wide world's end;
Methinks it is no journey.

TEWKESBURY ROAD

By John Masefield

It is good to be out on the road, and going one knows not where,
Going through meadow and village, one knows not whither nor why;
Through the gray light drift of the dust, in the keen cool rush of the air,
Under the flying white clouds, and the broad blue lift of the sky;

And to halt at the chattering brook, in the tall green fern at the brink
Where the harebell grows, and the gorse, and the fox-gloves purple and white;
Where the shy-eyed delicate deer troop down to the pools to drink,
When the stars are mellow and large at the coming on of the night.

O! to feel the warmth of the rain, and the homely smell of the earth,
Is a tune for the blood to jig to, a joy past power of words;
And the blessed green comely meadows seem all a-ripple with mirth
At the lilt of the shifting feet, and the dear wild cry of the birds.

IF ONCE YOU HAVE SLEPT ON AN ISLAND

By Rachel Field

If once you have slept on an island
You'll never be quite the same;
You may look as you look the day before
And go by the same old name,

You may bustle about in street and shop;
  You may sit at home and sew,
But you'll see blue water and wheeling gulls
  Wherever your feet may go.

You may chat with the neighbors of this and that
  And close to your fire keep,
But you'll hear ship whistle and lighthouse bell
  And tides beat through your sleep.

Oh, you won't know why, and you can't say how
  Such change upon you came,
But—once you have slept on an island
  You'll never be quite the same!

THE SEA GIPSY

By Richard Hovey

I am fevered with the sunset,
I am fretful with the bay,
For the wander-thirst is on me
And my soul is in Cathay.

There's a schooner in the offing,
With her topsails shot with fire,
And my heart has gone aboard her
For the Islands of Desire.

I must forth again tomorrow!
With the sunset I must be
Hull down on the trail of rapture
In the wonder of the Sea.

SEA FEVER

By John Masefield

I must go down to the seas again, to the lonely sea and the sky,
And all I ask is a tall ship and a star to steer her by;
And the wheel's kick and the wind's song and the white sail's
    shaking,
And a gray mist on the sea's face, and a gray dawn breaking.

I must go down to the seas again, for the call of the running tide
Is a wild call and a clear call that may not be denied;
And all I ask is a windy day with the white clouds flying,
And the flung spray and the blown spume, and the sea-gulls crying.

I must go down to the seas again, to the vagrant gipsy life,
To the gull's way and the whale's way where the wind's like a
whetted knife;
And all I ask is a merry yarn from a laughing fellow-rover,
And quiet sleep and a sweet dream when the long trick's over.

EEL-GRASS

By Edna St. Vincent Millay

No matter what I say,
All that I really love
Is the rain that flattens on the bay,
And the eel-grass in the cove;
The jingle-shells that lie and bleach
At the tide-line, and the trace
Of higher tides along the beach:
Nothing in this place.

A VISIT FROM THE SEA

By Robert Louis Stevenson

Far from the loud sea beaches
Where he goes fishing and crying,
Here in the inland garden
Why is the sea-gull flying?

Here are no fish to dive for;
Here is the corn and lea;
Here are the green trees rustling.
Hie away home to sea!

Fresh is the river water
And quiet among the rushes;
This is no home for the sea-gull
But for the rooks and thrushes.

Pity the bird that has wandered!
  Pity the sailor ashore!
Hurry him home to the ocean,
  Let him come here no more!

High on the sea-cliff ledges
  The white gulls are trooping and crying,
Here among rooks and roses,
  Why is the sea-gull flying?

THE NORTHERN SEAS

By William Howitt

Up! Up! let us a voyage take;
  Why sit we here at ease?
Find us a vessel tight and snug,
  Bound for the Northern Seas.

I long to see the Northern Lights,
  With their rushing splendors, fly,
Like living things, with flaming wings,
  Wide o'er the wondrous sky.

I long to see those icebergs vast,
  With heads all crowned with snow;
Whose green roots sleep in the awful deep,
  Two hundred fathoms low.

I long to hear the thundering crash
  Of their terrific fall;
And the echoes from a thousand cliffs,
  Like lonely voices call.

There shall we see the fierce white bear,
  The sleepy seals aground,
And the spouting whales that to and fro
  Sail with a dreary sound.

There may we tread on depths of ice,
  That the hairy mammoth hide;
Perfect as when, in times of old,
  The mighty creature died.

And while the unsetting sun shines on
Through the still heaven's deep blue,
We'll traverse the azure waves, the herds
Of the dread sea-horse to view.

We'll pass the shores of solemn pine,
Where wolves and black bears prowl,
And away to the rocky isles of mist
To rouse the northern fowl.

Up there shall start ten thousand wings,
With a rushing, whistling din;
Up shall the auk and fulmar start—
All but the fat penguin.

And there, in the wastes of the silent sky,
With the silent earth below,
We shall see far off to his lonely rock
The lonely eagle go.

THE SAILOR'S CONSOLATION

By Charles Dibdin

One night came on a hurricane,
The sea was mountains rolling,
When Barney Buntline turned his quid,
And said to Billy Bowling:

"A strong nor'wester's blowing, Bill—
Hark! don't ye hear it roar now?
Lord help 'em! how I pities all
Unhappy folks on shore now!

"Foolhardy chaps who live in town—
What danger they are all in,
And now are quaking in their beds,
For fear the roof should fall in.

"Poor creatures! how they envies us,
And wishes, I've a notion,
For our good luck, in such a storm,
To be upon the ocean.

"Then as to them kept out all day
  On business from their houses,
And late at night are walking home
  To cheer their babes and spouses,

"While you and I upon the deck
  Are comfortably lying,
My eyes! what tiles and chimney pots
  About their heads are flying!

"And often have we seen or heard
  How men are killed or undone
By overturns in carriages
  And thieves and fires in London;

"We've heard what risks all landsmen run
  From noblemen to tailors,
So, Billy, let's thank Providence
  That you and I are sailors."

THE BELL BUOY

By Rudyard Kipling

They christened my brother of old—
  And a saintly name he bears—
They gave him his place to hold
  At the head of the belfry-stairs,
  Where the minster-towers stand
And the breeding kestrels cry.
  Would I change with my brother a league inland!
(Shoal! 'Ware shoal!) Not I!

In the flush of the hot June prime,
  O'er sleek flood-tides afire,
I hear him hurry the chime
  To the bidding of checked Desire;
  Till the sweated ringers tire
And the wild bob-majors die.
  Could I wait for my turn in the godly choir?
(Shoal! 'Ware shoal!) Not I!

When the smoking scud is blown—
  When the greasy wind-rack lowers—
Apart and at peace and alone,

He counts the changeless hours.
He wars with darkling Powers
(I war with a darkling sea);
Would he stoop to my work in the gusty mirk?
(Shoal! 'Ware shoal!) Not he!

There was never a priest to pray,
There was never a hand to toll,
When they made me guard of the bay,
And moored me over the shoal.
I rock, I reel, and I roll—
My four great hammers ply—
Could I speak or be still at the Church's will?
(Shoal! 'Ware shoal!) Not I!

The landward marks have failed,
The fog-bank glides unguessed,
The seaward lights are veiled,
The spent deep feigns her rest:
But my ear is laid to her breast,
I lift to the swell—I cry!
Could I wait in sloth on the Church's oath?
(Shoal! 'Ware shoal!) Not I!

At the careless end of night
I thrill to the nearing screw;
I turn in the clearing light
And I call to the drowsy crew;
And the mud boils foul and blue
As the blind bow backs away.
Will they give me their thanks if they clear the banks?
(Shoal! 'Ware shoal!) Not they!

The beach-pools cake and skim,
The bursting spray-heads freeze,
I gather on crown and rim
The gray, grained ice of the seas,
Where sheathed from bitt to trees,
The plunging colliers lie.
Would I barter my place for the Church's grace?
(Shoal! 'Ware shoal!) Not I!

Through the blur of the whirling snow,
  Or the black of the inky sleet,
The lanterns gather and grow,
  And I look for the homeward fleet.
  Rattle of block and sheet—
"Ready about—stand by!"
  Shall I ask them a fee ere they fetch the quay?
(Shoal! 'Ware shoal!) Not I!

I dip and I surge and I swing
  In the rip of the racing tide,
By the gates of doom I sing,
  On the horns of death I ride.
  A ship-length overside,
Between the course and the sand,
  Fretted and bound I bide
Peril whereof I cry.
Would I change with my brother a league inland?
(Shoal! 'Ware shoal!) Not I!

A SEA SONG

By Allan Cunningham

A wet sheet and a flowing sea,
  A wind that follows fast,
And fills the white and rustling sail
  And bends the gallant mast;
And bends the gallant mast, my boys,
  While, like the eagle free,
Away the good ship flies, and leaves
  Old England on the lee.

"O for a soft and gentle wind!"
  I heard a fair one cry;
But give to me the snoring breeze
  And white waves heaving high;
And white waves heaving high, my lads,
  The good ship tight and free—
The world of waters is our home,
  And merry men are we.

There's tempest in yon hornèd moon,
And lightning in yon cloud;
But hark the music, mariners!
The wind is piping loud;
The wind is piping loud, my boys,
The lightning flashes free,
While the hollow oak our palace is,
Our heritage the sea.

MESSMATES

By Henry Newbolt

He gave us all a good-bye cheerily
At the first dawn of day;
We dropped him down the side full drearily
When the light died away.
It's a dead dark watch that he's a-keeping there,
And a long, long night that lags a-creeping there,
Where the Trades and the tides roll over him.
And the great ships go by.

He's there alone with green seas rocking him
For a thousand miles round;
He's there along with dumb things mocking him,
And we're homeward bound.
It's a long lone watch that he's a-keeping there,
And a dead cold night that lags a-creeping there,
While the months and the years roll over him
And the great ships go by.

I wonder if the tramps come near enough
As they thrash to and fro,
And the battle-ships' bells ring clear enough
To be heard down below;
If through all the lone watch that he's a-keeping there,
And the long, cold night that lags a-creeping there,
The voices of the sailor-men shall comfort him
When the great ships go by.

DRAKE'S DRUM

By Henry Newbolt

Drake he's in his hammock an' a thousand mile away,
(Capten, art tha sleepin' there below?)
Slung between the round shot in Nombre Dios Bay,
An' dreamin' arl the time o' Plymouth Hoe.
Yarnder lumes the island, yarnder lie the ships,
Wi' sailor lads a-dancin' heel-an'-toe,
An' the shore-lights flashin', an' the night-tide dashin'
He sees et arl so plainly as he saw et long ago.

Drake he was a Devon man, an' ruled the Devon seas,
(Capten, art tha sleepin' there below?)
Rovin' tho' his death fell, he went wi' heart at ease,
An' dreamin' arl the time o' Plymouth Hoe,
"Take my drum to England, hang et by the shore,
Strike et when your powder's runnin' low;
If the Dons sight Devon, I'll quit the port o' Heaven,
An' drum them up the Channel as we drummed them long ago."

Drake he's in his hammock till the great Armadas come,
(Capten, art tha sleepin' there below?)
Slung atween the round shot, listenin' for the drum,
An' dreamin' arl the time o' Plymouth Hoe.
Call him on the deep sea, call him up the Sound,
Call him when ye sail to meet the foe;
Where the old trade's plyin' an' the old flag's flyin',
They shall find him, ware an' wakin', as they found him long ago!

THE OLD SHIPS

By James E. Flecker

I have seen old ships sail like swans asleep
Beyond the village which men still call Tyre,
With leaden age o'ercargoed, dipping deep
For Famagusta and the hidden sun
That rings black Cyprus with a lake of fire;
And all those ships were certainly so old—
Who knows how oft with squat and noisy gun,
Questing brown slaves or Syrian oranges,

The pirate Genoese
Hell-raked them till they rolled
Blood, water, fruit and corpses up the hold.
But now through friendly seas they softly run,
Painted the mid-sea blue or shore-sea green,
Still patterned with the vine and grapes in gold.

But I have seen,
Pointing her shapely shadows from the dawn
An image tumbled on a rose-swept bay,
A drowsy ship of some yet older day;
And, wonder's breath indrawn,
Thought I—who knows—who knows—but in that same
(Fished up beyond Aeaea, patched up new
—Stern painted brighter blue—)
That talkative, bald-headed seaman came
(Twelve patient comrades sweating at the oar)
From Troy's doom-crimson shore,
And with great lies about his wooden horse
Set the crew laughing, and forgot his course.

It was so old a ship—who knows, who knows?
—And yet so beautiful, I watched in vain
To see the mast burst open with a rose,
And the whole deck put on its leaves again.

REQUIEM

By Robert Louis Stevenson

Under the wide and starry sky,
Dig the grave and let me lie.
Glad did I live and gladly die,
  And laid me down with a will.

This be the verse you grave for me:
Here he lies where he longed to be,
Home is the sailor, home from the sea,
  And the hunter home from the hill.

Looking Forward

ORPHEUS WITH HIS LUTE

By William Shakespeare

Orpheus with his lute made trees,
And the mountain tops that freeze,
  Bow themselves when he did sing:
To his music, plants and flowers
Ever sprung; as sun and showers
  There had made a lasting spring.

Everything that heard him play,
Even the billows of the sea,
  Hung their heads, and then lay by.
In sweet music is such art,
Killing care and grief of heart
  Fall asleep, or, hearing, die.

HARK! HARK! THE LARK!

By William Shakespeare

Hark! hark! the lark at heaven's gate sings,
And Phoebus 'gins arise,
His steeds to water at those springs
On chaliced flowers that lies;
And winking Mary-buds begin
To ope their golden eyes;
With everything that pretty bin,
My lady sweet, arise:
Arise, arise.

FIDELE

By William Shakespeare

Fear no more the heat o' the sun
Nor the furious winter's rages;
Thou thy worldly task hast done,
Home art gone and ta'en thy wages:
Golden lads and girls all must,
As chimney-sweepers, come to dust.

Fear no more the frown o' the great,
Thou art past the tyrant's stroke;
Care no more to clothe, and eat;
To thee the reed is as the oak:
The scepter, learning, physic, must
All follow this, and come to dust.

Fear no more the lightning flash,
Nor the all-dreaded thunder-stone;
Fear not slander, censure rash;
Thou hast finish'd joy and moan:
All lovers young, all lovers must
Consign to thee, and come to dust.

JOG ON, JOG ON

By William Shakespeare

Jog on, jog on, the footpath way,
And merrily hent the stile-a;
A merry heart goes all the day,
Your sad tires in a mile-a.

CARDINAL WOLSEY'S SPEECH TO CROMWELL

By William Shakespeare

Cromwell, I did not think to shed a tear
In all my miseries; but thou hast forced me,
Out of thy honest truth, to play the woman.
Let's dry our eyes: and thus far hear me, Cromwell;
And—when I am forgotten, as I shall be,
And sleep in dull cold marble, where no mention
Of me more must be heard of—say I taught thee;
Say Wolsey—that once trod the ways of glory,
And sounded all the depths and shoals of honor—
Found thee a way, out of his wreck, to rise in;
A sure and safe one, though thy master missed it.
Mark but my fall, and that that ruined me.
Cromwell, I charge thee, fling away ambition:
By that sin fell the angels; how can man, then,
The image of his Maker, hope to win by't?
Love thyself last: cherish those hearts that hate thee:
Corruption wins not more than honesty.
Still in thy right hand carry gentle peace,
To silence envious tongues. Be just, and fear not;
Let all the ends thou aim'st at be thy country's,
Thy God's, and truth's; then if thou fall'st, O Cromwell!
Thou fall'st a blessed martyr. Serve the king;
And—pr'ythee, lead me in:
There take an inventory of all I have,
To the last penny; 'tis the king's; my robe,
And my integrity to heaven, is all
I dare now call mine own. O Cromwell, Cromwell!
Had I but served my God with half the zeal
I served my king, he would not in mine age
Have left me naked to mine enemies!

SHALL I COMPARE THEE TO A SUMMER'S DAY?

By William Shakespeare

Shall I compare thee to a summer's day?
Thou art more lovely and more temperate:
Rough winds do shake the darling buds of May,
And summer's lease hath all too short a date:
Sometime too hot the eye of heaven shines,
And often is his gold complexion dimmed:
And every fair from fair sometime declines,
By chance, or nature's changing course, untrimmed.
But thy eternal summer shall not fade,
Nor lose possession of that fair thou ow'st,
Nor shall death brag thou wander'st in his shade,
When in eternal lines to time thou grow'st;
So long as men can breathe, or eyes can see,
So long lives this, and this gives life to thee.

INTEGER VITAE

By Thomas Campion

The man of life upright,
Whose guiltless heart is free
From all dishonest deeds,
Or thought of vanity;

The man whose silent days
In harmless joys are spent,
Whom hopes cannot delude,
Nor sorrow discontent;

That man needs neither towers
Nor armor for defense,
Nor secret vaults to fly
From thunder's violence;

He only can behold
With unaffrighted eyes
The horrors of the deep
And terrors of the skies;

Thus, scorning all the cares
  That fate or fortune brings,
He makes the heaven his book,
  His wisdom heavenly things;

Good thoughts his only friends,
  His wealth a well-spent age,
The earth his sober inn
  And quiet pilgrimage.

SWEET CONTENT

By Thomas Dekker

Art thou poor, yet hast thou golden slumbers?
    O sweet content!
Art thou rich, yet is thy mind perplexed?
    O punishment!
Dost thou laugh to see how fools are vexed
To add to golden numbers, golden numbers?
O sweet content! O sweet, O sweet content!
  Work apace, apace, apace, apace;
  Honest labor bears a lovely face;
 Then hey nonny nonny, hey nonny nonny!

Can'st drink the waters of the crispèd spring?
    O sweet content!
Swimm'st thou in wealth, yet sink'st in thine own tears?
    O punishment!
Then he that patiently want's burden bears
No burden bears, but is a king, a king!
O sweet content! O sweet, O sweet content!
  Work apace, apace, apace, apace;
  Honest labor bears a lovely face;
 Then hey nonny nonny, hey nonny nonny!

FOLDING THE FLOCKS

By John Fletcher

Shepherds all, and Maidens fair,
Fold your Flocks up; for the Air
'Gins to thicken, and the Sun
Already his great course hath run.
See the Dew-Drops how they kiss
Every little Flower that is:
Hanging on their Velvet Heads,
Like a Rope of Crystal Beads.
See the heavy Clouds low falling,
And bright Hesperus down calling
The dead Night from under Ground,
At whose rising, Mists unsound,
Damps and Vapors fly apace,
Hov'ring o'er the smiling Face
Of these Pastures, where they come,
Striking dead both Bud and Bloom;

Therefore, from such Danger, lock
Ev'ry one his lovèd Flock;
And let your Dogs lie loose without,
Lest the Wolf come as a scout
From the Mountain, and, ere day,
Bear a Lamb or Kid away;
Or the crafty, thievish Fox
Break upon your simple Flocks:
To secure yourself from these
Be not too secure in ease;
Let one Eye his watches keep,
While the other Eye doth sleep;
So shall you good Shepherds prove,
And deserve your Master's love.
Now, good night! may Sweetest Slumbers
And soft Silence fall in numbers
On your Eye-lids: So farewell;
Thus I end my Evening knell.

TO MEADOWS

By Robert Herrick

Ye have been fresh and green;
  Ye have been fill'd with flowers;
And ye the walks have been
  Where maids have spent their hours.

Ye have beheld how they
  With wicker arks did come
To kiss and bear away
  The richer cowslips home.

Ye've heard them sweetly sing,
  And seen them in a round:
Each virgin like a Spring,
  With honeysuckles crown'd.

But now we see none here
  Whose silv'ry feet did tread
And with dishevelled hair
  Adorn'd this smoother mead.

Like unthrifts, having spent
  Your stock, and needy grown,
Ye're left here to lament
  Your poor estates, alone.

TO DAFFODILS

By Robert Herrick

Fair daffodils, we weep to see
  You haste away so soon;
As yet the early-rising sun
  Has not attain'd his noon.
      Stay, stay
  Until the hasting day
      Has run
  But to the evensong;
And, having pray'd together, we
  Will go with you along.

We have short time to stay, as you,
  We have as short a spring;
As quick a growth to meet decay,
  As you, or anything.
    We die
  As your hours do, and dry
    Away
  Like to the summer's rain;
Or as the pearls of morning's dew,
  Ne'er to be found again.

GOING A-MAYING

By Robert Herrick

Get up, get up for shame! The blooming morn
Upon her wings presents the god unshorn:
  See how Aurora throws her fair
  Fresh-quilted colors through the air:
  Get up, sweet-slug-a-bed, and see
  The dew-bespangled herb and tree!
Each flower has wept and bowed toward the east,
Above an hour since, yet you not drest,
  Nay, not so much as out of bed?
  When all the birds have matins said,
  And sung their thankful hymns, 'tis sin,
  Nay, profanation, to keep in,
Whenas, a thousand virgins on this day,
Spring, sooner than the lark, to fetch in May.

Rise, and put on your foliage, and be seen
To come forth, like the Spring-time fresh and green,
  And sweet as Flora. Take no care
  For jewels for your gown or hair:
  Fear not; the leaves will strew
  Gems in abundance upon you:
Besides, the childhood of the day has kept,
Against you come, some orient pearls unwept.
  Come, and receive them while the light
  Hangs on the dew-locks of the night.
  And Titan on the eastern hill
  Retires himself, or else stands still
Till you come forth! Wash, dress, be brief in praying:
Few beads are best, when once we go a-Maying.

Come, my Corinna, come; and coming, mark
How each field turns a street, each street a park,
  Made green, and trimmed with trees; see how
  Devotion gives each house a bough
  Or branch! each porch, each door, ere this,
  An ark, a tabernacle is,
Made up of white-thorn neatly interwove,
As if here were those cooler shades of love.
  Can such delights be in the street,
  And open fields, and we not see't?
  Come, we'll abroad: and let's obey
  The proclamations made for May.
And sin no more, as we have done, by staying,
But, my Corinna, come, let's go a-Maying.

There's not a budding boy or girl, this day,
But is got up, and gone to bring in May.
  A deal of youth, ere this is come
  Back and with white-thorn laden home.
  Some have despatched their cakes and cream,
  Before that we have left to dream:
And some have wept, and woo'd, and plighted troth,
And chose their priest, ere we can cast off sloth:
  Many a green-gown has been given,
  Many a kiss, both odd and even:
  Many a glance, too, has been sent
  From out the eye, love's firmament:
Many a jest told of the keys betraying
This night, and locks picked: yet we're not a-Maying.

Come, let us go, while we are in our prime,
And take the harmless folly of the time!
  We shall grow old apace, and die
  Before we know our liberty.
  Our life is short, and our days run
  As fast away as does the sun.
And as a vapor, or a drop of rain,
Once lost, can ne'er be found again.
  So when you or I are made
  A fable, song, or fleeting shade,
All love, all liking, all delight,
  Lies drowned with us in endless night.
Then, while time serves, and we are but decaying,
Come, my Corinna, come, let's go a-Maying.

DEATH THE LEVELER

By James Shirley

The glories of our blood and state
  Are shadows, not substantial things;
There is no armor against fate;
  Death lays his icy hand on kings:
      Scepter and Crown
      Must tumble down,
And in the dust be equal made
With the poor crooked scythe and spade.

Some men with swords may reap the field,
  And plant fresh laurels where they kill;
But their strong nerves at last must yield;
  They tame but one another still:
      Early or late
      They stoop to fate,
And must give up their murmuring breath,
When they, pale captives, creep to death.

The garlands wither on your brow,
  Then boast no more your mighty deeds;
Upon Death's purple altar now,
  See where the victor-victim bleeds:
      Your heads must come
      To the cold tomb,
Only the actions of the just
Smell sweet, and blossom in their dust.

SONG: ON MAY MORNING

By John Milton

Now the bright morning-star, Day's harbinger,
Comes dancing from the East, and leads with her
The flowery May, who from her green lap throws
The yellow cowslip and the pale primrose.
Hail, bounteous May, that dost inspire
Mirth, and youth, and warm desire!
Woods and groves are of thy dressing;
Hill and dale doth boast thy blessing.
Thus we salute thee with our early song,
And welcome thee, and wish thee long.

EVENING IN PARADISE

By John Milton

Now came still Evening on, and Twilight gray
Had in her sober livery all things clad;
Silence accompanied; for beast and bird—
They to their grassy couch, these to their nests,
Were slunk, all but the wakeful nightingale;
She all night long her amorous descant sung;
Silence was pleased: now glowed the firmament
With living sapphires: Hesperus, that led
The starry host, rode brightest, till the Moon,
Rising in clouded majesty, at length
Apparent queen, unveiled her peerless light,
And o'er the dark her silver mantle threw.

ON HIS BLINDNESS

By John Milton

When I consider how my light is spent
  Ere half my days, in this dark world and wide;
  And that one talent which is death to hide,
  Lodged with me useless, though my soul more bent
To serve therewith my Maker, and present
  My true account, lest he returning chide;
  Doth God exact day-labor, light denied,
  I fondly ask? But Patience, to prevent
That murmur, soon replies, God doth not need
  Either man's work or his own gifts; who best
  Bear his mild yoke, they serve him best: his state
Is kingly; thousands at his bidding speed,
  And post o'er land and ocean without rest;
  They also serve who only stand and wait.

SONG OF THE EMIGRANTS IN BERMUDA

By Andrew Marvell

Where the remote Bermudas ride
In the ocean's bosom unespied,
From a small boat that row'd along
The listening winds received this song:

"What should we do but sing His praise
That led us through the watery maze
Unto an isle so long unknown,
And yet far kinder than our own?
Where He the huge sea-monster wracks,
That lift the deep upon their backs,
He lands us on a grassy stage,
Safe from the storms, and prelates' rage:
He gave us this eternal Spring
Which here enamels everything,
And sends the fowls to us in care
On daily visits through the air.
He hangs in shades the orange bright
Like golden lamps in a green night,
And does in the pomegranates close
Jewels more rich than Ormus shows:
He makes the figs our mouths to meet,
And throws the melons at our feet;
But apples plants of such a price,
No tree could ever bear them twice!
With cedars chosen by His hand
From Lebanon He stores the land;
And makes the hollow seas that roar
Proclaim the ambergris on shore.
He cast (of which we rather boast)
The Gospel's pearl upon our coast;
And in these rocks for us did frame
A temple where to sound His name.
O let our voice His praise exalt
Till it arrives at Heaven's vault,
Which then perhaps rebounding may
Echo beyond the Mexique bay!"

—Thus sung they in the English boat
A holy and a cheerful note:
And all the way, to guide their chime,
With falling oars they kept the time.

DIVINE ODE

By Joseph Addison

The spacious firmament on high,
With all the blue ethereal sky,
And spangled heavens, a shining frame,
Their great Original proclaim:
Th' unwearied Sun from day to day
Does his Creator's power display,
And publishes to every land
The work of an Almighty hand.

Soon as the evening shades prevail,
The moon takes up the wondrous tale,
And nightly to the listening Earth
Repeats the story of her birth:
Whilst all the stars that round her burn,
And all the planets in their turn,
Confirm the tidings as they roll,
And spread the truth from pole to pole.

What though in solemn silence all
Move round the dark terrestrial ball?
What though nor real voice nor sound
Amidst their radiant orbs be found?
In Reason's ear they all rejoice,
And utter forth a glorious voice,
Forever singing as they shine,
"The Hand that made us is divine."

PEACE

By Henry Vaughan

My soul, there is a country
  Afar beyond the stars,
Where stands a wingèd sentry
  And skillful in the wars;
There, above noise and danger,
  Sweet peace sits crowned with smiles,
And one born in a manger
  Commands the beauteous files.

He is thy gracious friend,
  And (O my soul, awake!)
Did in pure love descend,
  To die here for thy sake.
If thou canst get but thither,
  There grows the flower of peace,
The rose that cannot wither,
  Thy fortress, and thy ease.
Leave then thy foolish ranges;
  For none can thee secure,
But one, who never changes,
  Thy God, thy life, thy cure.

THE SHEPHERD BOY SINGS IN THE VALLEY OF HUMILIATION

By John Bunyan

He that is down needs fear no fall,
  He that is low, no pride;
He that is humble ever shall
  Have God to be his guide.

I am content with what I have,
  Little be it or much:
And, Lord, contentment still I crave,
  Because Thou savest such.

Fullness to such a burden is
  That go on pilgrimage:
Here little, and hereafter bliss,
  Is best from age to age.

SOLITUDE

By Alexander Pope

Happy the man, whose wish and care
A few paternal acres bound,
Content to breathe his native air
    In his own ground.

Whose herds with milk, whose fields with bread,
Whose flocks supply him with attire;
Whose trees in summer yield him shade,
    In winter, fire.

Blest, who can unconcern'dly find
Hours, days, and years, slide soft away
In health of body, peace of mind,
Quiet by day;

Sound sleep by night; study and ease
Together mix'd, sweet recreation,
And innocence, which most does please
With meditation.

Thus let me live, unseen, unknown;
Thus unlamented let me die;
Steal from the world, and not a stone
Tell where I lie.

THE SEASONS

By William Blake

To Spring

O thou with dewy locks, who lookest down
Thru the clear windows of the morning, turn
Thine angel eyes upon our western isle,
Which in full choir hails thy approach, O Spring!

The hills tell one another, and the listening
Valleys hear; all our longing eyes are turned
Up to thy bright pavilions: issue forth,
And let thy holy feet visit our clime.

Come o'er the eastern hills, and let our winds
Kiss thy perfumèd garments; let us taste
Thy morn and evening breath; scatter thy pearls
Upon our lovesick land that mourns for thee.

Oh, deck her forth with thy fair fingers; pour
Thy soft kisses on her bosom, and put
Thy golden crown upon her languished head,
Whose modest tresses were bound up for thee!

To Summer

O thou who passest through our valleys in
Thy strength, curb thy fierce steeds, allay the heat
That flames from their large nostrils! Thou, O Summer,
Oft pitches here thy golden tent, and oft
Beneath our oaks has slept, while we beheld
With joy thy ruddy limbs and flourishing hair.

Beneath our thickest shades we oft have heard
Thy voice, when Noon upon her fervid car
Rode o'er the deep of heaven. Beside our springs
Sit down, and in our mossy valleys, on
Some bank beside a river clear, throw thy
Silk draperies off, and rush into the stream!
Our valleys love the Summer in her pride.

Our bards are famed who strike the silver wire:
Our youth are bolder than the southern swains,
Our maidens fairer in the sprightly dance.
We lack not songs, nor instruments of joy,
Nor echoes sweet, nor water clear as heaven,
Nor laurel wreaths against the sultry heat.

To Autumn

O Autumn, laden with fruit, and stained
With the blood of the grape, pass not, but sit
Beneath my shady roof; there thou mayst rest,
And tune thy jolly voice to my fresh pipe,
And all the daughters of the year shall dance!
Sing now the lusty songs of fruits and flowers:

"The narrow bud opens her beauties to
The sun, and love runs in her thrilling veins;
Blossoms hang round the brows of Morning, and
Flourish down the bright cheek of modest Eve,
Till clustering Summer breaks forth into singing,
And feathered clouds strew flowers round her head.

"The Spirits of the Air live on the smells
Of fruit, and Joy, with pinions light, roves round
The gardens, or sits singing in the trees."
Thus sang the jolly Autumn as he sat;
Then rose, girded himself, and o'er the bleak
Hills fled from our sight; but left his golden load.

To Winter

O Winter! bar thine adamantine doors:
The north is thine; there hast thou built thy dark
Deep-founded habitation. Shake not thy roofs,
Nor bend thy pillars with thine iron car.

He hears me not, but o'er the yawning deep
Rides heavy; his storms are unchained, sheathed
In ribbèd steel; I dare not lift mine eyes;
For he hath reared his scepter o'er the world.

Lo! now the direful monster, whose skin clings
To his strong bones, strides o'er the groaning rocks:
He withers all in silence, and in his hand
Unclothes the earth, and freezes up frail life.

He takes his seat upon the cliffs—mariner
Cries in vain. Poor little wretch, that deal'st
With storm!—till heaven smiles, and the monster
Is driven yelling to his caves beneath Mount Hecla.

NIGHT

By William Blake

The sun descending in the west,
The evening star does shine;
The birds are silent in their nest,
And I must seek for mine.
The moon, like a flower
In heaven's high bower,
With silent delight
Sits and smiles on the night.

Farewell, green fields and happy grove,
Where flocks have ta'en delight:
Where lambs have nibbled, silent move
The feet of angels bright;
Unseen they pour blessing
And joy without ceasing
On each bud and blossom,
On each sleeping bosom.

They look in every thoughtless nest
  Where birds are cover'd warm;
They visit caves of every beast,
  To keep them all from harm:
    If they see any weeping
    That should have been sleeping
    They pour sleep on their head,
    And sit down by their bed.

When wolves and tigers howl for prey,
  They pitying stand and weep,
Seeking to drive their thirst away
  And keep them from the sheep.
    But, if they rush dreadful,
    The angels, most heedful,
    Receive each mild spirit,
    New worlds to inherit.

And there the lion's ruddy eyes
  Shall flow with tears of gold:
And pitying the tender cries,
  And walking round the fold:
    Saying, "Wrath by His meekness,
    And, by His health, sickness,
    Are driven away
    From our immortal day.

"And now beside thee, bleating lamb,
  I can lie down and sleep,
Or think of Him who bore thy name,
  Graze after thee, and weep.
    For, wash'd in life's river,
    My bright mane for ever
    Shall shine like the gold
    As I guard o'er the fold."

LUCY

By William Wordsworth

Three years she grew in sun and shower;
Then Nature said, "A lovelier flower
    On earth was never sown;
This child I to myself will take;
She shall be mine, and I will make
    A lady of my own.

"Myself will to my darling be
Both law and impulse: and with me
    The girl, in rock and plain,
In earth and heaven, in glade and bower,
Shall feel an overseeing power
    To kindle or restrain.

"She shall be sportive as the fawn
That wild with glee across the lawn
    Or up the mountain springs;
And hers shall be the breathing balm,
And hers the silence and the calm
    Of mute insensate things.

"The floating clouds their state shall lend
To her; for her the willow bend;
    Nor shall she fail to see
Even in the motions of the storm
Grace that shall mold the maiden's form
    By silent sympathy.

"The stars of midnight shall be dear
To her; and she shall lean her ear
    In many a secret place
Where rivulets dance their wayward round,
And beauty born of murmuring sound
    Shall pass into her face.

"And vital feelings of delight
Shall rear her form to stately height,
    Her virgin bosom swell;
Such thoughts to Lucy I will give
While she and I together live
    Here in this happy dell."

Thus Nature spake—The work was done—
How soon my Lucy's race was run!
She died, and left to me
This heath, this calm and quiet scene;
This memory of what has been,
And never more will be.

DAFFODILS

By William Wordsworth

I wander'd lonely as a cloud
That floats on high o'er vales and hills,
When all at once I saw a crowd,
A host of golden daffodils,
Beside the lake, beneath the trees
Fluttering and dancing in the breeze.

Continuous as the stars that shine
And twinkle on the milky way,
They stretch'd in never-ending line
Along the margin of a bay:
Ten thousand saw I at a glance
Tossing their heads in sprightly dance.

The waves beside them danced, but they
Out-did the sparkling waves in glee:
A poet could not but be gay
In such a jocund company!
I gazed—and gazed—but little thought
What wealth the show to me had brought:

For oft, when on my couch I lie
In vacant or in pensive mood,
They flash upon that inward eye
Which is the bliss of solitude;
And then my heart with pleasure fills,
And dances with the daffodils.

THE SOLITARY REAPER

By William Wordsworth

Behold her, single in the field,
Yon solitary Highland Lass!
Reaping and singing by herself;
Stop here, or gently pass!
Alone she cuts, and binds the grain,
And sings a melancholy strain;
O listen! for the vale profound
Is overflowing with the sound.

No nightingale did every chaunt
More welcome notes to weary bands
Of travelers in some shady haunt,
Among Arabian sands:
A voice so thrilling ne'er was heard
In spring-time from the cuckoo-bird,
Breaking the silence of the seas
Among the farthest Hebrides.

Will no one tell me what she sings?
Perhaps the plaintive numbers flow
For old, unhappy, far-off things,
And battles long ago:
Or is it some more humble lay,
Familiar matter of today?
Some natural sorrow, loss, or pain,
That has been, and may be again?

Whate'er the theme, the maiden sang
As if her song could have no ending;
I saw her singing at her work,
And o'er the sickle bending—
I listened motionless and still,
And, as I mounted up the hill,
The music in my heart I bore,
Long after it was heard no more.

BREATHES THERE THE MAN

By Sir Walter Scott

Breathes there the man, with soul so dead,
Who never to himself hath said,
  This is my own, my native land!
Whose heart hath ne'er within him burned,
As home his footsteps he hath turned
  From wandering on a foreign strand?
If such there breathe, go mark him well:
For him no minstrel raptures swell;
High though his titles, proud his name,
Boundless his wealth as wish can claim;
Despite those titles, power, and pelf,
The wretch, concentered all in self,
Living, shall forfeit fair renown,
And, doubly dying, shall go down
To the vile dust from whence he sprung,
Unwept, unhonored, and unsung.

KUBLA KHAN

By Samuel Taylor Coleridge

In Xanadu did Kubla Khan
A stately pleasure-dome decree:
Where Alph, the sacred river, ran
Through caverns measureless to man
  Down to a sunless sea.
So twice five miles of fertile ground
With walls and towers were girdled round:
And there were gardens bright with sinuous rills
Where blossom'd many an incense-bearing tree;
And here were forests ancient as the hills,
Enfolding sunny spots of greenery.

But oh! that deep romantic chasm which slanted
Down the green hill athwart a cedarn cover!
A savage place! as holy and enchanted
As e'er beneath a waning moon was haunted
By woman wailing for her demon-lover!
And from this chasm, with ceaseless turmoil seething
As if this earth in fast thick pants were breathing,

A mighty fountain momently was forced:
Amid those swift half-intermitted burst
Huge fragments vaulted like rebounding hail,
Or chaffy grain beneath the thresher's flail;
And 'mid these dancing rocks at once and ever
It flung up momently the sacred river.
Five miles meandering with a mazy motion
Through wood and dale the sacred river ran,
Then reach'd the caverns measureless to man,
And sank in tumult to a lifeless ocean:
And 'mid this tumult Kubla heard from far
Ancestral voices prophesying war!

The shadow of the dome of pleasure
Floated midway on the waves;
Where was heard the mingled measure
From the fountain and the caves.
It was a miracle of rare device,
A sunny pleasure-dome with caves of ice!

A damsel with a dulcimer
In a vision once I saw:
It was an Abyssinian maid,
And on her dulcimer she played,
Singing of Mount Abora.
Could I revive within me
Her symphony and song,
To such a deep delight 'twould win me
That with music loud and long,
I would build that dome in air,
That sunny dome! Those caves of ice!
And all who heard should see them there
And all should cry, Beware! Beware!
His flashing eyes, his floating hair!
Weave a circle round him thrice,
And close your eyes with holy dread
For he on honey-dew hath fed,
And drunk the milk of Paradise.

ABOU BEN ADHEM

By Leigh Hunt

Abou Ben Adhem (may his tribe increase!)
Awoke one night from a deep dream of peace,
And saw, within the moonlight in his room,
Making it rich, and like a lily in bloom,
An angel writing in a book of gold:
Exceeding peace had made Ben Adhem bold,
And to the presence in the room he said,
"What writest thou?"—The vision rais'd its head,
And with a look made all of sweet accord,
Answer'd, "The names of those that love the Lord."
"And is mine one?" said Abou. "Nay, not so,"
Replied the angel. Abou spoke more low,
But cheerly still; and said, "I pray thee, then,
Write me as one that loves his fellow men."
The angel wrote, and vanished. The next night
It came again with a great wakening light,
And show'd the names whom love of God had blest,
And lo! Ben Adhem's name led all the rest.

THE CLOUD

By Percy Bysshe Shelley

I bring fresh showers for the thirsting flowers,
  From the seas and the streams;
I bear light shade for the leaves when laid
  In their noon-day dreams.
From my wings are shaken the dews that waken
  The sweet buds every one,
When rocked to rest on their mother's breast,
  As she dances about the sun.
I wield the flail of the lashing hail,
  And whiten the green plains under,
And then again I dissolve it in rain,
  And laugh as I pass in thunder.

I sift the snow on the mountains below,
  And their great pines groan aghast;
And all the night 'tis my pillow white,
  While I sleep in the arms of the blast.

Sublime on the towers of my skiey bowers,
  Lightning my pilot sits,
In a cavern under is fettered the thunder,
  It struggles and howls at fits.

Over earth and ocean, with gentle motion,
  This pilot is guiding me,
Lured by the love of the genii that move
  In the depths of the purple sea;
Over the rills, and the crags, and the hills,
  Over the lakes and the plains,
Wherever he dream, under mountain or stream,
  The Spirit he loves remains;
And I all the while bask in heaven's blue smile,
  Whilst he is dissolving in rains.

The sanguine sunrise, with his meteor eyes,
  And his burning plumes outspread,
Leaps on the back of my sailing rack,
  When the morning star shines dead,
As on the jag of a mountain crag,
  Which an earthquake rocks and swings,
An eagle alit one moment may sit
  In the light of its golden wings.
And when sunset may breathe, from the lit sea beneath,
  Its ardors of rest and of love,
And the crimson pall of eve may fall
  From the depths of heaven above,
With wings folded I rest, on mine airy nest,
  As still as a brooding dove.

That orbèd maiden with white fire laden,
  Whom mortals call the Moon,
Glides glimmering o'er my fleece-like floor,
  By the midnight breezes strewn;
And wherever the beat of her unseen feet,
  Which only the angels hear,
May have broken the woof of my tent's thin roof,
  The Stars peep behind her and peer.
And I laugh to see them whirl and flee,
  Like a swarm of golden bees,

When I widen the rent in my wind-built tent,
  Till the calm rivers, lakes, and seas,
Like strips of the sky fallen thro' me on high,
  Are each paved with the moon and these.

I bind the Sun's throne with a burning zone,
  And the Moon's with a girdle of pearl;
The volcanoes are dim, and the stars reel and swim,
  When the Whirlwinds my banner unfurl.
From cape to cape with a bridge-like shape,
  Over a torrent sea,
Sunbeam-proof, I hang like a roof,
  The mountains its columns be.
The triumphal arch thro' which I march
  With hurricane, fire, and snow,
When the Powers of the air are chained to my chair,
  Is the million-colored bow;
The Sphere-fire above its soft colors wove,
  While the moist Earth was laughing below.

I am the daughter of Earth and Water,
  And the nursling of the Sky;
I pass thro' the pores of the ocean and shores;
  I change, but I cannot die.
For after the rain when with never a stain,
  The pavilion of heaven is bare,
And the winds and sunbeams with their convex gleams,
  Build up the blue dome of air,
I silently laugh at my own cenotaph,
  And out of the caverns of rain,
Like a child from the womb, like a ghost from the tomb,
  I arise and unbuild it again.

TO A SKYLARK

By Percy Bysshe Shelley

Hail to thee, blithe spirit!
  Bird thou never wert—
That from heaven or near it
  Pourest thy full heart
In profuse strains of unpremeditated art.

Higher still and higher
  From the earth thou springest:
Like a cloud of fire,
  The blue deep thou wingest,
And singing still dost soar, and soaring ever singest.

In the golden lightning
  Of the sunken sun,
O'er which clouds are brightening,
  Thou dost float and run,
Like an embodied joy whose race is just begun.

The pale purple even
  Melts around thy flight;
Like a star of heaven
  In the broad daylight,
Thou art unseen, but yet I hear thy shrill delight:

Keen as are the arrows
  Of that silver sphere,
Whose intense lamp narrows
  In the white dawn clear
Until we hardly see, we feel that it is there.

All the earth and air
  With thy voice is loud,
As, when night is bare,
  From one lonely cloud
The moon rains out her beams, and heaven is overflow'd.

What thou art we know not;
  What is most like thee?
From rainbow clouds there flow not
  Drops so bright to see
As from thy presence showers a rain of melody.

Like a poet hidden,
  In the light of thought,
Singing hymns unbidden,
  Till the world is wrought
To sympathy with hopes and fears it heeded not:

Like a high-born maiden
  In a palace tower,
Soothing her love-laden
  Soul in secret hour
With music sweet as love which overflows her bower:

Like a glow-worm golden
  In a dell of dew,
Scattering unbeholden
  Its aërial hue
Among the flowers and grass which screen it from the view:

Like a rose embowered
  In its own green leaves,
By warm winds deflower'd,
  Till the scent it gives
Makes faint with too much sweet these heavy-wingèd thieves.

Sound of vernal showers
  On the twinkling grass,
Rain-awaken'd flowers,
  All that ever was
Joyous and clear and fresh—thy music doth surpass.

Teach us, sprite or bird,
  What sweet thoughts are thine:
I have never heard
  Praise of love or wine
That panted forth a flood of rapture so divine.

Chorus hymeneal
  Or triumphant chaunt,
Match'd with thine, would be all
  But an empty vaunt—
A thing wherein we feel there is some hidden want.

What objects are the fountains
  Of thy happy strain?
What fields, or waves, or mountains?
  What shapes of sky or plain?
What love of thine own kind? What ignorance of pain?

With thy clear keen joyance
  Languor cannot be:
Shadow of annoyance
  Never came near thee:
Thou lovest, but ne'er knew love's sad satiety.

Waking or asleep,
  Thou of death must deem
Things more true and deep
  Than we mortals dream,
Or how could thy notes flow in such a crystal stream?

We look before and after,
  And pine for what is not:
Our sincerest laughter
  With some pain is fraught;
Our sweetest songs are those that tell of saddest thought.

Yet, if we could scorn,
  Hate, and pride, and fear;
If we were things born
  Not to shed a tear,
I know not how thy joy we ever should come near.

Better than all measures
  Of delightful sound,
Better than all treasures
  That in books are found,
Thy skill to poet were, thou scorner of the ground!

Teach me half the gladness
  That thy brain must know,
Such harmonious madness
  From my lips would flow
The world should listen then, as I am listening now!

TO NIGHT

By Percy Bysshe Shelley

Swiftly walk over the western wave,
Spirit of Night!
Out of the misty eastern cave
Where, all the long and lone daylight,
Thou wovest dreams of joy and fear
Which makes thee terrible and dear—
Swift be thy flight!

Wrap thy form in a mantle gray
Star-inwrought!
Blind with thine hair the eyes of day,
Kiss her until she be wearied out:
Then wander o'er city and sea and land,
Touching all with thine opiate wand—
Come, long-sought!

When I arose and saw the dawn,
I sigh'd for thee;
When light rode high, and the dew was gone,
And noon lay heavy on flower and tree,
And the weary Day turn'd to his rest
Lingering like an unloved guest,
I sigh'd for thee.

Thy brother Death came, and cried
Wouldst thou me?
Thy sweet child Sleep, the filmy-eyed,
Murmur'd like a noon-tide bee,
Shall I nestle near thy side?
Wouldst thou me?—And I replied
No, not thee!

Death will come when thou art dead,
Soon, too soon—
Sleep will come when thou art fled;
Of neither would I ask the boon
I ask of thee, belovèd Night—
Swift be thine approaching flight,
Come soon, soon!

TO AUTUMN

By John Keats

Season of mists and mellow fruitfulness!
Close bosom-friend of the maturing sun;
Conspiring with him how to load and bless
With fruit the vines that round the thatch-eaves run;
To bend with apples the mossed cottage-trees,
And fill all fruit with ripeness to the core;
To swell the gourd, and plump the hazel shells
With a sweet kernel; to set budding more,
And still more, later flowers for the bees,
Until they think warm days will never cease,
For Summer has o'erbrimmed their clammy cells.

Who hath not seen thee oft amid thy store?
Sometimes whoever seeks abroad may find
Thee sitting careless on a granary floor,
Thy hair soft-lifted by the winnowing wind;
Or on a half-reaped furrow sound asleep,
Drowsed with the fumes of poppies, while thy hook
Spares the next swath and all its twinèd flowers;
And sometimes like a gleaner thou dost keep
Steady thy laden head across a brook;
Or by a cider-press, with patient look,
Thou watchest the last oozings, hours by hours,

Where are the songs of Spring? Ay, where are they?
Think not of them, thou hast thy music too,
While barrèd clouds bloom the soft-dying day
And touch the stubble-plains with rosy hue;
Then in a wailful choir the small gnats mourn
Among the river shallows, borne aloft
Or sinking as the light wind lives or dies;
And full-grown lambs loud bleat from hilly bourn;
Hedge-crickets sing, and now with treble soft
The redbreast whistles from a garden-croft,
And gathering swallows twitter in the skies.

WINTER

By John Keats

In a drear-nighted December,
Too happy, happy Tree,
Thy branches ne'er remember
Their green felicity:
The north cannot undo them,
With a sleety whistle through them;
Nor frozen thawings glue them
From budding at the prime.

In a drear-nighted December,
Too happy, happy Brook,
Thy bubblings ne'er remember
Apollo's summer look;
But with a sweet forgetting,
They stay their crystal fretting,
Never, never petting
About the frozen time.

Ah! would 'twere so with many
A gentle girl and boy!
But were there ever any
Writh'd not at passèd joy?
To know the change and feel it,
When there is none to heal it,
Nor numbèd sense to steal it,
Was never said in rhyme.

LA BELLE DAME SANS MERCI

By John Keats

Ah! what can ail thee, wretched wight,
  Alone and palely loitering?
The sedge is withered from the lake,
  And no birds sing.

Ah! what can ail thee, wretched wight,
  So haggard and so woe-begone?
The squirrel's granary is full,
  And the harvest's done.

I see a lily on thy brow,
  With anguish moist and fever-dew;
And on thy cheek a fading rose
  Fast withereth too.

"I met a lady in the meads,
  Full beautiful—a fairy's child;
Her hair was long, her foot was light,
  And her eyes were wild.

"I set her on my pacing steed,
  And nothing else saw all day long;
For sideways would she lean and sing
  A fairy's song.

"I made a garland for her head,
  And bracelets too, and fragrant zone;
She looked at me as she did love,
  And made sweet moan.

"She found me roots of relish sweet,
  And honey wild, and manna-dew;
And sure in language strange she said,
  'I love thee true.'

"She took me to her elfin grot,
  And there she gazed and sighèd deep,
And there I shut her wild sad eyes—
  So kissed to sleep.

"And there we slumbered on the moss,
  And there I dreamed—ah! woe betide,
The latest dream I ever dreamed,
  On the cold hill-side.

"I saw pale kings and princes too,
  Pale warriors—death-pale were they all;
Who cried, 'La Belle Dame Sans Merci
  Hath thee in thrall!'

"I saw their starved lips in the gloom,
  With horrid warning gapèd wide;
And I awoke, and found me here
  On the cold hill-side.

"And this is why I sojourn here,
Alone and palely loitering,
Though the sedge is withered from the lake,
And no birds sing."

ODE ON A GRECIAN URN

By John Keats

Thou still unravished bride of quietness,
Thou foster-child of Silence and slow Time,
Sylvan historian, who canst thus express
A flowery tale more sweetly than our rhyme:
What leaf-fringed legend, haunts about thy shape
Of deities or mortals, or of both,
In Tempe or the dales of Arcady?
What men or gods are these? What maidens loth?
What mad pursuit! What struggle to escape?
What pipes and timbrels? What wild ecstasy?

Heard melodies are sweet, but those unheard
Are sweeter; therefore, ye soft pipes, play on;
Not to the sensual ear, but, more endeared,
Pipe to the spirit ditties of no tone:
Fair youth, beneath the trees, thou canst not leave
Thy song, nor ever, can those trees be bare;
Bold Lover, never, never canst thou kiss,
Though winning near the goal—yet, do not grieve;
She cannot fade, though thou hast not thy bliss,
For ever wilt thou love, and she be fair!

Ah, happy, happy boughs! that cannot shed
Your leaves, nor ever bid the Spring adieu;
And, happy melodist, unweariѐd,
For ever piping songs for ever new;
More happy love! more happy, happy love!
For ever warm and still to be enjoyed,
For ever panting and for ever young;
All breathing human passion far above,
That leaves a heart high-sorrowful and cloyed,
A burning forehead, and a parching tongue.

Who are these coming to the sacrifice?
To what green altar, O mysterious priest,
Lead'st thou that heifer lowing at the skies,
And all her silken flanks with garlands dressed?
What little town by river or sea-shore,
Or mountain-built with peaceful citadel,
Is emptied of its folk, this pious morn?
And, little town, thy streets for evermore
Will silent be; and not a soul, to tell
Why thou art desolate, can e'er return.

O Attic-shape! fair attitude! with brede
Of marble men and maidens overwrought,
With forest branches and the trodden weed;
Thou, silent form! dost tease us out of thought
As doth eternity. Cold Pastoral!
When old age shall this generation waste,
Thou shalt remain, in midst of other woe
Than ours, a friend to man, to whom thou say'st,
"Beauty is truth, truth beauty,"—that is all
Ye know on earth, and all ye need to know.

AUTUMN

By Thomas Hood

I saw old Autumn in the misty morn
Stand shadowless like Silence, listening
To silence, for no lonely bird would sing
Into his hollow ear from woods forlorn,
Nor lowly hedge nor solitary thorn;
Shaking his languid locks all dewy bright
With tangled gossamer that fell by night,
Pearling his coronet of golden corn.

Where are the songs of Summer?—With the sun,
Oping the dusky eyelids of the south,
Till shade and silence waken up as one,
And Morning sings with a warm odorous mouth.
Where are the merry birds?—Away, away,
On panting wings through the inclement skies,
Lest owls should prey
Undazzled at noonday,
And tear with horny beak their lustrous eyes.

Where are the blooms of Summer?—In the west,
Blushing their last to the last sunny hours,
When the wild Eve by sudden Night is prest
Like tearful Proserpine, snatched from her flowers
To a most gloomy breast.
Where is the pride of Summer—the green prime—
The many, many leaves all twinkling?—Three
On the mossed elm; three on the naked lime
Trembling—and one upon the old oak-tree!
Where is the Dryad's immortality?
Gone into mournful cypress and dark yew,
Or wearing the long gloomy Winter through
In the smooth holly's green eternity.

The squirrel gloats on his accomplished hoard,
The ants have brimmed their garners with ripe grain,
And honey bees have stored
The sweets of Summer in their luscious cells;
The swallows all have winged across the main;
But here the Autumn melancholy dwells,
And sighs her tearful spells,
Amongst the sunless shadows of the plain.
Alone, alone,
Upon a mossy stone,
She sits and reckons up the dead and gone
With the last leaves for a love-rosary,
Whilst all the withered world looks drearily,
Like a dim picture of the drownèd past
In the hushed mind's mysterious far away,
Doubtful what ghostly thing will steal the last
Into that distance, gray upon the gray.

EARLY SPRING

By Alfred, Lord Tennyson

Once more the Heavenly Power
Makes all things new,
And domes the red-plowed hills
With loving blue;
The blackbirds have their wills,
The throstles too.

Opens a door in Heaven;
  From skies of glass
A Jacob's ladder falls
  On greening grass,
And o'er the mountain-walls
  Young angels pass.

Before them fleets the shower,
  And burst the buds,
And shine the level lands,
  And flash the floods;
The stars are from their hands
  Flung thro' the woods,

The woods with living airs
  How softly fann'd,
Light air from where the deep,
  All down the sand,
Is breathing in his sleep,
  Heard by the land.

O follow, leaping blood,
  The season's lure!
O heart, look down and up
  Serene, secure,
Warm as the crocus cup,
  Like snowdrops, pure!

Past, Future, glimpse and fade
  Thro' some slight spell,
A gleam from yonder vale,
  Some far blue fell,
And sympathies, how frail,
  In sound and smell!

Till at thy chuckled note,
  Thou twinkling bird,
The fairy fancies range,
  And, lightly stirr'd,
Ring little bells of change
  From word to word.

For now the Heavenly Power
  Makes all things new,
And thaws the cold, and fills
  The flower with dew;
The blackbirds have their wills,
  The poets too.

BUGLE SONG

By Alfred, Lord Tennyson

The splendor falls on castle walls
  And snowy summits old in story:
The long light shakes across the lakes,
  And the wild cataract leaps in glory.
Blow, bugle, blow, set the wild echoes flying,
Blow, bugle; answer, echoes, dying, dying, dying.

O hark, O hear! how thin and clear,
  And thinner, clearer, farther going!
O sweet and far from cliff and scar
  The horns of Elfland faintly blowing!
Blow, let us hear the purple glens replying:
Blow, bugle; answer, echoes, dying, dying, dying.

O love, they die in yon rich sky,
  They faint on hill or field or river:
Our echoes roll from soul to soul,
  And grow forever and forever.
Blow, bugle, blow, set the wild echoes flying,
And answer, echoes, answer, dying, dying, dying.

PROSPICE

By Robert Browning

Fear death?—to feel the fog in my throat,
  The mist in my face,
When the snows begin, and the blasts denote
  I am nearing the place,
The power of the night, the press of the storm,
  The post of the foe;
Where he stands, the Arch Fear in a visible form,
  Yet the strong man must go:
For the journey is done and the summit attained,
  And the barriers fall,

Though a battle's to fight ere the guerdon be gained,
  The reward of it all.
I was ever a fighter, so—one fight more,
  The best and the last!
I would hate that death bandaged my eyes, and forbore,
  And bade me creep past.
No! let me taste the whole of it, fare like my peers
  The heroes of old,
Bear the brunt, in a minute pay glad life's arrears
  Of pain, darkness and cold.
For sudden the worst turns the best to the brave,
  The black minute's at end,
And the elements' rage, the fiend-voices that rave,
  Shall dwindle, shall blend,
Shall change, shall become first a peace out of pain,
  Then a light, then thy breast,
O thou soul of my soul! I shall clasp thee again,
  And with God be the rest!

THE FORSAKEN MERMAN

By Matthew Arnold

Come, dear children, let us away;
  Down and away below!
Now my brothers call from the bay;
Now the great winds shoreward blow;
Now the salt tides seaward flow;
Now the wild white horses play,
Champ and chafe and toss in the spray.
  Children dear, let us away.
    This way, this way!

Call her once before you go—
  Call once yet!
In a voice that she will know:
  "Margaret! Margaret!"
Children's voices should be dear
  (Call once more) to a mother's ear;
Children's voices, wild with pain—
  Surely she will come again!
Call her once and come away.
  This way, this way!
"Mother dear, we cannot stay!

The wild white horses foam and fret."
  Margaret! Margaret!

Come, dear children, come away down.
  Call no more.
One last look at the white-wall'd town,
  And the little gray church on the windy shore.
  Then come down!
She will not come though you call all day.
  Come away, come away!

Children dear, was it yesterday
We heard the sweet bells over the bay?
In the caverns where we lay,
Through the surf and through the swell,
The far-off sound of a silver bell?
Sand-strewn caverns, cool and deep,
Where the winds are all asleep;
Where the spent lights quiver and gleam;
Where the salt weed sways in the stream;
Where the sea-beasts, ranged all round
Feed in the ooze of their pasture-ground;
Where the sea-snakes coil and twine,
Dry their mail and bask in the brine;
Where great whales come sailing by,
Sail and sail, with unshut eye,
Round the world for ever and aye?
    When did music come this way?
    Children dear, was it yesterday?

Children dear, was it yesterday
(Call yet once) that she went away?
Once she sate with you and me,
On a red gold throne in the heart of the sea,
And the youngest sate on her knee.
She combed its bright hair, and she tended it well,
When down swung the sound of a far-off bell.
She sigh'd, she look'd up through the clear green sea;
She said: "I must go, for my kinsfolk pray
In the little gray church on the shore today.
'Twill be Easter-time in the world—ah me!
And I lose my poor soul, Merman, here with thee."
I said, "Go up, dear heart, through the waves:
Say thy prayer, and come back to the kind sea-caves."

She smiled, she went up through the surf in the bay.
  Children dear, was it yesterday?

  Children dear, were we long alone?
"The sea grows stormy, the little ones moan;
Long prayers," I said, "in the world they say;
Come!" I said, and we rose through the surf in the bay.
We went up the beach, by the sandy down
Where the sea-stocks bloom, to the white-walled town.
Through the narrow paved streets, where all was still,
To the little gray church on the windy hill.
From the church came a murmur of folk at their prayers,
But we stood without in the cold blowing airs.
We climb'd on the graves, on the stones worn with rains,
And we gazed up the aisle through the small leaded panes.
  She sate by the pillar; we saw her clear:
  "Margaret, hist! come quick, we are here!
  Dear heart," I said, "we are long alone.
  The sea grows stormy, the little ones moan."
But, ah! she gave me never a look,
For her eyes were sealed to the holy book!
  Loud prays the priest; shut stands the door.
  Come away, children, call no more.
  Come away, come down, call no more.
  Down, down, down,
    Down to the depths of the sea!
  She sits at her wheel in the humming town,
    Singing most joyfully.
Hark what she sings: "O joy, O joy,
From the humming street, and the child with its toy!
From the priest, and the bell, and the holy well;
  From the wheel where I spun,
  And the blessed light of the sun!"

  And so she sings her fill,
  Singing most joyfully,
  Till the spindle drops from her hand,
  And the whizzing wheel stands still.
She steals to the window and looks at the sand,
  And over the sand at the sea;
  And her eyes are set in a stare;
  And anon there breaks a sigh,
  And anon there drops a tear,

From a sorrow-clouded eye,
And a heart sorrow-laden,
A long, long sigh;
For the cold strange eyes of a little Mermaiden
And the gleam of her golden hair.

Come away, away, children!
Come, children, come down!
The hoarse wind blows colder;
Lights shine in the town.
She will start from her slumber
When gusts shake the door;
She will hear the winds howling,
Will hear the waves roar.
We shall see, while above us
The waves roar and whirl,
A ceiling of amber,
A pavement of pearl.
Singing: "Here came a mortal,
But faithless was she:
And alone dwell for ever
The kings of the sea."

But, children, at midnight,
When soft the winds blow,
When clear falls the moonlight,
When spring-tides are low:
When sweet airs come seaward
From heaths starr'd with broom;
And high rocks throw mildly
On the blanch'd sands a gloom:
Up the still, glistening beaches,
Up the creeks we will hie,
Over banks of bright seaweed
The ebb-tide leaves dry.
We will gaze, from the sand-hills,
At the white, sleeping town;
At the church on the hill-side—
And then come back down.
Singing: "There dwells a loved one,
But cruel is she!
She left lonely for ever
The kings of the sea."

THE SHEPHERDESS

By Alice Meynell

She walks—the lady of my delight—
  A shepherdess of sheep.
Her flocks are thoughts. She keeps them white;
  She guards them from the steep;
She feeds them on the fragrant height,
  And folds them in for sleep.

She roams maternal hills and bright,
  Dark valleys safe and deep.
Into that tender breast at night
  The chastest stars may peep.
She walks—the lady of my delight—
  A shepherdess of sheep.

She holds her little thoughts in sight,
  Though gay they run and leap.
She is so circumspect and right;
  She has her soul to keep.
She walks—the lady of my delight—
  A shepherdess of sheep.

UP-HILL

By Christina Georgina Rossetti

Does the road wind up-hill all the way?
  Yes, to the very end.
Will the day's journey take the whole long day?
  From morn to night, my friend.

But is there for the night a resting-place?
  A roof for when the slow dark hours begin.
May not the darkness hide it from my face?
  You cannot miss that inn.

Shall I meet other wayfarers at night?
  Those who have gone before.
Then must I knock, or call when just in sight?
  They will not keep you standing at that door.

Shall I find comfort, travel-sore and weak?
  Of labor you shall find the sum.
Will there be beds for me and all who seek?
  Yea, beds for all who come.

BREDON HILL

By A. E. Housman

In summertime on Bredon
  The bells they sound so clear;
Round both the shires they ring them
  In steeples far and near,
  A happy noise to hear.

Here of a Sunday morning
  My love and I would lie,
And see the colored counties,
  And hear the larks so high
  About us in the sky.

The bells would ring to call her
  In valleys miles away:
"Come all to church, good people;
  Good people, come and pray."
  But here my love would stay.

And I would turn and answer
  Among the springtime thyme,
"Oh, peal upon our wedding,
  And we will hear the chime,
  And come to church in time."

But when the snows at Christmas
  On Bredon top were strown,
My love rose up so early
  And stole out unbeknown
  And went to church alone.

They tolled the one bell only,
Groom there was none to see,
The mourners followed after,
And to church went she,
And would not wait for me.

The bells they tolled on Bredon,
And still the steeples hum.
"Come all to church, good people,"—
Oh, noisy bells, be dumb;
I hear you, I will come.

TO A WATERFOWL

By William Cullen Bryant

Whither, 'midst falling dew,
While glow the heavens with the last steps of day,
Far, through their rosy depths, dost thou pursue
Thy solitary way?

Vainly the fowler's eye
Might mark thy distant flight to do thee wrong,
As, darkly painted on the crimson sky,
Thy figure floats along.

Seek'st thou the plashy brink
Of weedy lake, or marge of river wide,
Or where the rocking billows rise and sink
On the chafed ocean-side?

There is a Power whose care
Teaches thy way along that pathless coast,
The desert and illimitable air—
Lone wandering, but not lost.

All day thy wings have fanned,
At that far height, the cold thin atmosphere,
Yet stoop not, weary, to the welcome land,
Though the dark night is near.

And soon that toil shall end;
Soon shalt thou find a summer home, and rest,
And scream among thy fellows; reeds shall bend,
Soon, o'er thy sheltered nest.

Thou'rt gone, the abyss of heaven
Hath swallowed up thy form; yet, on my heart
Deeply hath sunk the lesson thou hast given,
And shall not soon depart.

He who, from zone to zone,
Guides through the boundless sky thy certain flight,
In the long way that I must tread alone
Will lead my steps aright.

THANATOPSIS

By William Cullen Bryant

To him who, in the love of Nature, holds
Communion with her visible forms, she speaks
A various language: for his gayer hours
She has a voice of gladness, and a smile
And eloquence of beauty; and she glides
Into his darker musings with a mild
And healing sympathy, that steals away
Their sharpness, ere he is aware. When thoughts
Of the last bitter hour come like a blight
Over thy spirit, and sad images
Of the stern agony, and shroud, and pall,
And breathless darkness, and the narrow house,
Make thee to shudder, and grow sick at heart—
Go forth under the open sky, and list
To Nature's teachings, while from all around—
Earth and her waters, and the depths of air—
Comes a still voice:—Yet a few days, and thee
The all-beholding sun shall see no more
In all his course; nor yet in the cold ground,
Where thy pale form was laid, with many tears,
Nor in the embrace of ocean, shall exist
Thy image. Earth, that nourished thee, shall claim
Thy growth, to be resolved to earth again;
And, lost each human trace, surrendering up
Thine individual being, shalt thou go
To mix forever with the elements;
To be a brother to the insensible rock,
And to the sluggish clod, which the rude swain
Turns with his share, and treads upon. The oak
Shall send his roots abroad, and pierce thy mold.

Yet not to thine eternal resting-place
Shalt thou retire alone—nor couldst thou wish
Couch more magnificent. Thou shalt lie down
With patriarchs of the infant world—with kings,
The powerful of the earth—the wise, the good,
Fair forms, and hoary seers of ages past,
All in one mighty sepulcher. The hills,
Rock-ribbed, and ancient as the sun; the vales
Stretching in pensive quietness between;
The venerable woods; rivers that move
In majesty, and the complaining brooks,
That make the meadows green, and, poured round all,
Old ocean's gray and melancholy waste—
Are but the solemn decorations all
Of the great tomb of man! The golden sun,
The planets, all the infinite host of heaven,
Are shining on the sad abodes of death,
Through the still lapse of ages. All that tread
The globe are but a handful to the tribes
That slumber in its bosom.—Take the wings
Of morning, pierce the Barcan wilderness,
Or lose thyself in the continuous woods
Where rolls the Oregon, and hears no sound
Save his own dashings—yet the dead are there!
And millions in those solitudes, since first
The flight of years began, have laid them down
In their last sleep—the dead reign there alone!
So shalt thou rest; and what if thou withdraw
In silence from the living, and no friend
Take note of thy departure? All that breathe
Will share thy destiny. The gay will laugh
When thou art gone, the solemn brood of care
Plod on, and each one, as before, will chase
His favorite phantom; yet all these shall leave
Their mirth and their employments, and shall come
And make their bed with thee. As the long train
Of ages glides away, the sons of men—
The youth in life's green spring, and he who goes
In the full strength of years, matron and maid,
The speechless babe, and the gray-headed man—
Shall, one by one, be gathered to thy side
By those who in their turn shall follow them.

So live, that when thy summons comes to join
The innumerable caravan which moves
To that mysterious realm, where each shall take
His chamber in the silent halls of death,
Thou go not, like the quarry-slave at night,
Scourged to his dungeon, but, sustained and soothed
By an unfaltering trust, approach thy grave
Like one who wraps the drapery of his couch
About him, and lies down to pleasant dreams.

FORBEARANCE

By Ralph Waldo Emerson

Hast thou named all the birds without a gun?
Loved the wood-rose, and left it on its stalk?
At rich men's tables eaten bread and pulse?
Unarmed, faced danger with a heart of trust?
And loved so well a high behavior,
In man or maid, that thou from speech refrained,
Nobility more nobly to repay?
O, be my friend, and teach me to be thine!

THE SNOW STORM

By Ralph Waldo Emerson

Announced by all the trumpets of the sky
Arrives the snow, and, driving o'er the fields,
Seems nowhere to alight; the whited air
Hides hills and woods, the river, and the heaven,
And veils the farmhouse at the garden's end.
The sled and traveler stopped, the courier's feet
Delayed, all friends shut out, the housemates sit
Around the radiant fireplace, enclosed
In a tumultuous privacy of storm.
Come see the north-wind's masonry.
Out of an unseen quarry evermore
Furnished with tile, the fierce artificer
Curves his white bastions with projected roof
Round every windward stake, or tree, or door.
Speeding, the myriad-handed, his wild work

So fanciful, so savage, naught cares he
For number or proportion. Mockingly,
On coop or kennel he hangs Parian wreaths;
A swan-like form invests the hidden thorn;
Fills up the farmer's lane from wall to wall,
Maugre the farmer's sighs; and, at the gate,
A tapering turret overtops the work.
And when his hours are numbered, and the world
Is all his own, retiring, as he were not,
Leaves, when the sun appears, astonished Art
To mimic in slow structures, stone by stone,
Built in an age, the mad wind's night-work,
The frolic architecture of the snow.

DAYBREAK

By Henry Wadsworth Longfellow

A wind came up out of the sea,
And said, "O mists, make room for me!"

It hailed the ships, and cried, "Sail on,
Ye mariners, the night is gone."

And hurried landward far away,
Crying, "Awake! it is the day."

It said unto the forest, "Shout!
Hang all your leafy banners out!"

It touched the wood-bird's folded wing,
And said, "O bird, awake and sing!"

And o'er the farms, "O chanticleer,
Your clarion blow; the day is near!"

It whispered to the fields of corn,
"Bow down, and hail the coming morn!"

It shouted through the belfry-tower,
"Awake, O bell! proclaim the hour."

It crossed the churchyard with a sigh,
And said, "Not yet! in quiet lie."

THE DAY IS DONE

By Henry Wadsworth Longfellow

The day is done, and the darkness
  Falls from the wings of Night,
As a feather is wafted downward
  From an eagle in his flight.

I see the lights of the village
  Gleam through the rain and the mist,
And a feeling of sadness comes o'er me,
  That my soul cannot resist:

A feeling of sadness and longing,
  That is not akin to pain,
And resembles sorrow only
  As the mist resembles the rain.

Come, read to me some poem,
  Some simple and heartfelt lay,
That shall soothe this restless feeling,
  And banish the thoughts of day.

Not from the grand old masters,
  Not from the bards sublime,
Whose distant footsteps echo
  Through the corridors of Time.

For, like strains of martial music,
  Their mighty thoughts suggest
Life's endless toil and endeavor;
  And tonight I long for rest.

Read from some humbler poet,
  Whose songs gushed from his heart,
As showers from the clouds of summer,
  Or tears from the eyelids start;

Who, through long days of labor,
  And nights devoid of ease,
Still heard in his soul the music
  Of wonderful melodies.

Such songs have power to quiet
  The reckless pulse of care,
And come like the benediction
  That follows after prayer.

Then read from the treasured volume
  The poem of thy choice,
And lend to the rhyme of the poet
  The beauty of thy voice.

And the night shall be filled with music,
  And the cares that infest the day,
Shall fold their tents, like the Arabs,
  And as silently steal away.

HYMN TO THE NIGHT

By Henry Wadsworth Longfellow

I heard the trailing garments of the Night
  Sweep through her marble halls!
I saw her sable skirts all fringed with light
  From the celestial walls!

I felt her presence, by its spell of might,
  Stoop o'er me from above;
The calm, majestic presence of the Night,
  As of the one I love.

I heard the sounds of sorrow and delight,
  The manifold, soft chimes,
That fill the haunted chambers of the Night,
  Like some old poet's rhymes.

From the cool cisterns of the midnight air
  My spirit drank repose;
The fountain of perpetual peace flows there—
  From those deep cisterns flows.

O holy Night! from thee I learn to bear
  What man has borne before!
Thou layest thy finger on the lips of Care,
  And they complain no more.

Peace! Peace! Orestes-like I breathe this prayer!
  Descend with broad-winged flight,
The welcome, the thrice-prayed for, the most fair,
  The best-belovèd Night!

SNOW-BOUND

By John Greenleaf Whittier

The sun that brief December day
Rose cheerless over hills of gray,
And, darkly circled, gave at noon
A sadder light than waning moon.
Slow tracing down the thickening sky
Its mute and ominous prophecy,
A portent seeming less than threat,
It sank from sight before it set.
A chill no coat, however stout,
Of homespun stuff could quite shut out,
A hard dull bitterness of cold,
That checked, mid-vein, the circling race
Of life-blood in the sharpened face,
The coming of the snow-storm told.
The wind blew east: we heard the roar
Of ocean on his wintry shore,
And felt the strong pulse throbbing there
Beat with low rhythm our inland air.

• • •

Unwarmed by any sunset light
The gray day darkened into night,
A night made hoary with the swarm,
And whirl-dance of the blinding storm,
As zig-zag wavering to and fro
Crossed and recrossed the wingèd snow:
And ere the early bedtime came
The white drift piled the window-frame,
And through the glass the clothes-line posts
Looked in like tall and sheeted ghosts.

• • •

The old familiar sights of ours
Took marvelous shapes; strange domes and towers

Rose up where sty or corn-crib stood,
Or garden wall, or belt of wood;
A smooth white mound the brush-pile showed,
A fenceless drift what once was road;
The bridle-post an old man sat
With loose-flung coat and high cocked hat;
The well-curb had a Chinese roof;
And even the long sweep, high aloof,
In its slant splendor, seemed to tell
Of Pisa's leaning miracle.

• • •

All day the gusty north wind bore
The loosening drift its breath before;
Low circling round its southern zone,
The sun through dazzling snow-mist shone.
No church-bell lent its Christian tone
To the savage air, no social smoke
Curled over woods of snow-hung oak.
A solitude made more intense
By dreary-voicèd elements.
The shrieking of the mindless wind,
The moaning tree-boughs swaying blind,
And on the glass the unmeaning beat
Of ghostly finger-tips of sleet.
Beyond the circle of our hearth
No welcome sound of toil or mirth
Unbound the spell, and testified
Of human life and thought outside.
We minded that the sharpest ear
The buried brooklet could not hear,
The music of whose liquid lip
Had been to us companionship,
And in our lonely life, had grown
To have an almost human tone.
As night drew on, and, from the crest
Of wooded knolls that ridged the west,
The sun, a snow-blown traveler, sank
From sight beneath the smothering bank,
We piled with care, our nightly stack
Of wood against the chimney-back—
The oaken log, green, huge and thick,
And on its top the stout back-stick;

The knotty fore-stick laid apart,
And filled between with curious art
The ragged brush; then hovering near,
We watched the first red blaze appear,
Heard the sharp crackle, caught the gleam
On whitewashed wall and sagging beam,
Until the old rude-fashioned room
Burst flower-like into rosy bloom;
While radiant with a mimic flame
Outside the sparkling drift became,
And through the bare-boughed lilac tree
Our own warm hearth seemed blazing free.
The crane and pendent trammels showed,
The Turks' heads on the andirons glowed;
While childish fancy, prompt to tell
The meaning of the miracle,
Whispered the old rhyme: "Under the tree,
When fire outdoors burns merrily,
There the witches are making tea."

• • •

Shut in from all the world without,
We sat the clean-winged hearth about,
Content to let the north wind roar
In baffled rage at pane and door,
While the red logs before us beat
The frost-line back with tropic heat,
And ever, when a louder blast
Shook beam and rafter as it passed,
The merrier up its roaring draught
The great throat of the chimney laughed,
The house-dog on his paws outspread
Laid to the fire his drowsy head,
The cat's dark silhouette on the wall
A couchant tiger's seemed to fall;
And, for the winter's fireside meet,
Between the andirons' straddling feet,
The mug of cider simmered slow,
The apples sputtered in a row,
And close at hand the basket stood
With nuts from brown October's wood.

• • •

THE CHAMBERED NAUTILUS

By Oliver Wendell Holmes

This is the ship of pearl, which, poets feign,
Sails the unshadowed main—
The venturous bark that flings
On the sweet summer wind its purpled wings
In gulfs enchanted, where the Siren sings,
And coral reefs lie bare,
Where the cold sea-maids rise to sun their streaming hair.

Its webs of living gauze no more unfurl;
Wrecked is the ship of pearl!
And every chambered cell,
Where its dim dreaming life was wont to dwell
As the frail tenant shaped his growing shell,
Before thee lies revealed—
Its irised ceiling rent, its sunless crypt unsealed!

Year after year beheld the silent toil
That spread his lustrous coil
Still, as the spiral grew,
He left the past year's dwelling for the new,
Stole with soft step its shining archway through,
Built up its idle door,
Stretched in his last-found home, and knew the old no more.

Thanks for the heavenly message brought by thee,
Child of the wandering sea,
Cast from her lap, forlorn!
From thy dead lips a clearer note is born
Than ever Triton blew from wreathèd horn!
While on mine ear it rings,
Through the deep caves of thought I hear a voice that sings—

Build thee more stately mansions, O my soul,
As the swift seasons roll!
Leave thy low-vaulted past!
Let each new temple, nobler than the last,
Shut thee from heaven with a dome more vast
Till thou at length are free,
Leaving thine outgrown shell by life's unresting sea!

THE LAST LEAF

By Oliver Wendell Holmes

I saw him once before,
As he passed by the door;
And again
The pavement stones resound,
As he totters o'er the ground
With his cane.

They say that in his prime,
Ere the pruning-knife of Time
Cut him down,
Not a better man was found
By the Crier on his round
Through the town.

But now he walks the streets,
And he looks at all he meets
Sad and wan;
And shakes his feeble head,
That it seems as if he said,
"They are gone."

The mossy marbles rest
On the lips that he has prest
In their bloom;
And the names he loved to hear
Have been carved for many a year
On the tomb.

My grandmamma has said—
Poor old lady, she is dead
Long ago—
That he had a Roman nose,
And his cheek was like a rose,
In the snow.

But now his nose is thin,
And it rests upon his chin
Like a staff;
And a crook is in his back,
And a melancholy crack
In his laugh.

I know it is a sin
For me to sit and grin
At him here;
But the old three-cornered hat,
And the breeches and all that,
Are so queer!

And if I should live to be
The last leaf upon the tree
In the spring,
Let them smile, as I do now,
At the old forsaken bough
Where I cling.

TO ONE IN PARADISE

By Edgar Allen Poe

Thou wast all to me, love,
For which my soul did pine—
A green isle in the sea, love,
A fountain and a shrine,
All wreathed with fairy fruits and flowers,
And all the flowers were mine.

Ah, dream, too bright to last!
Ah, starry Hope! that didst arise
But to be overcast!
A voice from out the Future cries,
"On! on!"—but o'er the Past
(Dim gulf!) my spirit hovering lies
Mute, motionless, aghast!

For, alas! alas! with me
The light of Life is o'er!
No more—no more—no more—
(Such language holds the solemn sea
To the sands upon the shore)
Shall bloom the thunder-blasted tree,
Or the stricken eagle soar!

And all my days are trances,
And all my nightly dreams
Are where thy dark eye glances,
And where thy footstep gleams;
In what ethereal dances,
By what ethereal streams.

TO HELEN

By Edgar Allen Poe

Helen, thy beauty is to me
Like those Nicaean barks of yore,
That gently, o'er a perfumed sea,
The weary, wayworn wanderer bore
To his own native shore.

On desperate seas long wont to roam,
Thy hyacinth hair, thy classic face,
Thy Naiad airs, have brought me home
To the glory that was Greece
And the grandeur that was Rome.

Lo! in yon brilliant window-niche
How statue-like I see thee stand,
The agate lamp within thy hand!
Ah, Psyche, from the regions which
Are Holy Land!

THE SHEPHERD OF KING ADMETUS

By James Russell Lowell

There came a youth upon the earth,
Some thousand years ago,
Whose slender hands were nothing worth,
Whether to plow, or reap, or sow.

Upon an empty tortoise-shell
He stretched some chords, and drew
Music that made men's bosoms swell
Fearless, or brimmed their eyes with dew.

Then King Admetus, one who had
  Pure taste by right divine,
Decreed his singing not too bad
  To hear between the cups of wine:

And so, well pleased with being soothed
  Into a sweet half-sleep,
Three times his kingly beard he smoothed,
  And made him viceroy o'er his sheep.

His words were simple words enough,
  And yet he used them so,
That what in other mouths was rough
  In his seemed musical and low.

Men called him but a shiftless youth,
  In whom no good they saw;
And yet, unwittingly, in truth,
  They made his careless words their law.

They knew not how he learned at all,
  For idly, hour by hour,
He sat and watched the dead leaves fall,
  Or mused upon a common flower.

It seemed the loveliness of things
  Did teach him all their use,
For, in mere weeds, and stones, and springs,
  He found a healing power profuse.

Men granted that his speech was wise,
  But, when a glance they caught
Of his slim grace and woman's eyes,
  They laughed, and called him good-for-naught.

Yet after he was dead and gone,
  And e'en his memory dim,
Earth seemed more sweet to live upon,
  More full of love, because of him.

And day by day more holy grew
  Each spot where he had trod,
Till after-poets only knew
  Their first-born brother as a god.

SOURCES OF CONTEMPORARY POETRY IN VOLUME X

The Spicebush in March: Rhyme of November Stars: Stars, from Stars To-night, by Sara Teasdale. The Macmillan Company.

Fog, from Chicago Poems, by Carl Sandburg. Henry Holt & Company, Inc.

Velvet Shoes, from Collected Poems of Elinor Wylie, Alfred A. Knopf, Inc.

Stopping by Woods on a Snowy Evening: Canis Major: The Last Word of a Bluebird: The Runaway: The Pasture, from Collected Poems of Robert Frost, Henry Holt & Co., Inc.

The Moon's the North Wind's Cooky: Yet Gentle Will the Griffin Be: The Ghosts of the Buffaloes: The Old Horse in the City: A Dirge for a Righteous Kitten, from Johnny Appleseed, by Vachel Lindsay. The Macmillan Company.

The Night Will Never Stay, from Gypsy and Ginger, by Eleanor Farjeon. E. P. Dutton & Company, Inc.

Nature's Friend: A Child's Pet, from The Poems of W. H. Davies, Jonathan Cape, Ltd.

The Visitor: If Once You Have Slept on an Island, from Taxis and Toadstools, by Rachel Field. Doubleday, Doran & Company, Inc.

The Visitor, from Green Days and Blue Days, by Patrick R. Chalmers. The Norman Remington Company.

Seal Lullaby, from The Jungle Book: *Smugglers' Song,* from Puck of Pook's Hill: *The Bell Buoy,* from The Five Nations, all by Rudyard Kipling. Doubleday, Doran & Company, Inc.

A Fairy Went A-Marketing, from Fairies and Chimneys, by Rose Fyleman. Doubleday, Doran & Company, Inc.

Berries: The Ship of Rio: The Ogre: The Lost Shoe: Sam: Arabia, from Collected Poems of Walter de la Mare. Henry Holt & Company, Inc.

The Frog: The Python: The Yak, from The Bad Child's Book of Beasts, by Hilaire Belloc. Alfred A. Knopf, Inc.

Tarantella, from Sonnets and Verse, by Hilaire Belloc. Gerald Duckworth & Company, Ltd.

The Hens, from Under the Tree, by Elizabeth Madox Roberts. Viking Press, Inc.

Donnybrook: Seumas Beg, from Collected Poems of James Stephens. The Macmillan Co.

An Old Woman of the Roads, from Poems of Padraic Colum. The Macmillan Company.

Portrait of a Neighbor, from A Few Figs and Thistles, by Edna St. Vincent Millay. Harpers.

Eel-Grass, from Second April and Other Poems, by Edna St. Vincent Millay. Harpers.

Lepanto, from Collected Poems of G. K. Chesterton. Dodd, Mead & Company, Inc.

Nancy Hanks, from The Book of Americans, by Rosemary and Stephen Vincent Benét. Farrar & Rinehart, Inc.

Time, You Old Gypsy Man, from Poems by Ralph Hodgson. The Macmillan Company.

Romance, from The Dark Wind, by W. J. Turner. E. P. Dutton & Company, Inc.

The Song of Wandering Aengus, from Collected Poems of William Butler Yeats. The Macmillan Company.

Tewkesbury Road: Sea Fever, from Collected Poems of John Masefield. Macmillan Co.

Messmates: Drake's Drum, from Poems, New and Old, by Henry Newbolt. John Murray.

The Old Ships, from Collected Poems of James Elroy Flecker. Martin Secker & Warburg.

The Shepherdess, from Selected Poems of Alice Meynell. Charles Scribner's Sons.

Bredon Hill, from A Shropshire Lad, by A. E. Housman. Dodd, Mead & Company, Inc.

The Wind and the Moon, from Poems of George Macdonald, E. P. Dutton & Company, Inc.

ACKNOWLEDGMENTS

The publishers of THE JUNIOR CLASSICS express their appreciation to those publishers, agents, authors and artists who have granted permission for the use of copyrighted material appearing in these volumes. Acknowledgment is made to the following:

George Allen & Unwin, Ltd., publishers of the only authorized edition of John Ruskin's works: for permission to use "The King of the Golden River."

D. Appleton-Century Company: for permission to use the stories "The Little Humpbacked Horse" and "Wassilissa the Beautiful" from "Russian Wonder Tales" by Post Wheeler; "Prince Rabbit" by A. A. Milne from "Number Two Joy Street," illustrations by Hugh Chesterman; selections from "Uncle Remus, His Songs and Sayings" by Joel Chandler Harris, illustrated by A. B. Frost; "Gulliver the Great" from "Gulliver the Great and Other Dog Stories" by Walter A. Dyer; "Christmas with Queen Bess" from "Master Skylark" by John Bennett, with illustrations by Reginald Birch; "An Adventure with a Whale" from "The Cruise of the Cachalot" by Frank T. Bullen; for permission to use the poem "Columbus" by Joaquin Miller; for permission to use the illustration by Henry Pitz in "Beowulf Fights the Dragon" from "The Story of Beowulf" by Strafford Riggs.

Edward Arnold & Company, Ltd.: for permission to use in Canada "Prometheus the Firebringer" from "Orpheus with His Lute" by W. M. L. Hutchinson.

Rosemary and Stephen Vincent Benét: for permission to reprint the poem "Nancy Hanks," from "The Book of Americans" (copyright, 1933, by Rosemary and Stephen Vincent Benét).

Henry Beston: for permission to use the stories "The Lost Half Hour" and "The Seller of Dreams" from "The Firelight Fairy Book."

A. & C. Black, Ltd.: for permission to use in Canada the stories "The Little Humpbacked Horse," and "Wassilissa the Beautiful" from "Russian Wonder Tales" by Post Wheeler; permission to use illustration by Charles Folkard from "Mother Goose's Nursery Rhymes" by L. Edna Walker, for "Two Legs Sat upon Three Legs."

John Bennett: for permission to use "Christmas with Queen Bess" from "Master Skylark."

Bobbs-Merrill Company: for permission to use the poem "The Man in the Moon" by James Whitcomb Riley.

Messrs. Burns, Oates & Washbourne: for permission to use the poem "Lepanto" by Gilbert K. Chesterton.

Jonathan Cape, Ltd.: for permission to use in Canada the story "A Chinese Fairy Tale" from "Moonshine and Clover" by Laurence Housman; for permission to use the poems "Nature's Friend" and "A Child's Pet" by William H. Davies.

Mrs. Gilbert K. Chesterton: for permission to use the poem "Lepanto" by Gilbert K. Chesterton.

B. J. Chute: for permission to use her story "Head Over Heels" from "Shift to the Right" published by The Macmillan Company.

James Brendan Connolly: for permission to use "The Lone Voyagers," from "The Book of the Gloucester Fishermen."

Constable and Company, Ltd.: for permission to use in Canada selections from "Beasts and Saints" by Helen Waddell.

Coward-McCann, Inc.: for permission to use illustrations by Wanda Gág in "Snow White and Rose Red."

The Thomas Y. Crowell Company: for permission to use selections from "Stories of Norse Heroes" by E. M. Wilmot-Buxton; the story "The Boyhood of Cuchulain" from "Cuchulain, Hound of Ulster" by Eleanor Hull.

Curtis Brown Ltd.: for permission to use "Lassie Come-Home" by Eric Knight, first published in *Saturday Evening Post,* Dec. 17, 1938, reprinted here by permission of the author's estate.

John Day Company: for permission to use "The Lone Voyagers" from "The Book of the Gloucester Fishermen" by James Brendan Connolly.

Walter de la Mare: for permission to use his story "The Dutch Cheese"; and his poems, "Berries," "The Ship of Rio," "The Ogre," "The Lost Shoe," "Sam," and "Arabia."

J. M. Dent & Sons, Ltd.: for permission to use in Canada "King Arthur and the Round Table" from "Stories of King Arthur and the Round Table" by Beatrice Clay; "The Night Will Never Stay" and "Light the Lamps Up, Lamplighter" by Eleanor Farjeon.

Dodd, Mead & Company, Inc.: for permission to use selections from "The Story of Don Quixote," retold by Judge Parry; for permission to use "Buddy, Seeing Eye Pioneer" from Chapter 11 of "Dogs Against Darkness" by Dickson Hartwell; "The Monkey that Would Not Kill" by Henry Drummond; "Shipping Wild Animals" from "Trapping Wild Animals in Malay Jungles" by Charles Mayer; "My Friend Toto" by Cherry Kearton; "The Race for the South Pole" from "The Last Continent of Adventure" by Walter B. Hayward; for permission to use the poems "The Sea Gipsy" by Richard Hovey; "Bredon Hill" by A. E. Housman; "Lepanto" from "Collected Poems of G. K. Chesterton" (copyright, 1932, by Dodd, Mead & Company, Inc.); for permission to use the illustrations by Walter Crane for "Beauty and the Beast" from "Beauty and the Beast Picture Book"; illustration by Arthur Rackham for "Little One

Eye, Little Two Eyes, Little Three Eyes" from "Little Brother and Little Sister"; illustrations by Katharine Pyle for "Black Beauty."

Doubleday, Doran & Company, Inc.: for permission to reprint the stories "Billy Beg and the Bull" from "In Chimney Corners" by Seumas MacManus; "Conal and Donal and Taig," "The Old Hag's Long Leather Bag" and "Manis the Miller" from "Donegal Fairy Stories" by Seumas MacManus; "A Tale of Three Tails" from "Tales from the Silver Lands" by Charles J. Finger; "The Porcupine's Quills" and "How Rock-dweller the Chipmunk Gained His Stripes" from "Skunny Wundy" by Arthur C. Parker; "Taktuk, an Arctic Boy" by Helen Lomen and Marjorie Flack; "The Baker's Daughter" from "The Street of Little Shops" by Margery Bianco, with illustration by Grace Paull; "Polly Patchwork" by Rachel Field; "The New Pup" from "Penrod Jashber" by Booth Tarkington; "Leopards and Rhinos" from "In Brightest Africa" by Carl E. Akeley; "One Minute Longer" from "Buff, A Collie, and Other Dog Stories" by Albert Payson Terhune, with an illustration by Marguerite Kirmse from "The Heart of a Dog" by Albert Payson Terhune; "Coaly-Bay the Outlaw Horse" from "Wild Animal Ways" by Ernest Thompson Seton; "Daniel Boone's Rifle" from "The Long Rifle" by Stewart Edward White; for permission to use the poems "The Visitor" and "If Once You Have Slept on an Island" from "Taxis and Toadstools" by Rachel Field, with illustrations by the author (copyright, 1926, by Doubleday, Page & Company); "Smugglers' Song" from "Puck of Pook's Hill" (copyright, 1905, 1933, by Rudyard Kipling), reprinted with permission from Mrs. Kipling and Doubleday, Doran & Company, Inc.; "The Bell Buoy" from "The Five Nations" (copyright, 1903, 1931, by Rudyard Kipling), reprinted with permission from Mrs. Kipling and Doubleday, Doran & Company, Inc.; "Seal Lullaby" from "The Jungle Book" (copyright, 1893, 1921, by Rudyard Kipling), reprinted with permission of Mrs. Kipling and Doubleday, Doran & Company, Inc.

Gerald Duckworth & Company, Ltd.: for permission to use the poems "The Frog," "The Python," "The Yak," and "Tarantella" by Hilaire Belloc.

E. P. Dutton & Company, Inc.: for permission to use the stories "The Hare That Ran Away," "The Spirit That Lived in a Tree," "The Monkey That Saved the Herd," "The Elephant That Was Honored in Old Age," "The Faithful Friend," "The Banyan Deer," from "Eastern Stories and Legends" by Marie L. Shedlock; "King Arthur and the Round Table" from "Stories of King Arthur and the Round Table" by Beatrice Clay; "Bringing up Kari" from "Kari the Elephant" by Dhan Gopal Mukerji; for permission to use the poems "The Wind and the Moon" by George Macdonald; "The Night will Never Stay" from "Gypsy and Ginger," and "Light the Lamps Up, Lamplighter" by Eleanor Farjeon; "Romance," by W. J. Turner, from "The Dark Wind" (copyright, 1920, by E. P. Dutton & Co., Inc.); for permission to use illustrations by Katharine Pyle from "Granny's Wonderful Chair."

Eleanor Farjeon: for permission to reprint "Light the Lamps Up, Lamplighter."

Farrar and Rinehart: for permission to use "The Devil and Daniel Webster" by Stephen Vincent Benét; for permission to use illustration by J. W. Whymper from "The Life of Vice Admiral William Bligh" by George Mackaness in "The Voyage of the Bounty."

Rose Fyleman: for permission to use "A Fairy Went A-Marketing" from her book of poems, "Fairies and Chimneys"; and reprinted from *Punch,* by permission of the proprietors.

Wanda Gág: for permission to use her illustrations in "Snow White and Rose Red."

Wells Gardner, Darton & Co.: for rights for the use in Canada of the stories "Hunting the Calydonian Boar," "The Winning of Atalanta" and "The Divine Musician" from "Children of the Dawn"; for permission to use illustration by A. G. Walker in "The Proud King" from Darton's "Wonder Book of Old Romance"; for illustration by F. D. Bedford in "Embellishment" from "Old Fashioned Tales," by E. V. Lucas.

Hamlin Garland: for permission to use his story "The Prospector," from "They of the High Trails."

Lady Gilbert: for permission to use "Captain Reece" and "The Yarn of the Nancy Bell" by W. S. Gilbert.

Ginn & Company: for permission to use the illustrations by Hugh Thomson in "The Fight" from "Tom Brown's School Days" by Thomas Hughes, edited by Bradby.

Carl Glick: for permission to use his story "My Song Yankee Doodle" from *This Week, New York Herald Tribune.*

Harcourt, Brace & Company, Inc.: for permission to use the stories "Budulinek" and "Zlatovlaska the Golden-Haired" from "The Shoemaker's Apron," by Parker Fillmore; "Longshanks, Girth and Keen" from "Czechoslovak Fairy Tales" by Parker Fillmore; "How They Broke Away to Go to the Rootabaga Country" by Carl Sandburg; "A Chinese Fairy Tale" from "Moonshine and Clover" by Laurence Housman; "The Coyote and the Fox" and "Pah-Tay an the Wind-Witch" from "Taytay's Tales" by Elizabeth W. DeHuff; "Davy Crockett Legends" from "Davy Crockett" by Constance Rourke; "Abe Lincoln's Books" from "Abe Lincoln Grows Up" by Carl Sandburg; illustrations by Florence Ivins from "This Singing World" for "Seumas Beg" by James Stephens and "The Lost Shoe" by Walter de la Mare; illustration by James Daugherty, for the poem "Fog," by Carl Sandburg.

Harper & Brothers: for permission to use the stories "Living in W'ales" and "The Gardener and the White Elephants" from "The Spider's Palace" by Richard Hughes; "How Boots Befooled the King" and "King Stork" and illustration from "The Wonder Clock" by Howard Pyle; "The Stool of Fortune" and illustrations from "Twilight Land" by Howard Pyle; "A Miserable, Merry Christmas" from "Boy on Horseback" by Lincoln Steffens; "Mama and the Occasion" from "Mama's Bank Account" by Kathryn Forbes; "The Wild Bull" from "Herdboy of Hungary" by Alexander Finta and Jeannette Eaton; "Knighted by King Henry IV" from "Men of Iron" by Howard Pyle; "The Prospector" from "They of the High Trails" by Hamlin Garland; "Tom Chist and the Treasure Chest" and illustrations from "Howard Pyle's Book of Pirates"; "The Two-Twenty Low Hurdle Race" from "The Human Comedy" by William Saroyan; "Knapsack of Salvation" from "I'll Take the High Road" by Wolfgang Langewiesche; for permission to use illustrations by Michael Pertz from "Humpy" by Peter Ershov, for the story "The Little Humpbacked Horse."

George G. Harrap & Company, Ltd.: for permission to use in Canada selections from "Stories of Norse Heroes" by E. M. Wilmot-Buxton; for permission to use the story "Finn and Oisin" from "The High Deeds of Finn" by Thomas Rolleston.

Henry Holt & Company, Inc.: for permission to use the story "The Emperor's Vision" from "Christ Legends" by Selma Lagerlöf, translated by Velma S. Howard; selections from "Beasts and Saints" by Helen Waddell; selections from "Stories from the Chronicle of the Cid" by Mary Wright Plummer; "Thunderbird Limps Home" from "Here Is Your War" by Ernie Pyle; "A Saga of World War II," chapters from "The Raft" by Robert Trumbull; for permission to use the poems "Fog," by Carl Sandburg, from "Chicago Poems" (copyright, 1916, by Henry Holt & Company, Inc.); "Stopping by Woods on a Snowy Evening," "Canis Major," "The Last Word of a Bluebird," "The Runaway" and "The Pasture" from "Collected Poems of Robert Frost" (copyright, 1930, by Henry Holt & Company, Inc.); "Berries," "The Ship of Rio," with an illustration by W. Heath Robinson, "The Ogre," "The Lost Shoe," "Sam," and "Arabia" from "Collected Poems of Walter de la Mare" (copyright, 1920, by Henry Holt & Company, Inc.).

Houghton Mifflin Company: for permission to use the stories "The Proud King," "St. George and the Dragon," "The Bell of Justice," "William Tell," and "The Image and the Treasure" from "The Book of Legends" by Horace E. Scudder; the Robin Hood ballads from "English and Scottish Popular Ballads"; "The Departure of Telemachus" from "The Odyssey of Homer," edited by George Herbert Palmer; "The Battle of Roncesvalles" from "The Song of Roland" by Isabel Butler; "A Tragedy in Millinery" from "New Chronicles of Rebecca" by Kate Douglas Wiggin; "When Molly Was Six" by Eliza Orne White; "About Elizabeth Eliza's Piano" from "The Peterkin Papers" by Lucretia Hale; "Stickeen" by John Muir; "Emmeline" by Elsie Singmaster; "Salt-Water Tea" from "Johnny Tremain" by Esther Forbes; "Adrift on an Ice Pan" by Wilfred Thomason Grenfell; for permission to use the poems "The

Dandelions" by Helen Gray Cone; "The Visitor" by Patrick Chalmers; "Robinson Crusoe's Story" and "The Plaint of the Camel" by Charles E. Carryl; "Midsummer Song" by Richard Watson Gilder; "Farm-Yard Song" by J. T. Trowbridge; for permission to use illustration by Walter Crane in "The Chimaera" from "The Wonder Book for Boys and Girls" by Nathaniel Hawthorne; illustrations by A. B. Frost in "One Memorable Fourth" from "The Story of a Bad Boy" by Thomas Bailey Aldrich.

Mrs. Rudyard Kipling: for permission to use the poems, "Smugglers' Song," "The Bell Buoy" and "Seal Lullaby" by Rudyard Kipling.

Marguerite Kirmse: for permission to use illustration in "One Minute Longer" from "The Heart of a Dog" by Albert Payson Terhune.

Alfred A. Knopf, Inc.: for permission to use the stories "The Dutch Cheese" by Walter de la Mare; "Sarita and the Duendes" with illustration from "In Mexico They Say" by Patricia Fent Ross; "How the Coyote Danced with the Blackbirds" and "The Serpent of the Sea" from "Zuni Folk Tales" by Frank Hamilton Cushing; for permission to use first chapter of "Dawn Over Zero" by W. L. Laurence; for permission to use the poem "Velvet Shoes" from "Collected Poems of Elinor Wylie" (copyright, 1932, by Alfred A. Knopf, Inc.).

J. B. Lippincott Co.: for permission to use "MacArthur Scores Again" from "The Courage and the Glory" by John J. Floherty; "Summit of the World: The Fight for Everest" from "High Conquest" by James Ramsey Ullman.

Little, Brown & Company: for permission to use the stories "The Lost Half Hour" and "The Seller of Dreams" from "The Firelight Fairy Book" by Henry Beston; "Beowulf Fights Grendel" and "Beowulf Fights the Dragon" from "Beowulf" by John Carrington Cox; "Nelly's Hospital" from "Aunt Jo's Scrap Bag," by Louisa May Alcott; "The Story of the Four Little Children Who Went Round the World" by Edward Lear; "Sea Otter" from "Wild Folk" by Samuel Scoville, Jr.; "Leonidas" from "Men of Old Greece" by Jennie Hall; "Louisa Alcott, War Nurse" from "Invincible Louisa" by Cornelia Meigs; "Stover Plays Football" from "The Varmint" by Owen Johnson; for permission to use the poems "The Grass," "The Morns Are Meeker Than They Were," "The Bee," "A Narrow Fellow in the Grass," "A Bird Came Down the Walk" by Emily Dickinson, from "Poems for Youth"; "The Owl and the Pussy Cat," "The Jumblies," "The Pobble Who Has No Toes" and "The Courtship of the Yonghy-Bonghy Bò" by Edward Lear.

Liveright Publishing Corporation: for permission to use the stories "The Great Discoveries" and "Napoleon" from "The Story of Mankind" by Hendrik Willem Van Loon.

Longmans, Green & Co.: for permission to use the stories "Prometheus the Firebringer" from "Orpheus with His Lute" by W. M. L. Hutchinson; "Joan the Maid" by Andrew Lang and "The Story of Molly Pitcher" by Agnes Repplier, from "The Red True Story Book"; for permission to use illustration by

Henry J. Ford from Andrew Lang's "The Blue Poetry Book" for poem "Orpheus with His Lute" by William Shakespeare.

Lothrop, Lee and Shepard Company: for permission to use the stories "The Pumpkin Giant" from "The Pot of Gold" by Mary E. Wilkins; "What Happened to Inger Johanne" by Dikken Zwilgmeyer, translated by Emilie Poulsson; "The Lance of Kanana" by Harry W. French.

Greville Macdonald: for permission to reprint "The Wind and the Moon" by George Macdonald.

The Macmillan Company, New York: for permission to use the stories "The Light Princess" by George Macdonald, with illustrations by Dorothy Lathrop; "Two Youths Whose Father Was Under the Sea" from "The Big Tree of Bunlahy" by Padraic Colum; "St. Martin and the Honest Man," with illustration by Boris Artzybasheff, from "The Forge in the Forest" by Padraic Colum; "The Hunting of the Boar" from "The Island of the Mighty" by Padraic Colum; "Rustem and Sohrab" from "The Epic of Kings" by Helen Zimmern; selection from "The Adventures of Odysseus" retold by Padraic Colum; "Gulliver's Voyage to Lilliput" from "Gulliver's Travels" edited by Padraic Colum; "Ta-ming Wins the Short Sword" from "The Short Sword" by Violet M. Irwin; "The Miss Bannisters' Brother" from "Anne's Terrible Good Nature" by E. V. Lucas; "Susanna's Auction" from the French, with illustrations by Boutet de Monvel; "Buster," "Jim Crow" and "Zinnia and Her Babies" from "More About Animals" by Margery Bianco; "Jimmie, the Story of a Black Bear Cub" by Ernest Harold Baynes; "The Cat and the Captain" by Elizabeth Coatsworth; "King Cobra Takes the Stage," from "Thrills of a Naturalist's Quest" by Raymond L. Ditmars; "The Assault of Wings" from "Hoof and Claw" by Charles G. D. Roberts; "The Brown Wolf" from "The Brown Wolf and Other Jack London Stories"; "The Greek Slave and the Little Roman Boy" from "Buried Cities" by Jennie Hall; "The Mountain Man" from "Silent Scot" by Constance Lindsay Skinner; "The Tree of Jade" from "The Pool of Stars" by Cornelia Meigs; "Head Over Heels" from "Shift to the Right" by B. J. Chute; for permission to use illustrations by Eric Pape for "The Princess on the Pea" from "Andersen's Fairy Tales," and for "Aladdin" and "Ali Baba"; by Willy Pogany from "The Golden Fleece" by Padraic Colum, for "Prometheus the Firebringer."

The Macmillan Company: for permission to use the poems "The Spicebush in March," "Rhyme of November Stars" and "Stars," with an illustration by Dorothy Lathrop, from "Stars Tonight" by Sara Teasdale (copyright, 1930, by Sara Teasdale Filsinger); "Spring Quiet," "Who Has Seen the Wind?" "Summer Days," "O Lady Moon," "All Things Wait Upon Thee," "The City Mouse and the Country Mouse" and "Up-Hill" by Christina Rossetti; "The Moon's the North Wind's Cooky," "Yet Gentle Will the Griffin Be," "The Old Horse in the City," "A Dirge for a Righteous Kitten," and "The Ghosts of the Buffaloes" from "Johnny Appleseed" by Vachel Lindsay (copyright, 1913, 1914, 1917, 1925, 1928, by The Macmillan Company); "Donnybrook" and "Seumas Beg" from "Collected Poems" of James Stephens (copyright, 1909, 1912, 1915, 1918, 1925, 1926, by The Macmillan Company); "Robin Redbreast" and "The Fairies" by William Allingham; "The Owl," "The Eagle" and "Bugle Song" by Alfred Tennyson; "The Walrus and the Carpenter," "Jabberwocky," "The Mad Gardener's Song" and "The Three Badgers" by Lewis Carroll; "Time, You Old Gypsy Man" from "Poems" by Ralph Hodgson (copyright, 1917, by The Macmillan Company); "The Song of Wandering Aengus" from "Collected Poems" of William Butler Yeats (copyright, 1933, by The Macmillan Company), with an illustration by Wilfred Bromhall from "Silver Pennies" by Blanche Jennings Thompson; "Tewkesbury Road" and "Sea Fever" from "Collected Poems of John Masefield" (copyright, 1913, by Harper & Brothers; copyright, 1914, by The Century Company and the McClure publications; copyright, 1912, 1913, 1914, by The Macmillan Company; copyright, 1915, 1923, 1924, 1926, 1930, 1931, 1932, 1935, by John Masefield); "An Old Woman of the Roads" from "Poems" by Padraic Colum (copyright, 1916, 1922, 1927, 1930, 1932, by The Macmillan Company); for permission to use illustration by George Richards for "Yet Gentle Will the Griffin Be"; illustrations by Boris Artzybasheff from "The Fairy Shoemaker," for the poems "The Fairies" by William Allingham and "The Forsaken Merman" by Matthew Arnold; an illustration by Corydon Bell, from "Ring-A-Round," for "All Things Bright and Beautiful" by Cecil Frances Alexander; an illustration by Nancy Barnhart, from "The Listening Child," for "Hiawatha's Childhood"; illustration by Pamela Bianco, from "The Land of Dreams" by William Blake, for "Piping Down the Valleys Wild."

The Macmillan Company of Canada, Ltd.: for permission to use in Canada the poems "Smugglers' Song," "The Bell Buoy" and "Seal Lullaby" by Rudyard Kipling; "Captain Reece" and "The Yarn of the Nancy Bell" by W. S. Gilbert.

The Macmillan Company, Ltd., London: for permission to use the poems "Captain Reece" and "The Yarn of the Nancy Bell" by W. S. Gilbert; "The Forsaken Merman" by Matthew Arnold; "All Things Bright and Beautiful" by Cecil Frances Alexander.

Perry Mason Company: for permission to use the stories "My Fight with a Catamount" by Allen French; "Chased by the Trail" by Jack London.

Robert M. McBride & Company: for permission to use the story "Dick Turpin" from "Highwaymen" by Charles J. Finger.

Edna St. Vincent Millay: for permission to reprint her poems "Portrait by a Neighbor" from "A Few Figs and Thistles" (copyright, 1922, by Edna St. Vincent Millay) and "Eel-Grass" from "Second April and Other Poems" (copyright 1921, by Edna St. Vincent Millay).

Mrs. Abbie Leland Miller: for permission to use the poem "Columbus" by Joaquin Miller.

William Morrow & Company, Inc.: for permission to use the story "The Winning Bug" from "Split Seconds" by Jackson Scholz.

John Murray: for permission to use "An Adventure with a Whale" from "The Cruise of the Cachalot" by Frank T. Bullen; for permission to use "The Pied Piper of Hamelin," "How They Brought the Good News from Ghent to Aix" and "Prospice" by Robert Browning.

National Geographic Society for permission to use "Rounding the Cape in a Windjammer" by Alan Villiers.

Henry Newbolt: for permission to use his poems "Messmates" and "Drake's Drum."

Oxford University Press: for permission to use the poem "Sage Counsel" by A. T. Quiller-Couch.

Arthur C. Parker: for permission to use "The Porcupine's Quills" and "How Rock-Dweller the Chipmunk Gained His Stripes" from "Skunny Wundy."

G. P. Putnam's Sons: for permission to use text and illustrations for selections from "East o' the Sun and West o' the Moon" by Sir George W. Dasent; text and illustrations for selections from "English Fairy Tales," "More English Fairy Tales," "Indian Fairy Tales," and "Celtic Fairy Tales" by Joseph Jacobs; for permission to use the story "The Boy Viking, Olaf II of Norway" from "Historic Boys" by Elbridge S. Brooks; "The Making of an Explorer" from "Ends of the Earth" by Roy Chapman Andrews; "Flying Over the North Pole" from "Skyward" by Richard E. Byrd, with portrait of the author from "Little America"; "New York to Paris" from "We" by Charles A. Lindbergh; "With Helmet and Hose" from "Exploring with Beebe"; for permission to use illustration in "Brownie and the Cook"; the illustrations by John D. Batten in "Aladdin" and "Ali Baba"; for permission to use woodcut by Gwen Raverat from the "Cambridge Book of Poetry for Children," as illustration for "The Land of Story Books" by R. L. Stevenson.

Sir Arthur Quiller-Couch: for permission to use his poem "Sage Counsel."

Random House: for permission to use illustration by Rockwell Kent from "Moby Dick" for "An Adventure with a Whale."

Fleming H. Revell Company: for permission to use the story "Billy Topsail and the Devilfish" from "The Adventures of Billy Topsail" by Norman Duncan.

W. Heath Robinson: for permission to use his illustration for "A Ship of Rio" in "Peacock Pie" by Walter de la Mare; and for his illustrations of "A Midsummer Night's Dream" by Charles and Mary Lamb.

Charles Scribner's Sons: for permission to use the stories "The Emergency Mistress" from "The Floating Prince" by Frank R. Stockton; "Old Pipes and the Dryad" from "The Queen's Museum" by Frank R. Stockton; "Scarface" from "Blackfoot Lodge Tales" by George Bird Grinnell; "Roland and Oliver" from "The Story of Roland" by James Baldwin, with illustrations by Reginald Birch; "The Forging of the Sampo" from "The Sampo" by James Baldwin; "Gallegher" from "Gallegher and Other Stories for Boys" by Richard Harding Davis, with illustrations by Charles Dana Gibson; "A Cowboy and His Pony" from "Lone Cowboy" by Will James, with illustrations from "Smoky" by Will James; "Jody Finds the Fawn," chapters from "The Yearling" by Marjorie Kinnan Rawlings; for permission to use the poems, "Nearly Ready" by Mary Mapes Dodge; "Autumn Fires," "Windy Nights," "The Cow," "Winter Time," "Travel," "The Land of Counterpane," "The Land of Story Books," "The Vagabond," "Romance," "A Visit from the Sea" and "Requiem" by R. L. Stevenson; "The Shepherdess" by Alice Meynell; "The Duel" and "Wynken, Blynken and Nod" by Eugene Field; "The Chimpanzee," "The Ant," "The Elf and the Dormouse," and "A Bunny Romance" by Oliver Herford, with illustration by author for "A Bunny Romance" from "The Bashful Earthquake."

Martin Secker & Warburg, Ltd.: for permission to use the poem "The Old Ships" by James Elroy Flecker.

Frederick A. Stokes Company: for permission to use the stories "The Bun" and "Mr. Samson Cat" from "Picture Tales from the Russian" by Valery Carrick; "Arthur in the Cave" from "The Welsh Fairy Book" by W. Jenkyn Thomas; "Hunting the Calydonian Boar," "The Winning of Atalanta" and "The Divine Musician" from "Children of the Dawn" by Elsie Finnimore Buckley; for use of illustration by Victor Pérard for Washington Irving's "Rip Van Winkle."

Talbot Press, Ltd., Dublin: for permission to use "How the Son of the Gobhaun Saor Sold the Sheepskin" and "How the Son of the Gobhaun Saor Shortened the Road" from "Celtic Wonder Tales" by Ella Young.

Booth Tarkington: for permission to reprint the story of "The New Pup" from "Penrod Jashber."

This Week, New York Herald Tribune: for permission to use the story "My Song Yankee Doodle" by Carl Glick.

Viking Press, Inc.: for permission to use the poem "The Hens" from "Under the Tree" by Elizabeth Madox Roberts (copyright, 1922, 1930, by Viking Press, Inc.).

Alan Villiers: for permission to use "Rounding the Cape in a Windjammer."

Frederick Warne & Company: for permission to use illustrations by L. Leslie Brooke from Andrew Lang's "Nursery Rhyme Book" for various nursery rhymes carrying the initials L. L. B.; the Leslie Brooke illustrations for "The Three Little Pigs," "The Three Bears" and "Tom Thumb" from "The Golden Goose Book"; the F. D. Bedford illustration in "The Magic Fishbone."

John C. Winston Company: for permission to use in the story "New York to Paris" by Charles A. Lindbergh, the map from "The Book of Courage" by Hagedorn.

THE JUNIOR CLASSICS

READING GUIDE

Volume I

FAIRY TALES AND FABLES

At no limb of that great branching tree which is Children's Literature has the axe been more often laid than at that which represents the fairy tale. But there is something incontestably tough in its fiber. The sap never ceases to rise anew in it, and as long as there is a child to listen and a story-teller to speak, these tales, preserved so long in the memories of simple people—long before ever they were written down—are going to resist attack and survive as they have for centuries. Because they feed the imagination and cultivate in children the precious sense of wonder and delight, they are as necessary to them as any other good food, and he is poor indeed who misses them in youth.

So it seems fitting that this set of classics for children should begin with the folk tale and with fables, whose origin is equally shrouded in antiquity and whose characters are in equal degree known all over the world. "Dog in the manger," "belling the cat" and "sour grapes" are household words, and these stories, brief though they may be, are giant-sized wells of homely wisdom and ethical teaching.

From the folk lore of many lands the editors have chosen some of the old, old tales that children have loved for generations and to which grown-ups look back with especial fondness. The arrangement is by country, which makes it possible to catch the flavor peculiar to the soil in which the tale is rooted. The plots are well nigh universal, but no one could mistake the settings. The stories of Perrault reflect the grace and elegance of the French court for whose enjoyment they were designed; the Irish tales are full of the sly humor of that country of born story-tellers, that last retreat, so it is said, of the Good People; the Scandinavian stories of trolls and dwarfs could have no other background than mist-covered mountains and icy fiords; and as for the Japanese and Indian tales—you might be in another world. Even the traditional beginnings and endings have a flavor all their own: "Once upon a time" or "In a poor wood-cutter's hut" the English stories and the Grimms begin. "In a certain Tzardom," say the Russians, "across three times nine kingdoms. . . ." A typical Irish ending reads this way: "The marriage lasted nine days and nine nights. There were nine hundred fiddlers, nine hundred fluters, and nine hundred pipers and the last day and night of the wedding was better than the first."

Many favorites have had to be left out. The book list which follows supplements the selection. It includes not only the books from which the stories were taken, but others containing similar stories, and also a representation of the folk tales of other countries.

TALES FROM ENGLAND

English Fairy Tales, by Joseph Jacobs. G. P. Putnam's Sons.
More English Fairy Tales, by Joseph Jacobs. G. P. Putnam's Sons.
English Fairy Book, edited by Ernest Rhys. Frederick A. Stokes Company.
Fairy Gold, edited by Ernest Rhys. E. P. Dutton & Company, Inc.
English Fairy Tales, retold by Flora Annie Steel. The Macmillan Company.

TALES FROM IRELAND

Irish Fairy Book, compiled by Alfred Perceval Graves. Frederick A. Stokes Company.
Book of Celtic Stories, by Elizabeth Grierson. The Macmillan Company.
Celtic Fairy Tales, by Joseph Jacobs. G. P. Putnam's Sons.
More Celtic Fairy Tales, by Joseph Jacobs. G. P. Putnam's Sons.
Donegal Fairy Stories, by Seumas MacManus. Doubleday, Doran & Company, Inc.
In Chimney Corners, by Seumas MacManus. Doubleday, Doran & Company, Inc.
Donegal Wonder Book, by Seumas MacManus. Frederick A. Stokes Company.
Irish Fairy and Folk Tales, by William Butler Yeats. Modern Library, Inc.

TALES FROM GERMANY

Household Stories, by the Brothers Grimm, translated by Lucy Crane. The Macmillan Company.

Household Stories, by the Brothers Grimm, translated by Marian Edwardes. E. P. Dutton & Company, Inc.

Gone is Gone, by the Brothers Grimm, illustrated by Wanda Gág. Coward-McCann, Inc.

Tales from Grimm, by the Brothers Grimm, illustrated by Wanda Gág. Coward-McCann, Inc.

Fairy Tales, by the Brothers Grimm, translated by Mrs. Edgar Lucas. J. B. Lippincott Company.

The House in the Wood, by the Brothers Grimm, illustrated by Leslie Brooke. Frederick Warne & Company, Inc.

TALES FROM NORWAY

Fairy Tales from the Far North, by P. C. Asbjörnsen, translated by H. L. Braekstad. A. L. Burt Company, Inc.

Round the Yule Log, by P. C. Asbjörnsen. David Nutt.

Tales from the Fjeld, by P. C. Asbjörnsen, translated by Sir George W. Dasent. G. P. Putnam's Sons.

East o' the Sun and West o' the Moon, by Sir George W. Dasent. G. P. Putnam's Sons.

TALES FROM FRANCE

Fairy Tales, by Charles Perrault, illustrated by Charles Robinson. E. P. Dutton & Company, Inc.

Tales of Mother Goose, by Charles Perrault. D. C. Heath & Company.

The Sleeping Beauty and Other Fairy Tales, by Sir Arthur Quiller-Couch. Doubleday, Doran & Company, Inc.

TALES FROM CZECHOSLOVAKIA

Czechoslovak Fairy Tales, by Parker Fillmore. Harcourt, Brace & Company, Inc.

The Laughing Prince, by Parker Fillmore. Harcourt, Brace & Company, Inc.

Mighty Mikko, by Parker Fillmore. Harcourt, Brace & Company, Inc.

The Shoemaker's Apron, by Parker Fillmore. Harcourt, Brace & Company, Inc.

The Shepherd and the Dragon, by Bozena Némcová. Robert M. McBride & Company.

TALES FROM RUSSIA

Seven Simeons, by Boris Artzybasheff. Viking Press, Inc.
Tales of a Russian Grandmother, by Frances Carpenter. Doubleday, Doran & Company, Inc.
Picture Tales from the Russian, by Valery Carrick. Frederick A. Stokes Company.
More Picture Tales from the Russian, by Valery Carrick. Frederick A. Stokes Company.
Russian Fairy Tales from the Skazki, by Peter Nikolaevich Polevoi. Frederick A. Stokes Company.
Old Peter's Russian Tales, by Arthur Ransome. Thomas Nelson & Sons.
Russian Wonder Tales, by Post Wheeler. D. Appleton-Century Company.
Skazki: Tales and Legends of Old Russia, by Ida Zeitlin. Farrar & Rinehart, Inc.

TALES FROM INDIA

Fairy Tales from India, by Mary Eliza Frere, illustrated by Katharine Pyle. J. B. Lippincott Company.
Indian Fairy Tales, by Joseph Jacobs. G. P. Putnam's Sons.
The Talking Thrush, by W. H. Rouse. E. P. Dutton & Company, Inc.
Tales of the Punjab, by Flora Annie Steel. The Macmillan Company.

FABLES

Fables of Aesop, edited by Joseph Jacobs. The Macmillan Company.
Fables of Aesop, edited and illustrated by Boris Artzybasheff. Viking Press, Inc.
The Tortoise and the Geese, by Bidpai. Houghton Mifflin Company.
Fables, by Jean de La Fontaine. E. P. Dutton & Company, Inc.
Talking Beasts, edited by Kate Douglas Wiggin and Nora Archibald Smith. Doubleday, Doran & Company, Inc.

FOLK TALES OF OTHER COUNTRIES AND A FEW GENERAL COLLECTIONS

Welsh Fairy Book, by William Jenkyn Thomas. Frederick A. Stokes Company.
Scottish Fairy Book, by Elizabeth Grierson. Frederick A. Stokes Company.
Christmas Tales of Flanders, by Jean de Bosschère. Dodd, Mead & Company, Inc.
Tales of a Basque Grandmother, by Frances Carpenter. Doubleday, Doran & Company, Inc.

Three Golden Oranges, by Ralph Steele Boggs and Mary Gould Davis. Longmans, Green & Company.
Picture Tales from Spain, by Ruth Sawyer. Frederick A. Stokes Company.
Once There Was and Was Not, by George Ezra and Beatrice J. Dane. Doubleday, Doran & Company, Inc.
Danish Fairy Tales, by Svend Hersleb Grundtvig. The Thomas Y. Crowell Company.
Fairy Tales from the Swedish, by Nils Gabriel Djurklou. Frederick A. Stokes Company.
Tales from a Finnish Tupa, by James Clyde Bowman and Margery Bianco. George J. McLeod, Ltd.
Italian Fairy Book, by Anne Macdonell. Frederick A. Stokes Company.
The Polish Fairy Book, edited by Elsie Byrde. Frederick A. Stokes Company.
The Gypsy and the Bear, by Lucia M. Borski and Kate B. Miller. Longmans, Green & Company.
The Hungarian Fairy Book, edited by Nandor Pogány. Frederick A. Stokes Company.
The Foundling Prince, by Petre Ispirescu. Houghton Mifflin Company.
Wonder Tales from China Seas, by Frances Jenkins Olcott. Longmans, Green & Company.
Tales of a Chinese Grandmother, by Frances Carpenter. Doubleday, Doran & Company, Inc.
The Magic Bird of Chomo-Lung-Ma, by Sybille Noel. Doubleday, Doran & Company, Inc.
American Folk and Fairy Tales, edited by Rachel Field. Charles Scribner's Sons.
The Blue Fairy Book, by Andrew Lang. Longmans, Green & Company.
The Red Fairy Book, by Andrew Lang. Longmans, Green & Company.
Told Again, by Walter de la Mare. Alfred A. Knopf, Inc.
Tales of Laughter, by Kate Douglas Wiggin and Nora Archibald Smith, illustrated by Elizabeth MacKinstry. Doubleday, Doran & Company, Inc.
The Fairy Ring, by Kate Douglas Wiggin and Nora Archibald Smith. Doubleday, Doran & Company, Inc.
Tales Worth Telling, by Charles J. Finger. D. Appleton-Century Company.

Volume II

STORIES OF WONDER AND MAGIC

The second volume is the logical continuation of that which precedes it in that it contains a further selection of imaginative writing for children. With a few exceptions, however, notably the Arabian Nights tales, it contains stories that are the creation of a known author, even though modeled oftentimes on the old folk tales.

The field from which to select is not large. There are comparatively few outstanding examples of the so-called modern fairy tale. But the few that have laid hold upon the affections of the children are so firmly entrenched that under no circumstances could they be omitted. They are entitled to be called classics.

A wide range is represented, from the extravagances of the sheerest nonsense to the tender and exquisite creations of Hans Christian Andersen.

In the section entitled "Fun and Nonsense" will be found examples of one of the most difficult of arts—the writing of sheer nonsense, of absurdities so seriously and circumstantially presented as to seem not only believable but almost matter-of-course. Lewis Carroll, of course, belongs here but was claimed by another volume. "Uncle Remus" might with perfect propriety go into the folklore volume, yet no one can question the inclusion of Joel Chandler Harris' writing under the heading of "Fun."

Part Two ("From Old Story Books") is a selection from the work of some of the English writers of the nineteenth century, whose books, though written in a faintly didactic tone to suit the taste of an earlier day, preserve nevertheless their charm for this generation.

The third section of the volume ("Dreams and Enchantments") contains two favorite stories from the Arabian Nights, for which room could not be made in Volume I, and with them stories by certain English and American writers of today which have to a marked degree the element of magic and enchantment.

The fourth group of stories, those by Howard Pyle and Frank R. Stockton, have been accorded a special place because they represent, in the editors' minds, perhaps the highest point in imaginative writing for children reached by American authors. To many, Pyle is best known as one of our most famous illustrators. He should be recognized, too, for a writing style which equals his craftsmanship as an artist. While Stockton might easily have been included in the "Fun and Nonsense" section, his completely original stories full of absurdities and kindly yet shrewd humor entitle him to a special prominence in such a collection as this. The books of both writers form a mine of almost inexhaustible treasure for discriminating story-tellers.

The fifth and last part of the volume is given to the great Danish author, Hans Christian Andersen, whose fame grows with the years. Imagination, wit, philosophy, tenderness and beauty shine in every line of these wonderful stories. A complete Andersen belongs in the library of every child.

In the list which follows other stories of wonder and magic will be found.

FUN AND NONSENSE

Short Stories for Short People, by Alicia Aspinwall. E. P. Dutton & Company, Inc.

The Admiral's Caravan, by Charles E. Carryl. Houghton Mifflin Company.

Davy and the Goblin, by Charles E. Carryl. Houghton Mifflin Company.

The Magic Fishbone, by Charles Dickens. Frederick Warne & Company, Inc.

Uncle Remus, His Songs and His Sayings, by Joel Chandler Harris. D. Appleton-Century Company.

Nights with Uncle Remus, by Joel Chandler Harris. D. Appleton-Century Company.

Just So Stories, by Rudyard Kipling. Doubleday, Doran & Company, Inc.

Nonsense Books, by Edward Lear. Little, Brown & Company.

The Story of Doctor Doolittle, by Hugh Lofting. Frederick A. Stokes Company.

The Adventures of Pinocchio, by Carlo Lorenzini. Ginn and Company.

The House at Pooh Corner, by A. A. Milne. E. P. Dutton & Company, Inc.

Winnie the Pooh, by A. A. Milne. E. P. Dutton & Company, Inc.

Floating Island, by Anne Parrish. Harper & Brothers.

Tale of Peter Rabbit, by Beatrix Potter. Frederick Warne & Company, Inc.

Tale of Jemima Puddleduck, by Beatrix Potter. Frederick Warne & Co., Inc.

Roly-Poly Pudding, by Beatrix Potter. Frederick Warne & Company, Inc.

Rootabaga Pigeons, by Carl Sandburg. Harcourt, Brace & Company, Inc.

Rootabaga Stories, by Carl Sandburg. Harcourt, Brace & Company, Inc.

The Rose and the Ring, by William Makepeace Thackeray. The Macmillan Company.

Mary Poppins, by Pamela L. Travers. Reynal & Hitchcock, Inc.

Mary Poppins Comes Back, by Pamela L. Travers. Reynal & Hitchcock, Inc.

The Pot of Gold, by Mary E. Wilkins. Lothrop, Lee & Shepard Company.

FROM OLD STORY BOOKS

Granny's Wonderful Chair, by Frances Browne. E. P. Dutton & Company, Inc.
The Adventures of a Brownie, by Dinah Maria Craik. The Macmillan Company.
The Little Lame Prince, by Dinah Maria Craik. J. B. Lippincott Company.
The Brownies and Other Stories, by Juliana Horatia Ewing. Harcourt, Brace & Company, Inc.
Old Fashioned Fairy Tales, by Juliana Horatia Ewing. George Bell & Sons, Ltd.
The Good-Natured Bear, by Richard Henry Horne. The Macmillan Company.
Mopsa the Fairy, by Jean Ingelow. The Macmillan Company.
At the Back of the North Wind, by George Macdonald. The Macmillan Company.
The Princess and Curdie, by George Macdonald. The Macmillan Company.
The Princess and the Goblin, by George Macdonald. The Macmillan Company.
The Cuckoo Clock and the Tapestry Room, by Mary Louisa Molesworth. The Macmillan Company.

DREAMS AND ENCHANTMENTS

Arabian Nights, edited by Kate Douglas Wiggin and Nora Archibald Smith. Charles Scribner's Sons.
Arabian Nights' Entertainments, edited by Andrew Lang. Longmans, Green & Company.
The White Cat, by the Comtesse d'Aulnoy, illustrated by Elizabeth MacKinstry. The Macmillan Company.
Peter Pan in Kensington Gardens, by Sir James Matthew Barrie. Charles Scribner's Sons.
David Blaize and the Blue Door, by E. F. Benson. Doubleday, Doran & Company, Inc.
The Firelight Fairy Book, by Henry Beston. Little, Brown & Company.
The Starlight Wonder Book, by Henry Beston. Little, Brown & Company.
Shen of the Sea, by Arthur Bowie Chrisman. E. P. Dutton & Company, Inc.
The Big Tree of Bunlahy, by Padraic Colum. The Macmillan Company.
The King of Ireland's Son, by Padraic Colum. The Macmillan Company.
Tal, by Paul Fenimore Cooper. William Morrow & Company, Inc.
Broomsticks, by Walter de la Mare. Constable & Company, Limited.
The Three Mulla-Mulgars, by Walter de la Mare. Alfred A. Knopf, Inc.
Italian Peepshow, by Eleanor Farjeon. Frederick A. Stokes Company.
In Mexico They Say, by Patricia Fent Ross. Alfred A. Knopf, Inc.
Tales from Silver Lands, by Charles J. Finger. Doubleday, Doran & Company.
The Broom Fairies, by Ethel Mary Gate. Yale University Press.
The Wind in the Willows, by Kenneth Grahame. Charles Scribner's Sons.

Little Mr. Thimblefinger and His Queer Country, by Joel Chandler Harris. Houghton Mifflin Company.
Story of Aaron, by Joel Chandler Harris. Houghton Mifflin Company.
Doorway in Fairyland, by Laurence Housman. Harcourt, Brace & Company, Inc.
Moonshine and Clover, by Laurence Housman. Harcourt, Brace & Company.
Ching-Li and the Dragons, by Alice Woodbury Howard. The Macmillan Company.
A Little Boy Lost, by William Henry Hudson. Alfred A. Knopf, Inc.
The Wonderful Adventures of Nils, by Selma Lagerlöf. Henry Holt & Company, Inc.
Golden Spears, by Edmund Leamy. Longmans, Green & Company.
Nicholas, by Anne Carroll Moore. G. P. Putnam's Sons.
Five Children, by Edith Nesbit. Coward-McCann, Inc.
Fairy Caravan, by Beatrix Potter. David McKay Company.
The Children's Book, by Horace E. Scudder. Houghton Mifflin Company.
Tales from Timbuktu, by Constance Smedley. Harcourt, Brace & Company, Inc.
The Happy Prince, by Oscar Wilde. G. P. Putnam's Sons.
The Unicorn with Silver Shoes, by Ella Young. Longmans, Green & Company.

STORIES FROM PYLE AND STOCKTON

Pepper and Salt, by Howard Pyle. Harper & Brothers.
Twilight Land, by Howard Pyle. Harper & Brothers.
The Wonder Clock, by Howard Pyle. Harper & Brothers.
The Floating Prince, by Frank R. Stockton. Charles Scribner's Sons.
The Queen's Museum, by Frank R. Stockton. Charles Scribner's Sons.
The Reformed Pirate, by Frank R. Stockton. Charles Scribner's Sons.
Ting-a-Ling Tales, by Frank R. Stockton. Charles Scribner's Sons.

STORIES FROM ANDERSEN

Fairy Tales, by Hans Christian Andersen, translated by Mrs. Edgar Lucas. Macrae Smith Company.
Fairy Tales and Legends, by Hans Christian Andersen, illustrated by Rex Whistler. Oxford University Press.
Forty Stories, by Hans Christian Andersen, translated by M. R. James. J. B. Lippincott Company.
Stories and Tales, by Hans Christian Andersen, illustrated by V. Pedersen and M. L. Stone. Houghton Mifflin Company.
Wonder Stories, by Hans Christian Andersen, illustrated by V. Pedersen and M. L. Stone. Houghton Mifflin Company.

Volume III

MYTHS AND LEGENDS

This volume contains stories from mythology and legend which have special appeal for children.

The story of Phaeton was chosen from the great storehouse of classic Greek myth in Bulfinch's "Age of Fable," while the rendering of Orpheus was taken from the poetic and beautiful prose of W. M. L. Hutchinson. No collection of stories from the Greek would be complete without Kingsley. His simple, straightforward re-telling still holds the children in spite of paragraphs of moralizing which seem out-dated to us. Hawthorne's "Wonder Book" has been popular in American households for several generations and certainly no one would want a child to miss his delightful re-telling of the Baucis and Philemon story.

The sturdy myths of the Northern peoples follow the classic Greek tales.

To represent Eastern mythology the strongly ethical Buddha re-birth stories were chosen, and are presented in Miss Shedlock's dignified and beautiful rendering.

Next follow our own American Indian myths which have a special value and significance for American children. They are simple, full of action and color and a dry humor of understatement peculiar to the folk literature of this country. Myths of the Pueblo, Zuni, Iroquois and Blackfoot tribes are included.

The second half of the volume contains legends from many sources: old stories which have proved their appeal for the imaginative child.

It is hard to say what is history and what is legend in such a story as William Tell, and it is equally hard to tell what is myth or religious history and what legend in the saint stories. But that these latter are beautiful is certain, and the simplicity and childlike spirit of the saints of these beast legends, especially in the rendering of Helen Waddell, faithful to the original and reverent as it is, makes them especially suitable for a child.

Ella Young's stories are hard to place. They belong to ancient Irish literature and partake of the elements of fairy tale, hero tale and myth. They have a haunting beauty all their own and the author's style enhances it.

A list of additional titles of books of myths and legends follows.

STORIES FROM THE MYTHS OF GREECE AND ROME

Children of the Dawn, by Elsie Finnimore Buckley. Frederick A. Stokes Co.

Age of Fable, by Thomas Bulfinch. Lothrop, Lee & Shepard Company.

The Golden Fleece, by Padraic Colum. The Macmillan Company.

Gods and Heroes, by Robert Edward Francillon. Ginn and Company.

Tanglewood Tales, by Nathaniel Hawthorne. Houghton Mifflin Company.

Wonder Book for Boys and Girls, by Nathaniel Hawthorne, illustrated by Walter Crane. Houghton Mifflin Company.

The Golden Porch, by Winifred M. L. Hutchinson. Longmans, Green & Company.

Orpheus with His Lute, by W. M. L. Hutchinson. Longmans, Green & Company.

The Heroes, by Charles Kingsley, illustrated by the author. The Macmillan Company.

Old Greek Folk Stories Told Anew, by Josephine Preston Peabody. Houghton Mifflin Company.

Greek and Roman Mythology, by Jessie Mary Tatlock. D. Appleton-Century Company.

STORIES FROM THE NORSE MYTHS

In the Days of Giants, by Abbie Farwell Brown. Houghton Mifflin Company.

The Children of Odin, by Padraic Colum. The Macmillan Company.

Norse Stories Retold from the Eddas, by Hamilton Wright Mabie. Dodd, Mead & Company, Inc.

Stories of Norse Heroes, by Ethel M. Wilmot-Buxton. The Thomas Y. Crowell Company.

STORIES FROM THE JATAKA TALES OF INDIA

Jataka Tales, by Ellen C. Babbitt. D. Appleton-Century Company.

More Jataka Tales, by Ellen C. Babbitt. D. Appleton-Century Company.

Eastern Stories and Legends, by Marie L. Shedlock. E. P. Dutton & Company, Inc.

STORIES OF THE AMERICAN INDIAN

Zuni Folk Tales, by Frank Hamilton Cushing. Alfred A. Knopf, Inc.

Wigwam Evenings, by Charles Alexander Eastman. Little, Brown & Company.

Taytay's Tales, by Elizabeth Willis DeHuff. Harcourt, Brace & Company, Inc.
Blackfoot Lodge Tales, by George Bird Grinnell. Charles Scribner's Sons.
Indian Why Stories, by Frank Bird Linderman. Charles Scribner's Sons.
Zuni Indian Tales, by Aileen Nushbaum. G. P. Putnam's Sons.
Skunny Wundy, by Arthur Caswell Parker. Doubleday, Doran & Company, Inc.
Navaho Tales, by William Whitman. Houghton Mifflin Company.

OLD LEGENDS

The Swords of the Vikings, retold by Julia Davis Adams. E. P. Dutton & Company, Inc.
Once in France, by Marguerite Clément. Doubleday, Doran & Company, Inc.
The Forge in the Forest, by Padraic Colum. The Macmillan Company.
The Voyagers, by Padraic Colum. The Macmillan Company.
Wonder Book of Old Romance, by Frederick Joseph Harvey Darton. Frederick A. Stokes Company.
Truce of the Wolf, by Mary Gould Davis. Harcourt, Brace & Company, Inc.
Three and the Moon, by Jacques Dorey. Alfred A. Knopf, Inc.
The Sons o' Cormac, by Aldis Dunbar. E. P. Dutton & Company, Inc.
Tales of the Enchanted Islands of the Atlantic, by Thomas Wentworth Higginson. The Macmillan Company.
The Alhambra, by Washington Irving, Illustrated by Joseph Pennell. The Macmillan Company.
The Book of Wonder Voyages, edited by Joseph Jacobs. G. P. Putnam's Sons.
Christ Legends, by Selma Lagerlöf. Henry Holt & Company, Inc.
Battles and Enchantments, by Norreys Jephson O'Conor. Houghton Mifflin Company.
The Book of Legends, by Horace E. Scudder. Houghton Mifflin Company.
Stories from Old French Romance, by Ethel M. Wilmot-Buxton. Frederick A. Stokes Company.
Celtic Wonder Tales, by Ella Young. Talbot Press, Ltd.
The Wonder-Smith and His Son, by Ella Young. Longmans, Green & Company.

STORIES OF THE SAINTS

The Story of Saint Christopher, by John Ainsworth. The Macmillan Company.
The Book of Saints and Friendly Beasts, by Abbie Farwell Brown. Houghton Mifflin Company.
A Child's Book of Saints, by William Canton. E. P. Dutton & Company, Inc.
Legend of St. Columba, by Padraic Colum. Oxford University Press.

Ten Saints, by Eleanor Farjeon. Oxford University Press.
In God's Garden, by Amy Steedman. Macrae Smith Company.
Our Island Saints, by Amy Steedman. Thomas Nelson & Sons.
Beasts and Saints, by Helen Waddell. Henry Holt & Company, Inc.

Volume IV

HERO TALES

In this volume the editors have brought together some of the favorite hero tales read by boys and girls. Since these epic stories were told by bards and minstrels long before the invention of printing, there are a number of different versions from which to select. The reading list includes good re-tellings for each epic.

For the Odyssey, Padraic Colum's "Adventures of Odysseus" is perhaps the most widely read, although Alfred Church's "Odyssey for Boys and Girls" is still popular, especially with younger children. Butcher and Lang's translation of the Odyssey is a scholarly piece of work for adults and should be at hand for boys and girls who wish to progress from re-tellings to translations.

"The Story of Roland" by James Baldwin is an exceptionally popular book and shares the honors as a favorite with Howard Pyle's "Robin Hood." The editors included the beautiful poetic rendering of the "Battle of Roncesvalles" by Isabel Butler because interest in Roland is so great that boys and girls will read far beyond the versions prepared especially for children.

Howard Pyle's re-telling of the King Arthur legends is in text and illustrations unsurpassed. The version edited by Sidney Lanier has, from the time it was published (1880) been recognized as an exceptionally faithful rendering of the original Malory's "Morte D'Arthur."

Lady Gregory's rendering of the Irish epics of Finn and Cuchulain are unforgettably lovely and should be brought to the attention of any boy or girl who is ready for them after reading the simpler versions given in this volume. James Stephens tells only a portion of the Finn saga but does it in his own inimitable way. Ella Young's re-telling was too long to give in its entirety and accordingly could not be included in Volume IV, but it is of rare beauty, as is all her Irish folklore, and should on no account be missed.

THE ODYSSEY AND THE ILIAD

The Adventures of Odysseus and the Tale of Troy, retold by Padraic Colum. The Macmillan Company.

The Odyssey of Homer, translated by George Herbert Palmer. Houghton Mifflin Company.

The Odyssey for Boys and Girls, told from Homer by Alfred J. Church. The Macmillan Company.

The Odyssey Done into English Prose, by Samuel H. Butcher and Andrew Lang. The Macmillan Company.

The Iliad Done into English Prose, by Ernest Myers, Walter Leaf and Andrew Lang. The Macmillan Company.

The Iliad for Boys and Girls, told from Homer by Alfred J. Church. The Macmillan Company.

The Sunset of the Heroes: Last Adventures of the Takers of Troy, by Winifred M. L. Hutchinson. E. P. Dutton & Company, Inc.

THE EPIC OF KINGS

The Epic of Kings, by Helen Zimmern. The Macmillan Company.

The Story of Rustem, and Other Persian Hero Tales, retold by Elizabeth D. Renninger. Charles Scribner's Sons.

THE KALEVALA

The Sampo, by James Baldwin. Charles Scribner's Sons.

The Wizard of the North: Tales from the Kalevala, by Parker Fillmore. Harcourt, Brace & Company, Inc.

THE SONG OF ROLAND

The Story of Roland, by James Baldwin. Charles Scribner's Sons.

The Song of Roland, by Isabel Butler. Houghton Mifflin Company.

Stories of Charlemagne and the Twelve Peers of France, by Alfred J. Church. Seeley, Service & Company, Ltd., London.

THE CID

The Tale of the Warrior Lord: The Cid, by Merriam Sherwood. Longmans, Green & Company.

Stories from the Chronicle of the Cid, by Mary Wright Plummer. Henry Holt & Company, Inc.

BEOWULF

The Story of Beowulf, by Strafford Riggs. D. Appleton-Century Company.
Beowulf, by John Harrington Cox. Little, Brown & Company.

KING ARTHUR

The Boy's King Arthur, edited by Sidney Lanier, illustrated by N. C. Wyeth. Charles Scribner's Sons.
The Story of King Arthur and His Knights: The Story of the Champions of the Round Table: The Story of Sir Launcelot and His Companions: The Story of the Grail and the Passing of Arthur, by Howard Pyle. Charles Scribner's Sons.
Stories of King Arthur and the Round Table, by Beatrice Clay. E. P. Dutton & Company, Inc.

MABINOGION

The Island of the Mighty, by Padriac Colum. The Macmillan Company.

CUCHULAIN

Cuchulain, the Hound of Ulster, by Eleanor Hull. The Thomas Y. Crowell Company.
Cuchulain of Muirthemne, by Lady Augusta Gregory. Charles Scribner's Sons.
The Coming of Cuculain, by Standish O'Grady. George G. Harrap & Company, Ltd.
The Gates of the North, by Standish O'Grady. George G. Harrap & Company, Ltd.
The Triumph and Passing of Cuculain, by Standish O'Grady. George G. Harrap & Company, Ltd.

FINN

The High Deeds of Finn, by Thomas W. H. Rolleston. George G. Harrap & Company, Ltd.
Gods and Fighting Men, by Lady Augusta Gregory. Charles Scribner's Sons.
Irish Fairy Tales, by James Stephens. The Macmillan Company.
The Tangle-Coated Horse and Other Tales, by Ella Young. Longmans, Green & Company.

ROBIN HOOD

The Merry Adventures of Robin Hood, by Howard Pyle. Charles Scribner's Sons.
English and Scottish Popular Ballads, edited by Francis James Child. Houghton Mifflin Company.

Volume V

STORIES THAT NEVER GROW OLD

The stories in this volume are especially satisfying. They all invite reading and re-reading. They are stories the entire family will enjoy. They are stories that have stood the test of time.

The reading list is not long, but makes up in quality what it lacks in quantity. Some stories such as "Heidi," "Hans Brinker," "The Jungle Book," "Pinocchio" and Howard Pyle's "Robin Hood" could well be listed under "Stories That Never Grow Old," but they have already been given in the lists for other volumes of the Junior Classics.

There are several editions of most of these stories illustrated by different artists. In the selections included in Volume V and in the stories found in the reading list, the editors have taken great care to select the editions with fine format and illustrations. Only the Tenniel illustrations for "Alice in Wonderland" would be possible and Arthur Rackham's "Sleepy Hollow" and N. C. Wyeth's "Rip Van Winkle" are definitely first choice.

Alice's Adventures in Wonderland, by Lewis Carroll. The Macmillan Company.

Aucassin and Nicolette, translated by Andrew Lang. Holiday House.

The Bible for Young People, arranged from the King James version. D. Appleton-Century Company.

The Bold Dragoon, by Washington Irving, illustrated by James Daugherty. Alfred A. Knopf, Inc.

The Christmas Carol, by Charles Dickens, illustrated by Arthur Rackham. J. B. Lippincott Company.

David Copperfield, by Charles Dickens. Macrae Smith Company.

Don Quixote, by Miguel de Cervantes, retold by Judge Parry. Dodd, Mead & Company, Inc.

Gulliver's Travels, by Jonathan Swift, edited by Padraic Colum. The Macmillan Company.

Jackanapes, by Juliana Horatia Ewing, illustrated by Randolph Caldecott. E. P. Dutton & Company, Inc.

Kim, by Rudyard Kipling. Doubleday, Doran & Company, Inc.

The King of the Golden River, by John Ruskin. J. B. Lippincott Company.

The Legend of Sleepy Hollow, by Washington Irving, illustrated by Arthur Rackham. David McKay Company.
Pilgrim's Progress, by John Bunyan, illustrated by the Brothers Rhead. D. Appleton-Century Company.
Rip Van Winkle, by Washington Irving, illustrated by N. C. Wyeth. David McKay Company.
Robinson Crusoe, by Daniel Defoe, illustrated by Louis Rhead. Harper & Brothers.
The Swiss Family Robinson, by Johann David Wyss, illustrated by Louis Rhead. Harper & Brothers.
Tales, by Edgar Allan Poe. G. P. Putnam's Sons.
Tales from the Travels of Baron Munchausen, by Rudolph Erich Raspe. D. C. Heath & Company.
Tales from Shakespeare, by Charles and Mary Lamb, illustrated by Maud and Miska Petersham. The Macmillan Company.
The Water Babies, by Charles Kingsley, illustrated by Warwick Goble. The Macmillan Company.

Volume VI

STORIES ABOUT BOYS AND GIRLS

The editors have devoted one entire volume to stories about boys and girls because these stories are so eagerly sought after and read by children. It matters little from what country the story-children come if they are "real boys and girls."

During the last twenty-five years, publishers have recognized this keen interest by publishing stories about children from every corner of the globe. Each year adds new and attractive volumes to this field of children's literature.

Some of the authors of our time who have written good stories about boys and girls are Eliza Orne White, Lucy Fitch Perkins, Laura Ingalls Wilder, Ethel Parton, Katharine Adams and Elizabeth Coatsworth.

The stories selected for the reading list have been chosen primarily because of their story quality and the approval accorded them by the children themselves. "The Dutch Twins," for example, have no rival among the fifteen or more twins from other countries.

Some of these stories have been translated from the language of the country which they depict, *i.e.,* "Emil and the Detectives" from the German, "Johnny Blossom" and "What Happened to Inger Johanne" from the Norwegian, and "Susanna's Auction" and "Lady Green Satin and Her Maid Rosette" from the French.

The stories listed under "Older Boys and Girls" suggest the reading trends of many girls who are not yet ready for the adult novel, but are interested in people and social adjustments. "Dusky Day," "The Jumping-Off Place," "Meggy MacIntosh," "Winterbound" and "You Make Your Own Luck" will appeal especially to them.

FOR YOUNGER CHILDREN

Away Goes Sally, by Elizabeth Coatsworth. The Macmillan Company.

The Boys and Sally Down on a Plantation, by Rose B. Knox. Doubleday, Doran & Company, Inc.

Chi-Weé, by Grace Moon. Doubleday, Doran & Company, Inc.

Donkey John of the Toy Valley, by Margaret W. Morley. A. C. McClurg & Company.

The Dutch Twins, by Lucy Fitch Perkins. Houghton Mifflin Company.

Emil and the Detectives, by Erich Kästner. Doubleday, Doran & Company, Inc.

The Good Master, by Kate Seredy. Viking Press, Inc.

Heidi, by Johanna Spyri, translated by Helen B. Dole. Ginn and Company.

Jamaica Johnny, by Berta and Elmer Hader. The Macmillan Company.

Johnny Blossom, by Dikken Zwilgmeyer, translated by Emilie Poulsson. Pilgrim Press.

Lady Green Satin and Her Maid Rosette, by Elizabeth Martineau des Chesnez. The Macmillan Company.

The Little House in the Big Woods, by Laura Ingalls Wilder. Harper & Brothers.

The Peterkin Papers, by Lucretia P. Hale. Little, Brown & Company.

Petite Suzanne, by Marguerite De Angeli. Doubleday, Doran & Company, Inc.

Polly Patchwork, by Rachel Field. Doubleday, Doran & Company, Inc.

The Secret Garden, by Frances Hodgson Burnett. Frederick A. Stokes Company.

The Short Sword, by Violet Mary Irwin. The Macmillan Company.

Susanna's Auction, from the French, illustrated by L. M. Boutet de Monvel. The Macmillan Company.

Taktuk, an Arctic Boy, by Helen Lomen and Marjorie Flack. Doubleday, Doran & Company, Inc.

What Happened to Inger Johanne, by Dikken Zwilgmeyer, translated by Emilie Poulsson. Lothrop, Lee & Shepard Company.
When Molly Was Six, by Eliza Orne White. Houghton Mifflin Company.
What Katy Did, by Susan Coolidge. Little, Brown & Company.
Where Is Adelaide? by Eliza Orne White. Houghton Mifflin Company.

FOR OLDER BOYS AND GIRLS

The Adventures of Huckleberry Finn, by Mark Twain. Harper & Brothers.
The Adventures of Tom Sawyer, by Mark Twain. Harper & Brothers.
Boy on Horseback, by Lincoln Steffens. Harcourt, Brace & Co., Inc.
Caddie Woodlawn, by Carol Ryrie Brink. The Macmillan Company.
Downright Dencey, by Caroline Dale Snedeker, Doubleday, Doran & Co.
Dusky Day, by Florence C. Means. Houghton Mifflin Company.
Gallegher, by Richard Harding Davis. Charles Scribner's Sons.
Hans Brinker; or The Silver Skates, by Mary Mapes Dodge. Charles Scribner's Sons.
The Jumping-off Place, by Marian Hurd McNeely. Longmans, Green & Co.
Little Women, by Louisa May Alcott. Little, Brown & Company.
Mama's Bank Account, by Kathryn Forbes. Harcourt, Brace & Co., Inc.
Meggy MacIntosh, by Elizabeth Janet Gray. Doubleday, Doran & Company.
Midsummer, by Katharine Adams. The Macmillan Company.
My Song Yankee Doodle, by Carl Glick. *This Week, New York Herald Tribune.*
Penrod, His Complete Story, by Booth Tarkington, illustrated by Gordon Grant. Doubleday, Doran & Company, Inc.
Rebecca of Sunnybrook Farm, by Kate Douglas Wiggin. Houghton Mifflin Company.
Roller Skates, by Ruth Sawyer. The Macmillan Company.
The Story of a Bad Boy, by Thomas Bailey Aldrich. Houghton Mifflin Co.
Tabitha Mary, by Ethel Parton. Viking Press, Inc.
Winterbound, by Margery Williams Bianco. Viking Press, Inc.
Young Fu of the Upper Yangtze, by Elizabeth Foreman Lewis. John C. Winston Company.
You Make Your Own Luck, by Elsie Singmaster. Longmans, Green & Co.

Volume VII

THE ANIMAL BOOK

The editors found it difficult to define the scope of this volume since animals are such important characters in children's literature. Animal characters abound in fairy tales and folklore and have become almost human in such stories as "Peter Rabbit," "Wind in the Willows" and "Winnie the Pooh."

The selections in this volume are concerned with animals in their own world, sometimes personified, but always retaining their natural relationships with man and nature. A number of stories are by writers of ability who are also nature lovers, who observe animals in their native haunts and then write stories about them. Ernest Thompson Seton, Charles Roberts, Samuel Scoville, Herbert Saas and Henry Williamson belong with this group of writers.

In recent years scientists have brought back thrilling tales of their real adventures and have written about them so well that many boys and girls read them as eagerly as they do fiction. Carl Akeley and Raymond Ditmars are well-known contributors in this field.

Dhan Mukerji is in a class by himself. He is neither a scientist nor a hunter. His stories of the Indian jungle are vivid with realism, but are also filled with imagination and mystic beauty.

Rudyard Kipling's "Jungle Book" is a children's classic. No child should miss "Mowgli," "Toomai" or "Rikki-Tikki-Tavi."

One of the most beloved dog characters of recent years is Lassie from the story "Lassie Come-Home" by Eric Knight, so admirably shown in motion pictures. Marjorie Kinnan Rawlings' "The Yearling" also yields many touching incidents about Jody and his fawn Flag. But no less heroic are the Seeing Eye dogs from real life to whom leading their blind masters about and caring for them is very sober business, as told in book by Dickson Hartwell.

Since the days of "Black Beauty" stories about horses, dogs and other animals as the friends of mankind have been popular. The selections in Volume VII and the reading list are the best of these.

Three books on the reading list deal with animals scientifically and impersonally. They are "Animals on the March," "Ancient Animals" and "Vanishing Wilderness."

FOR YOUNGER CHILDREN

All About Pets, by Margery Williams Bianco. The Macmillan Company.

Ancient Animals, by William Wilcox Robinson. The Macmillan Company.

Animals of the Bible, by Dorothy P. Lathrop. Frederick A. Stokes Company.

Animals on the March, by W. Maxwell Reed and Jannette M. Lucas. Harcourt, Brace & Company, Inc.

Black Beauty, by Anna Sewell. Dodd, Mead & Company, Inc.

The Burgess Bird Book for Children, by Thornton Waldo Burgess. Little, Brown & Company.
The Cat and the Captain, by Elizabeth Coatsworth. The Macmillan Company.
Crazy Quilt, the Story of a Piebald Pony, by Paul Brown. Charles Scribner's Sons.
The Dog of Flanders, by Louise de la Ramée. The Macmillan Company.
The Handsome Donkey, by Mary Gould Davis. Harcourt, Brace & Co.
Hari, the Jungle Lad, by Dhan Gopal Mukerji. E. P. Dutton & Company, Inc.
Honk, the Moose, by Phil Stong. Dodd, Mead & Company, Inc.
Jimmie, the Story of a Black Bear Cub, by Ernest Harold Baynes. The Macmillan Company.
The Jungle Book, by Rudyard Kipling. Doubleday, Doran & Company, Inc.
Kari, the Elephant, by Dhan Gopal Mukerji. E. P. Dutton & Company, Inc.
Little Dog Toby, by Rachel Field. The Macmillan Company.
The Monkey That Would Not Kill, by Henry Drummond. Dodd, Mead & Company, Inc.
More About Animals, by Margaret Williams Bianco. Macmillan Company.
My Friend Toto, by Cherry Kearton. Dodd, Mead & Company, Inc.
Red Horse Hill, by Stephen W. Meader. Harcourt, Brace & Company, Inc.
The Second Jungle Book, by Rudyard Kipling. Doubleday, Doran & Co.
Spunky, the Story of a Shetland Pony, by Berta and Elmer Hader. The Macmillan Company.
Tales of the First Animals, by Edith B. Walker and Charles C. Mook. Farrar & Rinehart, Inc.
Toby Tyler; or, Ten Weeks with a Circus, by James Otis Kaler. Harper & Brothers.

FOR OLDER BOYS AND GIRLS

Animal Treasure, by Ivan T. Sanderson. Viking Press, Inc.
Bambi, by Felix Salten. Noble & Noble, Publishers, Inc.
Bob, Son of Battle, by Alfred Ollivant. Doubleday, Doran & Company, Inc.
The Call of the Wild, by Jack London. The Macmillan Company.
Dogs Against Darkness, by Dickson Hartwell. Dodd Mead & Company.
Gay-Neck, by Dhan Gopal Mukerji. E. P. Dutton & Company, Inc.
Ghond, the Hunter, by Dhan Gopal Mukerji. E. P. Dutton & Company, Inc.
Greyfriars Bobby, by Eleanor Atkinson. Harper & Brothers.
Gulliver the Great, and Other Dog Stories, by Walter Alden Dyer. D. Appleton-Century Company.
Herdboy of Hungary, by Alexander Finta and Jeanette Eaton. Harper & Brothers.
Here Comes Barnum, by P. T. Barnum, edited by Helen Josephine Ferris. Harcourt, Brace & Company, Inc.

Hoof and Claw, by Charles G. D. Roberts. The Macmillan Company.
In Brightest Africa, by Carl Akeley. Doubleday, Doran & Company, Inc.
Kindred of the Wild, by Charles G. D. Roberts. Doubleday, Doran & Co.
Lad: a Dog, by Albert Payson Terhune. E. P. Dutton & Company, Inc.
Lassie Come-Home, by Eric Knight. *Saturday Evening Post,* 1938.
Lions 'n Tigers 'n Everything, by Courtney Ryley Cooper. Little, Brown & Co.
Lost in the Jungle, by Paul Du Chaillu. Harper & Brothers.
Macaw: the Story of a Parrot, by Peggy von der Goltz. Farrar & Rinehart, Inc.
National Velvet, by Enid Bagnold. William Morrow & Company, Inc.
Red Heifer, by Frank D. Davison. Coward-McCann, Incorporated.
Safari, by Martin Johnson. G. P. Putnam's Sons.
Shasta of the Wolves, by Olaf Baker. Dodd, Mead & Company, Inc.
Smoky, the Cowhorse, by Will James. Charles Scribner's Sons.
Snakes Alive and How They Live, by Clifford H. Pope. Viking Press, Inc.
The Snow Goose, by Paul Gallico. Alfred A. Knopf, Inc.
Stickeen, by John Muir. Houghton Mifflin Company.
Strange Animals I Have Known, by Raymond Lee Ditmars. Harcourt, Brace & Company, Inc.
Tarka the Otter, by Henry Williamson. E. P. Dutton & Company, Inc.
Thrills of a Naturalist's Quest, by Raymond Lee Ditmars. The Macmillan Company.
Trapping Wild Animals in Malay Jungles, by Charles Mayer. Dodd, Mead & Company, Inc.
Vanishing Wilderness, by Francesca Raimonde La Monte and Micaela H. Welch. Liveright Publishing Corporation.
Way of the Wild, by Herbert Ravenel Sass. G. P. Putnam's Sons.
Wild Animals I Have Known, by Ernest Thompson Seton. Charles Scribner's Sons.
Wild Folk, by Samuel Scoville. Little, Brown & Company.
The Yearling, by Marjorie Kinnan Rawlings. Charles Scribner's Sons.

Volume VIII

STORIES FROM HISTORY

This volume represents another field of children's literature which has grown rapidly in recent years.

Stories with historic background have been popular with boys and girls of each generation beginning with the romances of Sir Walter Scott. The taste persists and new stories are published each year. Constance Skinner, Cornelia Meigs, Caroline Snedeker and

Rachel Field are well-known authors; however, Howard Pyle and John Bennett have not yet been surpassed in this field.

Modern boys and girls are not confined to stories for vivid writing in history. In recent years biography has become more colorful and alive. Stewart Edward White's "Daniel Boone, Wilderness Scout" was among the pioneers in good biography for children.

Cornelia Meigs, already accomplished in the story with historical background, has written "Invincible Louisa," a book that girls immediately claimed as their own. In "Abe Lincoln Grows Up" the publisher has made an inspiring book of Lincoln's early youth from Carl Sandburg's two-volume life of Abraham Lincoln.

Among the recent historical contributions are Esther Forbes' vivid and delightful stories of Revolutionary New England found in her books "Johnny Tremain" and "America's Paul Revere." Stephen Vincent Benét gave us a striking character story of Daniel Webster and his New Hampshire neighbors.

World War II furnishes graphic material, such as MacArthur's dramatic escape from the Philippines, told here by John J. Floherty, and a saga of three men in a raft who drifted for 34 days in the South Pacific, as recounted by Robert Trumbull.

The selections in this volume and the books on the reading list include stories with historical background and historical biography read by boys and girls of today. The four books listed as "Background" are modern presentations of world history.

BACKGROUND

A Child's History of the World, by Virgil M. Hillyer. D. Appleton-Century Company.

The Story of Mankind, by Hendrik Willem Van Loon. Liveright Publishing Corporation.

Unrolling the Map; the Story of Exploration, by Leonard Outhwaite. Reynal and Hitchcock, Inc.

The World We Live In, by Gertrude Hartman. The Macmillan Company.

AMERICA

The Voyages of Jacques Cartier, by Esther Averill. The Domino Press.

Barnaby Lee, by John Bennett. D. Appleton-Century Company.

The Story of Jack Ballister's Fortunes, by Howard Pyle. D. Appleton-Century Company.

The Young Trailers, by Joseph Altsheler. D. Appleton-Century Company.

Calico Bush, by Rachel Field. The Macmillan Company.
The Last of the Mohicans, by James Fenimore Cooper. Charles Scribner's Sons.
Young Lafayette, by Jeanette Eaton. Houghton Mifflin Company.
Johnny Tremain, by Esther Forbes, Houghton Mifflin Company.
The Covered Bridge, by Cornelia Meigs. The Macmillan Company.
Silent Scot, by Constance Lindsay Skinner. The Macmillan Company.
Daniel Boone, Wilderness Scout, by Stewart Edward White. Doubleday, Doran & Company, Inc.
Becky Landers, Frontier Warrior, by Constance Lindsay Skinner. The Macmillan Company.
Davy Crockett, by Constance Rourke. Harcourt, Brace & Company, Inc.
No Other White Men, by Julia Davis. E. P. Dutton & Company, Inc.
The Devil and Daniel Webster, by Stephen Vincent Benét. Farrar & Rhinehart, Inc.
The Oregon Trail, by Francis Parkman. Little, Brown & Company, Inc.
Wagons Westward, by Armstrong Sperry. John C. Winston Company.
The Pony Express Goes Through, by Howard R. Driggs. Frederick A. Stokes Company.
Abe Lincoln Grows Up, by Carl Sandburg. Harcourt, Brace & Company, Inc.
The Perfect Tribute, by Mary Raymond Shipman Andrews. Charles Scribner's Sons.
The Railroad to Freedom, by Hildegarde Hoyt Swift. Harcourt, Brace & Company, Inc.
Emmeline, by Elsie Singmaster. Houghton Mifflin Company.
Invincible Louisa, by Cornelia Meigs. Little, Brown & Company.
When the West Was Young, by Frederick R. Bechdolt. D. Appleton-Century Company.
High Adventure, by James Norman Hall. Houghton Mifflin Company.
Here Is Your War, by Ernie Pyle. Henry Holt & Company, Inc.
The Courage and the Glory, by John J. Floherty. J. B. Lippincott Company.
The Raft, by Robert Trumbull. Henry Holt & Company, Inc.

ENGLAND

Puck of Pook's Hill, by Rudyard Kipling. Doubleday, Doran & Company, Inc.
Rewards and Fairies, by Rudyard Kipling. Doubleday, Doran & Company, Inc.
The Talisman, by Sir Walter Scott. Houghton Mifflin Company.
Ivanhoe, by Sir Walter Scott. Houghton Mifflin Company.
King Richard's Land, by Leonard A. G. Strong. Alfred A. Knopf, Inc.
Men of Iron, by Howard Pyle. Harper & Brothers.
The Black Arrow, by Robert Louis Stevenson. Charles Scribner's Sons.
The Prince and the Pauper, by Samuel L. Clemens. Harper & Brothers.
Kenilworth, by Sir Walter Scott. The Thomas Y. Crowell Company.

Westward Ho! by Charles Kingsley. Charles Scribner's Sons.
Master Skylark, by John Bennett. D. Appleton-Century Company.
Merrylips, by Beulah M. Dix. The Macmillan Company.
Kidnapped, by Robert Louis Stevenson. Charles Scribner's Sons.
Young Walter Scott, by Elizabeth Janet Gray. Viking Press, Inc.
Lawrence; the Story of His Life, by Edward Robinson. Oxford University Press.

FRANCE

Gabriel and the Hour-Book, by Evaleen Stein. L. C. Page & Company.
Joan of Arc, by L. M. Boutet de Monvel. D. Appleton-Century Company.
The Girl in White Armor; the True Story of Joan of Arc, by Albert Bigelow Paine. The Macmillan Company.
The Boy Knight of Reims, by Eloise Lownsbery. Houghton Mifflin Company.
Quentin Durward, by Sir Walter Scott. Charles Scribner's Sons.
The Three Musketeers, by Alexandre Dumas. The Thomas Y. Crowell Co.
A Tale of Two Cities, by Charles Dickens. Dodd, Mead & Company, Inc.
The Reds of the Midi, by Felix Gras. D. Appleton-Century Company.
A Daughter of the Seine, by Jeanette Eaton. Harper & Brothers.
Falcons of France, by Charles Bernard Nordhoff and James Norman Hall. Little, Brown & Company.

OTHER COUNTRIES

Plutarch's Lives for Boys and Girls, edited by W. H. Weston. Thomas Nelson & Sons.
Men of Old Greece, by Jennie Hall. Little, Brown & Company.
Victor of Salamis; a Tale of the Days of Xerxes, Leonidas and Themistocles, by William Stearns Davis. The Macmillan Company.
The Spartan, by Caroline Dale Snedeker. Doubleday, Doran & Company, Inc.
Buried Cities, by Jennie Hall. The Macmillan Company.
The Lance of Kanana, by Harry W. French. Lothrop, Lee & Shepard Co.
The Story of Rolf and the Viking's Bow, by Allen French. Little, Brown & Company.
God's Troubadour; the Story of St. Francis of Assisi, by Sophie Jewett. The Thomas Y. Crowell Company.
The Story of Marco Polo, by Noah Brooks. D. Appleton-Century Company.
The Flame, Saint Catherine of Siena, by Jeanette Eaton. Harper & Brothers.
The Trumpeter of Krakow, a Tale of the Fifteenth Century, by Eric Philbrook Kelly. The Macmillan Company.
Courageous Companions, a Story of Magellan, by Charles J. Finger. Longmans, Green & Company.
The Dauntless Liberator, the Life of Simon Bolivar, by Phyllis Marschall and John Crane. D. Appleton-Century Company.

Volume IX

SPORT AND ADVENTURE

This entire volume and reading list are planned for the older boys and girls. Many of the books were not written specifically for children, but have been appropriated by them, a classic example being "Moby Dick." The authors of these stories of adventure are such masters as Rudyard Kipling, John Masefield, Jules Verne, Robert Louis Stevenson, Howard Pyle and John Buchan.

In the field of sport and school stories, William Heyliger, Ralph Barbour and Donal Haines are popular writers of today.

The only real representative of the mystery and detective story is the almost classic "Sherlock Holmes." However, "The Jinx Ship," "King Solomon's Mines" and "Ride in the Dark" are good.

Among the outstanding adventures in real life are Lindbergh's pioneer airplane flight across the Atlantic, air flights to the North and South Poles, the persistent and dramatic attempts to climb the summit of Mount Everest, and more recently the great scientific experiments on the atom bomb.

Other modern adventurers—and women are conspicuous among them—have been able to make actual experiences as interesting as fiction. Some of these writers are Amelia Earhart, Anne Lindbergh, Ann Axtell Morris, William Beebe and Roy Chapman Andrews.

STORIES

The Adventures of Sherlock Holmes, by A. Conan Doyle. Harper & Brothers.
The Bird of Dawning, by John Masefield. The Macmillan Company.
Captains Courageous, by Rudyard Kipling. Doubleday, Doran & Company.
A Dog at His Heels, by Charles J. Finger. John C. Winston Company.
The Half-back, by Ralph Henry Barbour. D. Appleton-Century Company.
The Half Deck, by George H. Grant. Little, Brown & Company.
The Heart of Little Shikara, by Edison Marshall. Little, Brown & Co.
Howard Pyle's Book of Pirates, by Howard Pyle. Harper & Brothers.
The Human Comedy, by William Saroyan. Harcourt, Brace & Co., Inc.
Jim Davis, by John Masefield. The Macmillan Company.
The Jinx Ship, by Howard Pease. Doubleday, Doran & Company, Inc.
King Solomon's Mines, by Henry Rider Haggard. Longmans, Green & Co.
Lumberjack, by Stephen W. Meader. Harcourt, Brace & Company, Inc.

Michael Strogoff, by Jules Verne. Charles Scribner's Sons.
Moby Dick, by Herman Melville. Dodd, Mead & Company, Inc.
Mutineers, by Charles Boardman Hawes. Little, Brown & Company.
Mutiny on the Bounty, by Charles Bernard Nordhoff and James Norman Hall. Little, Brown & Company.
The New Moon, by Cornelia Meigs. The Macmillan Company.
The Omnibus of Sport, by Grantland Rice and H. W. H. Powel. Harper & Brothers.
The Pearl Lagoon, by Charles Bernard Nordhoff. Little, Brown & Company.
Peggy Covers the News, by Emma Bugbee. Dodd, Mead & Company, Inc.
Prester John, by John Buchan. Houghton Mifflin Company.
Ride in the Dark, by Stephen W. Meader. Harcourt, Brace & Company, Inc.
Shift to the Right, by B. J. Chute. The Macmillan Company.
The Spirit of the Leader, by William Heyliger. D. Appleton-Century Co.
Split Seconds, by Jackson Volney Scholz. William Morrow & Company, Inc.
Stalky & Co., by Rudyard Kipling. Doubleday, Doran & Company, Inc.
Swallows and Amazons, by Arthur Ransome. J. B. Lippincott Company.
Swift Rivers, by Cornelia Meigs. Little, Brown & Company.
Team Play, by Donal H. Haines. Farrar & Rinehart, Inc.
Tom Brown's School Days, by Thomas Hughes. Ginn and Company.
Treasure Island, by Robert Louis Stevenson. Charles Scribner's Sons.
Twenty Thousand Leagues under the Sea, by Jules Verne. Charles Scribner's Sons.
The Varmint, by Owen Johnson. Little, Brown & Company.
The Will to Win, by Stephen W. Meader. Harcourt, Brace & Company, Inc.

STORIES FROM REAL LIFE

Adrift on an Icepan, by Sir Wilfred Thomason Grenfell. Houghton Mifflin Company.
Antarctic Icebreakers, by Lorene K. Fox. Doubleday, Doran & Company, Inc.
The Book of the Gloucester Fishermen, by James B. Connolly. John Day Company, Inc.
The Cruise of the Cachalot, by Frank Thomas Bullen. D. Appleton-Century Company.
Dawn Over Zero, by W. L. Laurence. Alfred A. Knopf, Inc.
Denmark Caravan, by Ruth Bryan Owen. Dodd, Mead & Company, Inc.
Digging in Yucatan, by Ann Axtell Morris. Doubleday, Doran & Company.
The Ends of the Earth, by Roy Chapman Andrews. G. P. Putnam's Sons.
The Epic of Mount Everest, by Sir Francis Edward Younghusband. Longmans, Green & Company.
Exploring with Beebe, by William Beebe. G. P. Putnam's Sons.
Exploring with Byrd, by Richard Evelyn Byrd. G. P. Putnam's Sons.

The Fun of It, by Amelia Earhart. Harcourt, Brace & Company, Inc.
Heroes of the Farthest North and Farthest South, by J. Kennedy MacLean. The Thomas Y. Crowell Company.
High Conquest, by James Ramsey Ullman. J. B. Lippincott Company.
I'll Take the High Road, by Wolfgang Langewiesche. Harcourt, Brace & Co., Inc.
Last Flight, by Amelia Earhart. Harcourt, Brace & Company, Inc.
Mountains and Men, by Leonard H. Robbins. Dodd, Mead & Co., Inc.
North to the Orient, by Anne Morrow Lindbergh. Harcourt, Brace & Co.
On the Bottom, by Edward Ellsberg. Dodd, Mead & Company, Inc.
Play the Game; the Book of Sport, edited by Mitchell V. Charnley. Harper & Brothers.
By Way of Cape Horn, by Alan J. Villiers. Charles Scribner's Sons.
This Business of Exploring, by Roy Chapman Andrews. G. P. Putnam's Sons.
The Voyages of Captain Scott, by Charles Turley. Dodd, Mead & Company.
We, by Charles A. Lindbergh. G. P. Putnam's Sons.

Volume X

POETRY

This volume contains a selection of the poems that are enjoyed by children and young people.

It is divided into three groups. The first includes famous old Mother Goose nursery rhymes and some of the old riddles that little children love to guess and to give to other children.

The second group contains a large and varied selection of poetry for those who have outgrown nursery rhymes. The poems are arranged by subject matter. First come those about nature and the seasons, then those about the animate world that the child sees all around him, then the poetry of fairyland and its inhabitants. Next comes a section devoted to the nonsense of Carroll and Lear and those who came after them. Following this is a group of poems about the child at home and at play and then a few poems about old friends of the children—Little Gustava, Hiawatha, Blake's Chimney Sweeper, Meddlesome Matty and others. The last two groups are a selection of famous old ballads and story-telling poems, including some familiar ones based on historical incidents, and, last of all, poems in the mood of romance and adventure.

Looking Forward—the third part of the volume—contains a

short selection of verse intended to be a foretaste of the riches in store for the poetry-loving child as he grows older. In this section, no attempt has been made to include the modern poets in the selection. In English poetry we have not gone beyond Housman and in American poetry we have stopped with Lowell. In the book list which follows, however, many contemporary poets have been included whose poetry appeals to young people.

Any anthology is bound to be disappointing, for what it leaves out, and many favorites had to be omitted for lack of room. In the inclusive supplementary list will be found most of the poems which readers may miss.

NURSERY RHYMES

Four and Twenty Blackbirds, edited by Helen Dean Fish. Frederick A. Stokes Company.

The Favourites of a Nursery of Seventy Years Ago, compiled by Edith Emerson Forbes. Houghton Mifflin Company.

Mother Goose's Melodies, edited by William A. Wheeler. Houghton Mifflin Company.

Nursery Rhyme Book, edited by Andrew Lang. Frederick Warne & Company.

Mother Goose's Nursery Rhymes, edited by Lavinia Edna Walter. The Macmillan Company.

The Only True Mother Goose. Lothrop, Lee & Shepard Company.

Sugar and Spice and All That's Nice, compiled by Mary Wilder Tileston. Little, Brown & Company.

Pinafore Palace, edited by Kate Douglas Wiggin and Nora Archibald Smith. Doubleday, Doran & Company, Inc.

POEMS OF CHILDHOOD AND YOUTH

Anthologies

Treasury of Verse for Little Children, edited by Madalen C. Edgar. The Thomas Y. Crowell Company.

The Cambridge Book of Poetry for Children, edited by Kenneth Grahame. G. P. Putnam's Sons.

The Little Book of Necessary Nonsense, compiled by Burges Johnson. Harper & Brothers.

The Blue Poetry Book, edited by Andrew Lang. Longmans, Green & Company.

A Book of Verses for Children, edited by Edward V. Lucas. Henry Holt & Company, Inc.

Story-telling Poems, compiled by Frances Jenkins Olcott. Houghton Mifflin Company.

A Book of Famous Verse, edited by Agnes Repplier. Houghton Mifflin Co.

The Home Book of Verse for Young Folks, edited by Burton Stevenson. Henry Holt & Company, Inc.

Rainbow Gold, edited by Sara Teasdale. The Macmillan Company.

The Listening Child, compiled by Lucy W. Thacher. The Macmillan Company.

Rainbow in the Sky, compiled by Louis Untermeyer. Harcourt, Brace & Company, Inc.

The Posy Ring, edited by Kate Douglas Wiggin and Nora Archibald Smith. Doubleday, Doran & Company, Inc.

Golden Numbers, edited by Kate Douglas Wiggin and Nora Archibald Smith. Doubleday, Doran & Company, Inc.

Individual Poets

Robin Redbreast, by William Allingham. The Macmillan Company.

Songs of Innocence, by William Blake. G. P. Putnam's Sons.

Collected Verse, by Lewis Carroll. The Macmillan Company.

Poems by a Little Girl, by Hilda Conkling. Frederick A. Stokes Company.

Peacock Pie, by Walter de la Mare. Henry Holt & Company, Inc.

Down-a-Down-Derry, by Walter de la Mare. Henry Holt & Company, Inc.

Poems for Youth, by Emily Dickinson. Little, Brown & Company.

Joan's Door, by Eleanor Farjeon. Frederick A. Stokes Company.

Pointed People, by Rachel Field. The Macmillan Company.

Taxis and Toadstools, by Rachel Field. Doubleday, Doran & Company, Inc.

Fairies and Chimneys, by Rose Fyleman. Doubleday, Doran & Company, Inc.

The Bashful Earthquake, by Oliver Herford. Charles Scribner's Sons.

More Animals, by Oliver Herford. Charles Scribner's Sons.

Nonsense Books, by Edward Lear. Little, Brown & Company.

Johnny Appleseed, by Vachel Lindsay. The Macmillan Company.

Now We Are Six, by A. A. Milne. E. P. Dutton & Company, Inc.

When We Were Very Young, by A. A. Milne. E. P. Dutton & Company, Inc.

Under the Tree, by Elizabeth Madox Roberts. Viking Press, Inc.

Sing-Song, by Christina Rossetti. The Macmillan Company.

Early Moon, by Carl Sandburg. Harcourt, Brace & Company, Inc.

A Child's Garden of Verses, by Robert Louis Stevenson. Charles Scribner's Sons.

Original Poems for Infant Minds, by Ann and Jane Taylor. Frederick A. Stokes Company.

Stars Tonight, by Sara Teasdale. The Macmillan Company.

Skipping Along Alone, by Winifred Welles. The Macmillan Company.

LOOKING FORWARD

Anthologies

The Winged Horse, compiled by Joseph Auslander and F. E. Hill. Doubleday, Doran & Company, Inc.
Girl's Book of Verse, compiled by Mary Gould Davis. Frederick A. Stokes Company.
Come Hither, compiled by Walter de la Mare. Alfred A. Knopf, Inc.
Boy's Book of Verse, compiled by Helen Dean Fish. Frederick A. Stokes Company.
Lyra Heroica, compiled by William Henley. Charles Scribner's Sons.
The Open Road, compiled by Edward V. Lucas. Henry Holt & Company, Inc.
The Golden Treasury of Songs and Poems, compiled by Francis Turner Palgrave. The Thomas Y. Crowell Company.
The Oxford Book of English Verse, edited by Sir Arthur T. Quiller-Couch. Oxford University Press.
The Little Book of Modern Verse, compiled by Jessie Belle Rittenhouse. Houghton Mifflin Company.
Modern American Poetry, edited by Louis Untermeyer. Harcourt, Brace & Company, Inc.
Modern British Poetry, edited by Louis Untermeyer. Harcourt, Brace & Company, Inc.

Individual Poets

Book of Americans, by Rosemary and Stephen Vincent Benét. Farrar & Rinehart, Inc.
Collected Poems, by Rupert Brooke. Dodd, Mead & Company, Inc.
Complete Poetical Works, by Robert Browning. Houghton Mifflin Company.
Collected Poems, by Gilbert Keith Chesterton. Dodd, Mead & Company, Inc.
Collected Poems, by Walter de la Mare. Henry Holt & Company, Inc.
Poems of Emily Dickinson. Little, Brown & Company.
Branches Green, by Rachel Field. The Macmillan Company.
Pool in the Meadow, by Frances M. Frost. Harper & Brothers.
Collected Poems, by Robert Frost. Henry Holt & Company, Inc.
The Bab Ballads, by Sir William S. Gilbert. The Macmillan Company.
Complete Poetical Works, by John Keats. Houghton Mifflin Company.
Complete Verse, by Rudyard Kipling. Doubleday, Doran & Company, Inc.
Complete Poems, by Henry Wadsworth Longfellow. Houghton Mifflin Co.
Poetical Works, by James Russell Lowell. Houghton Mifflin Company.
Lays of Ancient Rome, by Thomas Babington Macaulay. E. P. Dutton & Co.
Poems, by John Masefield. The Macmillan Company.
Reynard the Fox, by John Masefield. The Macmillan Company.

Poems Selected for Young People, by Edna St. Vincent Millay. Harper & Brothers.

Collected Poems, by Alfred Noyes. Frederick A. Stokes Company.

White April, by Lizette Woodworth Reese. Farrar & Rinehart, Inc.

Goblin Market, by Christina Rossetti. J. B. Lippincott Company.

Early Moon, by Carl Sandburg. Harcourt, Brace & Company, Inc.

Poetical Works, by Sir Walter Scott. The Macmillan Company.

Sonnets, by William Shakespeare. The Macmillan Company.

Complete Poetical Works, by Percy Bysshe Shelley. Houghton Mifflin Co.

Collected Poems, by James Stephens. The Macmillan Company.

Collected Poems, by Sara Teasdale. The Macmillan Company.

Poetical Works, by Alfred Tennyson. The Macmillan Company.

Blossoming Antlers, by Winifred Welles. Viking Press, Inc.

Complete Works, by John Greenleaf Whittier. Houghton Mifflin Company.

Complete Poetical Works, by William Wordsworth. The Macmillan Co.

Collected Poems, by William Butler Yeats. The Macmillan Company.

LIST OF ARTISTS

WHOSE ILLUSTRATIONS APPEAR IN THE JUNIOR CLASSICS

Artzybasheff, Boris

Some of the finest work in contemporary illustration in the field of children's books has come from the hand of this American of Russian parentage, whose drawings are found in our most widely popular books and our leading magazines.

Barnhart, Nancy

This American artist's work is characterized by delicacy, yet she displays a sureness of technique and a sympathy towards her subject which make her pictures altogether charming.

Batten, John D.

Celebrated English painter, muralist and illustrator, some of whose finest work is found in his illustrations for children's books. He is particularly happy in the fanciful humorous pictures for fairy tales.

Bedford, Francis Donkin

English artist who has been eminent in British and American book illustration for a number of years. He is numbered among that distinguished group who have illustrated Dickens' books.

Bell, Corydon

The work of this mid-western American artist displays a delightful conceit and technical mastery that gives it an unusual appeal to children.

Bianco, Pamela

Beginning at a very early age, Miss Bianco has achieved wide fame. Her work has been marked by an unusual charm and a mastery of technique. Her pictures will be found in a number of the principal galleries in England and America.

Birch, Reginald

He has illustrated a large number of books always with distinction. His drawings exhibit a liveliness of rendering, a flavor and spirit unique with him.

Boutet de Monvel, Louis Maurice

One of the most celebrated French artists, he obtained popular fame through his illustrations for children's books and for his water colors which exhibit great charm and delicacy of technique. He is also known to thousands for his murals illustrating scenes from the life of Jeanne d'Arc.

Brock, H. M.

This artist has long been a popular favorite with children. A member of the Royal Institute of Painters in Watercolors, an artist for *Punch* and many other magazines, his is one of the prominent names in English art.

Bromhall, Wilfred

Mr. Bromhall has been most successful in catching the spirit of fantasy with the essential lightness of touch in his illustration of the poem, "Song of the Wandering Aengus."

Brooke, L. Leslie

This Englishman whose work attains a particular excellence in his pictures of animals is one of the outstanding juvenile artists of our day. His drawings in color for such stories as the "Three Bears" and "Three Little Pigs" and for many nursery rhymes are celebrated throughout the realm of children's literature.

Caldecott, Randolph

This great English artist is considered to have given more pleasure and enjoyment to children and grown-ups through his pictures for children's classics than any other artist who ever lived. He possessed a whimsicality and originality that has never been matched. The Caldecott Medal is awarded each year for the most distinguished American picture book for children.

Carrick, Valery

Mr. Carrick of Russian-English parents has found a most interesting field for his talents, for his books are written from Russian peasant tales which he translates into English and illustrates with his delightfully different and fascinating pictures.

Chappell, Warren

Illustrator, typographer, and type-cutter, Mr. Chappell was born in Richmond, Virginia, and graduated from the University of Richmond. He studied at the Art Students' League and at the Technische Lehranstalt, Germany. He was an associate of Rudolf Koch at the Offenbacher Werkstatt and instructor in Graphic Arts at the Art Students' League and at the Colorado Springs Fine Arts Center. He was also associate instructor of Drawing and Composition under Boardman Robinson. He is the author of "The Anatomy of Lettering" and "Illustrations Made with a Tool."

Charlton, George

A celebrated English artist whose work is found in nearly all of the principal galleries of Europe. He is also the illustrator of many fine volumes, including leading children's books.

Chesterman, Hugh

This English artist is able to capture an airy mood in his drawings for children's stories which give them a strong appeal to boys and girls alike from the youngest to the oldest.

Corner, J. M.

This widely known Scandinavian artist has done some of his finest work in the illustration of Norwegian fairy and folk tales. He has very happily caught their fascination and spirit in his pictures.

Crane, Walter

One of the most famous English artists of all time, his work was influenced by Botticelli, the early Florentines and Japanese art. He possessed an extraordinary genius for design and an appreciation of color which have made his pictures classic masterpieces.

Cruikshank, George

As a caricaturist and satirist, his is probably the best known name in English art. Ruskin wrote enthusiastically of his genius. We know him better as the genial and humorous illustrator of the classic children's stories and of Dickens' books.

Curtis, Dora

This splendid artist is particularly successful in catching the mood and feeling of a narrative she is illustrating. Excellent examples of her work are found in her pictures for the King Arthur stories.

Daugherty, James

American illustrator of many outstanding books for adults and children and painter of murals. His work is found in public and semi-public buildings throughout the United States.

Doré, Gustave

Probably the most universally popular of French illustrators. When Doré was 15, his drawings were exhibited in the Salon at Paris, and the critics immediately noted his remarkable technical skill. For many years he enjoyed an amazing success for his work. Prolific and imaginative, Doré blended into his best work a skill in drawing and breadth of idea unsurpassed in pictorial art.

Doyle, Richard

English artist who is known to us principally through his illustrations of Dickens' books and his humorous and whimsical pictures of elves and fairies. He belongs to that great company of *Punch* artists. Collections of his work are in the British Museum and the National Portrait Gallery, Edinburgh.

Dürer, Albrecht

The greatest of all German engravers and one of the master painters of the world, it was he who gave us engraving as we know it today by introducing light and shade into his pictures and thus molding his figures.

Field, Rachel

Her talents range over a wide field as editor, novelist, author of children's stories, illustrator, and writer of verse and plays. She was awarded in 1929 the John Newbery Medal for the most distinguished contribution to literature for children.

Flack, Marjorie

This American artist has maintained a uniformly high standard of work in the many children's books which she has illustrated. Her technique is above reproach and she most successfully catches the spirit of the stories.

Flaxman, John

English illustrator and sculptor, a leader of the Classic revival in England. Flaxman worked for twelve years designing Wedgwood pottery, but it was his illustrations for "The Iliad" and "The Odyssey" that made his name secure as a great artist. Flaxman was elected to the Royal Academy and a special chair of Sculpture was created for him.

Folkard, Charles James

This English artist has enjoyed a long and distinguished career. He has written and illustrated many books for children and grown-ups. He has also created well-known comic characters for newspapers.

Ford, Henry J.

This eminent English artist has done unusually fine work in portraying historical characters for children's books and stories.

Frölich, Lorenz

A celebrated Danish artist who has illustrated many books by Danish, Norwegian and Swedish authors. He is particularly happy in his picturing of Scandinavian legends which give him a splendid opportunity to show his unusual talents.

Frost, Arthur Burdett

This famous American illustrator depicts types with a quaintness and homeliness in their creation true to the American scene. Frost has become an immortal in American art for his drawings are more and more cherished as the years go by.

Furniss, Harry

This British artist is internationally known as a political cartoonist and caricaturist. He has also illustrated a number of the most popular books of our time, always with excellent draftsmanship and with a rare sense of humor.

Gág, Wanda

Many thousands of people during recent years have laughed over Wanda Gág's books such as "Millions of Cats" and "Snippy and Snappy," which have a sense of humor almost universal in its appeal.

Gellert, Hugo

It is given to Gellert to be able to catch a likeness with a sharpness and brilliance that makes his work outstanding.

Gibson, Charles Dana

American illustrator, considered one of the masters of pen and ink drawing. Gibson became an illustrator for several popular magazines, among them the old "Life" and "Collier's," in which appeared many of his famous "Gibson Girl" drawings, depicting the well-groomed American girl.

Gilbert, Sir William

This celebrated Englishman is nearly as famous for his delightful pictures which he has drawn for such poems as "The Yarn of the Nancy Bell" and the "Bab Ballads" as for his collaborations with Sir Arthur Sullivan in "Pinafore," "The Mikado," "The Pirates of Penzance" and other operas.

Grant, Gordon

American painter and illustrator. He is widely known for his handling of marine and shipping subjects in oil and watercolors. His etchings also are of unusual interest. Grant painted the famous picture, the *Constitution,* for the Navy Department.

Hall, Thomas Victor

American artist, in pen and ink, oil and water color, and illustrator for books, newspapers and magazines. His juvenile illustrations have caught the swing of action and the lightness of flight.

Heighway, Richard

This Englishman is a miniature painter of distinction, who has exhibited at the Royal Academy in London. But he probably is best known for his illustrations for Aesop's Fables. To these animal characters he has given a human understanding that makes them very real and adds much to the enjoyment of the tales.

Herford, Oliver

American illustrator and author of many books for children and grown-ups. Possessing a keen sense of the ridiculous and a rare originality, his books for many years have had a wide popularity.

Hoffmann, Heinrich

German physician but best known to us as a humorist. He has written many books and illustrated them in an absurdly delightful vein. The best known of these is "Struawelpeter," translated as "Clean Peter," and regarded as a children's classic.

Huard, Charles

Well-known illustrator of Scandinavian legends, he is particularly noted for his illustrations for the "Heroes of Asgard." One of these is the full-page illustration in "How the Fenris Wolf Was Chained."

James, Will

American illustrator and author, was born in the west and lived in the western and Canadian ranges a great part of his life. Drawing his inspiration from this vital environment, he has given to his stories and drawings a virility and picturesqueness.

Jones, Wilfred

He is a noted artist in a variety of mediums. His skilled draftsmanship, his mastery in the handling of colors and his sympathetic treatment of the subjects which he illustrates, have made his pictures of interest.

Kent, Rockwell

This artist is represented in the principal museums of North and South America and Europe. He is one of our most prominent landscape and figure painters, as well as an illustrator of note, frequently contributing to magazines and books.

Kipling, Lockwood

Father of Rudyard Kipling, the great English writer, he attained wide fame in his own right as a painter and illustrator. For many years curator of the Lahore Museum in India, his first interest was in Indian and Oriental subjects.

Kirmse, Marguerite

There has been no one in the long history of art who has pictured so well the Scottie and his canine friends. As an etcher, she gives to English and American art a new distinction.

Kittelsen, Theodor

This famous Norwegian artist, painter, caricaturist, satirist and illustrator is ranked among the greatest illustrators that any country has produced. He pictured with rare characterization the Norwegian trolls, the goblins and demons who play such important parts in Scandinavian folk tales and legends. He was the master of grotesque humor and fantasy.

Lathrop, Dorothy

Miss Lathrop stands high among American women illustrators. Her drawings exhibit a delicacy and variety of detail which have been the willing handmaidens of a fertile imagination.

Lear, Edward

This English humorist wrote his "Nonsense Books" very informally for the young son of the Earl of Derby, but they proved so entertaining and successful that they have been read and enjoyed by thousands of children of every land.

Leech, John

With Cruikshank, he belongs to that illustrious company of illustrators of Dickens' stories and, in some ways, he is the greatest of the group for his talents had a wide range. Leech also attained great fame as a caricaturist and etcher.

Lenski, Lois

Illustrator of books for children, painter and author in her own right, her work exhibits a rare originality, imagination and humor. She has also done most creditable work as a painter and muralist.

Lewis, Allen

Mr. Lewis is the designer of the endpapers for The Junior Classics. No one of this generation has done more distinguished work in wood engraving. His best work is found in book illustrations, contributed to many of our finest contemporary publications. Mr. Lewis has been a practising artist for more than thirty years and has taught for a good portion of this time at the Art Students' League in New York.

Moe, Louis

Danish painter and illustrator, perhaps best known for his enchanting illustrations for fairy and folk tales of the North and his fascinating drawings of animals.

O'Connor, Henry M.

This native New England painter and etcher has a keen understanding not only of his art, but also of the Gloucester fishermen whom he so successfully portrays. His pictures seem to carry the salty tang and reflect the spirit and courage of men who go down to the sea in ships.

Pape, Eric

American painter and illustrator, the founder of the Eric Pape School of Art, has exhibited over two hundred of his paintings in the leading galleries of Europe and America and he has illustrated many books and stories for magazines.

Papé, Frank C.

This English artist brings to the pictures which he draws for children's stories a fine technique, a splendid sense of the dramatic, and an understanding of the child point of view—all of which makes his illustrations particularly successful.

Paull, Grace A.

This young American artist has devoted much of her attention to the illustration of books for children in which work she has shown a remarkable talent.

Pedersen, V.

This American artist has illustrated many of the classic stories for children. In his pictures for Andersen's fairy tales in The Junior Classics, he combines fanciful, whimsical treatment with a mysterious quality which appeals strongly to the child.

Pellicer, D. J. Luis

This Spanish artist has illustrated with complete sympathy and understanding the great masterpiece of his country, "The Cid." His illustrations are rare examples of an eloquent simplicity in art.

Pérard, Victor

The work of this modern painter and illustrator has appeared extensively in leading magazines and books, while his paintings hang in a number of the principal galleries in America and abroad.

Perts, Michael J.

The illustrations for the "Little Hump-Back Horse" contribute greatly to the enjoyment the child obtains from this charming story. This Latvian artist grasps with rare ability the atmosphere and spirit of the narrative.

Pitz, Henry C.

This American artist has reached the front rank very rapidly. The Dana Gold Medal for Watercolors and the Purchase Prize for lithography among other awards have been bestowed upon him in recognition of an unusual talent.

Pogâny, Willy

Painter, etcher, illustrator, sculptor and recipient of numerous medals and awards here and abroad, Pogány has illustrated over seventy volumes, among which are many children's books. He has also designed numerous stage productions and painted notable murals.

Pyle, Howard

This famous American illustrator has set the standard of our pictured conception of pirates, buccaneers, knights in armor, colonial squires and men of dauntless courage. His drawings give to a narrative a new gusto, authenticity and freshness.

Pyle, Katharine

Thirty books of fairy tales, stories and verse have come from her pen, either as illustrator or as author, and sometimes both, and all have possessed that consistent quality of imagination which has given them a strong appeal to the child reader.

Rackham, Arthur

English artist preeminent among modern illustrators of children's books. His pictures are in the Tate Gallery in London and in the National Collections at Barcelona, Vienna and Melbourne, and his work has received gold medals at Milan and Paris. Rackham stands unique among modern living illustrators for the quaintness and grace and the imaginative quality of his art.

Raverat, Gwendolen Mary

Miss Raverat is among the foremost of present day English engravers. She is a Fellow of the Royal Society of Painter Etchers and is the art critic of the well known English magazine *Time and Tide*.

Richards, George

This American artist is most successful in combining authentic technique and a fanciful touch which are so dominantly essential in the illustration of stories designed for child readers.

Robinson, William Heath

One of the most celebrated English artists, he has illustrated many beautiful books in England and America. Typical of his work are his pictures for a "Midsummer Night's Dream" which catch the airy, elfinlike quality with which Shakespeare imbued his characters. Robinson has been a frequent contributor to magazines.

Sandford, Joseph E.

This American has done creditable work in typographic decoration for which he exhibits a special talent, and in the creation of lovely designs for books and magazines.

Shields, Frank

Born in New York, he attended Columbia University and received his art training from the National Academy of Design. His knowledge of, and interest in, animals came while he was staff artist for the American Museum of Natural History. His work has appeared in the leading magazines and as illustrations for many books.

Steele, Frederic Dorr

The adventures of Sherlock Holmes would be far the poorer without illustrations by Steele, whose drawings have become so closely associated with these famous detective stories.

Taylor, Rebecca Lindon

This American etcher has made a fine portrait of Admiral Richard Evelyn Byrd, which accompanies the story "Flying Over the North Pole."

Tenniel, Sir John

No name is better known among children and their parents than that of this famous English illustrator and cartoonist who drew the pictures for

"Alice in Wonderland." So essential are Tenniel's drawings that this famous classic would lose much of its enjoyment for us without them.

Thomson, Hugh

Mr. Thomson is particularly successful in his illustrations for boys' books. The pictures for "The Fight" are masterpieces of boy psychology for they contain the gusto, spirit, and the challenge so dear to boyhood.

Torrey, Helen

Black and white animals on paper seem to emerge almost as real moving, breathing beings when this modern American artist draws them. Zinnia, the kitten, becomes bosom companion of many children readers.

Van Loon, Hendrik Willem

Dutch-American author, journalist, lecturer, correspondent and editor, has had a tremendous following wherever books are read. His pictures become part and parcel of his stories and make his text intensely interesting.

Verbeck, E.

This Irish artist is well known in his native country as a painter and illustrator. He has been consistently successful in the latter for his pictures accentuate the spirit and humor of the Irish stories.

Walker, A. G.

This artist brings into his illustrations a romance and a pageantry particularly suitable for the classic stories of knighthood and chivalry.

Werenskiold, Eric

This eminent Norwegian artist was of tremendous influence on art in his native land. Werenskiold possessed a searching method in his painting which gave his work as a portraitist, great fidelity. To the children of America, however, his fame rests upon his delightful illustrations for Norwegian legends and fairy tales.

Whymper, Josiah Wood

This English artist was an eminent figure in his native country for many years because of his remarkable work as a painter in water colors and as an engraver. His pictures are found in a number of the leading galleries in his own country and abroad.

Young, Florence Liley

This American painter and illustrator's work is marked by a lilt, humor and gaiety that adds much to the enjoyment of the text of the stories.

INDEX OF TITLES

Titles of poems are printed in *italics*.
Volumes are indicated by Roman numerals.

Abbot Gerasimus and the Lion, The, III, 339
Abe Lincoln's Books, VIII, 300
Abou Ben Adhem, X, 280
About Elizabeth Eliza's Piano, VI, 268
Adrift on an Ice Pan, IX, 297
Adventure with a Whale, An, IX, 362
Adventures of Odysseus, The, IV, 15
After Blenheim, X, 211
Aladdin, II, 187
Ali Baba, II, 230
Alice's Adventures in Wonderland, V, 1
All Things Bright and Beautiful, X, 51
All Things Wait upon Thee, X, 58
Allen-A-Dale, X, 200
Andrew Coffey, I, 73
Answer to a Child's Question, X, 61
Ant, The, X, 132
Apples of Youth, The, III, 207
Arabia, X, 237
Argonauts, The, III, 50
Arming of Pigwiggen, The, X, 77
Arthur in the Cave, III, 326
Arthur O'Bower, X, 23
As I Was Going to St. Ives, X, 24
As I Went Through the Garden Gap, X, 23
Ass in the Lion's Skin, The, I, 324
Assault of Wings, The, VII, 322
Atalanta, The Winning of, III, 133
Autumn, X, 291
Autumn, To, X, 287
Autumn Fires, X, 38
Baker's Daughter, The, VI, 120
Banyan Deer, The, III, 267
Barbara Frietchie, X, 224
Battle at Roncesvalles, The, IV, 171
Beauty and the Beast, I, 234
Bee, The, X, 56
Before Sleeping, X, 151
Bell Buoy, The, X, 248
Bell of Justice, The, III, 318
Beowulf Fights Grendel, IV, 225
Beowulf Fights the Dragon, IV, 239
Berries, X, 83
Billy Beg and the Bull, I, 98
Billy Topsail and the Devilfish, IX, 68
Bird Came Down the Walk, A, X, 62
Black Beauty, VII, 211
Black Bull of Norroway, The, I, 56
Blood Horse, The, X, 72
Blow, Wind, Blow! X, 7
Blue Beard, I, 229
Bonnie George Campbell, X, 171
Bonny Barbara Allan, X, 175
Boots Who Made the Princess Say "That's a Story," I, 204
"Bounty," The Voyage of the, IX, 367
Boy Viking, Olaf II of Norway, The, VIII, 86
Boyhood of Cuchulain, The, IV, 344
Breathes There the Man, X, 278
Bredon Hill, X, 300
Bremen Town Musicians, The, I, 162
Bringing Up Kari, VII, 280
Brown Wolf, VII, 306
Brownie and the Cook, II, 81
Buddy, Seeing Eye Pioneer, VII, 107
Budulinek, I, 248
Bugle Song, X, 294
Bun, The, I, 274
Bunny Romance, A, X, 132
Buster, VII, 3
Butterfly's Ball, The, X, 52
Bye, Baby Bunting, X, 11
Canis Major, X, 49

Cap o' Rushes, I, 37
Captain Reece, X, 99
Cardinal Wolsey's Speech to Cromwell, X, 259
Cat and Mouse in Partnership, I, 139
Cat and the Captain, The, VII, 179
Cat on the Dovrefell, The, I, 197
Chambered Nautilus, The, X, 311
Chased by the Trail, IX, 110
Child's Pet, A, X, 69
Children's Hour, The, X, 143
Chimaera, The, III, 157
Chimney Sweeper, The, X, 163
Chimpanzee, The, X, 131
Chinese Fairy Tale, A, II, 252
Christmas Carol, A, V, 312
Christmas with Queen Bess, VIII, 137
Cid, The Chronicle of the, IV, 183
Cinderella, I, 215
City Mouse and the Garden Mouse, The, X, 67
Clean Clara, X, 109
Cloud, The, X, 280
Coaly-Bay, the Outlaw Horse, VII, 286
Cock and the Pearl, The, I, 352
Columbus, X, 217
Come, Let's to Bed, X, 7
Come Unto These Yellow Sands, X, 76
Conal and Donal and Taig, I, 77
Concord Hymn, X, 223
Constant Tin Soldier, The, II, 350
Courtship of the Yonghy-Bonghy-Bò, The, X, 115
Cow, The, X, 68
Cowboy and His Pony, A, VII, 93
Coyote and the Fox, The, III, 273
Cradle Hymn, X, 151
Crow and the Pitcher, The, I, 348
Cuchulain, The Boyhood of, IV, 344
Curly Locks! X, 7
Daffodils, X, 276
Daffodils, To, X, 263
Daffy-Down-Dilly, X, 4
Dandelions, The, X, 30
Daniel Boone's Rifle, VIII, 198
Davy Crockett Legends, VIII, 210
Dawn Over Zero, IX, 236
Day Is Done, The, X, 306
Daybreak, X, 305
Death, the Leveler, X, 266
Departure of Telemachus, The, IV, 3
Destruction of Sennacherib, The, X, 207
Devil and Daniel Webster, The, VIII, 323
Dick Turpin, IX, 166
Diddle, Diddle Dumpling, X, 8
Diller, a Dollar, A, X, 3
Ding, Dong, Bell, X, 5
Dirge for a Righteous Kitten, A, X, 68
Divine Musician, The, III, 128
Divine Ode, X, 269
Dog and the Shadow, The, I, 346
Dog in the Manger, The, I, 354
Doll in the Grass, The, I, 187
Don Quixote, V, 266
Donnybrook, X, 49
Drake's Drum, X, 252
Dream, A, X, 57
Duel, The, X, 126
Dutch Cheese, The, II, 152
Eagle, The, X, 67
Early Spring, X, 292
Eel-Grass, X, 245
Elegy on the Death of a Mad Dog, An, X, 98
Elephant That Was Honored in Old Age, The, III, 263
Elf and the Dormouse, The, X, 134
Elfin Mound, The, II, 320
Elves and the Shoemaker, The, I, 111
Embellishment, VI, 231
Emergency Mistress, The, II, 288
Emmeline, VIII, 248
Emperor's Vision, The, III, 330
Epitaph on a Robin Redbreast, An, X, 63
Evening in Paradise, X, 267

Fable, A, x, 71
Fairies, The, x, 85
Fairies of the Caldon Low, The, x, 86
Fairy Went A-Marketing, A, x, 89
Faithful Friend, The, III, 265
Farewell, The, x, 196
Farmer and the Money Lender, The, I, 321
Farm-Yard Song, x, 154
Fidele, x, 258
Field of Boliauns, The, I, 62
Fight, The, IX, 59
Finn and Oisin, IV, 319
Fir-Tree, The, II, 342
Fisherman and His Wife, The, I, 166
Flour of England, Fruit of Spain, x, 24
Flying Dutchman, The, III, 323
Flying Over the North Pole, IX, 225
Fog, x, 38
Folding the Flocks, x, 262
Forbearance, x, 304
Forging of the Sampo, The, IV, 119
Forsaken Merman, The, x, 295
Fox and His Wife, The, x, 15
Fox and the Cat, The, I, 349
Fox and the Crow, The, I, 351
Fox and the Grapes, The, I, 352
Fox and the Stork, The, I, 347
Friend in the Garden, A, x, 60
Frog, The, x, 136
Frog He Would A-Wooing Go, A, x, 18
Frog Prince, The, I, 135
Frost, The, x, 39
Full Fathom Five, x, 76
Gallegher, VI, 336
Gardener and the White Elephants, The, II, 30
Gathering Song of Donald Dhu, x, 197
Ghosts of the Buffaloes, The, x, 228
God's Judgment on a Wicked Bishop, x, 186
Going A-Maying, x, 264
Gold Bug, The, V, 158
Gold-Giving Serpent, The, I, 326
Golden Bird, The, I, 175
Golden Goose, The, I, 142
Golden Touch, The, III, 142
Good Night and Good Morning, x, 145
Goose-Girl, The, I, 156
Goosey, Goosey, Gander, x, 14
Grass, The, x, 34
Grasshopper and the Cricket, To the, x, 56
Great A, Little a, x, 5
Great Discoveries, The, VIII, 124
Greedy Shepherd, The, II, 89
Greek Slave and the Little Roman Boy, The, VIII, 10
Gudbrand on the Hillside, I, 189
Gulliver the Great, VII, 294
Gulliver's Voyage to Lilliput, V, 210
Hansel and Grethel, I, 113
Hare That Ran Away, The, III, 259
Hark! Hark! the Lark! x, 258
Harp That Once Through Tara's Halls, The, x, 209
Head Over Heels, IX, 86
Helen, To, x, 314
Hens, The, x, 141
Hercules and the Wagoner, I, 353
Hereafterthis, I, 52
Hey! Diddle, Diddle, x, 13
Hiawatha's Childhood, x, 158
Hick-a-more, Hack-a-more, x, 24
Higgley-Piggley, x, 7
History of Tom Thumb, The, I, 31
Hobyahs, The, I, 49
Homer, The Odyssey of, IV, 1
House That Jack Built, The, x, 20
Housekeeper, The, x, 59
How All-Father Odin Became Wise, III, 203
How All Things Began, III, 197
How Boots Befooled the King, II, 260

How Hermod Made a Journey to the Underworld, III, 246
How Loki Was Punished at Last, III, 251
How Rock-Dweller the Chipmunk Gained His Stripes, III, 283
How the Coyote Danced with the Blackbirds, III, 287
How the Fenris Wolf Was Chained, III, 214
How the Leaves Came Down, x, 36
How the Pride of Thor Was Brought Low, III, 219
How the Son of the Gobhaun Saor Shortened the Road, III, 356
How the Son of the Gobhaun Saor Sold the Sheepskin, III, 352
How They Broke Away to Go to the Rootabaga Country, II, 54
How They Brought the Good News from Ghent to Aix, x, 208
How Thor's Hammer Was Lost and Found, III, 230
Hudden and Dudden and Donald O'Neary, I, 66
Humpty Dumpty, x, 6
Hunting of the Boar, The, IV, 299
Hunting of the Calydonian Boar, The, III, 85
Husband Who Was to Mind the House, The, I, 198
Hushaby, Baby, x, 12
Hymn to the Night, x, 307
Hynde Horn, x, 176
I Had a Little Nut-Tree, x, 8
I Had a Little Pony, x, 10
I Have a Little Sister, x, 24
If Once You Have Slept on an Island, x, 243
Image and the Treasure, The, III, 321
Inchcape Rock, The, x, 188
Integer Vitae, x, 260
Jabberwocky, x, 118
Jack and Jill, x, 8
Jack and the Beanstalk, I, 19
Jack Sprat, x, 8
Jackanapes, V, 111
Jay and the Peacock, The, I, 354
Jim Crow, VII, 13
Jimmie, the Black Bear Cub, VII, 17
Joan the Maid, VIII, 108
Jody Finds the Fawn, VII, 358
Jog On, Jog On, x, 259
John Gilpin, x, 90
Jumblies, The, x, 113
June, x, 34
Kalevala, The, IV, 117
King Arthur and the Round Table, IV, 253
King Cobra Takes the Stage, VII, 126
King of Denmark's Ride, The, x, 201
King of the Golden River, The, V, 88
King o' the Cats, I, 47
King Stork, II, 267
Kitten and the Falling Leaves, The, x, 69
Knapsack of Salvation, IX, 100
Knighted by King Henry IV, VIII, 101
Kubla Khan, x, 278
La Belle Dame Sans Merci, x, 288
Lad Who Went to the North Wind, The, I, 201
Lady Moon, x, 45
Lamb, The, x, 70
Lambikin, The, I, 328
Lance of Kanana, The, VIII, 20
Land of Counterpane, The, x, 141
Land of Story-Books, The, x, 139
Landing of the Pilgrim Fathers, The, x, 219
Lassie Come-Home, VII, 343
Last Leaf, The, x, 312
Last Word of a Bluebird, The, x, 62
Legend of St. Christopher, The, III, 336

Leonidas, VIII, 1
Leopards and Rhinos, VII, 138
Lepanto, X, 203
Light Princess, The, II, 95
Light the Lamps Up, Lamplighter, X, 50
Lion and the Mouse, The, I, 350
Lion and the Unicorn, The, X, 13
Little Anklebone, I, 341
Little Billee, X, 107
Little Black Boy, The, X, 161
Little Bo-Peep, X, 8
Little Boy Blue, X, 4
Little Gustava, X, 152
Little Humpbacked Horse, The, I, 283
Little Jack Horner, X, 5
Little Miss Muffet, X, 5
Little Nancy Etticote, X, 24
Little One Eye, Little Two Eyes, Little Three Eyes, I, 121
Little Polly Flinders, X, 9
Little Red Riding-Hood, I, 206
Living in W'ales, II, 26
Lochinvar, X, 202
Lone Voyagers, The, IX, 348
Long Legs, Crooked Thighs, X, 24
Longshanks, Girth, and Keen, I, 264
Lord Ullin's Daughter, X, 198
Lost Doll, The, X, 143
Lost Half-Hour, The, II, 143
Lost Shoe, The, X, 162
Louisa Alcott, War Nurse, VIII, 307
Lucy, X, 275
Lucy Gray, X, 194
Lullaby of an Infant Chief, X, 148
Mabinogian, The, IV, 297
MacArthur Scores Again, VIII, 345
Mad Gardener's Song, The, X, 122
Magic Fishbone, The, II, 1
Making of an Explorer, The, IX, 245
Mama and the Occasion, VI, 373
Man in the Moon, The, X, 127
Man, the Boy, and the Donkey, The, I, 345
Manis the Miller, I, 92
March, X, 28
Meadows, To, X, 263
Meddlesome Matty, X, 165
Meg Merrilies, X, 166
Messmates, X, 251
Midsummer Night's Dream, A, V, 145
Midsummer Song, A, X, 154
Minstrel Boy, The, X, 210
Miraculous Pitcher, The, III, 177
Miserable, Merry Christmas, A, VI, 367
Miss Bannisters' Brother, The, VI, 21
Mistress Mary, Quite Contrary, X, 10
Molly Whuppie, I, 41
Monkey That Saved the Herd, The, III, 261
Monkey That Would Not Kill, The, VII, 198
Moon's the North Wind's Cooky, The, X, 48
Morns Are Meeker Than They Were, The, X, 37
Moti Guj—Mutineer, VII, 358
Mountain Man, The, VIII, 156
Mr. Miacca, I, 17
Mr. Samson Cat, I, 278
Mr. Vinegar, I, 26
Munchausen, Tales from the Travels of Baron, V, 194
My Fight with a Catamount, VII, 150
My Friend Toto, VII, 35
My Song Yankee Doodle, VI, 384
Nancy Hanks, X, 226
Napoleon, VIII, 223
Narrow Fellow in the Grass, A, X, 59
Nature's Friend, X, 58
Nearly Ready, X, 28
Nelly's Hospital, VI, 106
New Pup, The: A Penrod Story, VI, 316
New York to Paris, IX, 215
Night, X, 273
Night, Hymn to the, X, 307
Night, To, X, 286

Night Will Never Stay, The, x, 46
Nightingale, The, II, 359
North Wind Doth Blow, The, x, 6
Northern Seas, The, x, 246
Nose, The, I, 150
Nurse's Song, x, 145
O Captain! My Captain! x, 227
O Lady Moon, x, 43
O, Wert Thou in the Cauld Blast, x, 234
Ode on a Grecian Urn, x, 290
Odysseus, The Adventures of, IV, 15
Ogre, The, x, 149
Old Gaelic Lullaby, x, 146
Old Hag's Long Leather Bag, The, I, 83
Old Horse in the City, The, x, 46
Old Ironsides, x, 224
Old King Cole, x, 6
Old Mother Hubbard, x, 16
Old Pipes and the Dryad, II, 302
Old Ships, The, x, 252
Old Woman and Her Pig, The, I, 9
Old Woman of the Roads, An, x, 167
On His Blindness, Milton, x, 267
One Memorable Fourth, VI, 298
"One Minute Longer," VII, 268
Orpheus with His Lute, x, 257
Ouphe of the Wood, The, II, 70
Outlaw, The, x, 238
Over Hill, Over Dale, x, 75
Owl, The, x, 67
Owl and the Pussy-Cat, The, x, 111
Pah-tay and the Wind Witch, III, 275
Passionate Shepherd to His Love, The, x, 233
Pasture, The, x, 142
Paul Revere's Ride, x, 220
Peace, x, 269
Pease Pudding Hot, x, 6
Perseus, III, 20
Phaeton, III, 3
Pied Piper of Hamelin, The, x, 178
Pin, The, x, 164
Piping Down the Valleys Wild, x, 27
Plaint of the Camel, The, x, 130
Pobble Who Has No Toes, The, x, 112
Polly Patchwork, VI, 11
Poor Dog Tray, x, 71
Porcupine's Quills, The, III, 278
Portrait by a Neighbor, x, 170
Prince Rabbit, II, 33
Princess on the Pea, The, II, 319
Princess Whom Nobody Could Silence, The, I, 183
Procession of the Flowers, The, x, 33
Prometheus the Firebringer, II, 10
Prospector, The, IX, 120
Prospice, x, 294
Proud King, The, III, 309
Pumpkin Giant, The, II, 45
Puss in Boots, I, 209
Pussy-Cat, Pussy-Cat, x, 6
Python, The, x, 135
Queen of Hearts, The, x, 7
Race for the South Pole, The, IX, 316
Raft, The. *See* A Saga of World War II.
Rapunzel, I, 146
Rat's Wedding, The, I, 331
Red-Headed League, The, IX, 190
Requiem, x, 253
Rhyme of November Stars, x, 40
Riddle, A, x, 137
Riddle, A, x, 138
Ride a Cock-Horse, x, 13
Rip Van Winkle, V, 296
Robin Goodfellow, x, 78
Robin Hood and Allen a Dale, IV, 367
Robin Hood and Little John, IV, 363
Robin Hood and the Curtal Friar, IV, 370
Robin Hood, Death of, IV, 374
Robin Redbreast, x, 66
Robinson Crusoe's Story, x, 105
Rockabye, Baby, x, 12

Roland and Oliver, IV, 143
Romance, X, 233
Romance, X, 237
Rounding Cape Horn in a Windjammer, IX, 377
Runaway, The, X, 73
Rustem and Sohrab, IV, 89
Saga of World War II, A, VIII, 359
Sage Counsel, X, 131
Sailor's Consolation, The, X, 247
St. Christopher, The Legend of, III, 336
St. Colman and the Cock, the Mouse, and the Fly, III, 345
St. Cuthbert's Birds, and Bartholomew, the Hermit of Farne, III, 343
St. George and the Dragon, III, 315
St. Godric and the Hunted Stag, III, 342
St. Kevin and the Blackbird, III, 346
St. Martin and the Honest Man, III, 347
St. Moling and the Fox, III, 344
St. Werburga of Chester and the Wild Geese, III, 341
Salt-Water Tea, VIII, 173
Sam, X, 169
Sarita and the Duendes, II, 175
Scarface, III, 298
Sea Fever, X, 244
Sea Gipsy, The, X, 244
Sea Otter, VII, 333
Sea Song, A, X, 250
Seal Lullaby, X, 61
Seasons, The, X, 271
Seller of Dreams, The, II, 137
Serpent of the Sea, The, III, 291
Seumas Beg, X, 168
Shall I Compare Thee to a Summer's Day? X, 260
Shepherd Boy Sings in the Valley of Humiliation, The, X, 270
Shepherd of King Admetus, The, X, 314
Shepherdess, The, X, 299
Ship of Rio, The, X, 129
Shipping Wild Animals, VII, 116
Simple Simon Met a Pieman, X, 4
Sing a Song of Sixpence, X, 3
Sir Patrick Spens, X, 172
Skeleton in Armor, The, X, 213
Skylark, To a, X, 282
Sleeping Beauty in the Wood, The, I, 223
Smugglers' Song, X, 240
Snow-Bound, X, 308
Snow Storm, The, X, 304
Snow-White and Rose-Red, I, 128
Solitary Reaper, The, X, 277
Solitude, X, 270
Solomon Grundy, X, 8
Solomon John Goes for Apples, VI, 270
Song of the Emigrants in Bermuda, X, 267
Song of Roland, The, IV, 141
Song of Wandering Aengus, The, X, 231
Song of Winter, A, X, 41
Song: On May Morning, X, 266
Spicebush in March, The, X, 29
Spider and the Fly, The, X, 54
Spirit That Lived in a Tree, The, III, 257
Spring, X, 29
Spring Quiet, X, 30
Squire's Bride, The, I, 193
Stars, X, 48
Stickeen, VII, 158
Stool of Fortune, The, II, 277
Stopping by Woods on a Snowy Evening, X, 43
Stories from the Chronicle of the Cid, IV, 185
Story for a Child, A, X, 190
Story of Augustus Who Would Not Have Any Soup, The, X, 108
Story of Balder the Beautiful, The, III, 238
Story of Molly Pitcher, The, VIII, 194

Story of the Four Little Children Who Went Round the World, The, II, 13
Story of the Three Bears, The, I, 4
Story of the Three Little Pigs, The, I, 1
Stover Plays Football, IX, 1
Summer Days, X, 36
Summit of the World: The Fight for Everest, IX, 272
Susanna's Auction, VI, 1
Sweet Content, X, 261
Swineherd, The, II, 354
Taffy Was a Welshman, X, 9
Taktuk, an Arctic Boy, VI, 125
Tale of Three Tails, A, II, 158
Ta-ming Wins the Short Sword, VI, 241
Tarantella, X, 236
Teeny-Tiny, I, 29
Telemachus, The Departure of, IV, 3
Tewkesbury Road, X, 243
Thanatopsis, X, 302
Thanksgiving Day, X, 156
There Was a Crooked Man, X, 11
There Was a Little Man, X, 13
There Was a Man, and He Had Nought, X, 14
There Was an Old Woman Lived Under a Hill, X, 11
There Was an Old Woman Toss'd up in a Basket, X, 10
There Was an Old Woman Who Lived in a Shoe, X, 8
Thirty White Horses, X, 23
This Is the Way the Ladies Ride, X, 12
Three Badgers, The, X, 124
Three Bears, The, I, 4
Three Little Kittens, The, X, 14
Three Little Pigs, The Story of the, I, 1
Three Wishes, The, I, 45
Thunderbird Limps Home, VIII, 340
Tiger, The, X, 74
Tiger, the Brahman, and the Jackal, The, I, 338
Time, You Old Gypsy Man, X, 235
Tinder-Box, The, II, 326
To a Skylark, X, 282
To a Waterfowl, X, 301
To Autumn, X, 287
To Daffodils, X, 263
To Helen, X, 314
To Market, to Market, X, 11
To Meadows, X, 263
To One in Paradise, X, 313
To the Grasshopper and the Cricket, X, 56
To Night, X, 286
Tom Chist and the Treasure Chest, IX, 138
Tom o' Bedlam, X, 242
Tom Sawyer Whitewashes the Fence, VI, 285
Tom Thumb, The History of, I, 31
Tom Tit Tot, I, 11
Topsy-Turvy World, X, 97
Tragedy in Millinery, A, VI, 274
Travel, X, 140
Travels of Baron Munchausen, Tales from the, V, 194
Tree of Jade, The, VIII, 233
Two Legs Sat upon Three Legs, X, 23
Two-Twenty Low Hurdle Race, The, IX, 77
Two Youths Whose Father Was Under the Sea, The, II, 167
Ugly Duckling, The, II, 333
Uncle Remus, II, 60
Up-Hill, X, 299
Vagabond, The, X, 232
Velvet Shoes, X, 42
Visit from St. Nicholas, A, X, 157
Visit from the Sea, A, X, 245
Visitor, The, X, 81
Visitor, The, X, 80
Vowels, The, X, 137
Voyage of the "Bounty," The, IX, 367
Walrus and the Carpenter, The, X, 119

Wassilissa the Beautiful, I, 300
Waterfowl, To a, X, 301
Wee, Wee Man, The, X, 76
What Happened to Inger Johanne, VI, 177
When I Was a Bachelor, X, 4
When Molly Was Six, VI, 33
Where Are You Going, My Pretty Maid? X, 10
Where the Bee Sucks, X, 75
Who Has Seen the Wind? X, 32
Who Stole the Bird's Nest? X, 63
Why the Bear is Stumpy-Tailed, I, 200
Why the Fish Laughed, I, 315
Wild Bull, The, VII, 81
William Tell, III, 319
Willie Winkie, X, 146
Wind and the Moon, The, X, 44
Wind in a Frolic, The, X, 31
Windy Nights, X, 40
Winning Bug, The, IX, 39
Winning of Atalanta, The, III, 103
Winter, X, 41
Winter, X, 288
Winter, A Song of, X, 41
Winter-Time, X, 142
With Helmet and Hose, IX, 255
Wolf and the Lamb, The, I, 355
Wolf and the Seven Little Goats, The, I, 107
Woodman and the Serpent, The, I, 356
Wraggle Taggle Gypsies, The, X, 241
Wreck of the Hesperus, The, X, 192
Wynken, Blynken and Nod, X, 147
Yak, The, X, 136
Yarn of the "Nancy Bell," The, X, 102
Yearling, The. *See* Jody Finds the Fawn.
Ye Mariners of England, X, 211
Yet Gentle Will the Griffin Be, X, 47
Zinnia and Her Babies, VII, 8
Zlatovlaska the Golden-Haired, I, 254

INDEX OF AUTHORS

Names of authors are printed in capitals. Titles of poems are printed in *italics*. Volumes are indicated by Roman numerals.

ABBOTT, JACOB
Embellishment, VI, 231

ADDISON, JOSEPH
Divine Ode, X, 269

AESOP'S FABLES
The Man, the Boy, and the Donkey, I, 345
The Dog and the Shadow, I, 346
The Fox and the Stork, I, 347
The Crow and the Pitcher, I, 348
The Fox and the Cat, I, 349
The Lion and the Mouse, I, 350
The Fox and the Crow, I, 351
The Cock and the Pearl, I, 352
The Fox and the Grapes, I, 352
Hercules and the Wagoner, I, 353
The Dog in the Manger, I, 354
The Jay and the Peacock, I, 354
The Wolf and the Lamb, I, 355
The Woodman and the Serpent, I, 356

AKELEY, CARL E.
Leopards and Rhinos, VII, 138

ALCOTT, LOUISA M.
Nelly's Hospital, VI, 106

ALDRICH, THOMAS BAILEY
One Memorable Fourth, VI, 298

ALEXANDER, CECIL FRANCES
All Things Bright and Beautiful, X, 51

ALLINGHAM, WILLIAM
Robin Redbreast, X, 66
The Fairies, X, 85

ANDERSEN, HANS CHRISTIAN
The Princess on the Pea, II, 319
The Elfin Mound, II, 320
The Tinder-Box, II, 326

ANDERSEN, HANS CHRISTIAN
The Ugly Duckling, II, 333
The Fir-Tree, II, 342
The Constant Tin Soldier, II, 350
The Swineherd, II, 354
The Nightingale, II, 359

ANDREWS, ROY CHAPMAN
The Making of an Explorer, IX, 245

ARABIAN NIGHTS (From the),
Aladdin, II, 187
Ali Baba, II, 230

ARNOLD, MATTHEW
The Forsaken Merman, X, 295

ASBJÖRNSEN, PETER CHRISTEN
The Golden Bird, I, 175
The Princess Whom Nobody Could Silence, I, 183
The Doll in the Grass, I, 187
Gudbrand on the Hillside, I, 189
The Squire's Bride, I, 193

BALDWIN, JAMES
The Forging of the Sampo, IV, 119
Roland and Oliver, IV, 143

BAYNES, ERNEST HAROLD
Jimmie, the Black Bear Cub, VII, 17

BEAUMONT, MME. JEANNE-MARIE LEPRINCE DE
Beauty and the Beast, I, 234

BEEBE, WILLIAM
With Helmet and Hose, IX, 255

BELLOC, HILAIRE
The Python, X, 135
The Frog, X, 136
The Yak, X, 136
Tarantella, X, 236

BENÉT, ROSEMARY
Nancy Hanks, x, 226

BENÉT, STEPHEN VINCENT
The Devil and Daniel Webster, VIII, 323

BENNETT, JOHN
Christmas with Queen Bess, VIII, 137

BESTON, HENRY
The Seller of Dreams, II, 137
The Lost Half-Hour, II, 143

BIANCO, MARGERY WILLIAMS
The Baker's Daughter, VI, 120
Buster, VII, 3
Zinnia and Her Babies, VII, 8
Jim Crow, VII, 13

BLAKE, WILLIAM
Piping Down the Valleys Wild, x, 27
A Dream, x, 57
The Lamb, x, 70
The Tiger, x, 74
Nurse's Song, x, 145
Little Black Boy, The, x, 161
The Chimney Sweeper, x, 163
The Seasons, x, 271
Night, x, 273

BROOKS, ELBRIDGE S.
The Boy Viking, Olaf II of Norway, VIII, 86

BROWNE, FRANCES
The Greedy Shepherd, II, 89

BROWNING, ROBERT
The Pied Piper of Hamelin, x, 178
How They Brought the Good News from Ghent to Aix, x, 208
Prospice, x, 294

BRYANT, WILLIAM CULLEN
To a Waterfowl, x, 301
Thanatopsis, x, 302

BUCKLEY, ELSIE FINNIMORE
The Hunting of the Calydonian Boar, III, 85
The Winning of Atalanta, III, 103
The Divine Musician, III, 128

BULFINCH, THOMAS
Phaeton, III, 3

BULLEN, FRANK T.
An Adventure with a Whale, IX, 362

BUNYAN, JOHN
The Shepherd Boy Sings in the Valley of Humiliation, x, 270

BURNS, ROBERT
The Farewell, x, 196
O, Wert Thou in the Cauld Blast, x, 234

BUTLER, ISABEL [translator]
The Battle at Roncesvalles, IV, 171

BYRD, RICHARD EVELYN
Flying Over the North Pole, IX, 225

BYRON, GEORGE GORDON, LORD
The Destruction of Sennacherib, x, 207

CAMPBELL, THOMAS
Poor Dog Tray, x, 71
Lord Ullin's Daughter, x, 198
Ye Mariners of England, x, 210

CAMPION, THOMAS
Integer Vitae, x, 260

CARRICK, VALERY
The Bun, I, 274
Mr. Samson Cat, I, 278

CARROLL, LEWIS (Charles Lutwidge Dodgson)
Alice's Adventures in Wonderland, V, 1
Jabberwocky, x, 118
The Walrus and the Carpenter, x, 119

CARROLL, LEWIS (Charles Lutwidge Dodgson)
The Mad Gardener's Song, x, 122
The Three Badgers, x, 124

CARRYL, CHARLES E.
Robinson Crusoe's Story, x, 105 . .
The Plaint of the Camel, x, 130

CERVANTES, MIGUEL DE
Don Quixote, v, 266

CHALMERS, PATRICK R.
The Visitor, x, 81

CHESTERSON, GILBERT K.
Lepanto, x, 203

CHILD, LYDIA MARIA
Who Stole the Bird's Nest? x, 63
Thanksgiving Day, x, 156

CHUTE, B. J.
Head Over Heels, IX, 86

CLAY, BEATRICE
King Arthur and the Round Table, IV, 253

COATSWORTH, ELIZABETH
The Cat and the Captain, VII, 179

COLERIDGE, SAMUEL TAYLOR
Answer to a Child's Question, x, 61
Kubla Khan, x, 278

COLUM, PADRAIC
The Adventures of Odysseus, IV, 15
The Hunting of the Boar, IV, 299
Gulliver's Voyage to Lilliput [editor], v, 210
Two Youths Whose Father Was Under the Sea, The, II, 167
St. Martin and the Honest Man, III, 347
An Old Woman of the Roads, x, 167

CONE, HELEN GRAY
The Dandelions, x, 30

CONNOLLY, JAMES B.
The Lone Voyagers, IX, 348

COOLIDGE, SUSAN
How the Leaves Came Down, x, 36

CORNWALL, BARRY
The Blood Horse, x, 72

COWPER, WILLIAM
John Gilpin, x, 90

COX, JOHN HARRINGTON [editor]
Beowulf Fights Grendel, IV, 225
Beowulf Fights the Dragon, IV, 239

CRAIK, DINAH MARIA MULOCH
Brownie and the Cook, II, 81

CUNNINGHAM, ALLAN
A Sea Song, x, 250

CUSHING, FRANK HAMILTON
How the Coyote Danced with the Blackbirds, III, 287
The Serpent of the Sea, III, 291

DASENT, SIR GEORGE WEBB
The Cat on the Dovrefell, I, 197
The Husband Who Was to Mind the House, I, 198
Why the Bear Is Stumpy-Tailed, I, 200
The Lad Who Went to the North Wind, I, 201
Boots Who Made the Princess Say "That's a Story," I, 204

DAVIES, WILLIAM H.
Nature's Friend, x, 58
A Child's Pet, x, 69

DAVIS, RICHARD HARDING
Gallegher, VI, 336

DE HUFF, ELIZABETH WILLIS
The Coyote and the Fox, III, 273
Pah-tay and the Wind Witch, III, 275

DEKKER, THOMAS
Sweet Content, x, 261

DE LA MARE, WALTER
The Dutch Cheese, II, 152
Berries, x, 83
The Ship of Rio, x, 129
The Ogre, x, 149

De la Mare, Walter
The Lost Shoe, x, 162
Sam, x, 169
Arabia, x, 237

Dibdin, Charles
The Sailor's Consolation, x, 247

Dickens, Charles
The Magic Fishbone, ii, 1
A Christmas Carol, v, 312

Dickinson, Emily
The Grass, x, 34
The Morns Are Meeker Than They Were, x, 37
The Bee, x, 56
A Narrow Fellow in the Grass, x, 59
A Bird Came Down the Walk, x, 62

Ditmars, Raymond L.
King Cobra Takes the Stage, vii, 126

Dobell, Sydney
The Procession of the Flowers, x, 33

Dodge, Mary Mapes
Nearly Ready, x, 28

Doyle, Sir Arthur Conan
The Red-Headed League, ix, 190

Drayton, Michael
The Arming of Pigwiggen, x, 77

Drummond, Henry
The Monkey That Would Not Kill, vii, 198

Duncan, Norman
Billy Topsail and the Devilfish, ix, 68

Dyer, Walter A.
Gulliver the Great, vii, 294

Emerson, Ralph Waldo
A Fable, x, 71
Concord Hymn, x, 223
Forbearance, x, 304
The Snow Storm, x, 304

Ewing, Juliana Horatia
Jackanapes, v, 111
A Friend in the Garden, x, 60

Fanshawe, Catherine M.
A Riddle, x, 138

Farjeon, Eleanor
The Night Will Never Stay, x, 46
Light the Lamps Up Lamplighter, x, 50

Field, Eugene
The Duel, x, 126
Wynken, Blynken and Nod, x, 147

Field, Rachel
Polly Patchwork, vi, 11
The Visitor, x, 80
If Once You Have Slept on an Island, x, 243

Fillmore, Parker
Budulinek, i, 248
Zlatovlaska the Golden-Haired, i, 254
Longshanks, Girth, and Keen, i, 264

Finger, Charles J.
A Tale of Three Tails, ii, 158
Dick Turpin, ix, 166

Finta, Alexander, with Jeanette Eaton
The Wild Bull, vii, 81

Flack, Marjorie, and Helen Lomen
Taktuk, an Arctic Boy, vi, 125

Flecker, James Elroy
The Old Ships, x, 252

Fletcher, John
Folding the Flocks, x, 262

Floherty, John J.
MacArthur Scores Again, viii, 345

Forbes, Esther
Salt-Water Tea, viii, 173

Forbes, Kathryn
Mama and the Occasion, vi, 373

French, Allen
My Fight with a Catamount, vii, 150

French, Harry W.
The Lance of Kanana, viii, 20

Frost, Robert
Stopping by Woods on a Snowy Evening, x, 43
Canis Major, x, 49
The Last Word of a Bluebird, x, 62
The Runaway, x, 73
The Pasture, x, 142

Fyleman, Rose
A Fairy Went A-Marketing, x, 89

Garland, Hamlin
The Prospector, ix, 120

Gilbert, William S.
Captain Reece, x, 99
The Yarn of the "Nancy Bell," x, 102

Gilder, Richard Watson
A Midsummer Song, x, 154

Glick, Carl
My Song Yankee Doodle, vi, 384

Goldsmith, Oliver
An Elegy on the Death of a Mad Dog, x, 98

Gould, Hannah Flagg
The Frost, x, 39

Grenfell, Sir Wilfred
Adrift on an Ice Pan, ix, 297

Grimm, William and Jacob
The Wolf and the Seven Little Goats, i, 107
The Elves and the Shoemaker, i, 111
Hansel and Grethel, i, 113
Little One Eye, Little Two Eyes, Little Three Eyes, i, 121
Snow-White and Rose-Red, i, 128
The Frog Prince, i, 135
Cat and Mouse in Partnership, i, 139
The Golden Goose, i, 142

Grimm, William and Jacob
Rapunzel, i, 146
The Nose, i, 150
The Goose-Girl, i, 156
The Bremen Town Musicians, i, 162
The Fisherman and His Wife, i, 166

Grinnell, George Bird
Scarface, iii, 298

Hale, Lucretia P.
About Elizabeth Eliza's Piano, vi, 268
Solomon John Goes for Apples, vi, 270

Hall, Jennie
Leonidas, viii, 1
The Greek Slave and the Little Roman Boy, viii, 10

Harris, Joel Chandler
Uncle Remus, ii, 60

Hartwell, Dickson
Buddy, Seeing Eye Pioneer, vii, 107

Hawthorne, Nathaniel
The Golden Touch, iii, 142
The Chimaera, iii, 157
The Miraculous Pitcher, iii, 177

Hayward, Walter B.
The Race for the South Pole, ix, 316

Hemans, Felicia Dorothea
The Landing of the Pilgrim Fathers, x, 219

Herford, Oliver
The Chimpanzee, x, 131
The Ant, x, 132
A Bunny Romance, x, 132
The Elf and the Dormouse, x, 134

Herrick, Robert
To Meadows, x, 263
To Daffodils, x, 263
Going A-Maying, x, 264

Hodgson, Ralph
Time, You Old Gypsy Man, x, 235

HOFFMAN, HEINRICH
The Story of Augustus, Who Would Not Have Any Soup, X, 108

HOLMES, OLIVER WENDELL
Old Ironsides, X, 224
The Chambered Nautilus, X, 311
The Last Leaf, X, 312

HOOD, THOMAS
Autumn, X, 291

HOUGHTON, LORD (Richard Monckton Milnes)
Lady Moon, X, 45
Good Night and Good Morning, X, 145

HOUSMAN, ALFRED EDWARD
Bredon Hill, X, 300

HOUSMAN, LAURENCE
A Chinese Fairy Tale, II, 252

HOVEY, RICHARD
The Sea Gipsy, X, 244

HOWITT, MARY
The Spider and the Fly, X, 54
The Fairies of the Caldon Low, X, 86

HOWITT, WILLIAM
The Wind in a Frolic, X, 31
The Northern Seas, X, 246

HUGHES, RICHARD
Living in W'ales, II, 26
The Gardener and the White Elephants, II, 30

HUGHES, THOMAS
The Fight, IX, 59

HULL, ELEANOR
The Boyhood of Cuchulain, IV, 344

HUNT, LEIGH
To the Grasshopper and the Crickett, X, 56
Abou Ben Adhem, X, 280

HUTCHINSON, W. M. L.
Prometheus the Firebringer, III, 10

INGELOW, JEAN
The Ouphe of the Wood, II, 70

IRVING, WASHINGTON
Rip Van Winkle, V, 296

IRWIN, VIOLET M.
Ta-ming Wins the Short Sword, VI, 241

JACOBS, JOSEPH
The Old Woman and Her Pig, I, 9
Tom Tit Tot, I, 11
Mr. Miacca, I, 17
Jack and the Beanstalk, I, 19
Mr. Vinegar, I, 26
Teeny-Tiny, I, 29
The History of Tom Thumb, I, 31
Cap o' Rushes, I, 37
Molly Whuppie, I, 41
The Three Wishes, I, 45
The King o' the Cats, I, 47
The Hobyahs, I, 49
Hereafterthis, I, 52
The Black Bull of Norroway, I, 56
The Field of Boliauns, I, 62
Hudden and Dudden and Donald O'Neary, I, 66
Andrew Coffey, I, 73
Why the Fish Laughed, I, 315
The Farmer and the Money Lender, I, 321
The Ass in the Lion's Skin, I, 324
The Gold-Giving Serpent, I, 326

JAMES, WILL
A Cowboy and His Pony, VII, 93

JOHNSON, OWEN
Stover Plays Football, IX, 1

KEARTON, CHERRY
My Friend Toto, VII, 35

KEATS, JOHN
Meg Merrilies, X, 166
To Autumn, X, 287
Winter, X, 288
La Belle Dame Sans Merci, X, 288
Ode on a Grecian Urn, X, 290

KINGSLEY, CHARLES
Perseus, III, 20
The Argonauts, III, 50
The Lost Doll, X, 143

KIPLING, RUDYARD
Moti Guj—Mutineer, VII, 358
Seal Lullaby, X, 61
Smugglers' Song, X, 240
The Bell Buoy, X, 248

KNIGHT, ERIC
Lassie Come-Home, VII, 343

LAGERLÖF, SELMA
The Emperor's Vision, III, 330

LAMB, CHARLES
The Housekeeper, X, 59

LAMB, CHARLES and MARY
A Midsummer Night's Dream, V, 145

LANG, ANDREW
Joan the Maid, VIII, 108

LANGEWIESCHE, WOLFGANG
Knapsack of Salvation, IX, 100

LAURENCE, W. L.
Dawn Over Zero, IX, 236

LEAR, EDWARD
The Story of the Four Little Children Who Went Round the World, II, 13
The Owl and the Pussy-Cat, X, 111
The Pobble Who Has No Toes, X, 112
The Jumblies, X, 113
The Courtship of the Yonghy Bonghy-Bo, X, 115

LEPRINCE DE BEAUMONT, MME. JEANNE-MARIE
Beauty and the Beast, I, 234

LINDBERGH, CHARLES AUGUSTUS
New York to Paris, IX, 215

LINDSAY, VACHEL
Yet Gentle Will the Griffin Be, X, 47

LINDSAY, VACHEL
The Moon's the North Wind's Cooky, X, 48
The Old Horse in the City, X, 64
A Dirge for a Righteous Kitten, X, 68
The Ghosts of the Buffaloes, X, 228

LOMEN, HELEN, and MARJORIE FLACK
Taktuk, an Arctic Boy, VI, 156

LONDON, JACK
Brown Wolf, VII, 306
Chased by the Trail, IX, 110

LONGFELLOW, HENRY WADSWORTH
The Children's Hour, X, 143
Hiawatha's Childhood, X, 158
The Wreck of the Hesperus, X, 192
The Skeleton in Armor, X, 213
Paul Revere's Ride, X, 220
Daybreak, X, 305
The Day Is Done, X, 306
Hymn to the Night, X, 307

LOWELL, JAMES RUSSELL
June, X, 34
The Shepherd of King Admetus, X, 394

LUCAS, EDWARD VERRALL
The Miss Bannisters' Brother, VI, 21

LUTHER, MARTIN
Cradle Hymn, X, 151

MACDONALD, GEORGE
The Light Princess, II, 95
The Wind and the Moon, X, 44

MACMANUS, SEUMAS
Conal and Donal and Taig, I, 77
The Old Hag's Long Leather Bag, I, 83
Manis the Miller, I, 92
Billy Beg and the Bull, I, 98

MARLOWE, CHRISTOPHER
The Passionate Shepherd to His Love, X, 233

MARVEL, ANDREW
Song of the Emigrants in Bermuda, x, 267
MASEFIELD, JOHN
Tewkesbury Road, x, 243
Sea Fever, x, 244
MAYER, CHARLES
Shipping Wild Animals, VII, 116
MEIGS, CORNELIA
The Tree of Jade, VIII, 233
Louisa Alcott, War Nurse, VIII, 307
MEYNELL, ALICE
The Shepherdess, x, 299
MILLAY, EDNA ST. VINCENT
Portrait by a Neighbor, x, 170
Eel-Grass, x, 245
MILLER, JOAQUIN
Columbus, x, 217
MILLER, WILLIAM
Willie Winkie, x, 146
MILNE, ALAN ALEXANDER
Prince Rabbit, II, 33
MILTON, JOHN
Song: On May Morning, x, 266
Evening in Paradise, x, 267
On His Blindness, x, 267
MOORE, CLEMENT C.
A Visit from St. Nicholas, x, 157
MOORE, THOMAS
The Harp That Once Through Tara's Halls, x, 209
The Minstrel Boy, x, 210
MORE, HANNAH
A Riddle, x, 137
MUIR, JOHN
Stickeen, VII, 158
MUKERJI, DHAN GOPAL
Bringing Up Kari, VII, 280
NASHE, THOMAS
Spring, x, 29
NEWBOLT, HENRY
Messmates, x, 251
Drake's Drum, x, 252
NORTON, CAROLINE ELIZABETH
The King of Denmark's Ride, x, 201
PALMER, GEORGE HERBERT [translator]
The Departure of Telemachus, IV, 3
PARKER, ARTHUR C.
The Porcupine's Quills, III, 278
How Rock-Dweller the Chipmunk Gained His Stripes, III, 283
PARRY, JUDGE EDWARD ABBOTT
Don Quixote [retold], v, 334
PERRAULT, CHARLES
Little Red Riding-Hood, I, 206
Puss in Boots, I, 209
Cinderella, I, 215
The Sleeping Beauty in the Wood, I, 223
Blue Beard, I, 229
PLUMMER, MARY WRIGHT
Stories from the Chronicle of the Cid, IV, 185
POE, EDGAR ALLAN
The Gold Bug, v, 158
To One in Paradise, x, 313
To Helen, x, 314
POPE, ALEXANDER
Solitude, x, 270
POULSSON, EMILIE [translator]
What Happened to Inger Johanne, VI, 177
PYLE, ERNIE
Thunderbird Limps Home, VIII, 340
PYLE, HOWARD
How Boots Befooled the King, II, 260
King Stork, II, 267
The Stool of Fortune, II, 277
Knighted by King Henry IV, VIII, 101
Tom Chist and the Treasure Chest, IX, 138
QUILLER-COUCH, SIR ARTHUR
Sage Counsel, x, 131

RANDS, WILLIAM BRIGHTY
Topsy-Turvy World, x, 97
Clean Clara, x, 109

RASPE, RUDOLPH ERICH
Tales from the Travels of Baron Munchausen, v, 194

RAWLINGS, MARJORIE KINNAN
Jody Finds the Fawn, VII, 358

REPPLIER, AGNES
The Story of Molly Pitcher, VIII, 194

RILEY, JAMES WHITCOMB
The Man in the Moon, x, 127

ROBERTS, CHARLES G. D.
The Assault of Wings, VII, 322

ROBERTS, ELIZABETH MADOX
The Hens, x, 141

ROGERS, SAMUEL
An Epitaph on a Robin Redbreast, x, 62

ROLLESTON, THOMAS WILLIAM
Finn and Oisin, IV, 319

ROSCOE, WILLIAM
The Butterfly's Ball, x, 52

ROSS, PATRICIA FENT
Sarita and the Duendes, II, 175

ROSSETTI, CHRISTINA G.
Spring Quiet, x, 30
Who Has Seen the Wind? x, 32
Summer Days, x, 36
O Lady Moon, x, 43
All Things Wait upon Thee, x, 58
The City Mouse and the Garden Mouse, x, 67
Up-Hill, x, 299

ROURKE, CONSTANCE
Davy Crockett Legends, VIII, 210

RUSKIN, JOHN
The King of the Golden River, v, 88

SANDBURG, CARL
How They Broke Away to Go to the Rootabaga Country, II, 54
Abe Lincoln's Books, VIII, 300
Fog, x, 38

SAROYAN, WILLIAM
The Two-Twenty Low Hurdle Race, IX, 77

SCHOLZ, JACKSON
The Winning Bug, IX, 39

SCOTT, SIR WALTER
Lullaby of an Infant Chief, x, 148
Gathering Song of Donald Dhu, x, 197
Allen-A-Dale, x, 200
Lochinvar, x, 202
The Outlaw, x, 238
Breathes There the Man, x, 278

SCOVILLE, SAMUEL, JR.
Sea Otter, VII, 333

SCUDDER, HORACE E.
The Proud King, III, 309
Saint George and the Dragon, III, 315
The Bell of Justice, III, 318
William Tell, III, 319
The Image and the Treasure, III, 321
The Flying Dutchman, III, 323

SETON, ERNEST THOMPSON
Coaly-Bay, the Outlaw Horse, VII, 286

SEWELL, ANNA
Black Beauty, VII, 211

SHAKESPEARE, WILLIAM
Winter, x, 41
Over Hill, Over Dale, x, 75
Come Unto These Yellow Sands, x, 76
Where the Bee Sucks, x, 75
Full Fathom Five, x, 76
Orpheus With His Lute, x, 257
Hark! Hark! the Lark! x, 258

SHAKESPEARE, WILLIAM
Fidele, x, 258
Jog On, Jog On, x, 259
Shall I Compare Thee to a Summer's Day? x, 260
Cardinal Wolsey's Speech to Cromwell, x, 259
SHEDLOCK, MARIE L.
The Spirit That Lived in a Tree, III, 257
The Hare That Ran Away, III, 259
The Monkey That Saved the Herd, III, 361
The Elephant That Was Honored in Old Age, III, 263
The Faithful Friend, III, 265
The Banyan Deer, III, 267
SHELLEY, PERCY BYSSHE
The Cloud, x, 280
To a Skylark, x, 282
To Night, x, 286
SHIRLEY, JAMES
Death, the Leveler, x, 266
SINGMASTER, ELSIE
Emmeline, VIII, 248
SKINNER, CONSTANCE LINDSAY
The Mountain Man, VIII, 156
SOUTHEY, ROBERT
God's Judgment on a Wicked Bishop, x, 186
The Inchcape Rock, x, 188
After Blenheim, x, 211
STEEL, FLORA ANNIE
The Lambikin, I, 328
The Rat's Wedding, I, 331
The Tiger, the Brahman, and the Jackal, I, 338
Little Anklebone, I, 341
STEFFENS, LINCOLN
A Miserable, Merry Christmas, VI, 367
STEPHENS, JAMES
Donnybrook, x, 49
Seumas Beg, x, 168
STEVENSON, ROBERT LOUIS
Autumn Fires, x, 38
Windy Nights, x, 40
The Cow, x, 68
The Land of Story-Books, x, 139
Travel, x, 140
The Land of Counterpane, x, 141
Winter-Time, x, 142
The Vagabond, x, 232
Romance, x, 233
A Visit from the Sea, x, 245
Requiem, x, 253
STOCKTON, FRANK R.
The Emergency Mistress, II, 288
Old Pipes and the Dryad, II, 302
SWIFT, JONATHAN
Gulliver's Voyage to Lilliput, V, 210
The Vowels, x, 137
TARKINGTON, BOOTH
The New Pup: a Penrod Story VI, 316
TAYLOR, ANN
The Pin, x, 164
Meddlesome Matty, x, 165
TAYLOR, BAYARD
A Story for a Child, x, 190
TEASDALE, SARA
The Spicebush in March, x, 29
Rhyme of November Stars, x, 40
Stars, x, 48
TENNYSON, ALFRED, LORD
The Owl, x, 67
The Eagle, x, 67
Early Spring, x, 292
Bugle Song, x, 294
TERHUNE, ALBERT PAYSON
"One Minute Longer," VII, 268
THACKERAY, WILLIAM MAKEPEACE
Little Billie, x, 107
THAXTER, CELIA
Little Gustava, x, 152
THOMAS, W. JENKYN
Arthur in the Cave, III, 326
TROWBRIDGE, JOHN TOWNSEND
Farm-Yard Song, x, 154

TRUMBULL, ROBERT
A Saga of World War II, VIII, 359
TURNER, WALTER J.
Romance, X, 237
TWAIN, MARK (Samuel Langhorne Clemens)
Tom Sawyer Whitewashes the Fence, VI, 285
ULLMAN, JAMES RAMSEY
Summit of the World: The Fight for Everest, IX, 272
VAN LOON, HENDRICK WILLEM
The Great Discoveries, VIII, 124
Napoleon, VIII, 223
VAUGHAN, HENRY
Peace, X, 269
VILLIERS, ALAN J.
Rounding Cape Horn in a Windjammer, IX, 377
WADDELL, HELEN
The Abbot Gerasimus and the Lion, III, 339
St. Werburga of Chester and the Wild Geese, III, 341
St. Godric and the Hunted Stag, III, 342
St. Cuthbert's Birds and Bartholomew, Hermit of Farne, III, 343
St. Moling and the Fox, III, 344
St. Colman and the Cock, the Mouse, and the Fly, III, 345
St. Kevin and the Blackbird, III, 346
WHEELER, POST
The Little Humpbacked Horse, I, 283
Wassilissa the Beautiful, I, 300
WHITE, ELIZA ORNE
When Molly Was Six, VI, 33
WHITE, STEWART EDWARD
Daniel Boone's Rifle, VIII, 198
WHITMAN, WALT
O Captain! My Captain! X, 227
WHITTIER, JOHN GREENLEAF
Barbara Frietchie, X, 224
Snow-Bound, X, 308
WIGGIN, KATE DOUGLAS
A Tragedy in Millinery, VI, 274
WILKINS, MARY E.
The Pumpkin Giant, II, 45
WILMOT-BUXTON, E. M.
How All Things Began, III, 197
How All-Father Odin Became Wise, III, 203
The Apples of Youth, III, 207
How the Fenris Wolf Was Chained, III, 214
How the Pride of Thor Was Brought Low, III, 219
How Thor's Hammer Was Lost and Found, III, 230
The Story of Balder the Beautiful, III, 238
How Hermod Made a Journey to the Underworld, III, 246
How Loki Was Punished at Last, III, 251
WORDSWORTH, WILLIAM
March, X, 28
The Kitten and the Falling Leaves, X, 69
Lucy Gray, X, 194
Lucy, X, 275
Daffodils, X, 276
The Solitary Reaper, X, 277
WYLIE, ELINOR
Velvet Shoes, X, 42
YEATS, WILLIAM BUTLER
The Song of Wandering Aengus, X, 231
YOUNG, ELLA
How the Son of the Gobhaun Saor Sold the Sheepskin, III, 356
How the Son of the Gobhaun Saor Shortened the Road, III, 352
ZIMMERN, HELEN
Rustem and Sohrab, IV, 89
ZWILGMEYER, DIKKEN
What Happened to Inger Johanne, VI, 177